Bliss and the Art of Forever

ALSO BY ALISON KENT

Hope Springs Novels

The Second Chance Café
Beneath the Patchwork Moon
The Sweetness of Honey

A Hope Springs Novel

Bliss and the Art of Forever

ALISON KENT

Montlake
Romance

Published by Montlake Romance, Seattle

www.apub.com
Amazon, the Amazon logo, and Montlake Romance are trademarks of Amazon.com, Inc., or its affiliates.

ISBN-13: 9781477828618
ISBN-10: 1477828613

Cover design by Anna Curtis
Library of Congress Control Number: 2014957337

Printed in the United States of America

*To chocolate. To coffee.
To the man in my life who puts up
with my love of both.
And whom I love because he puts up with me.*

*And for Jedi
Who needs a bookstore of his own.*

Thanks, too, to Shannon W. for the tip on tribal tats!

CHAPTER ONE

Inked script at his nape. Colored sleeves beneath his rolled cuffs. Elaborate artwork in his oxford's open collar. Her imagination wandered to his back and his chest, to his shoulders. His biceps. His abs. The tattoos were symbolic, not simply cosmetic, and part of the biker culture, leaving her to wonder how important the club had been to his life before he'd walked away.

Tats intrigued her—the creativity, the significance, the commitment—even when the man wearing the ink was her student's father, and off-limits. This particular man also wore, not a beard, but an unkempt scruff framing a devilish smile. His hair was long, pulled back in a disheveled sort of knot. It had her thinking of Heathcliff, tortured and haunted and wild on the moors.

Had her, too, wanting to rescue him.

Hands curled over the edge of her desk as she leaned back against it, Brooklyn Harvey looked out at her class of kindergartners. The fifteen five- and six-year-olds sat on the floor in a semicircle, their rapt attention on Callum Drake. Rather than using the full-sized chair she'd offered him, he'd lowered his six-foot-plus frame into one of those from the pint-sized collage table. Watching him fold himself to sit had been as breathtaking as watching him walk through the door.

She'd met Adrianne Drake's grandparents, Shirley and Vaughn, at orientation before school started, and visited with them again at parents' night, and at the Halloween costume party, and when they'd eaten lunch with the girl on Grandparents' Day, and at Christmas. But today, over halfway into the school year, was the first time she'd seen Adrianne's father for herself.

After months of his daughter's chatter, and details dropped by the older Drakes about their son, Brooklyn had found herself wanting to know more about him. But the man who'd arrived right on time for story hour left her speechless, because none of the photos she'd seen—the success of his business put him in the local spotlight on a regular basis—had him looking like he'd walked out of a foggy Irish landscape, green eyed and larger than life, with a touch of ginger tinting his dark brown hair.

When she'd read his name on the sign-up sheet for her Dads Love Books, Too! reading program, she'd been surprised. And a little bit apprehensive. Involving the parents in their children's learning experience was an important part of her curriculum.

But was exposing her students to a member of a biker gang—okay, an *ex-member* of a biker gang—a smart thing to do? Would other parents object should they get wind of a man with his background, celebrity or not, upstanding citizen or not, interacting with their children in her classroom?

And then she'd thought about Adrianne Drake. The girl was one of the most well-adjusted children Brooklyn had ever taught. She was bright, and gave serious thought to her questions and her answers. She was kind to her classmates, and responsive when Brooklyn asked for help. Yes, the girl's grandparents were an influential and hands-on part of her life, but she lived full-time with her father. She adored her father. She rarely stopped talking about her father.

In the end, that had been the deciding factor in Brooklyn's e-mailing Callum the details to confirm the date. She'd needed to meet the man who, as a single parent burdened with the baggage of a sketchy past, was rearing such a precious, and precocious, little girl.

Now that she had, well, she had more questions than answers. At the top of her list: Why was this man unattached? It couldn't be a lack of women throwing themselves at him, based on his looks alone. Then there was his career. His chocolate shop, Bliss, a locally owned small business, was often spotlighted by the *Hope Springs Courant*. A lot of women had a thing for men whose work drew that sort of acclaim.

More important, however, why hadn't he found time before now to visit his daughter at school? What about today's story hour was so different from the other activities she'd arranged to involve her students' parents?

But mostly, why was she letting herself notice him as anything besides Adrianne Drake's father when she was very happily single and intent on staying that way? The idea of going through another loss, no matter Artie's black-humored insistence that should he die in the line of duty, she mourn him no more than two years . . . she wasn't ready. She didn't know if she'd ever be.

She supposed it should make her feel better that she wasn't the only one captivated by the man. The three homeroom mothers had stopped setting up poststory treats—conversation heart–topped minicupcakes and heart-shaped cookies, both from Butters Bakery, and cute little candies with a chocolate shell and a root beer filling, from Callum's confectionery—to listen to the chocolatier introduce himself to the members of her class.

It was hard for Brooklyn to wrap her head around his transition from biker to candy maker, but she had no trouble picturing him in chef whites, the tats at his nape and the base of his throat suggesting she'd like what she'd find if she freed the buttons of his coat, parted the sides, pushed the garment off his shoulders, outlined the designs first with a fingertip, then her tongue—

"Okay," Callum said, his deep voice drawing Brooklyn's gaze and a heated blush. "Are we ready for a story now?"

"Yes!" cried a chorus of exuberant voices.

He looked to Brooklyn for guidance. She picked up a flat marble paperweight carved to look like an owl and nodded for him to begin, because nodding didn't require her to speak, and the owl gave her something to do with her hands. Good grief. What was wrong with her? Yes, he was pretty. Oh, he was pretty. And intriguing. And so very hot.

But Brooklyn had plans. Big plans. A week after the school year ended, she was going to be on her way to Italy with no idea when she'd return. Ships crossing in the night, she and Callum Drake. Or in this case, crossing in a kindergarten classroom.

He opened the picture book his daughter handed him, facing the pages of *The Bunny Who Loved Chocolate* toward his rapt audience. Adrianne sat in the center of the front row, her corkscrew blond pigtails brushing her shoulders, her crooked front tooth taking nothing away from her grin. She had eyes only for her dad, and Brooklyn stanched the catch tugging at her heart. He was doing such a good job as a father.

"Opie was a bunny whose fur was colored . . ."

"Blue!" The children called out the answer, and Callum turned the page.

"The same color as the sky where his friends the birds . . ."

"Flew!"

An awkward sentence, but it worked for the rhyme. Brooklyn looked from Callum to his daughter and watched Adrianne mouth the words. They'd obviously shared this story many times. The girl anticipated then mimicked the faces he made and the rhythm with which he read, and Brooklyn couldn't deny the smile teasing her own lips. Or her fascination with the movement of his.

"Opie loved chocolate, and all candy . . ."

"Too!"

"But he only had lettuce, and didn't know what to . . ."

"Do!"

Pushing off her desk and leaving the owl behind, Brooklyn circled the room to the snack table still needing to be readied. Callum was through four pages now, and only sixteen remained. She probably knew the story as well as Adrianne did. "Can I help with anything?" she whispered to one of the moms.

"Oh, no, we're fine." Bethany Patzka, who'd donated a tray of vegan granola and dried fruit clusters, leaned closer, bringing her fingers to her mouth to hide her words. "Just a little bit distracted, if you know what I mean. The kids are absolutely worshiping that man, and he looks like he could eat them for breakfast."

"I'd like to give him something to eat for breakfast," Lindsay Webber, the second volunteer and mother of Adrianne Drake's best friend, Kelly, put in, eliciting a sharp groan from the third.

Brooklyn looked at Callum. His gaze came up and met hers, and she pressed her hand to her throat to hide the throb of her pulse at the base. Surely he hadn't heard; he was half a room away.

But the words were out there, as was the sound, and both had her mind going places it didn't need to. Places she'd avoided for ages because she'd made her peace with being alone.

She'd had twelve years with the most wonderful man she'd ever known. Twelve years traveling the globe, and cooking breakfast for dinner, and watching every Bruce Willis movie ever made multiple times.

Until the roof of a burning building had collapsed, trapping Artie and another member of his firefighting crew and turning her world upside down. The love of her life had been gone for almost two years, and that was that.

Which didn't explain why was she thinking about Callum Drake's tats, his green eyes and ginger hair, and how his skin would taste smeared with chocolate.

~

Another hour, Brooklyn decided, and she was calling it quits. School had been dismissed for the four-day weekend, though since no one she knew actually celebrated Presidents' Day, it was less a holiday than it was a paid day off.

She'd stayed late the last three afternoons to put her classroom in order and get her lesson plans in tip-top shape. Organizing her work life made it a lot easier to enjoy her personal life guilt-free. She planned to do a lot of enjoying over the upcoming break, even if Valentine's Day fell smack in the middle of it.

The idea of a single day set aside for shallow, meaningless rituals of love had never sat well with her, even before meeting Artie. It was one of the things they'd shared, even if, ironically, the date itself ended up having a special meaning for them, and they'd used the it in other ways.

For Artie, it had been work. Every year he'd volunteered to swap shifts with any buddy who'd felt pressured to devote the day to romance. Then he'd chuckled about the poor soul not understanding the rewards of said devotion practiced daily. *You don't just brush your teeth after eating cotton candy. You see to the things that matter every day.* Artie, practical to the core.

For Brooklyn, it had been doing nothing but anything she wanted. A movie at Hope Springs' small art house theater after school. Antique shopping in Gruene and a solo dinner at the Gristmill restaurant. If she had the day off, a book in the backyard hammock. An afternoon nap in the same. And if the cold weather had been too much to bear, she'd done her reading and napping on the sofa in front of a fire.

Doing nothing but anything she wanted was exactly how she planned to spend the next four days, starting with lunch tomorrow at Two Owls Café with Jean Dial. Her next-door neighbor, a schoolteacher herself, though retired, loved Two Owls as much as Brooklyn, and they made a date of it monthly.

They had great fun swapping recipes and cooking tips and school district gossip, and discussing the medieval romances they both read until the spines cracked and the pages fell out. But Brooklyn enjoyed even more so listening to Jean's stories—and advice—from forty years in the teaching trenches.

After lunch it would be home again for a movie marathon with a six-pack of Kaylie Keller's brownies. The owner of Two Owls had made a name for herself and her Austin bakery with an incredible selection of the treats; now having sold the Sweet Spot and moved to Hope Springs, she offered a variety on the café's buffet for dessert.

As far as what to watch while nibbling through all that chocolate, Brooklyn was thinking the original Die Hard trilogy, followed by *Unbreakable*. Oh, how Artie had loved *Unbreakable*. She pulled in a deeply felt breath and shuddered with it. The long afternoons she and her husband had spent cuddled up on the couch watching those movies and, as newlyweds, season after season of *Moonlighting* on VHS . . .

Eyes closed, she allowed the sadness its moment, then shook it off. Artie had been gone two years. She would always miss him. She would always love him. But he'd made her promise, should anything happen to him, that she wouldn't stop living her life because he'd lost his. That was the last thing he'd wanted. And she'd done her best to respect his wishes, but once in a while, just every so often, she had to give grief its due.

Anyway, she mused, crossing from the classroom's cubbies to her desk, a Friday spent with Bruce Willis and brownies required she do something on Saturday to counter the calories and sloth. Most of her friends would be busy with their significant others, leaving her on her own. Which wouldn't be such a bad thing if, since Artie's death, she hadn't fallen into a rut.

It hadn't happened overnight. But it had happened. She'd initiated fewer outings with friends—dinners, shopping, shows—and turned down more and more invitations. It was easier to stay in and read her medieval romances or watch her Bruce Willis films than feel like a third wheel—or like a walking reminder to other firefighters' wives of what they and their men faced daily.

She had coworkers to whom she was close, and friends she'd met in yoga class, and neighbors, sure, but a rut being the dull and boring routine that it was, well, not to be defensive, but books and movies did make for great company. Though, she mused, a cat might be even better. Two cats. A clowder of cats. A glaring of cats. A whole freaking clutter of cats.

Thankfully, she'd be on her way to Italy soon, and seeing Artie's family there, because knowing that many terms for a group of said felines was a pretty good sign sloth was the least of her worries. This trip, as hard as it would be, was going to be good for her, because honestly, she needed to remember how to have fun.

Reaching for her trash can, she dusted her hands free of used staples and bent tacks. "Maybe I'll do something outrageous tomorrow. Like buy myself chocolate for Valentine's Day."

"Valentine's Day isn't Valentine's Day without chocolate."

At the deep male voice, she spun, reaching for her scissors, yet realizing instinctively she wouldn't need them. What criminal sort announced himself before committing his crime? Also, after today's story hour, she knew that voice well. She imagined she'd be a long time forgetting it.

She turned from her desk, forgoing the weapon. Callum Drake stood in her doorway, wispy twists of hair hanging loose from the knot on the back of his head to brush his cheeks. He had a forearm on either side of the frame, his feet in the hall as if he were a vampire awaiting an invitation.

For a very long moment she wondered how safe it would be to offer him one. "Mr. Drake," she finally said. "You scared me." She brought her hand to the base of her throat, less frightened than . . . other things. Things that had no business in this classroom. "What're you doing here?"

"Callum," he said, his shrug careless and lazy, but also hesitant, as if he wasn't sure, or was having second thoughts about whatever he'd come for. "Or Cal. Or C.B."

"C.B.?"

"Bennett," he said, and grinned, a devastating flash of teeth and charm. "My middle name. Friends used to call me that, but it's been a while, so . . ."

Callum Bennett Drake. Irish biker. Candy maker. Daddy to a six-year-old moppet. *Deep breath, Brooklyn. Deep breath. You have plans and no room in your life for a rogue.* "Callum it is."

His grin deepened. "Addy told me you'd been staying late all week. I was hoping you might still be here."

Addy. She'd forgotten his daughter telling her he used the nickname. She'd also forgotten telling the class she'd be preholiday cleaning after school, using the chore as a lesson in rewards. All she had to do was put in the time, and voilà, she had the long weekend free.

She waved him inside, wondering what he wanted. She preferred to discuss her students' progress during official parent-teacher conferences. "She told me she'd be at her grandparents' this weekend because you were working."

He pushed off the frame, seeming to gain six inches of height as he did, though at least some of that was due to the biker boots he wore. Black leather, silver buckles, tough stitching. "I dropped her off earlier, and I'll pick her up Sunday morning. Shop's closed the rest of the long weekend, so she gets two days with my folks and two days with me. And yeah. I'll be at Bliss till the clock tolls the end of Valentine's Day."

That would be Saturday night, yet instead of working, here he was. "Of course. All those last-minute shoppers." She pictured him again in chef's whites, though there was nothing wrong with the oxford and the blue jeans and the black leather he had on now. "All that chocolate temptation."

A dimple cut deep into his scruffy cheek. "Mmm, not so much."

"Familiarity breeding contempt?"

His laugh was a visceral, vital sound that echoed. "Gotta watch my figure—"

Because having every woman in the room watching it for you isn't enough?

"—what with having a six-year-old keeping me on my toes."

"Now, *that* I can relate to," she said, a blush heating her cheeks. She was *so* very glad he couldn't read her mind.

She returned to removing the artwork from above the cubbies, conscious of his gaze on her as she reached to pluck the staples and tacks. December's theme had been snowmen and sleds. Last year, for January, she'd used fireworks because she couldn't deal with clocks depicting the passage of time.

February was easy, with flowers and chubby little cupids and all things Valentine's Day, but two weeks spent looking at candy hearts was enough. She wanted her class to come back from the weekend to find portraits of past presidents, not just the pink and red of fabricated love.

"Looks like you're doing a good job. Keeping up with the kids, I mean. Not . . . your figure."

"Thanks. I think," she said, and looked over.

He scrunched up one side of his face. "That didn't come out right. You're figure's just fine."

"Thanks," she repeated, this time holding the caveat. "You were really good with them, you know."

He crossed his arms, leaned a shoulder against the end of the cubbies. "If I can't manage one hour of one day reading a book and answering questions, I should be shot. You're the pro, doing it all day long every day."

"I enjoy it," she said, because it was true. "Seeing their young minds working through problems, reaching conclusions. Using the skills they're learning. Though this *is* kindergarten, so I'm not sure they've got it in them yet to save the world. Still, when you think about it, our future really is in their hands." Then she shrugged because it seemed a silly thing to say.

He considered her for a moment. "You have any of your own? Kids?"

If she had a nickel for every time she'd been asked that question . . . She turned to him, pressing the hearts and cupids she held to her chest. "No. I don't. But that seems to be the leap most people make."

"It's an easy one, considering."

Because her chosen career meant she wanted children of her own? "I love what I do. But I also love leaving it here at the end of the day. That's why I'm still here now. So I can enjoy the four days I have off."

He nodded, and thankfully, changed the subject. "What're you doing with the break?"

"A whole lot of nothing," she said, slipping the construction paper cutouts into a huge manila envelope.

"You want to take a tour of my shop?"

An extra-chubby cupid slipped free and floated to the floor. "Your shop?"

All he did was nod.

"I don't understand—"

"You've been asking Addy about me," he said, a dark brow arching above eyes that were an even deeper green without the morning light from the room's windows to brighten them. "You asked her if I help her with her homework."

Hmm.

"You asked her if I talk to her about the stories we read."

Uh-oh.

"You asked her if she rides with me. And if she has a helmet."

"I ask all my students about their parents," she said, vowing never to ask Adrianne Drake anything again.

"Do you?" Those words in that voice . . . they heated the air, a flame licking at the oxygen between them.

"Of course," she said, waving off his query as she bent to retrieve the art. "It helps give me a sense of how involved they are in the education process." *Lame, Brooklyn. Really, really lame.*

He scuffed the toe of one boot against the floor. "And my not showing up before now makes you think I'm not involved?"

Fine. Okay. She turned to face her sins head-on. "You're right. I've been curious. Adrianne's situation isn't particularly unique, but it is . . . interesting."

He worked the words around in his mouth as if he found them unpleasant, then said, "Because I have sole custody? Or because of my history?"

Brooklyn nodded, but rather than press either point, she moved to less volatile ground. "And the fact that you're a chocolatier."

That seemed to settle well enough. "Then the timing is perfect for you to see me in my element, what with Saturday being—"

"Valentine's Day. I know," she said, realizing the holiday probably brought him a tidy little profit. "And with your business consisting primarily of online orders, which I know from your parents, not your daughter"—*though also from gossip and from googling you*—"you're no doubt up to your eyeballs packing boxes for last-minute shipping."

"I'm actually up to my eyeballs making the product to go in the boxes." He shoved his fists in his jeans' pockets, his shoulders hunched as if he were exhausted already. "I've had a couple of middle school kids helping me out after school with the surge. Addy's pediatrician's son, Grady. One of his friends, Jo."

"I thought there were laws against child labor." She teased him, a change of mood while she did her best to ignore the gap beneath the buttons of his shirt. The way he was standing gave her a glimpse of the bare skin above his belt. And it was so, *so* hard not to stare at his very tight abs, the dusting of hair there, and what looked like tattooed red, green, and gold scales . . .

He shrugged, the motion widening the gap. A lizard? A dragon? A snake? And what were the words clinging to the spikes along its back? She would need to get closer to see, and, well, that wasn't going to happen, was it?

"I figure it's no worse than hiring them to mow my lawn," he said. "If I had a lawn. Addy and I live in a loft in the textile district, though with the way she likes to talk, you probably know that."

Actually, she didn't, but the old cotton warehouses near the Guadalupe River, now trendy living spaces, were the sort of place she could picture him: the freight elevators, the original brick, the crank casement windows. The warehouses were funky and fun. Not staid and suburban. Not dull and boring. Probably not a cat to be found.

"Anyway, I've got a full-time employee working the front counter, and a temp helping her out this week. The rest is all me."

"You do everything by hand?"

"The artisan pieces?" He nodded. "It's a quality-control thing. And my reputation."

"A true craftsman."

He twisted his hips just so, and she heard something pop. "With the bad back to show for it."

Ouch. "That must take a lot of hours."

"Six days a week. Ten-hour days. Thousands of chocolates weekly."

"Impressive," she said, thinking about the physical toll such exacting work must take. And that on top of his being a single dad. Maybe he didn't have a woman in his life because he didn't have time.

"So? You want to take a look around before I get back to work? Set your mind at ease and all?" That grin, again. The dimple. The scruff. The glorious temptation. "Wouldn't want you thinking I sit Addy on a stool at the kitchen counter in the mornings and spread her toast with cocoa butter."

"I've actually seen your shop. Several times." She'd just never seen him while there.

"The open-to-the-public part, sure. Not where the magic happens."

The way he said the words . . . She swallowed, cleared her throat to ask, "When—" but was interrupted.

"Now? Before I dig in for the next fifty-six hours?" He gestured toward the storybook still sitting on the chair. "Gotta make up the time lost to Opie and his quest for chocolate."

So he'd come to school to read to her class when he needed to be working? And now he wanted to spend more of his valuable time on her? "We don't have to do this today. Not when you're so busy. Really. I'm not worried about Adrianne. Another time will be fine. We can wait—"

A sharp shake of his head, and, "Let's not."

She heard her breath catch, heard herself saying "Okay" before she could think through his invitation. Or his insistence that they do this now. Or about anything other than the tone of his voice, the push in his words. The sense of urgency coiling inside of her. "Let me get my keys—"

"Leave your car. We'll take my bike."

She glanced down at her gray wool pants, her deep cherry sweater, her black ballet flats. Then she glanced at his jeans, his jacket, his thick leather boots. The tease of his tattoo. A snake would be too clichéd. She liked the idea of a dragon. "I'm not sure I'm dressed for your bike," she said, tucking her hair behind her ear. "Not to mention I don't have a helmet."

"I brought an extra."

Because he'd expected her to come with him? To say yes? To jump? He was making this too easy. Her agreeing. Going along. Giving in. She wasn't sure she should do any of those things. But she wasn't quite ready to buy a litter box or a scratching post, either.

"Okay." Leaving her room decorations undone, she grabbed her purse and her keys and her peacoat, locking her sanity into her classroom along with the cutouts of Cupid and his stupid red hearts.

Then she walked with Callum Bennett Drake down the empty hallway and out the front door to his Harley, proving to herself—and to anyone else wondering—that she wasn't dull and boring at all.

CHAPTER TWO

Callum had always loved women who were good sports, who could deal with getting messy, who didn't flinch from a challenge. Turned out Brooklyn Harvey was all of those things and more. That, he hadn't expected. Addy's ramblings made her teacher sound like an old maid. He'd half imagined he'd find her in orthopedic shoes and a cat-hair cardigan.

Since day one of the school year he'd listened to his daughter go on about Ms. Harvey: how her teacher's glasses were just like her grandmother's, how their hair was the exact same color and their eyes, too, how they both baked the *bestest* sugar cookies in the world. How she would never disobey Ms. Harvey or Grammy; she didn't want to sit in their time-out chairs.

Oh, had little Miss Adrianne Drake been wrong. Maybe not about the cookies or time-out, but the rest . . . her teacher wasn't old, though it was his leaping logic that had twisted that conclusion out of his daughter's words. Unmarried, yes. That he knew from an overheard *no significant other* comment his mother had made. Why she was single was anyone's guess, but he wouldn't deny being glad. Or deny his being glad was a problem.

Her hair was naturally blond like his daughter's, not highlighted like his mother's. And, yes, the shape of their glasses was similar, but Brooklyn's accentuated bright blue eyes with lashes even longer than Addy's. His little girl had inherited hers from her mother. Thankfully she hadn't ended up with anything more. Or anything worse.

Neither of his parents had mentioned how young Brooklyn was, how sharp. How hot in her sexy librarian frames . . . not that they'd ever say that. They were careful not to say anything that might cause him to lose focus. No matter how many times he'd told them he was done with club life. No matter the success of his business demanding he stay put. His mother, at least, still believed he was ruled by bad choices. Which was pretty funny considering she'd made almost all of his for him while he was growing up.

With his history? He couldn't blame them. He was hardly a poster child for doing the right thing. But now he had Addy. She was his and she was everything. He was done screwing up, or doing anything that didn't have her best interests at heart. He couldn't lose her. He wouldn't lose her.

He would not lose her.

Crushing the thought, he signaled for a left turn, then leaned into it, the rumble of the bike an echo of the take-no-prisoners mood brought on by his thoughts. Brooklyn leaned, too, as if she'd been riding with him for years. Having her wrapped around him made the trip go by faster than he liked. He kept to the speed limit, enjoying the flex of her fingers as she held him tight.

She'd bound her hair at her nape beneath the helmet, but still she pressed her shielded face to his back as they rode. Her breasts, too. Her thighs. It had been a long time since he'd ridden with a woman behind him. Even longer since the woman was one who felt as good as Brooklyn did.

He wasn't sure he was ready to give a name to the reason he'd gone back to the school after dropping Addy off at his folks'. He picked her up most days; it was their thing, their time. Dad and daughter and a quick ride to either Bliss or his parents' home. He hated foisting her off on her grandparents, and only did so when he had no choice.

Most workdays he kept her with him after school. Perk of being the boss. She had a desk of her own in the storeroom, and liked it better than sitting on a stool in the corner of the kitchen with her hair in a net while he worked, though she did that, too, telling him about her day, asking him about the candy, reminding him how boring his life would be without her. For the most part she was happy to entertain herself. And she let him know via intercom when she wasn't.

She had books to read, and plenty of crayons and colored pencils, and yeah, she had a tablet PC and since four years old had known how to find what she wanted to watch on Netflix, how to play memory games with Disney princesses, or paint pictures with a touch of a finger. He wasn't so proud about all of that, letting technology babysit.

But he hadn't come to Hope Springs expecting his mother and his father to raise his little girl, even though he'd be in dire straits without them. Addy's *interesting* situation—wasn't that how Brooklyn had put it?—was his to deal with. Being a single father was hardly where he'd expected to find himself at thirty-four, but he wouldn't change it for the world. It was a good life, this business of being a dad. And being a chocolatier wasn't too shabby.

For the most part, his folks had forgiven him his past, and sooner or later he'd make his own peace with the things he'd done. Work kept him busy, and family took up the rest of his time. He hadn't thought much about not having a woman in his life until today, and he'd done so pretty much at the moment he'd walked into his daughter's classroom and seen Brooklyn Harvey sitting on the front of her desk, her legs crossed, all those curious wide eyes turned her way as she used giant Lego bricks to demonstrate fractions of wholes.

Who knew he had a thing for teachers? Or for this particular one anyway. He wanted to say he'd gone back this afternoon intending to thank her for having him . . . but that was a lie, and he knew it. He'd gone back because he wanted to see her again, to talk to her without an audience. To try and figure out why she'd looked at him as if she wanted to get him out of his clothes.

And why, after leaving, he'd been unable to erase the idea of her doing so out of his mind. *That one's simple, hotshot. All work and no play has made you a very dull boy.*

He eased the bike to a stop behind the store and killed the engine, waiting for Brooklyn to climb down before kicking the stand into place. The small shopping center backed up to a private through street, across which were the rear entrances and employee parking lots for the *Hope Springs Courant*, the post office, and the Dollar General. Bliss sat between Butters Bakery and an empty space he'd heard had been leased for a coffee shop.

The location was great for him, and for the others; the stores on the adjoining blocks drove foot traffic past their front doors. Then again, traffic was less a concern for him than it would be for an espresso bar. He did more than ten times the online business he did with his storefront. And last he knew, Peggy Butters didn't ship, though with his own success in doing so, he'd made his pitch to convince her there was a mint to be made.

"Why did you sign up for story hour today when this is such a busy time for you?" It was the first thing Brooklyn said after pulling off the helmet and shaking out her hair.

"Because I make candy and it seemed appropriate?" The truth was his mother had filled out the form. He'd learned of the obligation when Brooklyn had e-mailed to confirm with a list of instructions. Not that he would've backed out; Addy was too excited. He just wished his mother had asked him whether or not he could make time to go.

"Appropriate, maybe," she said, following him to the back door. "But not exactly business smart."

"Yeah, well. What can I say?" He stopped flipping through the keys on his ring and held up his pinkie. "Addy loves Valentine's Day. And Addy's got me right here."

The smile that played across Brooklyn's face caught him like a sucker punch, and it hit him again how much trouble he was courting here, inviting her out of his daughter's life and into his when he and Addy were settled and happy and he'd sworn he was done with upheavals. Brooklyn being more than Addy's teacher would be a big one.

"I've really enjoyed teaching her," she was saying, smoothing a hand over her helmet-mussed hair. "She'll be one of my fondest memories from my last year in Hope Springs."

Again with the sucker punch, this one making it hard for him to breathe. "What do you mean, your last year?"

The motion of her hand slowed. Her smile slowed, too. "I'm quitting," she said, and he frowned.

"What do you mean, you're quitting?"

She lowered her hand to her side, toying with her sweater's hem; was he making her nervous? "I gave notice before school started."

"What about Addy?" It was the only thing he could think about, his little girl and how much she adored her teacher.

"Adrianne will be in first grade next year. I wouldn't be her teacher even if I were still here."

"Oh, right." Duh. He started thumbing through his keys again, not liking her news or his reaction. *Because, you know, it makes perfect sense to hate her resigning when this is Addy's only year with her, and you met her for the first time today.* "What're you gonna do?"

She lifted her gaze, tucked her hair behind her ear. "More than likely I'll still be teaching, but I'll be doing it in Italy. I'm going there in June."

"What do you mean, you're going to Italy?" And at that he was just about ready to strangle himself. Her meaning—all of her meanings—were obvious. For some reason, he was being particularly slow.

She watched him fumble with the keys until he finally found the one he wanted. "I used to be married. My husband's family is there, and they're really the only family I have anymore. He died two years ago. On the job. He was a firefighter. And as a wedding gift, as strange as it sounds, he'd taken out an insane amount of life insurance. Enough that I can afford to work with his cousin in an English language program she's starting. If I'm a good fit."

"I'm sorry," he said. "About your husband," he added. Then he shoved the key into the lock while processing all she'd just told him. She wasn't just unmarried. She was a widow. For some reason, that had him seeing her with more gravitas and less, well, lust.

"Thank you."

It was a simple exchange—*I'm sorry. Thank you.*—and it covered the basics, but he felt as if the words conveyed nothing, as if he needed to offer something deeper, as if she deserved hearing something more.

But all he could come up with was, "Italy, huh. What part?"

"Cinque Terre. Vernazza, actually. It's on the Italian Riviera."

"Bet that's gorgeous," he said, gesturing for her to go inside. The back door opened into the shop's shipping center and stockroom. The shelves running the length of the space held plain cardboard cartons, tape, packing peanuts, and Bliss's custom-designed candy boxes, along with polycarbonate molds, paint rollers, bowls, peels, scrapers, and air-brushing supplies.

All these years later Callum still found himself awed by those personalized boxes: the particular shade of dark sepia matte he'd taken forever to choose, Bliss's name and logo gold-foiled on the front, his signature printed inside each lid. The interior packaging that kept the chocolates secure.

Stupid, really, to be so proud of a box, but there it was. Proof positive that, bad choices or not and against all odds, he'd made this work.

A laptop and printer sat on a desk flush with one of the shorter walls, and flush to the opposite was a similar desk, though this one and its child-sized chair sat closer to the ground. The surface held Addy's puzzles and glue sticks and sticker books and the set of bendable toy characters from the Disney movie *Frozen* his mother had insisted her granddaughter have.

It was that desk that drew Brooklyn's attention. "Adrianne must love this. Her own space. Her favorite things." She reached down and picked up the Olaf snowman figurine. "Does she still sleep with the plush version?"

He nodded, not quite sure what to think of her knowing his daughter that well. "I'll put a platform beneath the desk as she gets older, raise it until she doesn't need it anymore, though I guess by then she'll be old enough to catch rides home with friends rather than having her old man pick her up."

"On his Harley. You forgot that part," she said, one brow teasingly arched.

"Yeah, well . . ."

"I don't think she'll ever be too old for that."

"She's not the one I'm worried about," he said, grumbling as he added, "I've already found five gray hairs this week."

She laughed, then asked, "Does she spend a lot of time here?"

"Unless I've got something going on, like Valentine's Day, she hangs out most days after school while I work." He looked around, leaning a shoulder against a shelf. "It's not usually so crowded or so cluttered in here. I like to run a tight ship, but Valentine's Day always gets out of hand."

"And it's driving you crazy, isn't it?"

Like she wouldn't believe. "C'mon. You've seen Addy's domain. Let me show you mine." He led her into the rear hallway and pointed toward the various doors. "Restrooms, kitchen, showroom, the closet that serves as my office. Take your pick."

Brooklyn stepped into the space painted the same Irish cream as the walls in the shop, set off with molding in the same matte sepia as Bliss's boxes, and hung with photos of his portfolio of colorful artisanal candies. The door closed behind them, but she didn't move, standing to take a deep breath. "It smells amazing in here. You know that, don't you?"

It smelled like work. It smelled like his life.

It smelled like chocolate.

"I'm not sure I notice it anymore. Except sometimes doing laundry and catching a whiff on Addy's clothes. Makes me wonder what I smell like." And that was a thought best left right where it dropped, he decided, pushing open the door to the kitchen—the room took up a quarter of the leased space; two of its walls, the front and the left, faced the showroom—and avoiding the flurry of the shop.

Brooklyn walked to the window of one-way glass above his marble work counter. It looked out over the display case, from behind which Lena and the temp took care of the customers. "That's some kind of traffic. Two lines. Both five or six customers deep. And there's the door opening again." Arms crossed, she turned, the look on her face approving. "Very impressive, Mr. Drake. Especially since I know what those candies cost."

"Those candies are made by hand. With the highest quality ingredients to be had. They're worth every penny," he said, not minding at all that he sounded proud.

She took that in, considering him. He could nearly see her mind working behind her bright blue eyes. "What's your favorite?" she asked.

"To eat or to make?"

"Both."

Hmm. He'd never really thought about it. "The kid in me likes the Peanut Butter Crackle. I grind peanut brittle—and I make that, too—mixing it into a natural peanut butter I get from a supplier in upstate New York, then wrap it all up in a creamy milk chocolate."

"Yum," she said appreciatively. "And the adult in you?"

He walked toward her, put his hands on her shoulders, and spun her to face the showroom's display case, leaning close as he released her and catching a whiff of something soft and natural, perfume or soap or shampoo.

His gut tightened, and his heart thumped hard, and it took him several seconds to find his voice. Nope. This hadn't been a good idea at all. "See that shiny green geodesic dome? The shell's a dark bittersweet, but inside it's fresh lime juice and añejo tequila in a white chocolate ganache."

"The shell's chocolate? Even though it's green?"

"The green is cocoa butter." He pointed to the right and a row of scalloped rounds. "Just like the frosted white with the brown splatters on that one is cocoa butter."

"What flavor is that one?"

"S'mores."

"Seriously?" Her eyes, when she lifted her gaze to meet his, were wide and bright and so much like his daughter's that anyone who saw them together and didn't know the truth could easily mistake Brooklyn for Addy's mom.

Yep. Bad idea. Very bad idea, he mused, grinding his jaw. "I make the marshmallows, toast them, layer them with a milk chocolate ganache, and sprinkle on crushed graham cracker crumbs before sealing them up."

"No doubt you make the graham crackers, too."

He couldn't decide if what sounded like admiration was sarcasm instead, but he nodded as she glanced through the window again. "What about the orange speckles on the red one there?"

"That's a raspberry caramel."

"They don't look like chocolates at all." She shook her head, as if finding the concept hard to believe. "How do you do that?"

He thought back to the first artisan chocolates he'd seen at a shop in San Francisco, his fascination with them, and how it had grabbed hold. "The magic of iridescent powder and airbrushing the molds with red cocoa butter. I do that before pouring in the chocolate for the shell.

The shells harden, I pipe in the filling, cover it all with more chocolate, then let it set."

"You make it sound so simple," she said, and this time without a hint of anything but awe.

He liked that, coming from her, but he didn't stop to analyze why. "It's as simple as teaching kindergarten. Meaning once you've been doing it awhile, you know the ins and outs and all the things that can go wrong."

"What can go wrong?"

At the beginning? So many things he'd lost count. "Not tempering the chocolate correctly is the most obvious, but I've got a machine for that, even though I can pretty much tell the temperature by touch when I do it manually. Less obvious is coming up with a filling that seems like a good idea but ends up tasting like crap."

She stepped back from the window and looked at him. "Have you done that?"

"It's been a while, but yeah." When her expression grew questioning, he said, "Let's just say I won't be offering hot buttered rum popcorn again."

Her laughter filled the small kitchen. "That actually sounds really good."

"Sounds. Not tastes," he said, his hip braced against the center island as he watched her make a circle through the small room.

She ran a finger along the edge of the countertop range he used to prep some of the fillings. "It's so clean in here."

"That's because I worked as late as Addy would let me last night to get ahead, and I haven't dirtied anything up yet today. Stop by six hours from now and you'll be singing a different tune."

That earned him a rueful smile. "I guess that's my cue to go home."

He wasn't ready for her to, but she was right. "Our tours do include a complimentary sample, so before we head back, what's your pleasure?"

"Ooh, I'll have one of everything," she said, laughing as she returned to the window. Hands on the counter, she leaned forward, as if getting six inches closer would give her a better view.

She made him think of Addy, again, as if his daughter had inherited her traits: the way her eyes grew wide with excitement, the way she held her mouth to one side as if doing so helped her think.

Dangerous thoughts to be having, he realized, pushing them away to say, "We can go into the store, you know. Get you a better view."

But she shook her head. "Why don't you surprise me?"

"Okay," he said, though his ideas of what made good flavor combinations weren't what every customer enjoyed. "What do you like?"

"Something spicy. Cinnamon or cardamom, or even chilies."

He looked out at what was left in the cases, then knocked on the window. Lena Mining, his right-hand woman, held up one finger where she stood at the register counting out a customer's change before telling the others in line she'd be right back.

Moments later, she met him at the door, the longest swath of hair on her head falling over her right eyebrow and leaving the rings on the left brow—one silver, one bronze, one gold—exposed.

"Can you grab me a Queen Cayenne?" he asked.

"Sure thing, boss," she said.

Callum stayed where he was, and seconds later she returned, shocks of her multicolored hair sticking up in artful clumps. Makeup in the same bright pinks and blues shadowing her eyelids, she glanced over his shoulder at Brooklyn while handing him the candy in the brown glassine cup.

"She's Addy's teacher," he told her when her disconcertingly perceptive expression asked the question. "Don't be getting any ideas."

"Sure thing, boss," she said again. She said that a lot. Then she winked and returned to the store.

"She's cute," Brooklyn said, gesturing through the glass to where Lena was already at work filling a box for another customer.

"She's a pain in my ass, and I don't know what I'd do without her."
He offered her the candy. "Bottoms up."

"This is way too pretty to eat," she said, taking the pyramid-shaped
sweet from the paper and setting it on her palm, the kitchen's bright overhead lights picking up the molded brickwork of reds in the dark chocolate shell. "But something about it makes me think of Machu Picchu."

And then she popped the entire thing into her mouth and chewed.

He'd expected her to bite off the top, to listen to the crack of the
shell, to feel the sting of the pepper on her tongue. To look into the base
of the piece at the color of the creamy filling. To breathe deeply of the
chocolate and the chilies and the buttery ganache.

But nope. She tossed it back as if it were a handful of M&M'S.
And he loved it. Loved her smile as she savored the tastes. Loved her
eyes going big behind her glasses and her lips tightening when the heat
of the chilies hit.

Loved that she'd appreciated his artistry, but hadn't made it into a
big deal. She'd done what he'd wanted her to do. Enjoyed herself. And
that made him feel as if he'd made the best choice in the world with
his life.

∼

Though Brooklyn insisted she could make her own way back to the
school for her car, Callum insisted on taking her. She wouldn't have
minded the walk; it wasn't but a couple of miles. Or, though she
would've had to wait awhile, she could've used one of her taxi apps to
call for a car.

But no. Callum had brought her to Bliss, and, he said, he'd take her
back. She didn't put up much of an argument. Not really. She'd enjoyed
the wind blowing through the fabric of her clothes, tugging at the knot
of her hair. The bike growling beneath her like a big jungle cat.

The return trip was just as consuming, her legs open, her lower body pressed tightly to his, gripping his, clutching his. It was an incredibly intimate position to be in, while having nothing to do with the familiarity implied. Yet just for a moment, before they arrived, she let herself imagine what it would be like if he were doing more than taking her for a ride.

He stopped next to her car, the only one still parked in the teachers' lot, and waited for her to slide from the seat behind him. Once she was on her feet, her legs shaking, her heart tripping, he kicked the stand and pulled off his helmet, taking the second she handed him, one that truly was an extra, because it was too big for a six-year-old. He lashed it in place, his gripped between his thighs.

"I had fun," she said, flexing her fingers into her palms so she didn't reach for his hair. It was too long. It was in his face. She couldn't imagine him wearing it any other way. "And the candy . . . I can still taste the peppers. It's like they're sitting right at the back of my throat."

"But not too hot."

It was a statement, not a question, as if he'd worked long and hard to get the flavors just right. She imagined he had. "Perfectly hot. Especially since the chocolate is still there, too. Thank you for showing me what you do."

He nodded, holding tight to her gaze, his searching. "Do you feel better about Addy now?"

"I never felt bad about her. I see your influence in her every day. How polite she is. How inquisitive. I was more worried about you."

"Me?"

Tucking her hair behind her ear, she nodded. "I didn't want you to be missing out on these years with her."

For a moment she thought she'd gone too far. His hands tightened around the handlebars, and he looked away, his jaw clenched. But then he glanced back and said, "It's getting dark. Let me follow you home."

"You don't need to." She gestured toward her car, flinging away the nerves tickling the length of her limbs. "I'll be fine."

"Please," he said, and at last she nodded, and that was that.

The thrum of his bike vibrated behind her as she drove. The headlight pierced her car's back window like a beacon. His following her made her strangely anxious, when having spent the last hour with him, she should feel completely at ease. He wanted to make sure she got home safely. That was all.

She'd been getting herself home safely for years. Yet having Callum behind her, his big bike, his big body, his hands . . . what was wrong with her? He wasn't coming home with her to take her to bed. He was just being kind, she told herself, pulling into her driveway and hitting the button to open the garage, reminded again, as the door slid up, that she needed to replace the lightbulb.

She parked inside. She turned off the car. She climbed out.

He cut the bike's engine, and she turned into the stillness, her steps in sync with the beat of her heart and loud on the driveway's concrete. She should tell him thank you. Tell him good-bye. But those weren't the words she found tumbling into her mouth as she walked to where he straddled his bike.

"Would you like to come in? I can make you an espresso. Or I have Tia Maria. And illyquore. I don't think I have any Kahlúa, though I could open a bottle of wine . . ." And then she stopped because all she was doing was rambling about coffee liqueurs, and because he was standing now, and swinging his leg over the seat.

"I'll pass on the alcohol, but will take you up on the caffeine. I've got a long night ahead."

She answered with a nod and reentered the garage. Callum followed, and once he was inside, she hit the switch to lower the door. It creaked down behind him, and the last thing she saw before she was swallowed up by the darkness was the silhouette of his heavy boots moving toward her.

Clearing her throat of the nerves tickling there, she felt for the deadbolt and unlocked it, flipping on the lights as she stepped inside. She was across the room, having hit the button to heat the water in the espresso maker, when Callum closed the door.

"Do you work through the night often?" she asked, pushed to fill the silence. Being alone with him was trouble enough. Being alone with him in her kitchen . . .

The espresso maker hissed and steamed, then pounded the water through the capsule's packed grind. "Only a couple of times a year. Valentine's Day. Christmas. Oh, and Mother's Day, so three. I lucked out with Halloween. I'm too expensive. Though I do make some out-standing sugar skulls for the Day of the Dead."

What she wanted to know was how he'd fallen into making candy. What she said instead was, "I've got sugar and cream. Or I can steam milk and pour it in."

"I'm good with straight up," he said, then a grin pulled his mouth sideways. "Or 'yucky like dirt' as Addy calls it."

"How did you two end up in Hope Springs?" *Two*, because she was not going to ask about Adrianne's mother. "I know your parents live in town but I've always wondered if they played a part in your decision to open Bliss here."

He leaned against the counter beside her, his arms crossed. "You've wondered about me? Always?"

She was going to have to watch what she said around this one, she mused, handing him the tiny cup, the layer of crema atop the coffee visible through the clear glass, then gestured toward a chair at the table.

He took the cup from her hand, then took a seat while she made herself a latte. When she joined him, she'd found enough of her wits to answer. "I teach your daughter. I've met your parents. You're a famous chocolatier and you operate from the Texas Hill Country. Of course I've wondered about you."

There. He couldn't possibly pick through her response and find anything to tease her with. Could he?

He sat sideways to the table and he crossed his legs, his elbows braced on the chair arms, his drink held with the fingers of both hands as if he were playing an instrument. He made for such an incongruous picture. The *GQ* elegance of his posture. His *Sons of Anarchy* garb. His messy Heathcliff hair.

His hands were so large around the tiny espresso cup, and she thought about the delicate work he did with those long fingers, the exquisite chocolates he made. Thought about him running a brush through his daughter's long blond hair at bedtime. Thought about the children she and Artie had decided together they would never have because of the dangerous work Artie did.

They'd been right not to start a family, and she didn't regret their decision at all. How Callum managed on his own . . . then again, he had his parents close. She had no one left. It wasn't hard to understand how she'd fallen into a rut, when she had obligations to no one, and she was content with so little. "Mostly I've wondered why it took until today for you to visit Adrianne's class."

"You can thank my mother for that," he said, frowning as he stared down into his cup. "She signed me up for the story hour."

Interesting. "That doesn't explain where you were for the last six months. You know. At Halloween and at Christmas, when your parents were there for Adrianne."

"Working mostly," he said, sighing as he shrugged. "I didn't find out my mother had signed herself up for the Halloween or Christmas parties until after the fact. I mean, I knew about the parties from Addy, but not that I could've come. I'm new to this kid-in-school parenting thing, remember? And it's not like I've got neighbors keeping me posted." He leaned his head to one side and popped his neck, did the same on the other.

The motion gave her a better view of his neck and the words tattooed there. Which had her wondering again about the scales on his abdomen. And that thought had her hiding a private smile behind her cup as she brought it to her mouth. "You do go through the papers I send home, don't you?"

"Sure. Of course. But on the days I keep Addy with me, my mom usually stops by the shop after school to see her, so she goes through them first. She doesn't like my setup at Bliss. She thinks Addy would be better off staying with her until I get home."

Brooklyn hated that his mother's meddling had her rethinking her opinion of Shirley Drake, and threw out a bone. "Still, having your parents near has got to be a good thing."

"It's been good for Addy for sure. I mean, it's not like she wouldn't have survived day care. We all did. But my folks are great to step up at the last minute. Plus having them around has helped give Addy a good sense of family, and more stability, since otherwise it's just the two of us against the world."

There it was. The perfect opening. She could ask about Adrianne's mother and not feel as if she was stepping over the bounds of his privacy.

But not once had he, or his parents, or even his daughter, hinted at the woman's existence, leaving Brooklyn to hold her tongue. "It's good that you're close with them," she said, but then his mouth twisted again and she found herself adding, "If you *are* close with them."

"They're my parents," he said, and shrugged. "There's close. And then there's . . . close. As in way too far up in my business. My mother, anyway. Though with my best interests at heart, she says. And Addy's."

"I guess that's just how it is with families."

"Depends on the family," he said, leaving it at that as he drained his cup, set it on the table, and got to his feet. "Thank you for the coffee. It should get me through a few hours at least."

She set her own cup next to his and stood, too, resisting the urge to smooth down her hair, to check her sweater for wrinkles, to press the fabric of her pants with her palms. "I'd tell you not to work too hard . . ."

He smiled, a grin of deep dimples and eyes already too tired as he looked down at his feet. "I'm a lost cause."

"I don't believe that," she said, showing him out of the kitchen and through the living room to the front door. "Be careful," she said as she opened it.

"And you," he said, stepping out onto her porch.

"Me?"

"In Italy."

"That's four months from now." She couldn't bear the thought of this being their final good-bye. "You can come to Addy's end-of-year party and tell me then."

"We'll see," was all he said, leaving her with a wave, then walking down her driveway to his bike, and drawing her gaze to his stride, loose and rolling, his hips, his legs, his very tight—

"No." She whispered the word and shut the door, leaning her forehead against it and listening as Callum started the bike. Listening as he roared down the street. Listening until there was no more of him to hear.

She would not do this to herself—*she would not!*—tease herself, torture herself, with something her leaving meant she couldn't have. Even if she feared it might be the very thing she wanted.

Two Owls' Ultimate Chocolate Brownie Cake

For the cake:
1/2 pound room-temperature butter
2 cups granulated sugar
2 large eggs
2 cups all-purpose flour
1 teaspoon baking soda
6 tablespoons Dutch-processed cocoa powder
1/2 cup buttermilk
1/2 cup sour cream
1 teaspoon pure vanilla extract

Preheat oven to 350° (F). Grease and flour two 9-inch round cake pans and line with parchment paper, coating with nonstick spray.

In a large bowl, cream the butter and the sugar with an electric mixer until light and fluffy. Add the eggs and mix until thoroughly combined.

Into a medium bowl, sift the flour, the baking soda, and the cocoa powder.

In a small bowl, whisk together the buttermilk, the sour cream, and the vanilla.

With the mixer on low, add the dry ingredients and the liquid ingredients to the butter/sugar/egg mixture in three alternating batches. Divide the batter evenly between the pans.

Bake for 30–35 minutes, or until an inserted tester comes out clean from the center of the cakes, and the edges begin to pull away from the pans' sides. Transfer the pans to a cooling rack. Once cooled, carefully remove the cakes.

For the frosting:
1 stick softened butter
1/4 cup sifted Dutch-processed cocoa powder
8 ounces cream cheese
1 pound sifted powdered sugar
2 tablespoons buttermilk
1 teaspoon pure vanilla extract

Using an electric mixer, combine the butter, the cocoa powder, and the cream cheese at low speed, mixing until thoroughly combined. Increase the speed to high and cream the mixture until light and fluffy. Reduce the speed to low, slowly adding the powdered sugar, the buttermilk, and the vanilla.

Beat until the mixture is smooth. Frost the top of one cake layer. Cover with the second layer and spread the remaining frosting evenly over the top and the sides.

CHAPTER THREE

"I'm so sorry I'm late." Having hugged and helloed her way across the Two Owls Café dining room, Jean Dial tucked sunglasses with lenses the size of chrysanthemums into a nearly bottomless tote. A watch with a sunflower face battled two or three bracelets for real estate on her thin left wrist. She hung the bag on her chair back, but not before digging out two paperbacks. "Have you read either of these?"

"Ooh, I don't know. Let me take a look." Brooklyn scanned the titles and gave the back copy a cursory glance—the settings were Wales, 1157, and York, 1069—then said, "I don't think I have." She set both in the seat of the chair beside her with her purse. "Thank you. And you're not late. It's five minutes till noon."

"I was at the hairdresser's so long I guess it just feels that way. Pearl took a while to get started"—Jean patted the back of her silver bouffant, the charms on her bracelets jangling—"what with Maxine Mikels already in rollers and Peggy Butters getting a permanent wave. There was so much chatter, I'm surprised I didn't come out looking like Bozo the Clown. Of course, it didn't take Pearl long to finish, or me long to get out of there, once Shirley Drake came in and started carping on poor

Vaughn. That man is a saint, yet all Shirley's done since he retired is find fault with everything he doesn't get done, and everything he does."

Though she'd lived in Hope Springs for thirteen years, Brooklyn had yet to give up the Austin salon she'd trusted with her hair since grad school. She needed little more than a monthly trim, and enjoyed catching up with her college roommate when in the city, but her relationship with her stylist was sacred. It would be easier to grow her hair down to her feet than replace her.

And it was easier to think about doing so than let the mention of Shirley Drake have her mind drifting to Callum. "That surprises me. About Shirley. I've met them both, Shirley and Vaughn, at school functions, and they've seemed very much the happy couple."

Jean gave her a knowing look. "And how many times did Shirley pat Vaughn's wrist or knee and correct something he said? Or did she do all the talking, and not give him a chance to get a word in edgewise?"

At the time, Brooklyn had simply assumed Shirley Drake was intent on making a good impression as Adrianne's grandmother. But Jean's comments coming on top of Callum's remarks about his mother last night . . . "Let's not talk about the Drakes. Let's talk about how fabulous you look, as usual."

Taking the compliment in stride, Jean shook out her napkin and spread it across her lap. Woven by Kaylie Keller's best friend, Luna Caffey, née Meadows—the name behind the designer scarf line Patchwork Moon—the napkins and place mats coordinated perfectly with each room's color scheme. This particular eating nook, once a sitting room in the converted Victorian, was done up in the pale yellows and greens of spring. It was Brooklyn's favorite.

"I'm done teaching," Jean said, straightening the rings she wore on her pinkie and index fingers. "I sew and I garden. I don't know why I put myself through all this teasing and spraying . . . oh, who am I kidding? Of course I do. Their names are Maxine and Peggy and Pearl. It's hard to imagine going more than a couple of weeks without hearing the latest buzz."

"Anything good?" Brooklyn asked, smoothing her napkin and wondering what she would be doing when she reached Jean's age, whose gossip she would want to hear, what friends she would have to replace the ones with whom she'd lost contact.

"Oh, just what they think their husbands are doing for them tomorrow for Valentine's Day. All those surprises that don't ever seem to surprise." Eyes cast down, Jean lined up the cutlery just so on either side of her placeholder plate. "I never have been a fan of celebrating love with jewelry and candy and lingerie. Give me a good ol' bottle of bourbon any day. But I've also been without Mr. Dial for thirteen years. And that can make a difference."

"It can," Brooklyn said, though even when Artie had been alive she'd much preferred the practical gifts he'd given her year-round. Potted hibiscuses to plant along the side of their garage. A brand new cherry-red stand mixer just because she'd mentioned wanting one. Once he'd given her a fountain pen and a stack of yellow legal pads, knowing how she was with notes and lists and ideas she tended to jot on scraps and leave everywhere.

But Jean was just as practical as Artie had been, and rather than dwell on her loss, or Brooklyn's, or what might have been had death not interrupted, she reached for Brooklyn's hand and squeezed before pushing back her chair and asking, "Should we fill our plates?" then leading the way to the room set up with chafing dishes and signage—both decorative and descriptive.

The café's buffet of tossed salad with a selection of homemade dressings, fresh-baked hot rolls with sweet cream butter, local honey and jams, and piping-hot casseroles had Brooklyn realizing she'd skipped breakfast. Visiting Two Owls on an empty stomach was a very big, very bad mistake.

Today's entrées were vegetable lasagna, chicken spaghetti, and stacked pork enchiladas. Brooklyn knew from previous visits that Kaylie's father, Mitch Pepper, was the one who smoked the pork for hours before shredding it. His wife, Dolly, used a recipe handed down through generations of her family for the chicken dish. And the zucchini in the lasagna came from the Gardens on Three Wishes Road. The organic farm was owned by Kaylie's sister-in-law, Indiana, making Two Owls truly a family affair.

Brooklyn scooped up a small serving of each and added a roll to her plate along with a pat of butter and a spoonful of peach jam. She'd come back for salad later. Maybe. If she had room after the bread and the casseroles.

On the brownie bar, along with Cow Bells' vanilla bean and butterbrickle ice cream, was a new Ultimate Chocolate Brownie Cake and Two Owls' Number Ten Brownie Special. That one was packed with coconut and pecans, infused with orange zest and cayenne pepper, and topped with *dulce de leche*. Rumor had it Kaylie had been inspired to create the flavor combination by the man who was now her husband—a local contractor named Tennessee whom everyone called Ten.

Jean dished up a small plate of chicken spaghetti, then helped herself to a brownie and a slice of cake, topping each with a scoop of vanilla bean, an unabashed fan of having dessert first. Brooklyn would've done the same had she not already planned to spend the afternoon with multiple brownies in front of the TV at home.

"How's the packing going?" Jean asked, once they were seated again.

Buttering her hot roll, Brooklyn nodded. "I'm getting there. And I'm so glad I gave myself two whole semesters to do this. It's amazing the clutter that accumulates after twelve years of living in one place."

"Try thirty-two years," Jean said. "Curtis and I bought that house in 1983. I don't have enough time left in my life to go through everything I own. And I honestly don't want to," she added with a laugh. "So many things we didn't need. So much money wasted. I would love to go back and do it over again."

"You don't really think that, do you?" Brooklyn asked, having wondered often why she and Artie had bought so many books, only to read them once, and DVDs to replace VHS tapes, then left them sealed in their cases.

"We could've spent it so much more wisely," Jean said, scooting her dinner plate to the side. "Instead of Curtis investing in baseball cards and buffalo nickels and hand-tied fishing lures and electronics, we could've traveled like you and Artie did. Though I doubt getting rid of Curtis's hobbies would've funded us farther than Arkansas."

Brooklyn smiled. "It can definitely be costly, which is why I'm cutting all the corners I can. And if I sell my larger furniture pieces instead of storing them, I'll have that much more money to work with. Honestly," she added, reaching for her fork, "I'm debating getting rid of everything but what I'll need for the trip and the possible extended stay."

"Which side is winning?" Jean asked, scooping up a bite of brownie and melting ice cream with her spoon.

"I'm not sure." Brooklyn cut into her lasagna, shaking her head, wishing this decision were as easy as the one putting her on a plane four months from now. "If I knew when I was coming back, or even if I was coming back . . ."

"You have to eventually, don't you?" A concentrated frown. Another bite of dessert. "You can't stay in Italy forever."

Why not? The words sat for several seconds on the tip of her tongue. "I haven't thought much beyond June tenth, to tell you the truth." June 10th. The two-year anniversary of Artie's death. The date had been creeping up on her for months, and she was so ready to put it behind her.

"And come September?" Jean asked. "You're not going to miss those cherubic little faces looking up and hanging on your every word?"

Brooklyn thought about Adrianne Drake. And then, because she'd ridden behind him, and he'd given her chocolate, and he'd drunk espresso in her kitchen, holding the tiny cup with his large-boned hands, she thought about Callum Drake, too.

Teaching next year in Hope Springs would mean seeing Adrianne in the hallways and the cafeteria and on the playground, and wondering what had become of her father. "I will. But I'll have plenty of memories to look back on. And I owe Artie so much for making sure I'd be well taken care of monetarily."

"He was a good man, your Artie," Jean said, pointing at Brooklyn with her spoon instead of a finger. "And a good neighbor, checking the fluids in my car every weekend, as if I didn't know how to do it myself. Asking about the lawn any time my service was late. You remember that day Maxine came by, and you and Artie were outside, and he heard that noise under her hood? He took a look and saved her a small fortune by catching whatever was going wrong before it did."

The memory had Brooklyn smiling. Seemed like it had been an oil leak. "He liked taking care of things. Taking care of people."

"That's part of what made him so good at his job," Jean said, her gaze drawn to the photos of split-rail fences crossing pastures and prairies framed on the room's green pinstriped walls. "It's hard to believe the opening of this place was delayed so long because of a fire. I think about that and Artie every time I come here. Such a tragedy. Such a loss."

Her gaze on her plate, Brooklyn stilled. She knew the story of the house's third-floor turret having to be rebuilt after an electrical fire. But unlike Jean, she never thought about the fire when she came here. She did her best not to think about fires at all. As much as she'd loved reading to the crackle of flames in the fireplace at home, she hadn't used it since Artie's death, giving away the wood stacked on the patio and never buying more.

"It's okay that it still bothers you," she heard Jean saying. "To think about the fire. I can't pass an accident on the freeway without thinking about Curtis and his mangled car, and nearly losing my ability to breathe."

Bother. That hardly seemed a strong enough word. "Yes, but I feel like it's been long enough that I should have moved on."

Jean set down her spoon, and propped her elbows on the table, her fingers steepled below her sharp gaze, her bracelets tinkling against her watch face. "Why haven't you? I'm not saying you should have. Lord knows I'm not much of an example of how to get on with things, but maybe if you can put a name to why you're hanging on, you'll be able to let go."

Artie sharing his life with her had been everything that made their marriage fun. Except for going their own way for work, they'd been inseparable. When one cooked, the other came behind and cleaned. While one swabbed the toilet, the other took care of the tub. Brooklyn had weeded the flower beds while Artie had mowed. He'd moved the groceries from the car to the counter. She'd moved the groceries from the counter to the shelves.

They'd spent their days off together, even when that meant browsing different sections of the same bookstore, or one trying on clothes while the other waited outside the dressing room. Brooklyn buying new sheets and towels while Artie hit the hardware store. Meeting at the car loaded down with bags and heading for lunch, his shopping story turning into a whale of a tale between bites of his food. She'd be laughing until she couldn't breathe.

And there it was. She'd been without Artie for two long years, yet she'd kept his memory alive because she didn't know how to be alone. She gone from living with her parents until she'd finished grad school, to marrying Artie and living with him.

Was it any wonder she hadn't let go? She had no one else to hold on to, and wasn't sure her own two feet were steady. Sighing, she reached for her glass of iced tea. "Maybe I'm just not ready."

"I'd say the fact that you're going through and decluttering is a good sign you are."

"How did you know when you were ready?"

"Oh, honey. I'm still not. But I'm seventy-three years old. I was sixty when Curtis passed. I had forty years with the man in the flesh. Now he's with me in spirit. And I'm happy about that."

"You don't get lonely?"

"I have three children, six grandchildren. I have Maxine, Peggy, and Pearl. And I have you," she said, and Brooklyn's eyes threatened to sting. "I wasn't interested in marrying again. And though I enjoyed sharing Curtis's bed all those years, I wasn't terribly interested in sex after he died. Companionship, yes. I missed that. I still do. But I invite Alva Bean over for dinner every so often. He lost his wife four years ago. It's good for the both of us. Connecting. Laughing. But I'm too set in my ways for romance. You, on the other hand . . ."

"Oh, no. I'm just as set in my ways as you are." *I'm completely dull and boring. Just wait and ask my future cats.*

"But you *are* still interested in sex, I hope."

Brooklyn nearly sputtered her casserole. "I'm not ready to write off the possibility." And with that came thoughts of Callum again. Not Artie, whom she'd loved with her body as well as her heart and her mind, but Callum, after whom she lusted. "Actually, I did meet a man—"

"The one with the motorcycle?"

Jean was not a nosy neighbor, but Callum did ride a Harley. "You heard that, did you?"

"Hard not to."

"He followed me home from school to make sure I got there safely. Then he came in for a cup of coffee. That was it."

"I hope that was it," Jean said with a snort. "I heard him arrive, then heard him leave. He wasn't inside long enough for sex worth calling good."

"Jean!" Brooklyn laughed, but still her cheeks heated.

"Seventy-three years old, remember? I get to say what I think. Now, what's his name?"

Brooklyn hesitated; Jean had just made it clear how she felt about his mother. "His name is Callum. His daughter's in my class."

"So a little after-hours parent-teacher conference?" Jean asked, chuckling as she moved aside her empty dessert plate and reached for her chicken spaghetti. Then she stopped and looked up, frowning.

"Wait a minute. Callum. Do you mean Callum Drake? Shirley's son? The chocolatier?"

The heat blooming across her collarbone, Brooklyn nodded. "He came to class for story hour yesterday. Then he showed me his shop."

Jean considered her food. "I'm trying to remember if there was ever a father of a student I wanted to bring home. Of course, I was married all that time," she added, twirling a fork into the spaghetti. "I don't think Curtis would've liked very much me doing so."

Trying not to choke on the iced tea she'd just swallowed, Brooklyn said, "And this is why I will never give up having lunches with you, Mrs. Dial. It's like a meal and a show all in one."

But Jean's mind was elsewhere. "Do you know that young man's story? Why he's in Hope Springs? Why he's the one with custody of his little girl?"

"No," Brooklyn said, cutting into her enchilada. "We only met yesterday. And we talked mostly about his work and his daughter. A bit about his parents. I told him about Artie."

Jean arched a brow. "That's a lot of talk for a first date."

Brooklyn looked down at her plate with a quiet smile. "It wasn't a date. But no. I don't know his story. And I don't need to know." Though she was *so* very interested. "I assume he has one. Fathers don't usually get full custody."

"Shirley gives his history a sordid spin, but she does that with everything, so I'm not sure how much of what she says I believe. And I won't repeat any of the tales she's told at Pearl's because who knows if they're true. But I will say this."

Leaning forward, Jean covered Brooklyn's hand with her own and gave it a pat, her watch face slipping to the side of her wrist. "As good a man as your Artie was? From the facts I know to be true, not the ones embellished by his mother, Callum Drake is equally so."

~

Later that night found Brooklyn stuffed with brownies and thinking about good men. Not all the good men she'd known in her life, but Artie. And Callum. And her father, who'd loved her mother dearly, but had been clueless when it came to seeing where she needed help. Leaving her to the dinner dishes while he retired with a scientific journal didn't make him a bad man. Especially since Brooklyn had seen him pitch in when asked. But he had to be asked. For whatever reason, helping never occurred to him otherwise.

He'd been an academic, he and her mother both, which made Brooklyn's choice of profession somewhat fated. Theirs had been a house of learning: documentaries and discussion, books and brainstorming. Very little of what she'd read or watched had been for fun. Fun, her father said, was in thinking through puzzles, in solving problems strategically, in knowing things few others did. Even so, it wasn't about being smarter. Their family, he'd told her, simply used their minds more judiciously.

Artie had made her see fun differently. No. Artie had introduced her to fun. It hadn't made her think less of her father; it had made her appreciate Artie's love of life more. He'd had street smarts, and a four-year degree, and the sort of empathy her father didn't understand because her father read pages, not people.

And though she laughed at her susceptibility to the pull of the superficial, she couldn't deny the attraction of Artie's tattoos.

He'd had the most amazing series of firefighting tats on both arms and shoulders, and across his upper back. Helmets and hoses. Ladders and axes. Flags and eagles, and dates he never wanted to forget. Sadly, he'd lost a comrade during their eighth year of marriage; she'd gone with him when he'd added that one framed in a helmet shield.

Jean was right when she'd said Artie's need to take care of people had made him good at his job. That same compassion had been a big part of the reason she'd fallen in love with him. They'd met at a Labor Day barbecue thrown by his station's firefighters and their wives. Artie had been single, and Brooklyn the guest of a girlfriend whose brother worked Artie's same shift.

The brother had decided to play matchmaker. His matchmaking had worked. Brooklyn had been dazzled, swept off her feet. Artie had made sure she had enough to eat, that she was never without something to drink, that she met all of his friends and their families. That she learned everything about him time allowed. That he learned everything about her she was willing to share. That he had her number and her permission to call. He wanted to get together.

Oh, the memories, she mused, opening the hope chest at the foot of her bed and sitting on the floor in front of it. Thinking back to those early days never failed to bring on the tears. Sad tears, yes, but joyful ones, too. He'd been amazing. One of a kind. At least to her, coming from the world of academics, and she'd fallen hard.

The life of the party, her Artie. The jester. Always with a comeback, but never insulting or at another's expense. He'd been a big, bright light, and he'd shone down on her days, which were filled with term papers and textbooks, her nights, too. Her whole life, really. She could've majored in dull and boring. Until Artie had come along and saved her from herself. And from cats.

What he'd seen in her . . . it had taken her a long time to make sense of it. How he'd needed her quiet nature. They shouldn't have fit together; their personalities couldn't have been more dissimilar, their interests more diverse. Yet each brought to the relationship what the other was lacking, whether due to nurture or nature or something else. As much as she'd wanted to get to the bottom of their attraction, she'd finally managed to stop analyzing and simply enjoyed.

Later, she'd realized his clowning was a crutch. He'd used it to get through the dark side of his work, to take his mind off the destruction, the devastation, the loss; how could she blame him? She would never have been able to cope with the things he carried with him. Laughter, she supposed, was a better way to shore up his courage than drinking or drugs. That didn't make it any less addictive, or keep her from worrying when she found him in tears.

Shaking off the memories, she peered into the hope chest, trying to decide if she was up for more sorting and culling and packing tonight. She thought of Jean, living in the same place as long as she had. Brooklyn would've been only a year younger than Adrianne Drake when the Dials bought the house next door.

Of course, thinking of Adrianne had her thinking of Callum. On a regular Friday, Bliss would be closed by now, but with tomorrow being Valentine's Day, Adrianne would be with her grandparents while he worked late.

She wondered how many of his temp staff stayed late. Wondered, too, if Lena did. Then she reached into the hope chest for a stack of folders—she used the chest as a file cabinet for paperwork, storing tax records instead of her dreams—because what Lena and Callum did was not her business. And why she was even thinking there might be something between them, when neither had given off anything but an employer-employee vibe . . .

Enough. She had an entire house to organize and no time to moon over Callum Drake. Deciding to go through the files at the kitchen table, she grabbed the chest's lid to lower it, frowning as she caught sight of a sheet of paper stuck between the interior and its recessed tray. She tugged on the tray's hinges, then just sat there, staring.

How in the world had she forgotten tucking away the folder with all of her Cinque Terre notes? The ones she'd made after talking to Bianca, Artie's cousin who lived in Vernazza? Especially when the contents had played a vital role in her tendering her resignation after teaching for twelve years. She thought back to last summer . . .

She'd run out of shelf space on her living room's bookcases, and the books in her bedroom had become a hazard. Stacks leaned like the tower in Pisa against the side of her dresser, against the wall beside her dresser, and had spread across the top of her dresser like weeds. Then there were those taking over her vanity table, the ones she'd started shoving under the bed, and others filling the drawers of the bureau that had been Artie's.

The new case she bought, the first of what she feared would be many to line the house's long hall, meant rearranging her whole library—a collection of hardcovers and paperbacks and oversized art books in so many shapes it had taken her an entire weekend to sort them and shelve them, some staying in the living room, some remaining in the bedroom, some moving to their new home in the hall.

It was while transferring the books from the bureau that she'd unearthed the Bible bequeathed to Artie by his maternal grandmother. The family heirloom had been in the bottom drawer of the makeshift storage space for years; she remembered leaving it there with several of Artie's political thrillers when packing away some of his clothes.

Finding it the way she had, sitting on the floor in front of the bureau as she'd done so often when folding her husband's T-shirts and briefs . . . she'd been struck with myriad feelings, the most overwhelming being a sense of guilt. How had she been so remiss about keeping in touch with the members of his family since his death?

Artie had visited Italy several times before they'd married. His maternal grandparents had lived in Vernazza; his mother had grown up there, moving to the States at nineteen, where she'd married his father, and where Artie was born.

Artie had shared with Brooklyn his grandfather's stories: of fishing and swimming and sailing, of the sun and the lush olive groves and vineyards, of the gardens and the blue-green water he and his friends had taken for granted growing up. He'd told her how his grandfather couldn't wait until Artie, his namesake, his Arturo, was old enough to travel alone, to see it with his own eyes. To drink and breathe and relish the beauty of his Italy.

After she and Artie married, they'd made the trip four times, giving her the chance to meet and grow to love Pops and Zola before they'd passed on. Artie had wanted to visit more often. Instead, he'd put off his wishes while fulfilling hers, taking her to see One Tree Hill in Auckland, New Zealand, and the Royal Palace in Madrid. The Emerald Buddha in Bangkok, Thailand, and Norway's Urnes Stave Church in Ornes.

The memories made her feel so selfish. She loved Artie's family, his grandmother, his grandfather, his many cousins and their spouses and children. Time with them would've been the greatest gift she could've given Artie, but having grown up in such a sheltered environment, she'd wanted to see the world, and Artie had happily given it to her.

After running across the Bible, she'd e-mailed Bianca, Artie's cousin she'd grown closest to. Their correspondence had become a daily thing. When she'd learned about the floods that had struck Vernazza and Monterosso three years before, Brooklyn had been horrified by her failure to check in with the family sooner. And when she learned about the local church losing nearly everything, she mentioned the Bible to Bianca.

From there, the decision was made for her to bring the Bible with her when she visited in June. The village residents would be overjoyed to have it back in their midst. Talk had then turned to Brooklyn extending her visit, and staying to help Bianca with a new teaching initiative. Thinking now about those early days of planning her trip, the notes she'd jotted while researching housing and transportation . . .

Leaving the files in the hope chest, she headed to the kitchen, where she'd left the bottle of wine she'd opened earlier. Picking up her phone, she glanced at the clock, calculated the time difference, then scrolled through her contact list and hit Talk.

"Pronto?" came the answer less than thirty seconds later.

"Bianca? It's Brooklyn," she said, sitting as she reached for her wine. "Did I wake you?"

"Brooklyn! I'm just getting ready to turn in. *Come stai?*"

"*Sto Bene!* And you?"

"*Bene! Bene!* And looking very much forward to seeing you in June. It seems so far away, yet your visit is getting closer all the time. It is hard to believe your trip has been a year in the planning."

"I've been packing some of my belongings to store in my absence. I know several of the vases and figurines I have belonged to Grandmother Zola. Are there any you would like to have returned?"

"Oh, Brooklyn, yes. *Grazie*. I was just thinking about this the other day. Do you still have the majolica vase? The one with Adam and Eve and the goats and the cherubs?"

"And the creepy faces on the sides beneath the snake handles?" Brooklyn asked, and Bianca laughed.

"They are serpents. Not snakes. It's Adam and Eve!"

"Yes, I still have it." It was sitting in the corner of the living room, between two of her bookcases. The thing was gaudy and hideous and nearly three feet tall, but she'd kept it anyway. Because it had belonged to Zola.

"I would love to have that. Actually, Daniela is the one who would love to have it. I think it might be rather valuable and, well, you know Daniela."

"She's welcome to it." And all its dust, Brooklyn mused, cringing. "I'll go ahead and ship it to you. I'll be traveling light, so sending it ahead will be more expedient. And please let me know if you think of anything else."

They talked for another ten minutes, then rang off, their conversation leaving Brooklyn cheered, though still anxious; she had so much left to do, though in actuality, her anxiety was rooted elsewhere—in the two-year anniversary of Artie's death, when she would visit the family's vineyard and olive grove in Vernazza, and once there, scatter her late husband's ashes.

CHAPTER FOUR

Italy. Not the Golden Gate Bridge or the Great Lakes or the Grand Canyon. But Italy. Brooklyn was going to Italy with no definite plans to come back. Callum got that her husband's family was there, and she wanted to see them, but she couldn't make a quick trip of it? Tour the States if she needed a change of scenery? Teach someplace close if she was tired of Hope Springs?

He wanted to get to know her, but how smart was the investment of time and emotion when she was going to take off in a few months?

And, yeah. He couldn't believe this was where his mind had gone at the end of what had been a heinously busy Valentine's Day. Even without checking the receipts he knew he'd had a record one. But rather than celebrate the income and the exposure, he was stuck on Brooklyn Harvey leaving town.

What was wrong with him that he was making her life, her plans, her choices all about him? *That one's simple. She's everything good you could've had in your life all these years if you hadn't screwed up so completely.*

Sick of working with heart-shaped molds, he thought about tossing them instead of washing them. But replacing them next year would cost him, and he was done being stupid. Moving the polycarbonate trays from the marble work surface to the stainless-steel sink, he turned on the hot water and let it run, the room that he kept at a crisp sixty-five degrees growing damp from the steam.

Since day one of opening Bliss, end-of-day cleanup was on him. No candy mold unscrubbed. No floor tile unmopped. No bottle of colored cocoa butter unshelved. His daughter and his livelihood. He saw to every detail of both. At least the ones he knew about, and he *would* be having a talk with his mother—again—about backing off. As far as Bliss was concerned . . . maybe one day he'd let a crew handle things, but until then, iron fist, baby.

Shutting off the water, he headed out of the kitchen and into the store where his Roomba had been vacuuming for the last hour. This was his time to unwind, to put his world in order, to think. To process the day and assure himself it was exhaustion that had him imagining he'd heard the rumble of Harleys outside at the same time his father had stopped by this afternoon with Addy. He hadn't heard them. He couldn't have.

Addy was his. Officially. Legally. He'd spent every penny he could get his hands on to make sure he had sole custody. The money may have come from questionable sources. The evidence against the woman who'd carried his daughter nine months may have been enough to cost her her life. He didn't know. He didn't want to know. She was dangerous. She would've ruined Addy the way she'd very nearly ruined him.

A knock on the glass of the shop's front door brought his head around, loose strands of his hair flying into his face with the movement, his panicked heart slamming against the cage of his ribs. *Cool it, hotshot. It's not her. She's not here. Addy's safe.* He knew he was right, yet he couldn't rid himself of the fear that bubbled up in a hard, choking boil.

It wasn't Addy's mother. It was Addy's teacher. Brooklyn Harvey was standing on the sidewalk outside. She waved when she saw him looking at her, then wrapped her arms around herself and waited. And once he'd tamped down the dread that still lingered, he found himself smiling.

Found himself drinking her in and his emotions settling. It shouldn't be this good to see her. Though why in the world she was here . . .

She had to be cold. It was near midnight, and they might be in Texas, but it was the Hill Country and still February 14. Her sweater didn't appear thick enough to do its job, and though she had on jeans, she wasn't wearing socks with her flat slip-on shoes. He headed for the door, turning the locks at both the top and the bottom, and pushing it open.

"I'm sorry. I didn't think about you being all locked in," she said before he even got out a hello. "Though that answers that question."

"It's just a lock," he said, the cold rushing in and chilling him. "No big deal. Hang on. Let me turn down the music. What question?"

"Whether or not you wear chef whites."

It was so out of the blue, it left him looking down at his white coat and the stains of his work, at his black-and-white checkered pants Addy said were like her PopPop's crosswords, and wondering if she'd come for a particular reason, if she had something to say she couldn't do over the phone. If it was about Addy and couldn't wait.

"Is that what you came here to ask me? What I wear to work?" If so, he supposed it was better than asking him what he slept in.

Still standing near the door, she shook her head.

Well, something had brought her here. Once he'd turned down the music, he headed back to where she waited, and asked, "Are you okay?"

"It's not that important," she said. "And it could've waited, but I was thinking about it, and I couldn't sleep . . ." She pushed her hair from her face, tucked one side behind her ear, and shrugged.

"What is it?"

"I thought of a way for you to make up for all the class parties you've missed."

That's why she was here? Though the question he should be asking was why was she thinking of him while in bed? Was he the cause of her insomnia, or what she'd hoped would be a cure? "How 'bout I just promise to do a better job of keeping up next year?"

"You could do that," she said, canting her head as she studied him. "Or you could do a demonstration for the class. Show them how you made the candies you brought to story hour."

"A demonstration." He tried to wrap his mind around the idea. "Like here?"

Walking farther into the shop, she gestured toward his kitchen. "I know the window looking out over the register is one-way glass. What about the one on the side facing the shelves? The one behind the drawn blinds? That's a regular window, yes?"

He nodded.

She nodded, too, the motion an indicator of working out logistics. "There are only fifteen children in class. We always have three chaperones on our field trips. Mothers, fathers." She paused, added, "Grandparents."

Touché. "And you?" Because if he did this it would be for her. Addy would be bored silly; she'd seen it all before. And he couldn't imagine holding the interest of fourteen kids his daughter's age.

"And me. Of course." She looked up at the speakers in the ceiling, her brows drawn into a thoughtful vee. "Do you have one of those headsets like the chefs in Williams-Sonoma or HEB use for their cooking classes?"

"I don't, but I can get one." And then hope like hell he could figure out how to broadcast from the kitchen.

"That would be great, but only if it's not too much trouble." Her eyes were sparkling when she looked at him again. "Otherwise we'll work up a script."

"A script." Did she have an answer for everything?

"Just something simple," she said, waving one hand. "You explain to me beforehand what you'll be doing, and I'll do my best to describe the steps."

"I'm used to explaining things to Addy. I can probably make it pretty clear." Then he realized what he'd said and cringed. "For the kids, I mean. Not for you."

"Don't worry. I knew what you meant," she said. "Let me look at my calendar on Monday, then we can set up a date convenient for you."

"Can't wait," he said, and headed to the back hall for the mop since the Roomba had docked itself not long after Brooklyn arrived.

She laughed, a sound that said she saw right through him. "It'll be fun. I promise."

"I don't know," he said. "I'm thinking you skipped your college classes that taught you about fun."

"I didn't skip a single class in college," she said, arms crossed as she leaned against the corner of the kitchen's two walls.

"Exactly my point."

"Spend enough time with me," she said, her shrug self-deprecating, "and you'll see that fun is not, and never has been, my middle name."

He had a hard time believing that. He'd seen her excitement in the kitchen when he'd given her the candy on Thursday. Right after he'd seen the thrill of the ride in her eyes as she'd pulled off the helmet and shaken out her hair.

"In that case, can I sell you on the fun of doing dishes?" He asked the question jokingly; it was easier to keep things lighthearted than address the elephant in the room: What was she doing here at nearly midnight?

But she took it to heart. "Sure," she said, pushing away from the wall. "I'm happy to help if you need it."

He stood for a moment with the mop in his hand, listening to what sounded like a rumble in the distance. "You don't have to. That was just next on my to-do list. Lena does her best to keep it together when things are slow, but today was a mess."

"I don't mind. Whatever you need help with. Really." Then she stopped, as if realizing he'd checked out of the conversation, and asked, "Callum? Is everything okay?"

"Yeah." He shook off the distraction. "I just thought I heard . . ."

"Heard what?"

"Nothing." Because that's what it had been. Nothing. "Sounded like a Harley, but it's gone. It's been a long day. I'm punch-drunk."

She gestured over her shoulder with her thumb. "I can go—"

"No." He shook his head. "Don't. Please stay. But I'll do the dishes."

"You want me to clean up the shelves?" she asked, as she glanced around. "Dust and straighten things up?"

"Sure. Okay." He didn't want her straightening the shelves, but even more than that he didn't want to be left alone with his imagination. "There's a box of cloths in the far bottom cabinet, but don't worry too much about any of it. Lena will do it all over her way when we open again Tuesday morning."

Brooklyn laughed. "Having only seen her the one time, that doesn't surprise me. I got the sense she's incredibly efficient."

"Efficient's not even the half of it." The day Lena Mining had walked into his life he'd been able to let go of his worries about keeping the showroom running. Lena did that with whip-smart competence, allowing him to focus on his products. And the customers didn't seem to mind her multiple piercings, or the blue, pink, and purple chunks of her hair. "I can't imagine dealing with Valentine's Day without her."

"Do you believe in Valentine's Day?"

He looked over to where she squatted in front of the cabinet, not sure what she was asking. "Do I believe it exists? Do I believe people spend an exorbitant amount of money in the name of love? Do I believe Addy gets the biggest kick ever out of reading the words on conversation hearts?"

She glanced up, her black-framed gaze curious. "Is that a yes?"

"Do I believe there should be a single day set aside to celebrate love?" he asked, realizing as he did that he'd never actually been in love. He'd made love to a lot of women. He'd had fun with a lot of women. But the emotion had always been out of reach. He wasn't sure he knew why. "I'm all for anything that makes people feel good. It's not like giving a girlfriend flowers or candy on February fourteenth means her guy loves her any less the next day."

"If he loved her at all to begin with"—she toyed with a stack of chocolate bars imported from Hungary, then lined up their edges—"and didn't give the gift expecting something from her in return."

Sex. She was talking about—or avoiding talking about—sex. "I suppose that happens, but I'm just here to sell chocolate. Speaking of which . . ." He let the sentence trail, and she finally turned to look at him. "Did you buy any today?"

"Chocolate?"

He nodded. "I heard you talking to yourself when I came to your class on Thursday. You said you might."

"Oh. Right. That was mostly to keep from buying a cat."

"A cat?"

"It's a long story. A dull and boring story."

"No chocolates then."

"Candy, no. Though I had plenty of brownies leftover from lunch with a friend on Friday. Today I cleaned a little. I packed some. I figured since I've got enough time to go through everything before I leave, I need to do it right."

Packed. It was too soon for her to be packing for her trip. And a trip overseas, even one with no set return, didn't require her going through everything which meant . . .

"You're moving?" he asked, his heart in his throat nearly blocking the words.

"I think so. I might be. I haven't decided."

"Brooklyn . . ."

She answered with a soft laugh. "It's complicated. I'm not sure when I'll be back, which is why I didn't want the district holding my job. And really. My only ties to Hope Springs are sentimental. I don't have any family here. I lost touch with a lot of our friends after Artie died, and even more since. I'd miss Jean, of course. And others. But maybe it's time to move on."

The idea of Brooklyn being alone . . . he stared at the section of the floor he thought he'd just mopped, but it was dry, so he went over it again, slamming the mop head into the baseboard hard enough for the handle to bounce back and jab him. "What are you doing with your house?"

"That's where it gets complicated. I haven't decided whether to sell it or to rent it out."

"I guess that depends on whether or not you want to live there when you come back. If you come back."

"I'll end up somewhere eventually." She said it with a shrug. "But in the meantime I'm going through everything I own, tossing a lot of things. I still have Artie's tools, and most I'll never use. I don't even know what half of them do. I need to do something with those, at least."

He'd been renting the loft he and Addy called home for almost five years now, and they'd lived there on a shoestring, the money from Bliss going back into the business. Keeping to a budget meant moving would be a piece of cake. He couldn't imagine living for decades in the same house as his parents had done and sorting through years' worth of accumulated possessions.

He checked the supplies for the espresso machine in the cabinet beneath, then sponged out the sink before getting back to his mop. "I read somewhere that if you haven't used something in a year, toss it."

"I read the same, but for six months."

"That's kinda brutal. I've got T-shirts I haven't worn in six months."

Wiping down a shelf that held several books on the history of cacao, Brooklyn laughed. "Then you've got a more extensive wardrobe than I do."

"I just have a lot of ratty T-shirts. I've got some I wore in high school."

"And they still fit you?"

He shrugged. "Depends on your definition of *fit*."

Smiling, she moved to the next shelf and dusted around the demi-tasse cups used for sipping-chocolate. "It's what to do with the things I'm keeping that's the problem. If I hang on to the house, I'll just close it up and everything can stay there. But if I rent it, or sell it, I need to rent a storage space, too."

"So the packing is just proactive? In case you do move or rent?"

She nodded. "It's easier to go through everything now than at the last minute. Just in case. I'm looking at it as a long-overdue spring cleaning."

"How do you feel about having someone else live there?"

"If I still own it, you mean?"

"Own it and rent it, or sell it. Either way you won't be there and someone else will. Does that bother you?"

"I've never really thought about it like that," she finally said. "But, no. I don't think so."

"The place isn't a shrine, then?" he asked, thinking about her living there with her husband, then living there alone, falling out of touch with friends . . .

"A shrine? To Artie, you mean?"

"Or to the life you lived with him."

"Like I said, I still have some of his things." Her hands stilled for a moment before she finished repositioning the cups. "But no. No shrine. Just things we owned together."

That seemed a lot healthier than her continuing to worship the ground her husband had walked on. And thinking that made him feel like a jerk, especially since what lingered of her relationship with the man she'd been married to wasn't any of his business.

That didn't mean he wasn't curious. "You and your husband lived here a long time? In Hope Springs?"

"Eleven years." She dusted behind the row of fair-trade cocoa powder canisters. "I've been here now thirteen. We both lived in Austin when we met. I was finishing up grad school. He worked for the AFD. We moved here the year after we married. He would work a twenty-four-hour shift, then be off for forty-eight. He liked the separation of work and home."

"I get that."

"You never did tell me how you ended up here," she said, turning from the shelves and holding a dried cacao pod from a decorative tray of several.

"I came here for Addy," he said. She'd asked him on Thursday night in her kitchen, and he'd managed not to answer her then. He wasn't sure how much he wanted her to know about his past, but he was already feeling exposed, and since she was being honest . . .

"I'd been bartending in San Francisco, and I crashed with the owner and his wife for a while. Me and Addy both. I used the kitchen in his bar to run my business for about a year, most of that online."

"Adrianne must've been just a baby then," she said, facing him, the dust cloth crushed in her hands.

He nodded. "Straight from the hospital into a crash pad with her old man."

"Does Addy know her mother?"

His ears pricked as he listened again for the distinctive Harley rumble he thought he'd heard. "No, and she never will."

"How did you manage that?"

Oh the tangled webs we weave. "Cheryl didn't want her."

"What?" she asked, the question coming out on a choked breath.

He slapped the mop against the floor again and shoved it across the tiles. "I cut her out of my life in the hospital when she told me if I didn't want the kid, she was going to give it to someone who did. And that's a direct quote. She called our daughter *it*."

"Callum." Brooklyn stopped. Her eyes tearing. "I'm so terribly sorry."

"It happened. It's done with. I'd like to say I'm over it . . ." He shook his head, surprised he'd said that much. He didn't talk about Cheryl.

Ever. "I'm not, because who calls a newborn infant *it*, but I don't dwell on the past. Addy's mine, and that's all that matters."

"Well, it's obvious you're doing an amazing job with her," she said, adjusting her glasses. "She adores you, but I'm sure you know that. Not all of my students are lucky to have a father as involved as you are, though I suppose that comes with being a single parent."

"Right," he said with a snort. "I'm so involved I've missed how many things so far this year?"

She gave him a lopsided grin. "Fifty cents says you won't miss anything else."

"Fifty cents?" That made him smile. "That's all the faith you have in me?"

"I'd bet more but I'm saving all my money for my trip." She walked the length of the shelves, checking to see what she'd missed. "I want to kick myself for falling out of touch with Artie's family."

He supposed talking about her ex was better than talking about his. "Harvey's not an Italian name."

"His mother moved here from Vernazza when she was nineteen and married an American a year or two later. Artie was in college before he made his first trip to Italy. His mother never went back."

"Bad blood?"

She shook her head as if she didn't have an answer. "I never met her, but from what he told me, she and his father had pretty much cut themselves off from both of their families before he was born. There was some spousal abuse. Artie did what he could to help his mother, and stay out of his father's way, but he was young. He couldn't do much. He only knew about the family he had in Italy because of the letters his grandfather wrote." She paused, then waved off the rest of what she'd been going to say. "I can't imagine you want to hear all this."

The juxtaposition of his cushy upbringing with that of her husband . . . "Sounds like a rough way to grow up."

"He turned out okay, though he had moments he wasn't proud of, stealing food so he and his mom could eat, stealing money so she could pay bills." She swallowed, tucked back her hair. "I mean, his reasons were good, but still . . ."

Yeah. He was putting food on the table. Not stealing to get high. "He did what he had to do. Some of us can't even manage to do what we should."

"You would've been at the school for Addy's parties if you'd known," she said, tossing the disposable dust cloth into the trash can on the far side of the shelving unit. "I'm quite sure about that."

"I would've been. But that doesn't excuse me not being more on the ball. I've kinda relied on my parents to the point of letting them take care of things that aren't their responsibility. Trust me that it's not going to happen again." He rolled the mop and bucket back to the hallway door and left it there. "As tied up as I am with the shop, Addy comes first."

Frowning, she dropped her gaze to the floor. "If you're too busy to do the demonstration . . ."

Because of Bliss? "No. It's okay. It'll be fun."

"My idea of fun, anyway," she said, waving an arm toward the front door and heading that way. "And I can help you with whatever prep you need to do so it won't be so overwhelming."

"Do you make that offer to all the places who host your field trips?" he asked as he squatted to unlock the door.

"Nope," she said, tugging it open and letting in a blast of cold air. "Only the ones whose owners feed me chocolate. And have tattoos."

"You like the ink?"

"I'm curious about the sayings," she said, pointing to his neck, letting the door close, and remaining inside.

"I've got Nietzsche, Tolkien, and if you're more into science fiction than fantasy, I've got Frank Herbert. Then there's Lewis Carroll. Even Harper Lee."

She cocked her head, her expression broadcasting her curiosity when she said, "Really?"

He nodded, wondering if that look meant she was trying to guess what he'd chosen. *Dune*'s mind-killer passage about dealing with fear was obvious, but only if she knew the book and more about him. And the banter between Alice and the Cheshire Cat about mad people had seemed to fit his life at the time, though she wouldn't know that.

The Harper Lee might be harder, but Atticus talking to Jem about courage had stuck with him. He'd chosen the first two lines of Tolkien's "The Riddle of Strider" for the same reason, finding the sentiment about wandering but not being lost apropos when he'd gotten the ink.

But none of those tattoos were easily accessible. "How 'bout Tennyson?"

He pulled up his sleeve to show her the words. They were buried in a design that began just above his inner wrist and circled his forearm, before disappearing beneath his coat.

She took hold of his hand and read the quote for herself. "'To strive, to seek, to find, and not to yield.'" Then she ran her finger along the words, and onto the visuals around which they'd been wound. "Do these have anything to do with the motorcycle club?"

"The words or the pictures?" he asked, surprised at how steady his voice sounded, when her touch had him wound up inside.

"Both. Either."

"They did. Some I never had altered. Others were too gruesome, and I didn't want Addy freaking out."

"The wolf is nice," she said, holding his hand palm up in hers and tracing the animal's snout where it nudged against his wrist bone.

"Now it is," he said, staring at the back of its head, which used to be open, with skulls pouring out as if they'd been scraped of their flesh and humanity and eaten by the beast. He'd covered the wound with a scroll of parchment, then had the Tennyson line—the final one from *Ulysses*—inked on top.

But mostly he was staring at his hand in Brooklyn's. She held him like she would a baby bird, her palm barely cupped as if squeezing him too tightly might break him because he was fragile, and wild, and too new to his life not to jump away from what frightened him.

Funny about that, how such a gentle, nonthreatening, understanding touch made him want to leap.

He was just surprised by the direction he was thinking to go.

~

It was close to one a.m. when Brooklyn finally got home, and for the whole of the drive all she'd been able to think about was what in the world had compelled her to go to Bliss in the middle of the night? Okay, it hadn't really been the middle of the night, but it had been long after hours.

Calling would've been so much easier—and so much warmer—though doing so wouldn't have made much sense.

The fact that it *had been* after hours when she'd been struck with this insane idea made Callum still being at work a long shot. And her idea. Really? A kindergarten class field trip to his shop? Was she that desperate to see him? Apparently so. Midnight hadn't stopped her.

She'd gone because . . . did she even know? She could have easily talked to him next week about the field trip idea. Or, by then, she could have easily talked herself out of it. Bliss wasn't a big shop. Lining up a row of seven children in front of a row of eight at the window would work.

But the logistics of fitting fifteen five- and six-year-olds into Callum's confectionery wasn't the issue. The issue was her grabbing on to any reason to see him. This wasn't like her, this giving physical attraction more than its due. She refused to believe she was so . . . what? Sexually needy? That she'd invent reasons to see a man with whom she shared only chemistry?

Except that wasn't true, not at all. For one thing, they had his daughter in common, her education, her welfare, though the latter wasn't truly Brooklyn's purview but that of Adrianne's father. But more than both caring about the girl's well-being, well . . . what *were* their mutual interests?

Chocolate, obviously, though he was the expert and she was only there to enjoy the fruit of his labors. She'd never been on a motorcycle before riding behind him, and could add that to the list of things they enjoyed. And tattoos, even if she didn't think she'd ever be brave enough to get one.

But bigger than all of those things, he made her laugh, which few people did anymore, and in a different way than Artie had. Her sense of humor was, well, stunted if not lacking. Artie had known that and teased laughter from her as often as he could.

Callum wasn't a jokester, except at his own expense. He took himself seriously, but only when it mattered, and when it didn't, he had no problem making light. She liked that about him. She liked it a lot. She liked, too, the way he flirted. And that he included her in the fun. He wasn't performing. He didn't need an audience. A subtle thing, but it was there.

His grin spoke volumes, but his words came layered with so much meaning, requiring she peel back the ones she'd deciphered, and hope she could do the same with the next. She liked that depth. Liked that she couldn't take what he said at face value because the true gems in his words were buried. Liked a whole lot that he found solace in words, too. Enough so to mark himself permanently as if wearing them as armor against the world.

But attraction or not, she should not have gone to see him. It was February. She was leaving for Italy in June. Four months barely gave her enough time to get her house ready to list, the sign in the yard, and her possessions either sold or stored. And all her books . . .

Suddenly, she was extremely exhausted. And left pondering the fact that she was scheduled to leave town after meeting a man worth staying for.

Friday, May 26, 2006

"Please let me do something," Brooklyn said. "It's my anniversary, too, you know." She was sitting at the table in the kitchen of the Hope Springs house she and Artie shared, watching him very capably pull their dinner together.

He had already set the table, taken the lasagna he'd worked on all afternoon from the oven to cool, and put the fresh Italian loaf he'd baked earlier in to warm. Their kitchen smelled like a ristorante: *onions, tomatoes, oregano, and wine, and Brooklyn was starving. For the food. For her husband.*

He brought two glasses and the bottle he'd just opened to where she sat, and poured hers first. She reached for the stem, looking past it to the dark hair dusting the edge of his hand, his wrist. The tattoo on his forearm. It was new, and still healing. He had it inked to commemorate ten years on the job.

It was the Austin Fire Department symbol. Above and behind it flew the Texas state flag as well as the stars and stripes. An eagle perched on top, its talons gripping the emblem's edge, and the word Brotherhood *stretched across the center on a banner.*

She lifted her glass to her mouth and sipped, her gaze falling to his belt buckle against his flat stomach. She wanted to take him to bed. The lasagna could wait. But this was the first time in their five-year marriage that his shift hadn't fallen on their anniversary date. This was his night as much as it was theirs, and she wouldn't do anything to take away from their celebration.

"Drink," he told her. She raised her gaze; his smile was bright in his five o'clock shadow, and his brown eyes flashed. "That's what I want you to do. Drink and relax and enjoy dinner. Your gift to me."

"*Five years. You're supposed to give me wood,*" *she said, and when he snorted with laughter, she felt the heat of a blush rising. She loved that he could still make her blush.* "*Something made out of wood, you perv.*"

"*You love every pervy bit of me,*" *he said, heading back to the oven to check on the bread.* "*Or would that be every pervy inch?*"

He was right. She did. "*What I love is your lasagna,*" *she said, and sipped her wine. The bottle he opened was one of several they brought back from their last trip to Vernazza. They had plans to go again in June.*

He bent at the waist as he reached for the bread, and all she could think about was undressing him, climbing over him, onto him. She drained her wineglass and when she reached for the bottle to pour more, he was there, across from her, handing her a box enclosed in olive-green paper.

A ribbon of pink wrapped the box in a cross, and the tiny bow at the apex was the same pink sprinkled with glitter. She didn't want to open it. The package was pretty enough that she wanted to set it on the living room bookcase as a keepsake, but she sensed Artie's impatience.

"*C'mon. Open it.*"

The box was a rectangle, the size fitting of a fountain pen, but he'd given her a fountain pen before. She wasn't a jewelry person, though it might very well have held a bracelet. She couldn't imagine him buying a bracelet.

What she found inside was a bookmark. The label read "*Arte Legno,*" *whose products, she knew, were made in Italy of olive wood. The top of the bookmark was carved into an owl with big eyes, big ears, a tiny beak, and feathers that could've served as flat toothpicks.*

"*Oh, Artie,*" *she said, pressing her fingers to her lips.* "*I love it. It's adorable.*"

"*And me?*" *he asked.* "*Am I adorable?*"

"*Absolutely. And I love you, too.*"

"*Good,*" *he said, leaning across the table to kiss her quickly, then sitting back and sobering.* "*Because I need you to promise me something.*"

He rarely asked her for a promise, and when he did, it was almost always morbid and something she didn't want to give.

"It's our anniversary. Can the promise wait? I don't want to spoil the mood." Though his request had very nearly done so already.

He held up two fingers. *"Two years. If I go up in flames—"*

"Artie!" She hated how he talked about the dangers of his job. He tossed off the words so callously, when the picture he painted was her worst nightmare.

"No keepsakes," he said. *"No mementos. I don't want to think about you making this house into a shrine. Get rid of my clothes, any books of mine you won't read, any of the crap in the garage you won't use. Don't leave pictures of me on the bookcase—"*

Why was he saying this? What could have prompted him to be so grim on today of all days? "They're pictures of us. Artie, what's going on?"

But he ignored her. *"You know what you look like. You know what I look like. If you have to keep them, put them in an album. Or scan them and store them on a flash drive."*

She couldn't bear the thought of losing him, or of his wanting her to put him away. She loved him. He was her life. Emotion rose to choke her, and she put down her foot. *"I'm not getting rid of the owls."*

He glanced down at his plate, his forearms on the table's edge. A smile played over his face, and he laughed. *"The owls you can keep. But two years is more than enough time to get on with living. Even rigorous Catholic customs no longer require a lengthy mourning period. You're not Queen Victoria, and we're not living in the old country. Promise me."*

"I can't—"

"Brooklyn. This is important to me." He reached for his wine and drank. *"I want you to scatter my ashes someplace meaningful. Pops's olive grove and vineyard, or the Guadalupe or the Gulf. Wherever you want."*

"Oh, my God, Artie." She fought down a sob, her throat burning, her eyes aching, her chest feeling as if it would burst. *"Why are you asking me this now?"*

"Why not now? We're celebrating our marriage, our love. This . . . magic we have together." He took hold of her hand, and closed her fingers

in his, holding her gaze, his eyes solemn and red. "This is something I need from you because of that. You know I'm not sentimental—"

"You are the most sentimental person I know." She picked up the book-mark, ran her thumb over the tiny sticks carved to resemble feathers. "If this isn't you showing sentiment, I don't know what it is."

"I can show you even more," he said, his voice growing husky. "But we'll have to go to the bedroom."

"Why?" she asked, because he had her feeling out of sorts, and she was struck with the urge to prove them both so alive that death wouldn't dare visit. "Why can't you show me right here?"

He was leaning back in his chair, his legs spread, and he drained his wine. Then he returned his glass to the table, and scooted his chair from beneath. His hand went to his belt. Just the one hand, and he freed the buckle, then the button of his navy Dockers, then he opened his zipper. And he was hard when his fly parted.

She went to him, straddled him, wrapped her arms around his neck. Then he said "Promise me," and her heart froze, then jolted, and she said "I promise," pushing out of his lap and leaving the kitchen, leaving behind the lasagna and the wine and the bread.

Leaving behind the man she loved more than life itself with the very thing he'd wanted from her: her word that she'd let him go.

CHAPTER FIVE

After Brooklyn's Saturday night visit to Bliss, Callum became obsessed with Italy and Cinque Terre. He'd never been. He'd never planned to go. Hell, he'd never even heard of the place until Brooklyn had mentioned it, then he'd taken to Google the next time he'd had some free time, wanting to see exactly where it was she was going.

And now, well, her reasons were her own, but he couldn't stop thinking about walking the Sentiero Azzurro between the villages, eating gelato, drinking wine, looking down into the sea. Carrying Addy on his shoulders so she could see the vineyards and the terraced hills and the olive trees. Piggybacking her when her little legs got too tired to climb.

The idea of showing his daughter the world, being able to give her every advantage in life, every chance in life, every possible thing she might need to live the most amazing life . . . As much as he'd loved California, he'd had no choice but to move her out of that volatile environment. Coming to Hope Springs had made the best sense at the time.

Having his parents near allowed him to work the hours he needed. Their generosity, their availability, their delight in having a granddaughter . . . he'd be nowhere without them, or at least traveling a much harder road. As often as he and his mother clashed, and as aggravated as he got with her ignoring his instructions for Addy's care—giving her cookies she didn't need to eat, playing TV news she didn't need to hear—he owed her and his father a magnificent debt.

But his obsession with Cinque Terre was all such crap, because he was not taking Addy to the Italian Riviera. And even if he did, Brooklyn was going now, not later when he'd be able to, and the trip wouldn't be half as much fun without her. Though why he was jumping to that conclusion when he'd known her a whole four days . . .

Four days. And he'd only seen her on two of them: Thursday and Saturday. Friday he'd been elbow deep in chocolates and too busy to think, but Sunday he'd done nothing but crash on the futon and dream of Italy—and Brooklyn—while Addy curled up beside him and watched *Reading Rainbow*.

He was totally preoccupied by a woman he wasn't dating, a woman he hadn't slept with, a woman he'd done nothing but talk to. They'd talked a lot. And about a lot of things. He couldn't remember the last time he'd opened his mouth and let so many words spill out. He much preferred no one know where he'd been, what he'd done . . .

But he couldn't get Brooklyn Harvey out of his mind.

On one hand, he liked that she was there, tucking her hair behind her ear, smiling, making sure he was taking care of his girl. On the other . . . it was as if he hadn't learned a damn thing from his past. Jumping into situations because doing so made him feel good instead of making the best choice.

Right. Since life was all about feeling good. The years he'd lived with that attitude had messed up so many people's lives he'd lost count. And created one that left him breathless, that hitched at his heart anytime his thoughts drifted to her. Or when he first heard her voice in the mornings.

Speaking of which . . . "Adrianne Michelle! Breakfast is getting cold!"

"You don't have to yell, Daddy," she said, skipping her way around the kitchen bar to her stool. "I'm right here with my ears."

And there went his heart. *Thump, bomp. Thump, bomp.*

She'd slipped her feet into bright pink Crocs, no socks, of course, and pulled on pink leggings to match. Her top was long sleeved and long waisted, purple and black striped with whatever that flippy skirt-like thing attached was called. In the center of the top was a black giraffe with purple spots, its neck wound around that of a purple giraffe with black spots.

His mother bought a lot of Addy's clothes, even though he continually reminded her that he was perfectly capable, at which she always rolled her eyes before telling him not to be silly and to allow her to be a grandmother, please, since she'd missed so much of Addy's life already.

An exaggeration: Addy had turned six last month. He'd brought her to Hope Springs not long after her first birthday. So, yes. His mother had missed swaddling an infant, but she had years of grandmothering left.

What he wasn't perfectly capable of, and didn't mind admitting because it wasn't his thing, was dealing with his daughter's corkscrew hair. Yet he couldn't bring himself to cut it. The waves were his, unruly and with a mind of their own. Addy got a kick out of them both wearing theirs long.

The blond hair and blue eyes, and the lashes that brought to mind the thick bristles on a pastry brush, well, he shouldn't be thinking it, but they were a lot like Brooklyn's. It was just easier to think of Brooklyn than the truth of where his daughter's coloring had come from.

"Well, you and your ears need to eat your eggs," he said, scooping the scrambled mess from the skillet into a bowl, putting a slice of jam-smeared toast on a saucer to match. "We've got places to go and people to see."

"Silly Daddy," she said, clambering up to sit and setting her plush Olaf on the stool beside hers. "Ears can't eat eggs."

"Are you sure?" he asked, scraping the rest of the eggs onto his plate and tossing the skillet into the sink. "I've seen food in your hair many times. I thought your ears might have vomited."

"That is just yucky," she said, reaching for her toast with both hands and taking a bite before saying, mouth full, "You forgot my milk."

"So I did," he said, turning to the fridge for the carton and the cabinet for a cup.

"What people and places are we going and seeing?"

He smiled. "I have to pick up some supplies for Bliss in Austin."

"It takes hours and weeks to get to Austin," she said as she dug into her eggs, her brows drawn together as if she were calculating drive times. "You should just go shop at HEB. Grammy gets everything at HEB."

He chuckled. Little girls. "HEB doesn't sell what I need. They don't even sell everything Grammy needs. You know she has to go to Austin sometimes." Though often it was only so she could drop the name of the specialty store she'd visited and the item she'd purchased that she might use but once in a dish she'd seen Nigella Lawson cook.

"But you said we could go to the park and to the bookstore and to get ice cream. It will take forever to go to Austin," she whined. Then whined again. "You might be too tired and forget when we get back."

"How can I forget when I have you to remind me?"

"Sometimes Grammy forgets."

"Tell you what," he said, opening drawers until he found a pencil and a notepad and a roll of Scotch tape. He tore out one sheet and licked the pencil's lead. "I'm going to write a note this minute, and you can tape it on the dash of the truck. That way we'll both remember everything we need to do today. Both in Austin and in Hope Springs."

She seemed to like that idea, nodding as she picked up her milk. "Most important is ice cream."

"Ice cream. Got it," he said, biting into his toast and holding it with his teeth as he anchored the notepad in place with one hand and wrote with the other. "Do you know what flavor you want?"

"I want ten scoops of peppermint bubble gum."

"I'm not sure Cow Bells has peppermint bubble gum."

"Do so. Kelly Webber told me."

"Well, if Kelly Webber told you, then it must be true. But only one scoop. Not ten."

She gave him a huge huff, as if she were making the ultimate sacrifice. "And going to the park. Write that down."

"The park," he said, having returned his toast to his plate. "It's on the list."

"Write down the slide and the swings so I don't play too much on the monkey bars and forget."

"I won't let you forget."

"You might, so write it. And write down books. I want ten books."

Slide. Swings. Monkey bars. He wrote them all. Then he wrote *books*, but not ten. "How about three books?"

She took a moment to frown, then said, "But ten is more."

Good for her. "Ten *is* more but your bookshelves are too crowded already."

"I like ten."

So he'd noticed. "Tell you what. You can pick out three today," he said, writing the number beneath the rest of the items on the list, "then choose three from your shelf to give to someone who might need them."

"Kelly Webber might need them," she said matter-of-factly before leaning close to her bowl to scoop another bite of eggs into her mouth. "She doesn't have enough and Ms. Harvey says we need to read books every day."

And there went his heart again, though this time the thump came with a tightening of his gut. "Well if Ms. Harvey said it, it must be true."

"Everything Ms. Harvey says is true."

"Oh, really," he said, biting off half a piece of bacon.

"Duh. She's a teacher."

He'd have fun reminding Addy of that in fifteen years when she was deep into her cultural anthropology studies or whatever. Setting the list aside with the roll of tape, he tossed the pencil back into the drawer. "What's the best thing you've ever learned from Ms. Harvey?"

Addy set down her milk, her mouth twisted to one side. "About the moon. And the sun. And the shadows on the world. Like clips. With a lamp."

"*E*-clipse. And how the earth rotates on its axis around the sun, making day and night?"

She nodded as she shoved a whole strip of bacon into her mouth and chewed. "She had a soccer ball and a corn of pepper and then she had a lime with a stixis through it because the pepper was too small to twirl around."

He took a minute to translate her six-year-old speak. A lime on a stick representing the earth on its axis. A soccer-ball sun and a peppercorn Earth. Lego bricks for fractions. Portraits of presidents instead of conversation hearts.

Clever Brooklyn Harvey, using familiar objects to demonstrate the foreign—though for all he knew, having attended absolutely zero school functions, her props were standard in kindergarten instruction.

He wanted to kick himself for not paying more attention to what Addy was learning in school; blaming his mother for going through the notes from his daughter's teacher was just lame. He knew better.

He'd talked to Peggy Butters at Christmas when she was doubling up on her seasonal cookie baking. They'd joked then about mothers ordering goodies for class parties and passing them off as homemade.

Hell, he'd bought cookies decorated like jack-o'-lanterns himself for Addy to take to school at Halloween. And he'd helped her with her Olaf costume. How many little girls had dressed like *Frozen*'s Elsa, while his daughter had insisted on being the movie's snowman?

This was Addy's first year of school, and he was going to have to step up his game for the twelve of public education yet to come. If he didn't, all the rest of his efforts to provide for her wouldn't mean squat.

For five years his focus had been on establishing Bliss as *the* place for artisanal chocolates in the Hill Country. Maintaining his online business had been easier; that was no more than creating the supply to meet the demand that had continued to grow since he'd begun offering his wares in San Francisco.

The first few months he and Addy had been in Hope Springs, he'd cooked in this very kitchen, packaged boxes for shipment on folding tables lined up beneath the loft's long wall of windows.

He'd held interviews for his showroom help in his living room. He'd brought in a branding designer for his logo, an interior designer for the look of the shop. Experts in packaging, labeling, advertising.

He'd used the money he'd been handed by Duke Randall, the man who'd been his best friend in California. His mentor. His conscience and guide, and though she would never know it, Addy's uncle. He hadn't questioned where it had come from; he didn't want the answer. He'd needed it to give his daughter a good life, a safe life; he didn't want to know.

It had been worth it: the lack of sleep, the trial and error, dealing with new vendors and new employees, Lena as well as the occasional temp, and a new relationship with his mom and dad.

He'd do it all again. He'd do it ten times over.

Because he was doing it all for the little girl sitting at the bar drinking milk, eating bacon and eggs, and talking to a goofy-looking snowman. The little girl who was his whole life, who was his whole heart.

~

Sitting cross-legged in the far back corner of Cat Tales, the best new and used bookstore in the world, Brooklyn reached for a long-out-of-print Penelope Williamson title and read the description on the back. Or she tried to read the description on the back. The words weren't cooperating, keeping her from remembering if she'd read this one before. Mostly likely she had.

Still, there was a chance Jean had not. She added it to the stack at her hip on top of a Kathleen Woodiwiss, as if she needed yet another huge trade paperback on her not-even-a-year-old bookcase. She didn't, and she knew it. She also knew why she was here, and it had nothing to do with books.

Her visit was about her life turning upside down, first by Bianca's pleas that she stay in Italy to teach, and now by her attraction to Callum Drake.

When she worried about upcoming dates—a new school year, an annual checkup, an international flight—or when she needed a distraction—the amount of time she spent thinking about Callum proved she did—she browsed her two favorite bookstores: Cat Tales and Amazon. Her poor Kindle. Her poor credit card. Her poor not-even-a-year-old bookcase.

She reached for a Michelle Willingham book set in 1305 Scotland, only to find a pair of bright yellow eyes that belonged to the store's mascot staring at her from the shelf above. No way. Uh-uh. This was not a sign. But the big gray tabby using the row of books as a bed did explain why her eyes were suddenly watering.

"You're lying on my Willingham, sir. I hope you don't think you're going to get away with that."

He answered with a big yawn that seemed to be more about showing off his canines than anything.

"Oh. Is that so? You're a fan of mysterious stable boys and maidens and castles with no running water, too?"

Another teeth-baring yawn, and a long reaching stretch; then the cat eased from the shelf into her lap, curling up and making himself at home in the cradle of her crossed legs.

"No, no, no. This isn't happening," she said, laughing to herself as the cat began to purr, loudly, the rumble against her thighs bringing to mind Callum's bike. See? This was what she was talking about. Why couldn't she shake her thoughts of him?

It was ridiculous, this fascination. It wasn't like she hadn't known handsome men before. Artie's crew could've posed for a firefighter calendar and made buckets of cash.

Of course, her being Artie's wife meant none of them ever regarded her the way Callum had from her classroom door. Or later, in her kitchen. Thinking of how he'd looked at her after she'd downed the piece of chocolate at Bliss, or when she'd held his hand to get a closer look at his Tennyson tattoo . . .

How could she possibly be feeling so strongly about a man who'd only come into her life this weekend? And why was she going over this again when she'd told herself not two nights ago that none of the things between them could matter? Hope Springs had been her home for thirteen years, and in four months she'd be leaving for who knew how long? Callum was staying. His business was here, his family was here, his daughter went to school here.

No doubt one day he'd have a wife, and a passel of little red-headed Irish rogues running riot across an expanse of lawn as green as his homeland. Not that Ireland was actually his homeland, but she was sitting in the romance section, and dammit, she would give her imagination its due.

"I've been reading about too many knights on horseback crossing miles of rolling hills, cat. Do you see my problem?" The cat's purr grew louder, and he curled into an even tighter ball, as if settling in for the rest of the day, no matter Brooklyn's plans. "Good thing I don't really have anything going on. Unless you want to count paying for these books."

And, of course, sorting through the pile of clothes she'd started pulling from her closet yesterday morning and tossed to the bed, the mess requiring her to push the mountain aside to sleep last night.

She'd become such a pack rat the last two years. At first she blamed the lack of energy that had plagued her for months after Artie's death. Then she had nothing—or no one—to blame but herself.

She kept things neat, but she kept things she had no reason to. It seemed easier to move a blouse with a ragged buttonhole to the back of the closet than take it to the cleaners to be repaired.

And now half of the clothes hanging up were ones she hadn't worn in years. Some she hadn't worn but once. The items were perfect for someone handy with a needle and thread. Someone who didn't mind cuts and colors she was too old to wear. Someone who wouldn't have the memories of Artie loving how she looked in red . . .

"You, Brooklyn Harvey, are just plain lazy," she said, scratching behind the cat's ears. "Life isn't lived in books, you know. And it's not lived sitting on the floor of a bookstore. You're going to have to give me my legs, cat."

"Look, Daddy. It's Ms. Harvey! And she's got a cat!"

Hearing her name spoken with such excitement and in a voice that was part of her daily life, Brooklyn turned, grinning at the sight of Adrianne Drake running down the aisle and squatting next to her.

"Can I pet her?" the girl asked, her hands balled in her lap as if she could barely contain them. "What's her name?"

"I don't know *his* name," Brooklyn said. "But you'll need to ask your dad if petting him's okay." She waited a few seconds until her heart settled before lifting her gaze from Adrianne to her dad.

"Can I, Daddy? Please?"

Callum had been staring at the cat, but now looked at Brooklyn as if asking her permission, when Adrianne was his daughter, not hers. He was frowning, his eyes dark, as if uncertain, or caught off guard, his defenses down; strangely, she couldn't tell if what he was feeling was about his daughter and the cat, or about her.

"He's been completely friendly," she said, not wanting to make a wrong move. "But it's up to you. Is she allergic?"

He shook his head, then gave Adrianne a single nod. "Sit by Ms. Harvey and pet its back very softly."

"I will," Adrianne said, crossing her ankles and bending her knees and folding herself into a sitting position then reaching out with a tentative hand. "Hello, Mr. Kitty. You're very pretty. And you're very soft."

Brooklyn watched Callum's daughter stroke her hand down the cat's back repeatedly, watched the cat shudder as if the pleasure was nearly unbearable. The look on Adrianne's face said she was experiencing the same.

It wasn't quite as easy to look up and meet Callum's gaze; he wasn't anywhere near as transparent. He stood with his hands shoved in his jeans pockets, much as he had in her classroom last week.

His hair was messier today than it had been then, most of it in a knot but enough falling free that she wanted to tuck it back. And, while she was there, to pull aside his oxford's collar and read the inscription that ran in cursive letters from beneath one ear around his neck to the other.

"I didn't hear your bike." It was a struggle to get the words out. It was a struggle to breathe.

He shook his head, reached up with one hand to clear his hair from his face. Then he looked at his daughter and smiled, his dimples, like slivers of the moon, cut into the scruff on his face. "We're in the truck today. I've got a rebuilt '72 GMC. We had to go to Austin for supplies for the shop."

"That's right. I forgot the shop was closed for the holiday."

He gave a single nod. "Good thing, too. Addy didn't feel so hot yesterday. She spent most of it curled up on the futon watching *Reading Rainbow*. I had a feeling we might be putting off today's errands and seeing Dr. Barrow instead."

"No Dr. Barrow," Adrianne put in vehemently, her nose a little too close to the cat's for Brooklyn's peace of mind.

She put her own hand on the cat's head and scooted back, then reached out to sweep the girl's hair over her shoulders. "Well, I'm glad you're feeling better today, but I'm sorry you were sick yesterday."

"I wasn't sick," Adrianne replied matter-of-factly, her focus not the least bit diverted. "I didn't feel like a fireplace. I was just sleepy."

Like a fireplace? Brooklyn mouthed the words and Callum nodded, then said. "She didn't have a fever."

"Ah."

"Daddy?"

"Yes, pumpkin?"

"Can I get six books since I'm six years old?" she asked, causing Brooklyn to press her lips against a grin.

"Didn't we talk about this this morning?" he asked, getting a reluctant nod in answer. "And what did we decide?"

"That I could pick out three. And that I had to choose three from home to give to Kelly Webber. But, Daddy?"

"Yes, Addy?"

"Can Ms. Harvey come with us to get ice cream?"

"Fine with me," Callum said before Brooklyn could think of a way to let him off the hook. "Assuming Ms. Harvey likes ice cream."

"Oh, Daddy. Everybody likes ice cream." She scooted closer to Brooklyn's crossed legs and leaned toward the cat, whose purring was about to put Brooklyn to sleep. "You are just so silly all the time."

He looked at Brooklyn and shrugged as if no one could ever understand the things he had to put up with. "And there you have it. An invitation to ice cream with a girl who loves cats and her father who is silly all the time."

~

"That wasn't a planned ambush, you know," Callum said, walking beside Brooklyn on their way to the park, ice-cream cone in hand. His bag from Cat Tales swung from his free hand as Brooklyn's did from hers. "I had no idea you'd be at the bookstore."

"You couldn't have," she said, unable to get the picture of Callum shopping for books with his daughter out of her mind.

Leaving the cat in the medieval romances, they'd headed for the children's section. It was set up in the middle of the store, four walls of low shelves, with bean bag chairs, and fuzzy throw rugs, and books that weren't for sale but for reading. There were building blocks, and wooden trains, and plastic dinosaurs to ride on top.

Martha Prescott, the bookstore's owner, had taught at Hope Springs Elementary the same years as Jean Dial, though she'd retired earlier with one goal in mind: to instill a love of reading in children before they knew how to make out the words. Brooklyn couldn't remember a time she'd stopped by Cat Tales when every chair wasn't shared by two kids and every rug by three.

Callum had walked into the area scaled to his daughter's size and hunkered in front of the shelves. Adrianne had dropped to her knees beside him, pointing out the books she wanted to see. He'd flipped through the pages, smiling when she'd excitedly shown him one picture or another, teasingly tugging at the books she took from him to make a perfect stack of three to buy.

Brooklyn had been teaching kindergarten for thirteen years, and she couldn't remember ever being sucked into a father-daughter dynamic as she'd been into this one. Adrianne was adorable, yes, and Callum irresistible, true, but it was the bond between them, the absolute attention Callum gave his daughter, the complete trust Adrianne showed in him that Brooklyn couldn't get over. It filled her with so much hope and such absolute, unfathomable joy.

Their love was undeniable, and honest, and so beautifully transparent that it got to her, when letting it was a huge mistake, and for so many reasons. Her leaving being the biggest one. Which brought her back to the present.

She licked at the ice cream threatening to drip down her thumb to her wrist. "I didn't even decide until this morning that I was going."

"You did mention the other night that you had nothing to read."

"That wasn't exactly the truth. I have more books loaded on my e-reader than I'll ever get through in a lifetime. And let's not even talk about my bookshelves. I just wanted something . . . else."

"I'd say that makes perfect sense . . ."

"It doesn't. I know. I'm hopeless."

"No. Really it does." He lifted the bag with Adrianne's three books and the two military thrillers he'd bought for himself. "Three books at a time, and yet the shelves in Addy's bedroom look a whole lot like the ones in Cat Tales."

"That's not going to be any fun when you move. If you ever do move. Trust me." She thought of all the books she was going to have to pack. "Besides. At least you're not parking her in front of mindless television for hours on end."

"Sorry to disappoint you, but I do plenty of that. The parking, anyway. Not the mindless part so much. At least I hope not. At home and at the shop we have rules about what she can watch. It's when she stays at my mother's that I have to worry."

"Soap operas?"

He shook his head. "Twenty-four-hour news. I'm thirty-four years old, and I don't want *my* head filled with all the garbage those pundits spout. Addy hears too much, then asks questions, and I'm the one left to answer them."

He was thirty-four, which made her the older woman, him the younger man. Or such would've been the case if theirs was a relationship defined in those terms. It was not. "It's good that she's curious."

"Some things I'd rather her not be curious about," he said, glancing ahead where Adrianne had turned to run back toward them. "Not at six."

"Daddy! Daddy! I need you to hold my ice cream"—she held it out toward him—"so I can go swing!"

Callum looked at the mess of her sugar cone on the verge of collapse, then pointed toward the park's closest seating area. "I've got a better idea. You and me are going to sit on this bench while you finish your ice cream. Then you can swing."

"And Ms. Harvey, too?"

"I don't think Ms. Harvey will want to swing."

"Not swing, Daddy. Can she sit with us on the bench? And she can eat her ice cream and I can eat my ice cream, too."

"What about my ice cream?" he asked as he popped the last bite of his cone into his mouth.

"You don't have ice cream anymore," she said, and skipped down the sidewalk to the bench.

Callum followed, and Brooklyn ate the last of her cone on the way, then sat next to Adrianne. Callum tossed the book bag on his daughter's other side, digging into his front pocket for a tear-packet with a cleansing wipe. Adrianne finished off her ice cream and held out both hands, letting her father wash her fingers before she ran off to play.

When he caught Brooklyn watching him clean his own, he shrugged. "Being a father's a whole lot like being a Boy Scout."

"So I see," she said, then took the second packet he offered. "Thank you. The ice cream hit the spot. But that's it for me and caffeine today."

Laughing, he tossed the packets and wipes into the nearest trash can. "With that espresso machine of yours, I should've guessed you'd choose coffee."

"Is there any other flavor?" she asked.

He smiled, laugh lines like a starburst at the corners of his eyes. "What's your favorite? Kona? Blue Jamaican? Sumatran?"

Coffee. One of her favorite subjects. "So many people sing the praises of Kona, but I find it too . . . fruity, maybe? Too floral? I like Sumatra's earthiness, I guess it is. It's very . . . I don't know. Brooding, maybe?"

"It's the same with chocolates," he said as he sat beside her. "It's all about the soil. Well, and with coffee, how the beans are processed, though that plays a part in chocolate as well."

"How so?" she asked, knowing some of how chocolate and coffee got their flavors, but wanting to hear more from him.

"Well," he began, looking toward Adrianne, where she'd draped her midsection over the seat of a swing and was kicking up a cloud of dust as she dragged her feet through the dirt beneath. "In Hawaii you get these notes of banana and coconut, even lava. In Venezuela and Brazil," he added, leaning forward, his elbows on his knees, "you're going to taste mango and other tropical fruits. There are cocoa beans from Bolivia that have hints of licorice. And in Jamaica . . ." He paused and glanced over at her. "In Jamaica, you'll get notes of wood, earth, spice, and tobacco. Right up your alley."

She wasn't sure how she felt about him knowing her that well. "Do you have a favorite?"

"I like them all, and for different reasons," he said, and shrugged, twists of his hair blowing in the breeze. "How they pair with other flavors. How they behave when I work with them. How they smell. There's a chocolate maker in Italy," he said, waving at Adrianne as she flapped her arms to get his attention. "He owns his own cacao plantations in Venezuela, and he has a bar of unsweetened chocolate, no sugar at all, that's not the least bit bitter. He even roasts one particular cacao bean whole for eating. Dude is hard-core. Amazing stuff. I'm into him for thousands."

"You make chocolate sound like a drug," she said, and when he didn't answer right away, she looked from his daughter to meet his gaze.

It was solemn, his throat working as he swallowed, his jaw tight, his eyes harsh and dark. "Isn't it?"

He held her gaze for several long moments, his pulse ticking at his temple, hers beating sharply at the base of her throat. She wondered if he could see it there in her sweater's V-neck. Wondered, too, what he was thinking, if her comment about drugs had dragged up bad memories, and if she should have kept her mouth shut, or at least thought more carefully about what she was saying.

And to whom she was saying it. "In some ways, I suppose. Like coffee. And ice cream. We all have our passions. And passions, well, some are addictive." And now she was just making things worse. "I liked hearing you talk about it. The chocolate. I've never thought about—"

"Excuse me for interrupting," said a voice at Brooklyn's side. She turned from Callum, strangely thankful for the intrusion, to see an older woman with her arm crooked through that of an older man.

They were so cute together, small and stooped and comfortable, as if they'd been walking through parks arm in arm their whole lives. Something told her they had. "It's not a problem. Can we help you?"

"I saw you earlier, when you were eating your ice cream, and just had to tell you both what an adorable daughter you have."

Brooklyn blushed. "Oh, she's—"

"Thank you," Callum said before she could correct the woman's assumption. "We think so."

"I'll bet she's a handful, that little one." The woman smiled, shaking her head as she patted her companion's hand. "Those pigtails, that grin."

"She is that."

"Well, she's incredibly well behaved," the man leaned closer to say. "You've taught her well."

This time Brooklyn was the one to say, "Thank you," returning the couple's waves as they continued on their way. She waited until they were out of earshot before looking at Callum again. "Well, that was awkward."

"Not really," he said, leaning back against the bench and stretching out his arms. One of his hands touched her shoulder, but he didn't move.

She didn't move, either, just reached up to tuck her hair behind her ear. "Why did you let them believe we were a family?"

"They don't know us, it's doubtful they'll ever see us again, and it made them feel good. Besides, they were right about everything else. Addy is a handful, and you have taught her well."

ALISON KENT

"I'll take credit for what she's learned in class, but you're the one who's instilled all the things that make her who she is. Unless you want to credit your parents with some of that."

"Better than crediting her mother," he said, biting off a sharp curse, then saying, "Sorry. I usually do a better job of keeping the bad-mouthing to myself. I figure the less I say, the less chance Addy will hear something she shouldn't."

Another opening, but his comment was enough to convince Brooklyn not to press for more. She'd pressed enough on Saturday night; there was no reason, other than curiosity, for her to know anything more about the woman who'd given birth to Adrianne Drake. Callum wasn't married to her. As far as she understood, he never had been, and Adrianne's mother had given up all claims to the girl—

"Actually," he said, sitting forward again, "I'm still trying to deal with saying as much as I have to you."

She frowned and glanced over, but he was looking down at his hands, flexing them between his knees. "What?"

"I haven't even told my parents a quarter of what I've told you," he said, and raised his head, watching Adrianne fly off the end of the slide into a cloud of dirt.

Brooklyn didn't have time to process his admission, or deal with the sharp hitch in her chest, before the girl came rushing up to where they sat. Though Callum had cleaned the melted ice cream from her hands, they were still as grimy as her pink shoes and her ankles beneath her leggings.

"Daddy?" The word came out in a breathless rush as she collapsed across his thigh. "Can Ms. Harvey come over tonight and watch my *Frozen* DVD with us?"

Callum fought back a grin. "I don't think Ms. Harvey wants to watch *Frozen*, pumpkin."

"I would love to watch *Frozen*," Brooklyn hurried to say when Adrianne's eyes widened, "but I have plans tonight."

"Okay," the girl said, then bounced away again.

Callum shook his head and grinned. "Do you really have plans tonight? Or are you just the type to break a little girl's heart?"

She sputtered at that. "Actually, I was letting *you* off the hook. Though," she rushed to add, "I've had a huge mess of clothes for donation on my bed since yesterday, and I really need to get them sorted."

An old maid. That's what she was. Choosing to go through things she should've gotten rid of years ago instead of watching a movie with a chocolatier. *What is wrong with me?* Because surely something was.

Sane women, ones who were not old maids, not dull and boring, ones who did not own cats, who knew how to have fun, would always choose the Irish ex-biker with the hidden tattoos.

"Another time then. Because trust me. She'll want to watch it another. And another. And—"

"Another. Got it," she said, trying not to laugh at his pain.

CHAPTER SIX

"Grammy, can I feed the fish before I go to bed?"

Still in full makeup, shoes with low heels that made Callum think of golf tees, and hoop earrings the size of saucers, Shirley Drake turned from the deep stainless-steel sink and reached for an embroidered dish towel. Her gaze moved from Callum's, as he shut the kitchen door, to her granddaughter, as Addy twirled on her toes around the eating nook's circular table, dancing with her plush Olaf.

A hand at her hip, bracelets jangling inside her yellow gloves, she said, "Hello to you, too, Miss Adrianne."

"Hello to you, too, Grammy." The words were delivered with a mock exasperation, though knowing his chip-off-the-old-block little girl, Callum mused, there was probably very little *mock* to it. She pirouetted to a stop, knocking into one of the chairs, which bumped the table, causing the vase in the center to wobble and his mother to stiffen. "Did PopPop already feed them?"

"You'll have to ask your PopPop about that," came the answer.

"Okay. I will. PopPop!" Addy called for her grandfather at the top of her lungs and skipped out of the kitchen to find him.

Callum's mother shook her head, not a hair out of place, her toweled hand still on her hip. "That girl is one of a kind."

He used to think so. "After Thursday's story hour, I'd have to say she's pretty much an average six-year-old."

"She's no such thing. She's a Drake. And no Drake I've ever known has been anything close to average."

His mother had never been shy, and had always been insistent about what it meant to be a Drake, seeming to forget she'd married into the name and esteem, and ignoring the fact that her only child had failed at living up to her family creed. He'd skipped the prestigious university and the prestigious sports, charging his way through one defensive line after another on his way to a high school diploma and a football scholarship he'd never used.

Oh, he'd been smart enough for the Ivy League and athletic enough for rugby or lacrosse—sports that met with his mother's approval. But unlike either of his parents, he'd grown up in Texas. That meant pigskin and Friday night lights and cheerleaders with big hair.

It also meant Lone Star Beer. And smoking weed under the bleachers. Getting caught with his girlfriend buck naked in the bed of a pickup under the stars and ending up in county for public indecency.

"We'll see." It was the only response he could come up with. Nothing he said to his mother tonight would make a bit of difference. She only pulled out the Drake firepower when she was in a mood, and he was pretty sure he knew the cause. Her next words confirmed it.

"I didn't think you'd be doing any overnights for a while with Valentine's Day behind you," she said as she got back to doing the dishes. Meatloaf and mashed potatoes and cornbread. The smells of Monday's dinner, his father's favorite foods, still lingered—though after all these years, the menu was prepared more out of habit than love.

Callum heaved Addy's backpack onto the kitchen table, careful to avoid the vase. He'd stuffed in everything she'd need for school tomorrow, though he hoped to finish up at Bliss in time to get back and take her himself.

Then he'd need to catch a few *z*'s before he headed to the title company to sign away his life. Lena could set up for the day and handle things at Bliss till he got there. "I hadn't planned to. This just came up."

"*This* being . . ."

How was he supposed to explain Brooklyn Harvey to his mother when he couldn't explain her to himself?

He'd prefer his mother not know he'd done more than meet *Ms. Harvey* when he'd visited her class last week. Of course, since he hadn't thought to tell his daughter not to share the details of today's outing, his mother would no doubt know everything about the park and the bookstore and the ice cream before Addy got around to brushing her teeth.

Ah, well. "Saturday wiped me out of product. I'd like to get in a few trays to have ready for the morning. And I got an idea for a new filling when Addy and I were at the park today. It may get . . . complicated, working out the flavor."

"And you couldn't cook it up in your kitchen at home?" she asked, the sink water sloshing as she worked her way through the silverware, washing everything before loading the dishwasher. "Or here?"

He could have. He didn't want to. He needed to think and to pace and to blast the Killers over Bliss's speakers instead of the licensed jazz that usually played. "I don't have all the ingredients I'm going to need at home. Or here. I can take Addy with me—"

"So she can stay up too late and sleep on the couch in your office and be miserable tomorrow at school?" His mother shook her head, yanking at the faucet's sprayer head to squirt down the now empty sink. "No. She'll be better off here."

And . . . here we go. "Hang on a sec," he said, grabbing on to the back of the closest chair and leaning into it. "I know you didn't just say that."

"Oh, you know what I mean," she said, dismissing him with the wave of one hand, while wiping down the countertop with the other.

What she meant was he was still making bad choices, working overnight instead of spending time with his girl. "You didn't tell me how pretty Addy's teacher is."

"Is she?" she asked, though the question, lacking a single bit of inflection, could just as easily have been an offhanded remark.

He worked his jaw. There were so many things he wanted to say. So many things he shouldn't. "Surely you've noticed. You were there for Halloween, for Christmas. For who knows what else. You know, events I would've gone to had I known about them. Funny how the notes disappeared out of Addy's backpack. I'm actually kinda surprised you didn't sign yourself up for story hour."

"Don't be silly, Callum." She was done with the sink and the countertop now, and had found a different cleaner to use on the stove. "It was a story hour for fathers. I'm not Adrianne's father."

Rubbing a hand over his forehead did nothing but spread out his headache. "Not being her parents didn't stop you and Dad from going with her to parents' night."

She paused in her scrubbing, just long enough for Callum to notice, though she kept her head down, her eyes on her sponge as she asked, "Did Ms. Harvey tell you that?"

"Actually no. I remember Addy mentioning that you'd gone. I told myself then that I needed to pay better attention to her schedule."

Pursing her lips, she went back to the cleaning that seemed to be the only thing at the moment that mattered. "You can log in and see it all online."

Oh, well, that would've been nice to know. "Give me the URL and user name. I'll take a look."

"Your father has that saved on his laptop." Finished with her scrubbing, she pulled off her gloves, draping them over a rod inside the cabinet door beneath the sink. "There's a parent-teacher conference coming up in just over a month."

But no date, time, day of the week. He supposed he should be thankful she'd offered that much. Getting anything else out of her, and especially getting what he wanted—an apology, or an acknowledgment that she'd overstepped her bounds—was a fool's errand. "Is Dad busy?"

"He's in his study," she said with a distracted wave of one arm, having moved to the pantry for the broom. "Talking back to his TV."

"Thanks." Callum made his way from the kitchen through the dining room to his father's domain. He might never have lived in this particular house, though he'd lived with some of the same furniture, the same area rugs, the same paintings and drapes, but one thing had never changed: Vaughn Drake talking back to the TV.

"That is the biggest load of crap I've ever seen passed off as forensic science."

Arms crossed, Callum leaned a shoulder on the study's doorjamb. "I don't know why you keep watching that show, or any of the spin-offs. I've never heard you say a nice thing about it. Or to it."

"Hey, Cal." Muting the television, Callum's father turned in his recliner to glance over his shoulder, his wire-framed glasses sliding to the end of his nose. "I didn't know you were still here."

"Thought I'd dropped off the hellion and run, huh?" he asked, coming into the room and sitting on the fireplace hearth at his father's side.

"If she's a hellion, she gets it honestly," he said, settling back into his chair and leaving Callum to chew on some uncharitable thoughts about Addy's mother. "She at least asks about feeding the fish. You never did."

Callum hung his head and laughed. "I probably owe you a small fortune in goldfish."

"I've got it all jotted down in my ledger."

He wouldn't doubt it. His father was a CPA who'd grown up

charging his siblings interest when they'd borrowed his allowance. "Thanks for letting Addy sleep over tonight."

"No thanks necessary. Love having her."

"I know you do. But she's my daughter. My responsibility. This should be the last night for a while that I need to work," he said, cringing as he did, because no matter what he'd said to his mother, tonight wasn't about needing to work as much as it was about the candy he wanted to make for Brooklyn.

"Seems to me you're handling that responsibility just fine. But it does sound like you've been talking to your mother. Or at least listening to your mother, since she's usually the one to do the talking."

"Actually, she didn't have a lot to say. She was too busy cleaning."

His father harrumphed. "She was cleaning when I left for work this morning. She was cleaning when I got home. Maid service comes tomorrow."

"I should've guessed," Callum said, the picture from the big TV flickering to light the room.

His father let that settle, then asked, "You still set to close on the house in the morning?"

"Yes, sir."

"Even though you're working all night?"

"It's just signing the papers," Callum reminded him, thinking back to the hell he'd gone through to get to closing. "I was wide awake for the offer and the inspection and the never-ending mortgage process, and damn if I ever want to do that again as someone who's self-employed."

His father chuckled. "That place is big enough that it should last you awhile. When are you going to tell Addy?"

"That we're moving?" He shook his head. "I'm trying to decide if it would just be easier to get the whole house set up first. I mean, it's not like it's going anywhere. And I can't imagine a six-year-old hurricane living out of boxes."

"I don't think I've ever known anyone who wasn't jumping with joy to get settled after buying a new place."

Callum laughed. "I'll jump once I've recovered from Valentine's Day. Assuming I ever do. I figure we'll be moved in before the end of the school year. Addy's going to want all that space come summertime."

"You started interviewing for child care yet?"

"It's on my list. Shouldn't be too hard to find someone. I thought about talking to one of the high school counselors. Or the youth minister at Second Baptist. See if they could recommend someone."

His father nodded, then raised his hand and shook one finger, tapping it to his nose as he thought. "You know Billy Bower across the street? He mentioned the other day that his granddaughter was going to need a summer job. She's sixteen, I believe. I know she's got a car."

With the location of his new place, a car would be a necessity. "Thanks. I'll give him a call," he said, pushing to stand. "I'd better head out."

"See you at breakfast?"

Callum reached down to shake his father's offered hand. "Will there be bacon?"

Laughing, the older man clasped Callum's hand between both of his. "If I get to the kitchen before your mother, there will be."

~

Dropping her bag of books on the kitchen table, Brooklyn headed for her bedroom to change out of her pants that were sticky with ice cream and covered in cat hair, only to be reminded of the chore she'd left undone.

She was more than a little bit tempted to stuff every piece of clothing she'd left on her bed into a garbage bag to drop off later at the Second Baptist Church donation center, but that was just more of her being lazy.

She'd delayed the inevitable long enough. It was time to sort everything, keeping only what she wore regularly, and what she would need for her stay in Cinque Terre. The rest of the items had to go.

After she showered and changed, she dug in. Italy. Possibly for a year, or even more, depending on her fit with Bianca's teaching program. Brooklyn wouldn't want to take but maybe one or two dressy outfits; Artie's family were not jet-setters. She didn't see herself attending fashion week in Milan. There would be Christmas and Easter, and she'd need appropriate clothing for both.

Hiking, swimming, skiing . . . again, she could get by with very little, and buy anything she didn't set aside for Jean to send. Then there was the fact that she and Bianca had always worn the same size, so it was possible she could borrow clothing if she found herself in dire straits.

That made getting rid of her sporting gear and dressier pieces easy to do. She thought about the places she'd worn the outfits as she put them aside, knew the memories would stay with her, and that she'd likely never wear any of them again. Some of them she'd only worn once, when out with Artie, when traveling with Artie, and had been bought with Artie's appreciation in mind.

As much as she'd dressed for herself, she'd done so for him, too. He'd been generous with his admiration, and she'd blossomed because of his words. Even now, looking at the items, she could feel his fingers at her nape on the pull of a zipper, feel the heat of his breath as he leaned in for a kiss . . .

Honestly, she mused, shaking off the sensation. How had she let something like her closet get so out of hand? Though she shouldn't be surprised. Look at her bookcases. Her garage, though most of what remained out there had been Artie's, and too many of the tools were too valuable not to find them a home where they'd be used.

If her book buying—okay, book hoarding—hadn't gotten so bad that she'd needed the additional bookcase, prompting her to move the books out of the bureau where she'd found the family Bible, resulting in the call to Bianca last summer that had changed her currently rud-derless course . . .

She didn't even want to think how deep her dull and boring rut would've been by now. Maybe her owning so many books hadn't turned out to be such a bad thing. Tossing a pair of UGGs in with a pair of ski pants she didn't remember owning and adding a pair of Gore-Tex gloves, she decided the rest could wait for tomorrow, and cleared herself enough room to sleep.

She was as exhausted as a six-year-old who'd spent too much time on the park playground while her kindergarten teacher, mistaken by a stranger for her mom, had spent too much time growing infatuated with her dad.

~

Addy
Tuesday Morning

Ms. Harvey has a lot of rules for kindergarten. A lot, a lot, A LOT. Some of the rules are for all day long. Like:

- Talking stays on the playground. (*Unless we raise our hand.*)
- Other rules are only for mornings when we first get to school and are VERY IMPORTANT. Like:
- Walk to your seat with classroom steps. (*This means no running.*)
- Put your gloves and your hat in your coat pockets. Hang your coat on the hook in the cubby with your name. (*It's okay if you don't have gloves. And this is only for winter. NO ONE wears coats in summer.*)
- Put your snack in your cubby box, and your lunch if you brought it.

- Put your papers in your cubby sleeve.
- Put your backpack on your cubby floor.

But Daddy has rules, too. Lots and lots and LOTS of them. Like:

- Bedtime when the little hand is on the eight and the big hand on the twelve. (Or when there is an eight, two dots called a colon, and two zeroes. He says I have to learn both kinds of clocks to be smart.)
- Only one drink of water after teeth-brushing.
- Only one story before lights-out. (This rule is NOT FAIR though he's nice and lets me keep extra books under my extra pillow.)
- No sugar at breakfast.
- No TV at breakfast. (Daddy really doesn't like TV except for teaching TV since it's my job to learn EVERYTHING, he says.)
- Only THREE books at a time when we go to the book-store.
- No toys left in the big room when I'm done playing.

Even Grammy follows Daddy's rules. She always gives me scrambled eggs and ham or bacon and orange juice and toast with grape jam, but she says the juice and the jam are okay because they are made out of fruit sugar, and if Daddy has a problem with that he can take it up with her.

I don't know what that means, but I hope it's not bad, because Daddy told me to do something when I got to class and when I told him it would break Ms. Harvey's morning rules he said if she didn't like it she could take it up with him.

My stomach feels like a big ache is inside it and I want to burp, but I go to my chair and put my backpack on my table and unzip it. I'm supposed to hang up my coat now but Daddy says I have to obey him first this one time.

I hope Daddy's right. I don't want Ms. Harvey to be mad. And I really don't want to have to sit in the time-out chair and think about what I did wrong and how to not do it again. That is the WORST. Kelly Webber told me so and she should know. She sits there ALL THE TIME.

It's very hard to walk to Ms. Harvey's desk but I do it anyway and Kelly's eyes get all wide because I'm breaking the rules. My eyes feel like they're extra big, too, and when I look at Ms. Harvey's, hers are NOT HAPPY.

"My daddy told me it was okay to give you this before I took off my coat so I wouldn't forget and leave it in my backpack all day and ruin it."

Ms. Harvey takes the little box and holds it like she thinks it might break but that's silly because it's made out of paper even if the paper is sparkly like glass. "Thank you, Adrianne."

"It's okay it won't hurt you it's just some candy Daddy made and it won't break but he didn't want it to melt so am I in trouble for not taking off my coat?"

"No." She sets the box on her desk very carefully and looks at it while she's talking to me and I think she might cry and I wonder if she's afraid of Daddy. A lot of people are afraid of Daddy. Which is just SO silly.

"You're not in trouble," she finally says, looking at me and trying to smile, then looking at the box again. "But now that you've done what your father asked, you can hang your coat in your cubby and put your things away."

My stomach feels like it just plopped back where it goes. "Okay. I hope you like the chocolate. Daddy worked all night to make it and came to see me this morning at Grammy's so I could bring it to you."

"Well, I'm sorry you didn't get to see him last night."

"Oh, I saw him at supper before we went to Grammy's. Then I played Crazy Eights with PopPop and I won three times but then it was eight-colon-zero-zero and time for bed. PopPop read some of *Winnie-the-Pooh* but just one chapter. He said we'll read Harry Potter but probably not 'til I'm eight. I went to bed after that."

"I see."

Now Ms. Harvey looks like she wants to laugh, but that's SO MUCH BETTER than when she looks like she wants to cry. I go back to my chair with Kelly Webber watching me the whole time and I take off my coat and then it's not so hard to breathe.

Addy Drake's Ooey Gooey Cake

1 box pound cake mix
4 eggs
1 stick butter, melted
8 ounces cream cheese, softened
1 box powdered sugar (reserving 1/2 cup)

Preheat oven to 350° (F). Grease or spray a 13 x 9-inch baking pan and line with parchment paper, coating with nonstick spray.

Combine the pound cake mix with two of the eggs and the butter. Pat the cake mix "crust" evenly into the bottom of the prepared pan.

Mix the cream cheese with the remaining two eggs and the powdered sugar. Spread the cream cheese mixture on top of the cake mix "crust."

Bake 35–40 minutes. While warm, dust the top with the reserved 1/2 cup of powdered sugar. Let cool completely before cutting.

CHAPTER SEVEN

The box Callum had sent to school with Adrianne sat on Brooklyn's desk blotter all day. The blotter was a calendar, littered with colorful art representing her vocation and the season, with any appropriate holidays given their due.

Apples and pencils and falling orange leaves and green grass and the alphabet in bright block letters and numbers, too. Since the current month was February . . . hearts, of course. Dozens of them. Tiny ones in clusters. Puffy ones. Patterned ones and solids in pink and red and white.

The calendar had come with a laminated sheet for each month, and she'd used them every year she'd taught kindergarten in Hope Springs. She jotted notes and appointments with a dry-erase marker to keep her days on track.

She left herself reminders of things to discuss with her students' parents: their child's interest in a particular subject and how to encourage it, emotional reactions that seemed unprovoked and worried her, classroom incidents that might be blown out of proportion over the dinner table at home.

Each afternoon before leaving, she read over the scattered comments and wiped away the ones she'd taken care of, or that no longer required her attention, or those that by the end of the day had lost their pressing nature.

Today all she could focus on was the box. None of the words she'd written for herself made sense. Oh, she tried reading them, eraser in hand, ready to clear them away, but her gaze strayed to Callum's gift again and again.

The box was a three-inch cube with a fitted lid. The paper made her think of the signature Tiffany & Co. robin's-egg blue, but Callum's design was almost iridescent, a shimmering sort of pearl over a deep chocolate brown.

She'd seen dozens of similar boxes in his shop, sizes to hold four candies, to hold twenty, to hold six. To hold one. And that's what this was. Without opening the box, she knew. A single chocolate specifically for her. Because he'd listened to her and he'd learned something about her. Something he thought important, when nothing she'd told him mattered enough for this.

She knew that because she was getting to know him, the type of man he was, the business owner, the father, the son. His tats told her things, too. About what he considered important. He wouldn't put what he wanted to tell her into words, he wouldn't write a poem or a song. He wouldn't give her a purchased gift, though he might pick up a stone, or a leaf, or an acorn.

Her fingers shaking unaccountably, she lifted the lid, catching a glimpse of the underside as she did and looking closer. It was Callum's signature, and illegible, which made her smile, and she pressed her fingertips to the hollow of her throat, feeling her pulse there, as well as an unexpected sensation of choking. Of being unable to breathe, which was absolutely not okay.

This was what a crush felt like. An ill-timed and ill-suited fascination, because that was all this was. Her attraction to a man. The first man to have stirred her emotions since Artie. And the way they were stirred . . . what she was feeling . . . oh, but this was so very different from then.

It wasn't the same sense Artie had provided of everything being right in her world. Of security, of being settled, being safe. Safe. The word made her laugh. Her fingertips tingled and her stomach clenched and there was a hole opening beneath her, a cliff's edge inviting her to fall. Deep and dark and dangerous. Those were the sensations coiling through her as she ran her thumb over Callum's name.

She was so very tired of being alone.

There. She'd admitted it. Two years of eating dinner alone, going to the movies alone, climbing into bed alone was getting to her. And even though she'd already begun shedding the past, it had taken Callum Bennett Drake lowering his big body into a tiny little chair and reading to her class about a chocolate-loving bunny to tug free the ribbon she'd wrapped around her widowhood so neatly.

Enough. Four months and she'd be in Italy to scatter Artie's ashes. She had to do this her way, this moving on with her life. She couldn't let an Irish rogue slip into the opening she'd inadvertently made for him. That didn't mean she couldn't enjoy the fruit of his labors, so she took a cleansing breath and looked down.

The shape of the candy made her think of a pod, or a bean. No, a cherry. A coffee cherry. It was the size of the other artisan chocolates on display in Bliss. She knew the shell was chocolate, even though the color was more a Radical Red with a Mulberry shimmer, and brushstrokes of Jazzberry Jam. That made her laugh. Who but a kindergarten teacher would think in Crayola crayon colors?

Coffee. They'd talked about coffee at the park just yesterday. But nowhere in any of their conversations had he hinted at the sort of interest in her she would think necessary for this. Unless she'd missed it, which, sad to say, was not all that unlikely. Yes, she'd been moved by the way he'd looked at her, and more than once, but she'd never been good with signals; even when Artie had been the one broadcasting them, she'd never picked them up.

If that's what was happening with Callum . . . swallowing the nerves tickling the base of her throat, she bit into the candy, savoring the comfortable pleasure of warm coffee, like the first sip of her morning latte, though this one came with the added indulgence of chocolate.

That had her smiling, as she licked her fingers clean. Had her, too, determined to pay better attention, to watch for signs and clues. Not now as much as in the future. The timing was all wrong for her and Callum, but it would be nice to get to know him better, to climb out of her rut with the help of a man who appreciated good coffee, whose taste in artwork mirrored hers, and who found meaning in well-chosen words.

Hoping the Second Baptist Church donations center would still be open, Brooklyn headed there after school on Wednesday—finally—with the boxes she'd hauled to her car late Tuesday night before collapsing exhausted into bed. Who knew culling twelve years' worth of clothes from her closet and drawers would end up taking her three days?

She'd started going through her things on Sunday morning. Usually she went to church with Jean, but after Saturday night spent at Bliss with Callum, she'd failed to set her alarm; when Jean called at nine, she'd only just emptied the last of the milk into her espresso machine's foamer and was still half asleep.

She'd begged off; she didn't have time to get ready, and she truly wasn't feeling up to par, though that she blamed on her state of mind, not her body. Having Callum show her his Tennyson quote, leaving her to guess at the rest of his tattooed sayings, had her musing over how fitting they were, how personal.

Though really, she knew next to nothing about how he'd lived when he'd belonged to the club. What she knew about such groups came from the media, from books and movies; who hadn't heard of *Easy Rider*? Or the Hells Angels? Even *Sons of Anarchy*?

Strangely, she couldn't picture him in any of those situations, but she only knew him as Adrianne's father, who, on Monday, had crawled around the children's section of Cat Tales to help her pick out her limit of books. Who'd allowed her to have one scoop of ice cream, not the ten she'd asked for, not the three she'd countered with, just the one.

Who'd carried wet wipes to clean his daughter's hands, then let her get as messy as she'd wanted, swinging and sliding and climbing, until she turned from a mild-mannered six-year-old into an unholy terror and had to be carried cuddled against his neck all the way to their truck. Monday had been an extraordinary day, and so much better than normal.

But that line of thinking only served to remind Brooklyn of the rut she'd fallen into. It also served to distract her from finishing the clothes-sorting chore when she'd arrived home Monday night; she'd taken until last night to get it done. Not that it had gone any faster; she'd been thinking about Callum's gift of candy the entire time.

Now it was Wednesday, one day shy of a week since she'd met him, and he'd been constantly on her mind. The only other time she'd known this level of infatuation had been with Artie, and she could not let herself believe this was the same. Love was the last thing she was looking for, the last thing she had time for. Later. When she was herself again. She just wasn't ready. Not yet.

The donations center was in a small addition at the rear of the church's main building, next to the youth annex, which included the nursery and the choir's practice room. It was open late Wednesday for the convenience of members dropping off items before services. And it was manned with volunteers.

Today those volunteers were Dolly Pepper, whom she knew only from Two Owls Café, and Shirley Drake. For the briefest second, Brooklyn hesitated near the door, then made her way to the counter, behind which both women were sorting items from several boxes onto long folding tables. "Hello, Mrs. Pepper. Mrs. Drake."

Callum's mother looked up from checking the label inside a woman's cream linen suit coat, her face nearly expressionless. "Why, Ms. Harvey. What a surprise. It took me a minute to place you outside of the school. Dolly? This is my granddaughter Adrianne's kindergarten teacher, Brooklyn Harvey."

"Delighted, Ms. Harvey." Dolly extended her hand over the counter, her smile genuinely kind. "I know your name, of course," she said, leaving Brooklyn to wonder if she recognized it from the stories the *Hope Springs Courant* had run about the fire that had claimed Artie's life. "I'm so glad to finally have the pleasure of meeting you."

"Brooklyn, please."

"Dolly and her husband, Mitch, do a lot of the cooking at Two Owls," Shirley said, her gaze traveling from Dolly to Brooklyn and back as if making some sort of assessment.

Unable to imagine what Callum's mother would be assessing, Brooklyn simply responded, "Yes. I know. I eat there often."

"Have I seen you there with Jean Dial?" Dolly asked, pulling a pair of blue jeans from a now empty box and holding them up to examine.

Brooklyn nodded. "She's my next-door neighbor."

"Oh, lucky you." Dolly tossed the jeans onto a table with what looked like items of children's clothing. "Jeanie is an absolute saint. She's the reason Rick, my son, survived third grade actually reading at a third-grade level. I've baked her pumpkin muffins at Thanksgiving every year since."

"I've actually eaten those pumpkin muffins," Brooklyn said with a laugh. "You need to put them on the café's buffet for the holidays."

"You know, I might just mention that to Kaylie. Not that we don't already have more food than we know what to do with."

"I wonder how your daughter-in-law would feel about working with the church to make use of those leftovers," Shirley said, having hung the suit and moved on to inspecting the labels on the blouses from the same box.

"I believe she's talked to the city about doing just that. Unfortunately, it's more complicated than dropping off clothing, what with the health department regulating how food is dispensed to the public." Dolly folded down the flaps of the box and set it near a door that led to the donation center's warehousing area. "Anyway, Ms. Harvey. Brooklyn. Can we help you with something?"

Gesturing behind her toward the parking lot, Brooklyn said, "I've got several boxes of clothes and small tools. Everything's in good shape, some of the items never worn or used. Before I give it all to Goodwill, could y'all use it?"

"Oh, yes," Dolly said. "Tools are welcome. My stepson-in-law is forever looking for good deals for his employees. Let me give him a call and see if he wants me to set anything aside. And let me find Grady to unload your car."

Brooklyn watched Dolly go, then turned and offered an awkward smile to Callum's mother, who continued to check labels as she said, "Adrianne told me you went to the park with her and her father on Monday."

Tucking back her hair, Brooklyn nodded. "I ran into them at Cat Tales, though I guess it would be more accurate to say they ran into me. Jean and I swap paperback romances. Medieval-set. I was looking for anything we hadn't yet read." And why in the world was she explaining herself to Callum's mother? It wasn't like she'd kept her son out past his bedtime.

"And then you went to the park."

"After we went for ice cream, yes." Might as well get it all out on the table. "Adrianne invited me before Callum could stop her. But I have a feeling he doesn't tell her no very often."

"Not as often as he should."

"He seems like a devoted father."

"Oh, he is," Shirley said, shaking out a skirt she then held up to her waist as if she were shopping at Macy's. "It's one thing he's managed to do right."

"Bliss seems to be doing well. He did that, didn't he?" Defending Callum, whom she'd known but a week, to his mother, whom she'd come to associate with Adrianne's education, left her feeling rather unbalanced. In fact, this whole conversation needed to be reined in.

"Ask him sometime where he got the money."

Brooklyn crossed her arms, her purse swinging from its shoulder strap against her hip. "I don't think that's any of my business."

"I suppose not," Shirley said, discarding the skirt onto the pile of blouses, still not making eye contact, as if Brooklyn weren't really there. "But if you happen to run into him again, just keep it in mind."

"I'm sorry, but are you warning me away from your son?"

"I'm saying that my son doesn't always make the best choices."

Seriously? "And seeing me is a bad one?"

"Now that's just a silly thing to say.." She picked up a pair of pumps and checked the wear on the soles. "It's just that he's got his daughter to take care of and his business taking up the rest of his attention."

Meaning he didn't have time for a woman in his life. Was that what she was saying? Or was that what she feared? That she'd lose her son for a second time, and along with him her granddaughter?

"Mrs. Drake. I'm a friend of your son. Nothing more," Brooklyn said, wondering if the words rang truer for Callum's mother than they did in her own ears. "I teach his daughter. Those are the only relationships Callum and I have. Even Adrianne will tell you I turned down her offer to watch *Frozen* with them Monday night."

"I would think, as a teacher, you wouldn't get personally involved with your students' parents," Shirley said, the shoes still in her hands as she finally lifted her gaze to meet Brooklyn's, her expression harsh and judgmental.

"I don't," Brooklyn said, frowning. "As I told you, Adrianne and her father ran into me at the bookstore. The ice cream and the park . . ." *Who is making bad choices now?* "Those were one-time, spur of the moment things. I can't imagine they'll happen again."

The strange moment passed, leaving Brooklyn more wobbly than ever as she watched Shirley toss the shoes aside, then fold down the flaps of the empty box much as Dolly had done with hers. "I did tell Callum about the next parent-teacher conference. I'm happy to come along, or come instead, if it would be more conducive to the discussion."

Did the woman think Brooklyn was going to drag her son across her desk and have her way with him? "Since I haven't had the chance to go over Adrianne's work with her father, this will be the perfect opportunity for the two of us to do just that. But I do want to thank you for signing him up for the dads' story hour. The kids adored him. Like you said, he knows what he's doing with the kids."

It wasn't exactly what Callum's mother had said, but Brooklyn paraphrasing, or extrapolating, didn't seem like such a sin. Until Shirley Drake came back with, "He knows what he's doing with Adrianne. And I hope to heaven he keeps his expertise to that girl. The idea of him taking on more responsibility when he's already up to his eyeballs—"

"Here we go, Brooklyn," Dolly said, her timing saving Brooklyn from saying something she knew she'd regret. "I'm so sorry that took so long. Brooklyn Harvey, this is Grady Barrow. He'll unload your car for you."

Brooklyn shook the boy's hand. He was as tall as she was, probably no more than fourteen, with dark brown hair that fell over his forehead, and sparkling blue eyes. "Are you the same Grady who's been working at Bliss?"

"Yes, ma'am. Me and Jo helped Callum pack shipments to go out for Valentine's Day," he said, though all Brooklyn could hear was Callum's mother whispering, "Good Lord," under her breath, as if she didn't approve of her son's choice of temporary help.

Before Brooklyn could respond, Dolly stepped around the counter and began walking with her to her car. "We're having a bake sale and carnival on Friday night. Why don't you come? We're raising money to get the bell in the steeple fixed."

Brooklyn hesitated. She wasn't a church member, though she did attend with Jean. And the idea of spending more time with Callum's mother . . . "Oh, I don't know—"

"Yes, Shirley will be there, but she's working the cakewalk so she'll be too busy to care what you're doing. I could use some help at the refreshment station. We'll be selling Two Owls brownies along with some goodies from Butters Bakery. There's a dessert competition. I think Callum may have entered his chocolates. Orville and Merrilee Gatlin will be judging.

"Anyhow," she said, waving a hand as she walked, "Mitch and Kaylie do the baking and packaging for all the church functions, so I let them off the hook for having to sell. Say you'll come. You can take home any brownies we have left at the end of the night. They'll be wrapped up and ready to freeze."

"Oh, I don't need that kind of temptation looking at me every time I open the freezer door," Brooklyn said, laughing.

Dolly joined in. "Why do you think I'm sending them home with you instead of taking them home with me?"

"What about me?" Grady asked. "My mom's got lots of room in her freezer."

"Are you and Quinn coming to the carnival?" Dolly asked.

"I think so. As long as she gets off work in time."

"If she doesn't, you call me." Dolly wrapped an arm around him and hugged. "Mitch and I can pick you up on the way."

"Sweet," he said, then turned to the trunk of Brooklyn's car. "Let me go get the handcart. I'll be right back."

"He's a good boy," Dolly said, watching him jog back toward the youth annex building. "Proof right there that a single parent can do just as good a job as two."

Uh-oh. "How much of my conversation with Shirley did you hear?"

"Enough to tell you to ignore most of what she says. Callum's a fine man. A wonderful father. And sometimes I think he's a better son than Shirley Drake deserves."

"I'm not going to touch that with a pole of any length," Brooklyn said, though she feared she was beginning to agree.

"Good," Dolly said. "Because here comes Grady. The carnival opens at seven, so be here at six if you can. That gives us plenty of time to set up."

CHAPTER EIGHT

When Brooklyn opened the front door to Bliss Thursday evening, the store was empty. Callum stood behind the display case with Lena going over a printout of the month's sales by individual candy. They did this every other week, and should've done it on Monday, but the holiday weekend had thrown off more than his twice-monthly check of what flavors were selling best.

Some combinations were instant hits—Cookies and Cream, Spiced Praline, Caramel Rum—and he kept those in stock. Others, like the ones made with crushed sunflower seeds and honey, or orange and lavender . . . those had a much smaller, though devoted, following. His artisan chocolates had a three-week shelf life, but sold out long before, requiring he plan his schedule in advance. Having the ingredients on hand when he needed them was how he managed his inventory's rotation.

He bought his honey from the Gardens on Three Wishes Road, his organic butter from a farm in Bastrop, his fruit from local markets. He did what he could to support the Hill Country economy, but most ingredients required he do his shopping elsewhere.

Which was why he and Addy had gone to Austin Monday. Some of the more unconventional items he had shipped direct. Some he bought in specialty stores there. He liked picking out individual vanilla beans. The same with cardamom pods. And he was ridiculously picky when it came to rum.

This week he'd made two of Addy's favorites, Strawberry Shortcake and Toffee Crunch, and that after making the candy he'd had her take to Brooklyn. He hadn't made just the one, but he *had* gone through three batches of filling before he'd gotten the taste right. Then he'd made a full tray, using each row of the mold as a sandbox to get the look he wanted for the shell.

The browns and reds and copper. Spatters of liquid cocoa butter versus airbrushed iridescent powder versus random swipes of color with his fingertip. He'd spent a good four hours working to make the perfect candy to give her, his mind on his task but also on his life, his daughter's life, and where Brooklyn might fit in—and he had no idea why; she wasn't sticking around.

He did know where the inspiration had come from: the time they'd spent together on Monday. The bookstore. The ice cream. The park. He'd expected the day with Addy to be like all their others—full of nonstop nonsense and exhausting. Not that he would've changed it for the world, but adding Brooklyn to the mix had been damn great.

He'd actually expected to hear from her before now. Addy had confirmed delivery of the candy box on Tuesday, and it had been all he could do not to grill her that afternoon and Wednesday afternoon and even after school today about her teacher's reaction.

He'd thought Brooklyn would call during lunch, or come by after school. He'd thought she'd send a note home with Addy, a thank-you, or a fuck-off. He wasn't sure which he deserved.

Giving a woman a box of candy was one thing. Making a batch of candy with her in mind was another. But what he'd done . . . he'd shown a vulnerability he didn't like admitting to. He'd pushed himself into a part of her life where he didn't belong.

And why? Because she made his daughter happy? Because she made him happy? Made him wish what the old woman in the park had seen was true?

The door closed behind her, the canned jazz piped over the speakers barely registering over the beat of his heart. He held Brooklyn's gaze as he said, "Lena—"

"Sure thing, boss," she replied before he could ask her to check on Addy. She took the tablet and stylus from his hand, tucked the printout beneath, and left the register area, backing her way through the exit door into the rear hallway.

Callum blew out a loud puff of breath, not sure he was ready for this. Not sure what this was. Not sure he shouldn't just treat Brooklyn Harvey like he would any customer and stop trying to make something out of this attraction that left him bulldozed.

And . . . that wasn't going to happen. He looked from the hallway door to the floor, then with his hands at his hips, looked at her. He did so just in time to watch her tuck her hair behind her ear and tilt her head, frowning as she bent to look more closely into the case.

"Hey," he said because he was lame.

"Hi," she said in return.

"Are you here about Addy? Or . . ."

"I need a gift. For a friend." She walked along the front of the display case, looking at the chocolates, ignoring him. "It's her birthday. I thought since you do a good job of matching your patrons with your wares, you might suggest something."

Were they playing a game? Pretending she was a customer and he was a chocolatier? Was she digging to find out how he'd known to make her the candy he was thinking of calling Java Express? Not that it needed a name. He wasn't planning on making it again.

"Sure. I'll give it a shot. What does she like?"

"She's not much for spicy, or savory, at least when it comes to dessert, but she loves sweets of all kinds. Fruits are good. She makes the best chocolate chip cookies in the world, and brings them to work at least once a week."

"She's a teacher then?"

Brooklyn nodded. "She was. She's retired, though she still considers the school her second home. She taught third grade. And as much as she loved the job, that age, those kids . . . they drove her absolutely nuts. Oh, and she doesn't like nuts."

"Got it," he said, thinking of what might work. "Anything else?"

"She definitely enjoys her margaritas. And her White Russians. So something along those lines? I know you had some chocolates with alcohol."

"I do, yeah."

"What about something that resembles a coffee cherry? Maybe an iridescent sort of mulberry color? Filled with a ganache flavored with, I'm thinking, espresso, crushed beans, and coffee liqueur?"

His throat was tight when he said, "Brooklyn—"

"Why, Callum?" she asked, looking up at him at last, the glass case between them, her eyes behind her glasses as curious as they were torn. "That's all I want to know. It was beautiful. A work of art. And it tasted like the best part of every morning. It tasted like . . ." She waved her hand. "You need to offer that one along with the rest of these so everyone can buy one."

"I can't," he said, tensing up.

She frowned. "Why not?"

"Because it was for you."

"The first one, sure—"

"No. I don't have the mold anymore. I didn't write down the recipe."

"You can re-create the recipe. You can buy more molds."

"No. Not that one. Just . . . no," he said, not even sure why he was so adamant. Her candy—and it was hers, he would always think of it that way—would be a great addition to the current collection. She was right. But he couldn't make it again without thinking about her. And he didn't want to put himself through that on a regular basis. "But I'm happy to put together a selection for your friend. Do you want four? Six? Twenty?"

"Six will be fine," she said.

He nodded and grabbed a box, slipping his hand inside a disposable prep glove before reaching into the display case. "The tequila and lime I told you about the other day. The raspberry caramel. This one is Bourbon Peach. Lemon Curd. Banana Pudding. Punch Drunk, which has a sort of sangria center. That's six."

"And I'll take one of the Queen Cayenne for me. No. I'll take six."

He reached for a second box of the same size and tucked the pyramids inside. Then handed her the bag with both boxes and rang up her purchase.

"You didn't charge me enough," she said, holding tight to her credit card as he tried to take it from her hand.

"The Queen Cayennes are on the house," he told her.

"No," she said, and removed it from the bag. "I can't take it. Not if you don't let me pay."

"Fine," he said, not in the mood to argue, and especially not with her. He added the second box to her ticket and ran her card for the purchase. "Is that it? No chocolate bars from Java, Ghana, Madagascar, or Ecuador?"

"This should do me. Until next time," she said, and reached for her card.

He held on to it as she tugged, holding her gaze as well, his gut tightening as he asked, "Will there be a next time?"

"Are we talking about me running out of chocolate?" she asked, and he finally let go. "Or are you asking if I'll need another book? Another ice cream cone? A walk in the park? A candy that looks like a coffee cherry made just for me to commemorate the day?"

"You're overthinking things, Brooklyn," he said, pulling off his glove and tossing it in the trash. He should've known she'd try to make something out of what for him was nothing but a thank-you for the day. Right. That's all it was.

"Callum," she said, then stopped to clear her throat. "You took Adrianne to your parents' to spend the night so you could make me a chocolate you're not even going to sell in your shop. How exactly am I overthinking things?"

"You just are," he said, reaching beneath the counter for a clear glass mug, then stepping to the hot chocolate maker, nodding toward the nearest of the bistro tables set along the front wall for her to sit. She gave him a quick roll of her eyes, but she did.

Next time. Hell, how was he supposed to answer her question when he didn't even know what he'd meant asking her that? Why hadn't he left her comment alone? She was his daughter's teacher. She was leaving her job at the end of the year for the Italian Riviera.

Could there be a worse choice to make than starting up with someone who wouldn't be around to finish things? Even seeing her while she was still here . . . that wasn't smart, either. Monday at the park with Addy had proved that. His little girl was already nuts about her teacher.

To make Brooklyn a more important part of Addy's life than she already was, then rip her away?

He set the mug on a saucer, added a spoon, and carried the drink to her table. She smiled as he got close, and he thought it was too late to be worrying about choices. This one seemed as if it had been ripped out of his hands.

"What is this?" she asked, leaning close to the mug he set down and breathing deep of the rising steam. "It smells . . . spicy. But a sweet spice, not hot like the cayenne. And not cinnamon, either."

He enjoyed the way she worked to figure things out. "It's a white hot chocolate, with orange and cardamom."

"White cocoa?" she asked, and he nodded as she brought the cup to her mouth and sipped, closing her eyes as she swallowed.

He watched her throat work, watched her smile widen, and a dimple he'd never noticed before pulled at the right side of her mouth. Watched her lashes flutter, and her bright blue eyes sparkle behind the frames of her glasses that made him think of Clark Kent.

"I didn't mean to put you on the spot," she said, looking at him over the rim of the mug. "But your making that chocolate was just—"

"Did you have fun?" he asked. He was done talking about the chocolate, thinking about the chocolate. He was this close to being sorry that he'd made the chocolate, except that wasn't the truth at all. "On Monday?"

"I did, and would love for there to be a next time," she said, her expression softening as she looked down at her drink. "It was nice to do something different. I'm not in the habit of eating ice cream while walking to the park. In February."

"It was a little chilly," he said, relaxing. "Though you couldn't tell it by Addy."

"I'm so glad you're the one who'll be dealing with that particular sixteen-year-old and not me."

"Don't. Just don't," he said, slumping down in the too-small bistro chair, and with legs spread, rubbing both hands down his face.

She tossed back her head and laughed. "There's a reason I teach kindergarten and not high school. That right there is part of it. I prefer a hormone-free educational experience. There's so much extra room in their brains for things like spelling."

He huffed, and arched a brow. "Seeing the shorthand teenagers use for texting, not sure you're doing such a good job."

"That's hardly fair. But now that you mention it, kindergarten means I don't have to deal with smartphones, either. For the most part anyway." She picked up her spoon, stirred the chocolate, then licked away the foam before resting it on the saucer's edge. "I've had two students bring one to class. For emergencies only, of course. Or so claimed their parents, who didn't like me asking if there wasn't a way to lock down access to games."

"You can do that with apps and profiles, yeah," he said, lacing his hands behind his head. "I've been known to let Addy play on mine when we're stuck somewhere and she's bored. You know, modern parenting. Letting the electronics do the work."

"You realize that not once on Monday did she even ask to see your phone. Even when you used the alarm to give her fifteen more minutes to play. I'd say you're managing that temptation well."

He snorted and leaned forward. "You weren't there for the ride home. She was at her exhausted, grumpy, grimy, should-have-taken-a-nap six-year-old best. I almost gave it to her just to shut her up, but the mood she was in, I wouldn't have put it past her to toss it out her window."

She smiled at him over the rim of her mug as she lifted it. "Sounds like a sixteen-year-old in the making."

"You're just determined to ruin my day, aren't you?" he asked, then heard the words echo back. "Shit, Brooklyn. I didn't mean that at all. Not about you. It's just . . . the idea of being a father of a teenage girl is something I'd like to put off thinking about for the seven years it will take to happen."

"Don't forget about the Harley. And the long hair. And the tattoos. She's going to be the most popular girl in school because you're going to be the coolest dad." She sipped at her cocoa, then gestured toward him. "The tattoo on the back of your neck. The text. What does it say?"

He undid the top three buttons of his coat and opened it, pivoting in his seat and tugging down the collar so she could read the words that had been his creed for six years. Words he said to himself when he thought he'd hit a breaking point. When he thought he was all done.

"Hold on a sec," she said, the feet of her chair scraping on the floor as she moved to get closer, her fingers on his skin pushing aside his hair, and causing parts of him to tighten in response. She smelled like soap and something soft but not quite floral. Something green. Something nice.

"'He who has a why to live can bear almost any how.'" Once she'd read the words, she sat again, and he heard the clink of her mug on the saucer.

"It's Nietzsche," he said. And then he turned back around, watched her gaze follow the movement of his hands as he buttoned his coat. "And it's for Addy."

She lifted her gaze from his chest to meet his. "Is it true? You can bear the how because you have the why?"

If she knew the things he'd done to make sure no one could take his daughter from him . . . "No question."

"And if you didn't have her? Would you be here now?"

"Here in Hope Springs?" he asked, though he knew it wasn't what she wanted to know.

"If you didn't have Adrianne, would you have left the motorcycle club?"

"Honestly?" He shook his head. "I don't know. I'd like to think I would've gotten out before it was too late. Because it was always going to be too late. The minute I patched in . . . I was looking for something. For myself, maybe. And I wasn't smart about it. I thought . . ." He shook his head. "I don't know what I thought, what I was doing. I do know that I was a fuckup of the first degree until that girl was born."

"And now?"

"I get straightened out a little more each year. One day I might be a bona fide adult," he said, grinning. "Though making candy my livelihood doesn't sound like a grown-up thing to do, does it?"

"You smell like chocolate, by the way," she said, gesturing loosely toward his neck and his hair. "I noticed. When I was close."

He could get used to her being close. He really could. "Hazard of the job. Guess plumbers have the same problem."

. "No," she said, and laughed. "Plumbers have a much worse problem."

"Yeah, I suppose smelling like chocolate's not such a bad thing."

"I shouldn't have said anything. You smell . . . nice," she said, and he knew he was going to be in trouble if he didn't move.

He gestured over his shoulder. "I should probably go let Lena out of the storeroom."

"Oh," Brooklyn said, and got to her feet, reaching for the hot chocolate cup when it threatened to tumble to the floor. "I totally forgot she was here."

"A good cup of chocolate will do that for you," he said, taking it from her hand and walking her to the door.

"Thank you again. For the candy. And for the candy," she added, holding up her bag.

"You're welcome for the first. But I owe you the thanks for the second. We probably hit our daily sales goal today with that."

"Then I'm happy I stopped by."

"As am I," he said, letting her go without listing the many reasons why.

ALISON KENT

Bliss's Orange-Spiced White Hot Chocolate

3/4 cup white chocolate, chopped
(preferred: Askinosie Davao White Chocolate, 34% cocoa butter)
2 cups whole milk
2-inch strip of orange zest
3 green cardamom pods, crushed
1/2 teaspoon pure vanilla extract
dusting of nutmeg or cinnamon

Place the chopped white chocolate into a large pitcher or bowl.

Into a small saucepan over medium-low heat, pour the milk, then add the orange zest and the cardamom. Heat the mixture until the milk starts to steam, stirring frequently. When small bubbles appear around the saucepan's edge, remove it from the heat. Do not boil. Do not scorch.

Place a strainer over the pitcher or bowl containing the chocolate and pour in the milk. Discard the cardamom and the zest. Add the vanilla. Allow the mixture to sit for 30 seconds to soften the chocolate, then whip with a whisk or a submersion blender until smooth.

Pour into mugs and dust the top with nutmeg or cinnamon if desired.

CHAPTER NINE

Marker eraser in hand, Brooklyn read over the notes on her desk blotter, wiping away the ones she'd taken care of, then adding a short reminder for Monday's spelling exercise: plants and animals whose names began with the letter *B*. There weren't too few to be frustrating, or too many to overwhelm. She'd search out some images and print them this weekend. She added new ones each year and—

"Knock, knock."

At the sound of Callum's voice, and that of his knuckles on her door, she closed her eyes, her blood zinging just beneath her skin. After yesterday she wasn't sure she was ready to see him again. If she ever would be. If she even should. This was so much the wrong time to find herself wanting to get to know a man the way she wanted to know Callum Drake.

She loved what he'd done for her, making the chocolate, yet she didn't want the debt, the obligation, despite knowing in her heart there wasn't one. He hadn't asked anything of her. He hadn't even wanted to talk about it, why he'd made it, why he'd given to her, why he'd been thinking about her. He'd gifted it because he wanted to. Why was she so uptight?

It was really as simple as that.

It was really as complicated as that.

"Come in," she said, finally looking up and watching him walk into the room.

Today he wore jeans with the boots she'd grown used to seeing him in, and the same leather jacket he'd had on during their first ride. Instead of a wrinkled oxford, or clean and pressed chef whites, however, he was wearing a ratty T-shirt, one threadbare and faded, with six of the ten letters required to spell *high school* still visible where they arced across his chest.

And oh, what a chest. The thin gray cotton showed off his upper body, clinging like a second skin to his pecs and his abs and his neck and what she could see of his shoulders beneath the black leather. The man—because he was no high school boy—worked with his hands making candy, yet looked like he spent his days hefting bags of cocoa beans onto pack mules or into carts or whatever cacao farmers used to get their harvest out of the jungle, and she'd been staring too long.

"I cannot believe you can still fit into a shirt from high school."

"I'm not exactly sure I do," he said, opening the sides of his jacket to look down and giving her a much better view of the muscles she'd clung to when behind him on his bike. "But I need to weed through my own junk, so the T-shirts seemed a good place to start. That six-month thing."

"I hope I didn't guilt you into that."

"Nah." He strolled into the room as if he belonged there. As if he were a welcome part of her life. "Finally realized I'm going to need to get rid of a bunch of crap eventually just to make room for Addy's shoes."

Smiling, she opened her desk drawer and put away the eraser and the markers, too. "You probably have a few years before you have to worry about that."

"Her *Frozen* collection then," he said, crossing his arms and leaning back against the low bookshelf next to her desk. "The plushies. The figurines. The fast food tie-in toys. The coloring books. The costumes—"

That had her smile widening. "You may need a bigger loft."

"Actually, I've got that covered. And it's why I'm here." He paused and waited for her to look up, his eyes bright with secrets and the promise of fun. "I've been thinking about your storage issue. I may have a solution."

"Oh?"

"Got time for a ride?" He gave a nod toward the door, wisps of his hair escaping their knot to fall into his face. "Addy's at gymnastics until six."

"And you're done for the day?"

"Done enough."

If she agreed to go, would he have to make up the lost time? Because she didn't want to cause him trouble on that front. Or on any front . . . She glanced around her desk. "Give me five minutes to put everything away?"

"Sounds like a plan." He jerked his thumb toward the door and headed that way. "I'll wait outside."

"Callum?" she asked, before he got all the way there. "Does this mean we're going on your bike?"

"Is that okay?"

Since she'd changed from a skirt to pants at the last minute this morning . . . "Yes."

He grinned, said, "Good deal," then walked out of the room, leaving her to anticipate, well, so many things. The ride, the surprise, the heat of his body as she leaned into him. When was the last time she'd left school on a Friday afternoon and actually had something fun to look forward to?

Fun. Yes. This was going to be fun. And she was so ready for it she left everything on her desk right where it was.

～

They rode past the Caffey-Gatlin Academy, past the Gardens on Three Wishes Road, past the greenhouses and the undeveloped acreage on the other side that belonged to the farm. The long stretch of blacktop wound through the less populated parts of Hope Springs; if they kept going they'd wind up seeing Meadows Land, the sheep farm owned by Harry and Julietta Meadows, from which they provided the wool their daughter used in her Patchwork Moon scarves.

But Callum slowed long before they'd gone that far, turning into a winding paved driveway between sections of an honest-to-God white picket fence. Oh, the pickets were spaced too far apart to corral anything but livestock; a dog, even a large one, could easily wiggle through. But Brooklyn was pretty sure the fence was for show only, as it bordered a huge lawn, landscaped to perfection under the shade of pecans and oaks.

At the end of the driveway sat the house—a traditional two-story, with sandy red brick and white porch columns, deep eaves and a stone fireplace, paned windows and crape myrtles, and a wide circular drive in which Callum pulled to a stop. It was very suburban, though with a rural-sized lot. It was a place for a family, with a pool and room to run and outbuildings for storage and . . .

No. Surely he didn't mean . . .

"What do you think?" he asked once they'd both dismounted and removed their helmets, Brooklyn raising a hand to shade her eyes as she looked around.

Was this his house? "I'm not sure what I'm supposed to think. Or what I'm doing here. Or what this place is."

"This place is where Addy and I will be living as soon as I can get it outfitted and get us moved." He shrugged out of his leather jacket, draped it over the Harley's seat. "You're here because I've got tons of extra room perfect for storage. And you can think anything you want."

So . . . moving, which meant he was going to need to cull his T-shirts after all. A good thing, because the one he was wearing was driving her nuts. As far as his having room for her to use for storage . . . "This is yours. This house. You bought it."

"Yep," he said with a nod. "Closed on it Tuesday morning."

While she was looking at the candy he'd made just for her. And now he was offering her part of it to use. Free of charge. No obligation. No tit for tat. She took a deep breath. "You never mentioned that you'd bought a house."

"Didn't want to jinx it," he said with a shrug.

She remembered thinking how the warehouse district suited him. "Well, I'd be lying if I said this was you."

He laughed at that, a big uproar of humor. "You want a tour? I haven't been out here since the walk-through prior to signing away my life."

"Are you kidding?" This man . . . she'd never known anyone like him. So seemingly nonchalant about something that would have most people jumping for joy. Which had her wondering . . . had his old life, the one she knew so little about, made him this way? Too guarded to revel in his good fortune?

He walked toward the edge of the circular drive where a sidewalk led to the rear of the house, where a picnic table sat on a large patio to the side of the enclosed pool, and on to the outbuildings. "My dad's pretty incredulous that I'm not chomping at the bit to move."

That she could understand. She certainly would be. "What about your mom?"

"She doesn't know about it," he said, glancing at her with a bit of a sheepish grin. "I don't want her telling Addy."

"Adrianne doesn't know, either?"

He shook his head. "She'd be all over me asking how much longer till we move. We don't have a lot of furniture. She was still in a crib when I rented the loft. I want to make the house into at least a semblance of a home before I bring her here."

"I think bringing her here, with you, is how you make that happen," she told him, thinking with no small amount of hypocrisy about all of Artie's possessions she'd hung on to, when she had years' worth of memories to keep close.

"I know. But she's going to need a bigger bed. A real dresser instead of the stacked milk crates we've been using. More room for her books. And a bike. I've been promising her a bike for a year. She wants one with Olaf," he said as he started off down the sidewalk. "That movie's . . . how old now? Shouldn't she have moved on to the next big thing?"

Brooklyn followed, walking to his side when he waited. "How long has Cinderella been around? Snow White? Sleeping Beauty? Disney knows what they're doing. I'd say you're stuck with Olaf for a while."

He grunted. "An Olaf bike. Probably be easier to find a pony."

"You've definitely got the room for one," she said, her encompassing gesture taking in the whole of the lot.

"Maybe when she's sixteen," he said with a snort. "If we stay here ten years. Because a pony at six means I'll have to do the dirty work."

"You could always get her a cat," she offered teasingly.

"No cats. Cats are as high maintenance as ponies."

"I'm sure you could hire a service."

He shoved his hands in his pockets. "Floors, windows, pony rides, cats, and the care and feeding of a six-year-old on summer vacation. Craigslist, maybe?"

"With that pool?" she asked, nodding toward the fenced-off deck surrounding the kidney-shaped pool. "I can't imagine you won't have dozens of applicants."

"I do need to start looking. For the six-year-old care and feeding part at least. Or school's going to be out and I'm going to be boned. My dad did say a neighbor's granddaughter is looking for a summer job. And she has a car."

Hmm. If Brooklyn weren't going to Italy . . . no. *No, no, no, no, no.* She was Adrianne's teacher, not the help. She reached for a change of subject. "So your dad knows you're moving, but not your mom."

"Right. He's a CPA. Ran the numbers for me. And my mom"—he paused, as if working to find the right words—"she can be . . . difficult."

Brooklyn thought about her mother working full-time, keeping house full-time, being a wife full-time, dying two years before the husband she'd done her best to love. Thought, too, about Jean Dial's less than charitable remarks about Shirley Drake. Then about her own run-in with Callum's mother.

Hard to admit her thoughts were lacking much of what could be called charity. "Sometimes I think they're just tired."

"I imagine mine is. Being a busybody takes a lot of time and energy."

"Callum!"

"It's the truth. I was surprised when I came for story hour that you let me into the room. I figured she would've told you what she knows about my past and scared you off. Not that she knows everything. Not that she ever will."

Interesting, though not surprising. He was an ex-biker. Ex. She took that to mean he wanted to leave the past where it lay. "She's only hinted at bits and pieces of your life before Hope Springs."

"Enough to make you curious?"

"Hard not to be," she said, moving to sit on the picnic table's bench without admitting to how curious she actually was.

"I figure it's my mystique that pulls new customers into Bliss." He added a laugh as he leaned against the tree at the patio's edge. "I guess I should thank her for that."

"Until Wednesday, I don't think I'd ever seen her without your father. He may have kept her from speaking freely." Shirley had certainly had no problem speaking her mind without him.

"Wednesday?"

She looked down, watched the play of the trees' shadows on the ground. "I took some bags of clothing to the church donation center. She was working there with Dolly Pepper. But we had a few minutes alone to chat."

Callum dragged both hands down his face and groaned. "I'm afraid to ask."

"She thinks you're a good father." That much she'd give him. She didn't see any reason for him to know his mother had basically told her to keep her hands to herself.

"Well, that's something."

But the rest of what his mother had said . . . "She told me to ask you where you got the capital for Bliss."

He snorted. "Of course she did."

His response hardly set her at ease. "I didn't ask her. And she didn't tell me, though she was the one who brought it up. Just in case you were wondering."

He pushed away from the tree and came to stand in front of her, waiting for her to look up before asking, "Do you want to know?"

More than she could put into words. "It's none of my business."

"That's not what I asked you."

"Then, yes. I want to know, but," she hurried to add, "I'm not asking you to tell me."

"What happened in the past stays in the past? Is that it?"

Her past . . . it was part of her life daily. She was who she was because of who her parents had been, how they'd raised her, the life they'd given her. Because of the man she'd chosen to marry who was so different from anyone they would have wanted for her, lacking the higher education they prized. Yet he'd been the best man she'd ever known.

Jean Dial's words came back to her then. *As good a man as your Artie was? From the facts I know to be true, not the ones embellished by his mother, Callum Drake is equally so.* But what about the facts Jean didn't know?

"Do you want to tell me?" she asked. "Have you ever told anyone? How much *does* your mother actually know?"

"You're just full of questions today, aren't you, Ms. Harvey?" he asked as he sat beside her.

She crossed her legs, swinging her foot. Her toes caught the seam of his jeans and she stopped. "I'm an educator. It comes with the territory."

Elbows on his knees, he leaned forward, rubbing at the heel of one hand with the thumb of the other. "It's less about where the money came from than where it didn't."

"I'm not sure I understand."

"I started making chocolates after Addy was born. I think I told you I was in San Francisco then."

"Right. You were bartending. And living with the owners of the bar."

"Lainie and Duke. They were both in the club. That's where I met them. Lainie would watch Addy at night while I worked. Not a lot of watching to do when they're that young. Or so according to Lainie. She said it was no big deal. Anyhow," he said, lifting his gaze from his busy hands to look across the yard, "I was there with Addy during the day. We bunked in the living room. She had a playpen. I had the couch. I pretty much existed on catnaps. If she was quiet, I slept. When she wasn't . . ."

He shook his head, as if reliving those days. "There were a lot of times she wasn't. I walked her. I paced back and forth. I rocked her and bounced her. The TV was usually on, and I got hooked on cooking shows. Don't ask me why. Maybe having a kid, that little baby girl, and wanting the best for her. No way was I going to be able to give her a good life if I didn't change mine. Anyhow, I started thinking about what was in the formula I was feeding her. There was so much crap on the Internet about cow's milk and soy and vegetable oil and all the chemical additives. Not that there was much I could do about what she was eating then. It's not like I had the right equipment for breastfeeding. But how she ate later . . . that was going to be on me."

"And that's where the cooking shows came in."

"I figure most parents start out swearing to do things right. Then the kids find out about Happy Meals. One day, she couldn't have been but about four months old, I was sitting and rocking her and about to fall asleep, when this dude came on TV and started making candy. And not just chocolate bars but these exquisite little pieces of art."

"Like you make for Bliss."

ALISON KENT

He laughed. "I'm not sure anything I've ever created has come close
to what I saw that day. He had a local shop, and I stopped by there on
my way to the bar the next day. Spent about fifty bucks I couldn't afford
on the artisan chocolates he had on display. Took them back to the bar
and when I wasn't busy, I dissected them like you would a frog."

"You didn't eat them?"

"Oh, I ate them. Duke ate them. Lainie ate them. I told them what
I'd paid for them. Asked if they'd mind me using their kitchen to see
if I could make some of my own. I bought a couple of molds, some
really crappy chocolate, though I didn't know it at the time. It was a
big fat fail. Spent two months researching and experimenting before
I turned out something I was proud of. It was nothing compared to
what I'd bought from the dude I'd seen on TV. Or compared to what
I make now—"

"But you were on your way."

"I was on my way to being on my way."

A self-made man. A self-taught man. She pictured a younger Callum
in his jeans and his boots and his T-shirts, cooing to a baby Adrianne
while tempering chocolate. "How did you end up in Hope Springs?"

"Some shit happened," he said. "With Addy's mother. And I knew
I had to get out of California or spend the rest of my life looking over
my shoulder. Duke made it happen. Duke made all of it happen."

"He gave you the money."

"He gave me enough to get out of there and for a new start. It was
a lot of money. A *lot* of money." He went quiet, went back to worrying
one hand with the other, frowning and shaking his head. "I shouldn't
have taken it. If not for Addy, I wouldn't have. I mean, I don't know
all of what Duke was into, we didn't talk about it, but it wasn't hard to
guess, since I was into some of it, too."

"Drugs?"

He nodded as if finding no reason to deny what he'd done. It was
what it was. "His money got me and Addy here, and that's all I could

think about. I'd saved a lot of what I'd made tending bar. I did other odd jobs for guys in the club. Delivered packages. Picked up packages. They paid good money, and I never asked. Adding what was left from Duke to what I had got me started. And it seemed a lesser evil than being indebted to my folks. The fact that my dad even offered . . ."

Interesting how often he singled out his dad. "Did your mother know?"

"I'm not sure. I hadn't talked to my folks in a while. I hadn't seen them in ages. But I sent them a box of the chocolates I'd made in the bar's kitchen and told them that was what I was doing with my life. And I told them about Addy."

"They didn't know about her?"

He shook his head. "We weren't in touch. I wasn't married to her mother. We weren't really even in a relationship besides, well, the one that made Addy happen. Turns out I wasn't particularly proud of that, but I didn't know I felt that way until after she was born. Becoming a parent, being responsible for a life . . ." He reached down, swiped a stick off the ground. "It put a new spin on a lot of stuff. Including the whole extended-family thing, and wondering about relatives Addy might one day want to know. I'm surprised I didn't take up genealogy." He looked over, grinned. "That was a joke."

Brooklyn took a deep breath, thinking about the children she and Artie had decided not to have. How different things would be for her today if they had.

"Anyway, they wanted to meet her, and they really wanted me to come back to Texas. But there was a very big chance I'd fail. So it was easier to risk my own money, and what I had from Duke, than to take what my dad offered. I mean, I wasn't making the type of candy you can grab at the grocery store checkout, and Hope Springs is the size of a postage stamp. You can nearly buy a cheeseburger for what one of my artisan pieces costs."

"You put a lot of work into them."

"Work and the ingredients. Quality is not cheap. The chocolate. The liquors. I get pistachios from Sicily. Hazelnuts from Washington State. And every confection includes a touch of sea salt imported from Camargue, France."

"Sea salt," she said, and smiled to herself at all the things about chocolates she didn't know.

"It balances the sour and the bitter and the sweet. You don't even know it's there."

"You're pretty amazing, this wealth of knowledge you have."

"Not really. I read an article last year sometime about Cambridge offering a degree in chocolate. To research the melting point or something." He shrugged. "Not exactly my cuppa, but if I know things, it's because I've made a point to learn them, or had hands-on experience with them."

Every bit of his story was so clear, so straightforward . . . "Have you ever explained to your mother where the money came from? The same way you just explained it to me?"

He huffed and shook his head. "She wouldn't listen."

"Even knowing you accepted it because of Adrianne?"

"Addy is six years old, and my mother is still mad that I deprived her of the first year of her only grandchild's life."

"I can see that, I guess."

"Taking her side now?" he asked, arching a brow.

"It's not about taking sides," she told him. "It's about family. You think she's difficult, that she's"—*how had he put it?*—"up in your business too much. Maybe she's just having a hard time forgiving you for not telling her about Adrianne sooner. That first grandchild has got to be a big deal. All the little booties and tiny sleepers and knitted blankets. She missed out on that."

"Yeah. I guess," he said, breaking the stick into pieces then tossing them into the yard. "You and Artie never wanted kids?"

She waited for the catch in her throat to pass before answering. "Not while he was fighting fires."

"That would've been tough. Especially since . . ."

"Yeah." It was all she could say.

"Shit, Brooklyn. I'm sorry."

"It was a long time ago." Though it felt as if it were yesterday.

"Still. I need to learn to watch my mouth."

"And I need to get back to town," she said, standing. "I promised Dolly Pepper I'd help her tonight with the refreshment station at the Second Baptist Church's carnival."

Callum closed his eyes and chuckled. "And I promised Addy we'd go, and that I'd buy her ten tickets to the cakewalk. She wants to win my mother's Oreo cake, and since my mother's in charge of the booth . . ."

"I hope you like Oreos," she said, leading the way down the sidewalk as they returned to his bike. "Or at least have room in your freezer."

"My mom . . ." He stopped as he handed her a helmet, frowning down at his own. "She's not the least bit shy when it comes to sharing her ideas on, well, anything. But especially on how to keep me from screwing up again."

"Are you going to?"

"And risk losing everything? My business, my daughter . . . what do you think?"

She thought that Callum Bennett Drake would never make a wrong choice in his life again.

CHAPTER TEN

Brooklyn couldn't remember the last carnival she'd been to that wasn't a work-related event. For thirteen years she'd attended autumn and Halloween carnivals, bobbing for apples along with cakewalks; winter and Christmas carnivals, singing carols along with cakewalks; spring carnivals with sack races and yeah—cakewalks.

For tonight's refreshment table, she'd baked an old family favorite, a banana cake her mother had made often. The recipe had come from her maternal grandmother, and was just as easily made into a sheet cake as it was layers. The sheet allowed her to cut individual rectangles and wrap them much like the brownies from Two Owls Café.

"Thank you so much for bringing these," Dolly said, taking the basket Brooklyn carried and setting it against the wall of the church gymnasium along with the rest of the items to be set up for sale. "It certainly wasn't necessary but it is so very appreciated. Strange as it may seem, not everyone likes chocolate."

"Anything for the cause," Brooklyn said, looking around at the decorative streamers and balloons in pinks and reds as if someone had gotten a good deal after Valentine's Day. "I would hate to show up for the fun without contributing something."

"You're contributing your time, and that's plenty," Dolly said with a pat to Brooklyn's shoulder. "Especially since I don't believe you're a member here?"

"I'm not," she said, leaving her purse in a plastic bin next to Dolly's, which sat on top of the refreshment table's cash box. "Though I do come sometimes with Jean. My husband was Catholic, so I always went to mass with him. But I haven't been going anywhere regularly for years. I need to. For the fellowship as much as anything."

"Then I'm going to be sure and introduce you to everyone, even though teaching here for as long as you have means you probably know as many people as I do."

"It's a very real possibility," Brooklyn said, laughing as she took a stack of red-and-white-checked plastic tablecloths from Dolly's hand.

"Just spread these out over the tables. I think we'll set up the goodies on the sides, and we can sit at the one in the center to take payments. And don't worry about collecting the exact amount for the items. If someone is a dime or a quarter short, that's good enough," Dolly said, then sidled nearer to add, "Unless Shirley Drake is close enough to notice."

After the last week, Brooklyn wasn't surprised at the comment, just that Dolly had been the one to make it, though she understood—and sympathized with—the frustration behind the words. "I'm beginning to think the Shirley Drake I know from school as Adrianne's grandmother isn't the same Shirley you know from church and Jean knows from Pearl's."

Dolly took a deep breath, blew it out, pressed her hands to her cheeks. "Brooklyn, I'm so sorry. Please forgive me. I'm still on edge after volunteering with her on Wednesday afternoon, and I'm blowing off steam. I shouldn't be blowing it in your direction. Especially with you being such good friends with her son."

"I don't know that we're such good friends," Brooklyn said, snapping the first tablecloth into place and hoping to hide the color she felt in her cheeks. "I mean, we've only just met . . ."

Hearing Dolly's soft chuckle, she let the sentence trail; then Dolly added, "Get Tennessee and Kaylie to tell you about *just meeting*."

Brooklyn laughed, not quite ready to tell the other woman that she was right. That even now Brooklyn was wondering when Callum would get here, if they'd have time to talk, or if he'd be tied up with Adrianne and her efforts to win her grandmother's cake. "What about you and Mitch?"

"Well, we're older, not that age means anything, but we'd worked together and were friends for quite a while before we realized we'd fallen in love." Dolly stopped in the act of setting up chairs at the center table, and glanced wistfully across the gymnasium.

Standing next to Harry Meadows, Mitch was easy to spot, his salt-and-pepper hair buzzed short, his grin electric. The two men were arranging the station where they would slice brisket and sausage for sandwiches served on white bread with pickles and onions. "Still," Dolly said, "there was a spark there from the beginning. Hard to ignore when we were stepping over and around each other in Kaylie's kitchen."

Brooklyn let that sink in while she and Dolly finished laying out the refreshments, thinking, as they did, about the day she'd looked up after story hour to find Callum looming in her classroom door. And later, in his kitchen at Bliss, when he'd been so focused on her eating the spicy chocolate. Yeah, she mused, remembering the tingle of the chilies that had been only a little bit hotter than the look in his eyes. She understood sparks.

After lining up rows of cookies and brownies and cake bars—the noise in the gym growing progressively louder, the crowd larger, the aroma of barbecue more enticing, the banjo and fiddle music from the band on the lawn outside the main door competing with the noise from the carnival games—Brooklyn paid Dolly for one of Two Owls' new Crackle-Top Brownies, sneaking bites as she sold the donated desserts.

Dolly was true to her word, introducing Brooklyn to everyone who stopped at their table. There wasn't a person at the carnival the older woman didn't seem to know. Brooklyn couldn't remember ever meeting as many people in one night, or seeing as many homemade goodies in one place at one time. But not once in the ninety minutes since the carnival had started had she caught sight of Callum.

A couple of times while she'd been visiting with parents of children she'd taught in years past, she'd thought she heard his voice, but it had turned out to be her imagination. She'd even thought she'd caught a glimpse of his boots walking by, but they'd belonged to Luna's husband, Angelo Caffey.

Her disappointment had been keen. Also ridiculous; she'd decided to take up Callum on his offer and use his place for storage. The decision had come out of nowhere, though, she supposed, she'd made it the moment the words left his mouth. She wanted a reason to see him again, one that didn't have her using her class as camouflage. Like she'd said. Ridiculous.

And with that decision had come another: she would be putting her house up for sale, emptying it of everything she and Artie had owned. She'd keep only what she couldn't live without. Her books, of course. Their collection of owls. A few pieces of furniture she loved too much to part with and knew she'd never be able to replace.

Whether or not Callum had room for everything remained to be seen. But it was the right thing to do, this break, and knowing the things she cherished would be in the hands of a man she trusted . . . How quickly she'd made the leap from not knowing him, only just meeting him, shying away from their involvement, to relying on him to keep her belongings safe.

A sudden burst of what sounded like thunder had her looking up from her brownie to see several children running through the gym screeching like banshees. It wasn't the screeching she minded—the boisterous noise actually made her smile—or the thunderous slamming of feet on the floor; she was so used to seeing the same every day it almost didn't register.

What did register was the little ones paying no attention to their surroundings as they played, and the two elderly gentlemen, both relying on canes as they shuffled together, deep in conversation, right into their path. Her heart jolted, and she imagined brittle bones hitting the hard gymnasium floor as she pushed out of her chair.

Dolly was already on her feet and headed to avert the disaster. Peggy Butters's husband, Pat, beat her there, leaning forward to create a roadblock and catching the first of the kids to run by. The second dodged him, and the third, Kelly Webber, with Adrianne right on her heels, darted the other way, her outstretched hand snagging on Alva Bean's cane.

Wade Parker, who Brooklyn knew was a volunteer firefighter for Hope Springs, stepped in and steadied Alva with a hand on his shoulder, and Brooklyn managed to lean in and snare both Kelly and Adrianne before they skipped their way past the mishap they had no clue they'd almost caused.

Her pulse racing, she knelt in front of the girls, holding Adrianne's right shoulder and Kelly's left while each gripped the other's hand. It took a moment for her to find her breath and shake the adrenaline free. "Girls? I know this is a carnival and you're having all kinds of fun, but it's safer for everyone if you do your running on the grass outside."

"But Andrew Patzka pushed the top off of Kelly's snow cone with a stick because sugar is bad, then ran, so we had to chase him." Adrianne gestured with both hands as if the motivation of the group of kids was everything.

"You almost knocked down Mr. Bean," Brooklyn said, turning her head to where the elderly man was blotting his forehead with his handkerchief. "He doesn't move as fast as you do. You could have hurt him and hurt yourselves, too, if you fell while going so fast. Understand?"

"Yes, Ms. Harvey," the girls said in unison, heads hanging, lips quivering, tears welling.

"Good." Brooklyn hugged the two briefly, smiling at both as she asked, "Do you think you should tell Mr. Bean you're sorry?"

Both girls nodded. Both girls said, "Yes, Ms. Harvey," but before either could move, Adrianne's grandmother stepped in and pulled her away.

"You come with me, Adrianne. We'll let your father take care of this."

Adrianne tilted her head to look up at her grandmother, her expression torn and dismayed. "But Ms. Harvey said—"

"I don't care what Ms. Harvey said." Shirley Drake held Brooklyn's gaze as Brooklyn got to her feet, her face heating—*anger? embarrassment?*—until she was certain her cheeks were beet red. "This isn't the classroom."

"We're supposed to be *'spectful* of our teachers," Kelly put in, still holding tight to Adrianne's hand.

"What's going on?"

At the sound of Callum's voice, Brooklyn turned, wondering if she'd ever been so glad to see someone. She couldn't even mind that he'd arrived with Lindsay Webber. The other woman, her jeans tight, her shirt tight, her heels high, her perfume overwhelming, bent and lifted her daughter to her hip. Kelly's legs went around her mother's waist and her arms around her shoulders as she tucked her face to her neck.

Brooklyn looked from Callum to Lindsay to Shirley, then to Callum again, his gaze fixed fast on hers and making the skin at her nape grow damp. He was frowning, but with concern, not annoyance, his eyes sharp and bright. "What happened?"

"The girls were running—"

"The girls were being little girls," Shirley interrupted before Brooklyn could finish. "Nothing more."

Callum pulled Adrianne away from his mother and squatted in front of her. "Addy? Tell me what happened."

"Me and Kelly were chasing Andrew Patzka because he broke her snow cone and we almost caught him but we ran in front of Mr. Bean and he nearly fell and Ms. Harvey stopped us and told us not to run inside and Grammy yelled at Ms. Harvey—"

"I most certainly did not yell," Shirley said to her son as Callum stood. "I asked Ms. Harvey to let me deal with my granddaughter."

"Now, Shirley. You know that's not true. You didn't ask Brooklyn to do anything," Dolly put in from Brooklyn's side. "In fact, I'm quite certain I heard you say you didn't care what she said."

Brooklyn reached for Dolly's arm to keep her from adding more, but all Shirley Drake did was huff and turn to Callum. "Well?"

"C'mon, Addy," Callum said, his jaw tight as he ignored his mother and grasped his daughter's hand. "Let's go find Mr. Bean and apologize."

"Does Kelly have to apologize, too?" Adrianne's eyes grew even wider than they already were as she looked at her father, her emotions nearly breaking Brooklyn's heart.

"Kelly most certainly does," the girl's mother said, turning away with Callum, the two walking to the Hope Springs Emergency Services booth, where Alva Bean, who worked as a 911 dispatcher, now sat chatting with several city employees.

That left Brooklyn to return to the refreshment table with Dolly, but the two women had only gone a couple of steps when Shirley moved to block them. "I don't appreciate being made to look like a fool in front of my son."

"Was that directed at me?" Brooklyn asked. "Because I didn't say a word about you to your son, and if you were speaking to Dolly, she did nothing but repeat what you said to Adrianne."

"I told you before," Shirley said, lifting a warning finger, her eyes behind her narrow black frames as harsh as her voice, "you need to stay away from Callum."

Brooklyn had no idea how she'd misjudged this woman so completely, but she was through holding her tongue. "And I told you, I have no interest in Callum beyond his being the father of one of my students." But then the devil sitting on her shoulder made her add, "Though if there were more to our relationship, it would be our business, and not your concern."

"That's where you're wrong, *Ms.* Harvey. That is precisely where you are wrong." Shirley came closer. "Everything my son does affects my granddaughter, and Adrianne's well-being is most certainly my concern."

"It's mine as well. Which is why it was important to me that she understood what she had done wrong then, when it happened, not later when things had calmed down."

"It's not your place to discipline her."

"I didn't discipline her. That's up to her father, not me. But if Callum has a problem with my talking to her, I'll apologize to him." Because she owed this woman nothing.

"See that you do," Shirley said, then turned away, her kitten-heeled mules slapping against the gymnasium floor, before Brooklyn could gather her wits to respond. And, really, what was there to say? Callum's mother had made up her mind: Brooklyn was coming between her and her son.

The rest of the evening was uneventful, Brooklyn shaking off the tension and doing her best to enjoy the night—and the huge sliced-brisket sandwich, with potato salad and baked beans, Mitch Pepper set in front of her when he brought a similar plate to his wife.

Brooklyn didn't have much of an appetite, but she appreciated the kindness and dug in, Mitch entertaining her and Dolly with a story of feeding a young Kaylie her first plate of barbecue until both women were laughing around mouthfuls of food. And she'd actually gone two whole minutes without thinking about her encounter with Callum's mother, when he arrived to remind her.

"You okay?" he asked, his hands on the table as he leaned close to her, leaving Mitch and Dolly to their conversation.

"Sure. Why wouldn't I be?" she asked, taking another bite of potato salad, then reaching for her napkin with a shrug. She didn't know if he was here to complain about her overstepping with Adrianne, or to thank her for acting as quickly as she had, or to buy a piece of cake.

"My mother," was what he finally said. "Several people heard you and her talking after I left, and wanted me to know what she'd said." He shoved his hands in his pockets, frowning down, his eyes angry, the tic at his temple a visible beat. "I'm sorry for that, and for not thanking you sooner. You helped prevent what could've been a pretty nasty accident."

Funny how benign his posture, yet how dangerous the look in his eyes. "So was she right? About me needing to stay away from you?"

His jaw tight, he circled the table to hunker at her side, staring down at the floor. "She's rarely right about anything. Not anymore. And as far as you staying away from me?" He shook his head, reached up and rubbed at his jaw, then lifted his gaze. "She couldn't be more wrong. I really don't know what's going on with her—"

"She's jealous."

His mouth pulled curiously sideways, his dimple carving deep. "Jealous?"

"Of my time with you. My time with Adrianne. Though jealous probably isn't the right word. Resentful might be better. Maybe even scared."

Scraping a hand over his jaw, he shook his head. "I'd argue, but I'm not sure I'd get very far."

"Because you know I'm right," she said, reaching for a snickerdoodle the size of her hand in an effort to change the subject. "Cookie?"

"No thanks," he said with an exasperated groan. "I'm going to have an entire Oreo cake to deal with."

Part of her wanted to laugh. Part wanted to say *I told you so*. "So Adrianne won the cakewalk?"

"I'm not sure *won* is the right word. But, yeah. Addy got her wish. And I guess my mother got hers. She gets to be the good guy in her granddaughter's eyes. And I'm the bad guy who made Addy apologize." He shook his head. "I have *got* to get a new babysitter."

He looked so exhausted, dark half-moons under his eyes, the worry of a father, the regret of a son. *Oh, Brooklyn. What have you gotten yourself into?* "Actually, there is an after-school program at the elementary. I didn't even think to mention it earlier today when you were talking about Adrianne's care and feeding."

"Really?" he asked, his tone a mixture of hope and relief.

"It might be too late to get in this year but it wouldn't hurt to check." She couldn't believe she was going to say it, but she added, "Lindsay Webber could tell you about it. She leaves Kelly there when the hospital has her on days."

"Huh. Thanks." And then he gave her a twisted sort of grin. "I guess information about the program went home at the beginning of the year?"

"I'm pretty sure it went home at registration before school started."

Callum bit off a curse. "If I'd paid more attention to what was going on with Addy and school instead of Bliss . . ." He shook his head, cursed again. "Yeah, my mother got her hooks in deep, but I let her. And I don't need to be unloading on you. Sorry, and sorry for earlier, and thank you. I should've been paying better attention instead of stuffing my face with barbecue."

"Mr. Bean is okay," she said, realizing the depth of her investment in Callum's emotional battle. Realizing, too, and regretting, how soon she'd be pulling up stakes. "That's all that matters."

Just then, Grady Barrow came running up to Callum's side. "Hey, boss," he said, in a perfect imitation of Lena while giving a jerk of his chin to toss back his hair. "The Gatlins are about to announce the winners of the dessert competition."

Callum got to his feet, chucking the boy on the shoulder. "Well, I guess we'd better go see whose ass I'm going to kick the hardest."

"Sweet," Grady said, and trotted off, the soles of his sneakers squeaking against the gym's floor.

"You coming?" Callum turned to ask.

"Of course." Though she shouldn't enjoy his including her as much as she did. But just for tonight . . . "I've been waiting to see what you entered since Dolly mentioned that you had."

He gave her a sheepish shrug. "It was a sort of last-minute thing."

Now she was curious. "Do you really think your candy can kick the ass of any brownie Kaylie Keller decides to whip up? Or stand a chance against Peggy Butters's salted caramel macarons?"

He very nearly pouted. "Doesn't sound like you have much faith in my abilities."

He was so cute when he sulked. "Well, Jean did share the Bourbon Peach chocolate with me, so if you entered that one, I could see you having a chance."

"Nope. I entered the candy I made for you. The coffee cherry."

He'd entered her candy? The candy he wasn't going to make more of? The candy he wasn't going to sell? "I didn't think you saved the recipe."

"I didn't, but I made a whole tray. I actually made several whole trays, trying to get it right."

"And you entered them here instead of giving them to me?"

"I gave you the best in show," he said, then he held out his hand and she took it, thinking this might just be the greatest carnival of her entire life.

Shirley Drake's Oreo Cake

For the cake:
3/4 cup all-purpose flour
1/4 cup Dutch-processed cocoa powder
5/8 teaspoon baking soda
1/8 teaspoon salt
1/2 cup + 2 tablespoons granulated sugar
1/2 cup + 2 tablespoons sour cream
1/3 cup vegetable oil
1 large egg
1/2 teaspoon pure vanilla extract

Preheat oven to 350° (F). Grease and flour one 9-inch round cake pan and line with parchment paper, coating with nonstick spray.

Into a large bowl, sift the flour, the cocoa, the baking soda, and the salt.

In a medium bowl, whisk together until smooth the sugar, the sour cream, the eggs, the oil, and the vanilla.

Stir the wet ingredients into the dry ingredients until thoroughly combined. Pour the batter into the prepared pan and bake for 20–25 minutes, or until an inserted tester comes out clean from the middle of the cake.

Cool the cake in the pan for 15 minutes. Carefully remove the cake from the pan and cool completely on a wire rack.

For the frosting:
40 Oreo cookies (or more/less to taste)
4 cups whipping cream

2 tablespoons granulated sugar

1 tablespoon pure vanilla extract

Chop the cookies into pieces. Set aside.

In the bowl of a stand mixer fitted with a whip attachment, or using an electric mixer, whip two cups of cream on medium-high speed to soft peak, then spoon into a large bowl and refrigerate.

In the same mixer bowl, whip the remaining two cups of cream along with the sugar and the vanilla to soft peak. Fold into the already-whipped cream along with the chopped Oreos.

Slice the cake in half horizontally, creating two layers. Place the bottom layer on a serving plate and spread with one-third of the whipped cream and Oreo mixture. Top with the second cake layer and use the remaining whipped cream and Oreo mixture to frost the top and sides of the cake.

Chill the frosted cake for two hours before slicing to allow cookies to soften. (If transporting, carry the cake in an insulated shipping box with a frozen chill pack beneath the serving plate.)

CHAPTER ELEVEN

You know," Jean said the next morning from inside Brooklyn's garage. "You should think about wearing cobwebs in your hair more often. It's a very fetching look. A bit like St. Birgitta's cap."

"Thanks," Brooklyn said, not sure she wanted to look like the founder of the Bridgettine nuns. Reaching up, she brushed away the mess, praying she didn't find spiders. Though she had no one to blame but herself if she did. She was the one who'd let the arachnids have their way.

After a cloudy Friday night, Saturday had turned out bright and gorgeous, a perfect day to antique shop in Gruene, or read a book in the backyard hammock, or drive through the Hill Country with the windows down. Doing so on a Harley would've been even better. The sun shining, the wind whooshing by, the scents of cedar and juniper and pine in the air . . .

Instead she was cleaning out her garage. Or at least continuing the chore that would take a month's worth of weekends. She'd already donated most of Artie's smaller tools she had no use for, many going to Keller Construction via the Second Baptist Church earlier in the week.

Before listing the larger saws and drills and whatevers in the *Hope Springs Courant*, however, she'd invited Jean to take photos for her sons and anyone she thought might have use for the items. Photos involved moving things to where she could shoot them from all sides.

After two years of the pieces sitting untouched, there were a lot of cobwebs, and too many dust bunnies to count, and so much dirt Brooklyn wanted to hang her head in shame. Artie had kept the garage as clean as a firehouse; she couldn't remember the last time she'd swept it.

Jean walked around what Brooklyn thought was some sort of grinder. It was on a stand and together the pieces weighed what felt like a ton, and though she was certain Artie had used it, she had no idea what for. Sharpening knives or lawn-mower blades? Was that a thing one did?

"If either Jeffrey or Paul are interested in any of these items," Jean said, "you *will* take their money. I won't let you give away a single nail. Artie no doubt paid a handsome sum for whatever in the world everything in here is."

"I'm glad I'm not the only one clueless, though not knowing makes me feel like I should've been more involved in what he was doing," Brooklyn said, suppressing the sense of guilt that had taken root this morning when she'd opened the garage door and watched the day's sunlight hit the corners.

"Now, Brooklyn. Did Artie know what to do with every gadget in your sewing room?" Jean asked, not even waiting for an answer. "Of course he didn't. This was his domain. That's yours. I'm not saying he couldn't sew on a button. I'm quite sure he could. And if he'd had need to fill a bobbin he would've learned. Just like if you'd ever had a need to do something with this," she said, gesturing toward the grinder, "you would've done the same."

Leave it to Jean to use logic against Brooklyn's misgivings. "I guess you're right."

"Of course I'm right. I've lived long enough and well enough to teach even that Justin Beaver a thing or two."

Brooklyn smiled, letting the mistake, which knowing Jean might very well have been on purpose, stand. And then she was stopped from saying anything else by the rumble of a motorcycle engine coming close.

Jean heard it, too, cocking her head and grinning broadly. "I believe you may have a visitor on the way."

That, or she was hearing the same phantom Harley Callum had imagined last Saturday night. Still, she couldn't deny the rush of pleasure she felt at the sound. It was that crush thing again. That illicit thrill of his thinking about her when she could hardly get him out of her mind. "He's unexpected, if so."

"Those are the best kind," Jean said, taking a final picture of the grinder, then pocketing her phone. "I'm going to head home and get these sent to the boys, and to Alva, too. He may know someone who could use these things. I'll let you know what they say."

"Okay," Brooklyn said, her mind elsewhere, primarily on the state of her cobwebbed hair and clothes that were smeared with almost as much grease and dirt as the floor. "Thanks."

Moments later, Callum pulled into her driveway and shut off the engine, though every nerve in her body continued to zing to the thrum. He swung his leg over the bike and stood in profile as he reached for his helmet, his legs encased in faded jeans, heavy black boots on his feet, a tight T-shirt hugging his torso, his arms, his chest.

She closed her eyes, breathed deeply, opened them again in time to see him pull off the helmet, to see his hair shake free. He was wearing it loose today, and it fell in tight red-brown waves to the base of his neck, though not quite to his shoulders. He turned toward her then, lifting one hand and raking it out of his face. His smile very nearly killed her.

Another deep breath and she walked to the front of the garage. "Looks like you came by at just the wrong time."

He glanced over her shoulder, leaving her to look at his T-shirt. It was another worn long past its prime, and all the better for it. "For helping out a friend, you mean? Never the wrong time for that."

"It's Saturday. You should be making chocolate."

"I'm still basking in the glow of last night's dessert competition win. Besides, Bliss isn't even open yet. I can spare a few." He looked around the garage. "And you've got some kind of job on your hands."

She did, but he had his own to get to, if not now, then later, and unless he had time to ride back to the textile district, shower, and change . . . "It's my mess, I'll clean it, and you didn't come here to help, so . . ."

"I came to see if you wanted to make chocolate tonight," he said. "Addy's sleeping over with Kelly. I thought I'd play with some flavors."

Because, of course, for Callum Drake, work was play. "You want to make chocolate. In your free time."

"It's the only time I have to experiment," he said, and shrugged. "And Addy's going to be gone. What else am I going to do?"

"I don't know," she said, because she wanted more than anything to have fun with him—*Dear Lord, do I want to have fun with him*—but since she was leaving she wasn't sure doing so was a good idea. "Go for a long ride? Move some of your things to your house? Watch a ball game with your dad? Read a book?"

He seemed to think about her suggestions, then shook his head. "I'd rather make chocolate with you."

It was the *with you* that got to her. The words floated in front of her eyes, dancing there, spinning round and round until she was dizzy with the idea. "I'm not sure I can. The garage is going to take me all day—"

"Then let me help."

"It's chaos in here. You'll get filthy." *Oh, how weak that argument sounds.*

"A little dirt never hurt anyone."

She gave him a look. "We're not talking about a little."

"You, Brooklyn Harvey"—he leaned close and grinned—"worry too much."

He really needed to stop being so persuasive. And so incredibly cute. "What about your work chocolate, as opposed to your play chocolate?"

"I put in the overnight on Monday and cranked out an extra batch every day this week." His gaze curious, he walked farther into the garage. "Like I said. I'm good. And I've got Lena to let me know when I'm not."

Did he ever worry about anything? Of course he did. She knew he did, leaving her to take his word that he wasn't worried now. "Fine. But don't blame me when you can't fill all the orders that come in once everyone finishes what they bought for Valentine's Day."

"No blaming. Promise." That grin again. That *with you* still dancing. "Now what do you want me to do?"

They spent the next hour going through the tools in the garage. Callum knew the purpose for everything he picked up, and for the larger pieces she couldn't move and didn't recognize. She told him to take anything she hadn't offered to Jean's sons that he thought he might be able to use, but he was reluctant.

"I'm gonna wait till I get moved, pick up what I need as I need it."

If it was a matter of pride, doing things for himself, that was one thing. But if he didn't want what she had to give because her things had belonged to Artie . . . "I've got an entire home improvement store here, and it can be yours for free. Don't you think it's kinda dumb to spend the money?"

"Thanks, but no." He was shaking his head. "I've been making my own way a long time."

Still she argued. "Taking what I offer doesn't obligate you to me. I'm not going to haunt you and exact payment." But when he cocked his head and looked over, his expression one of finality, she said, "Okay. Craigslist it is."

"I'm sure Craig and his list will snap up everything Artie had."

So it *was* about Artie, she mused, trying to decide if that hurt her feelings, or if this was one of those molehill-and-mountain situations she needed to let go. "Jean and I were looking through things earlier, trying to decide what might be worth holding on to, but all I've ever used is a hammer and a screwdriver and a pair of pliers. Maybe the stepladder. And the tire pump."

This time he started in the back left corner of the garage and walked her through everything she owned. How he'd come to know the workings of machines she couldn't even identify . . . well, he was a guy, with guy genes, and he had belonged to a motorcycle club.

Oh, she knew the saws and the drills, and was well versed in using the lawn equipment, but she only had a vague idea of what one might do with a lathe, and couldn't imagine she would ever need a bench vise, a floor jack, an optical level, or even one of the five tool belts hung with ridiculously specific single-purpose gadgets, even though she did set aside a very cool laser measuring device.

It was noon when they reached the door that led into the kitchen. And as cool as it was outside, she was sweaty, grimy, and in desperate need of something to eat and to drink. "Would you like some lunch? I make a mean turkey club. Or do you need to get to work?"

"I'd love a sandwich," he said, adding, "or three. But yeah. I do need to head to the shop. And check in with my dad. He's got Addy today."

His dad. Not his mother. "Three I can do," she said. "You can take them with you, though I'm not sure you want to go to work looking like that. I think you're even filthier than I am. And your T-shirt's an insult to rats everywhere. That grease is never going to come out."

He tucked his chin to his chest and looked down. "One less item to wash. One less item to pack. Though you may have to feed me in the garage."

"Just dust off. You'll be fine. Except maybe your hair. It's as cobwebby as mine was earlier. C'mere."

He moved closer and she reached up, brushing the sticky strands from his temple. They caught on the backs of her fingers, and she reached higher to clear away more of the web, her hand slowing as she realized she was making things worse because she wasn't paying attention to the spider's work at all.

His hair wasn't the least bit coarse, as the unruly waves led her to believe. It was as soft as hers, though so much thicker; no wonder he wore it knotted on the back of his head. When his eyes sparked, she pulled her hand away to ask, "Why don't you cut it?"

"I do. Just not short. It's been this length as long as I can remember," he said, raking it back. "Addy loved to play with it when she was a baby, so I left it alone. I'd be holding her, my hair falling in my face, and she'd flail around trying to grab it like she would a mobile. Sometimes I'd actually catch thirty minutes of shuteye before she yanked too hard and tried to pull me bald."

The thought brought Brooklyn a tender smile, and she watched as he dug into his pocket for a black elastic, then wound his hair into a knot and secured it. Doing so pulled his shirt up his torso a good six inches, giving her a clear view of the tattoo that seemed to undulate behind the waist of his jeans.

"It's a dragon."

"What?"

"The tattoo on your stomach," she said, nodding down, lingering long enough to read the words there. "And it's the Bene Gesserit's litany against fear on the spine."

"Yeah. I've had that one awhile," he said, tugging at the shirt's hem to hide the image—unless he was hiding the words—and leaving it at that.

She wasn't going to press. "C'mon. You can wash up in the restroom. See what a mess my garage has made of your face."

He followed her into the house, and she showed him down the hall before returning to the kitchen to make lunch. Sub buns—though since she only had three, Callum would have to settle for two—turkey, bacon, tomatoes, lettuce, mayo, and Swiss cheese, because that's how she liked it.

She assembled the sandwiches, thinking as she did of fear being a mind-killer, as the tattoo's text said, and Callum, at some time in his life, needing the reminder not to give in to said fear. Had he been afraid of something specific, or was the danger inherent to the life of a biker involved with drugs enough to require the warning?

But since she wasn't going to ask—his pulling down his shirt to cover the ink took the subject off the table—she finished with the food, then went in search of her guest, finding him in the bathroom doorway, towel in hand, facing the bookcases that ran the length of the hall.

"You read all these?" he asked, catching sight of her.

"Most of them," she said with a nod, liking too much that he looked right at home in her house, with her towel, smelling of her bathroom's soap.

"No digital editions for you?"

"Oh, no," she said, dispelling the notion. "I have a Kindle." She let her gaze wander the shelves. "With a lot of the same titles loaded on it. Along with, oh, a thousand more?"

"You're kidding."

"I'm just your average bibliophile," she said laughingly.

"Is that the reason behind the story hours?" he asked as he stepped back into the bathroom to hang the towel on its rack.

"Yes and no. The story hours are for the kids, obviously, but my love of reading, and my belief in the importance of reading, is a part of it."

He leaned down, picked up a little steampunk owl that stood three inches high and had gears for eyes and riveted feathers. "You collect owls?"

"Not really." Not since Artie.

He returned the one owl, motioned to the others sitting on adjoining shelves. "The evidence says otherwise."

"It started as a joke," she said. "Before Artie and I were married. One of his coworkers said Artie was the wisest man he knew for marrying me, and it stuck. The first trip we took together, Artie bought me one carved out of marble and no bigger than my thumb. After that, we made it a thing to hunt down a locally crafted owl everywhere we went."

"You went to a lot of places," Callum said after looking over all of the shelves.

"We did." And that was all she wanted to say about that. Something he and his dragon tattoo should understand. "C'mon. Food's ready." She led him to the kitchen. "You want a glass of wine?"

"If you don't have a beer, sure."

"I do have a beer. Shiner Bock?"

"A beermaid after my own heart." He twisted off the top, then stopped and frowned. "What did I say?"

"Nothing. Artie. The way you opened the beer . . . I watched him stand there and do that about a thousand times." Ugh. What was with all her melancholy today? "Ignore me."

"It's okay. We've all got our demons," he said, lifting the bottle to his mouth. "Mine ride in on imaginary Harleys."

Oh, good. A change of subject. His memories instead of hers. "You said you'd thought you heard one when I came by Bliss the other night."

"It's no big deal," he said, except she'd known that night that it was. "I sometimes wonder if Addy's mother will come looking for her is all."

"Even though you have custody? And she told you she didn't want her?"

"That was six years ago. I'm not the same person I was then," he said, taking the plate with his sandwiches to the table. "I figure she's not, either, though I'm kinda hoping the radio silence means she's dead."

She cringed. Surely he wasn't serious. "You can't mean that," she said, sitting across from him, not quite as hungry as she was a moment ago. "What about Adrianne?"

"Addy has me."

Brooklyn looked down at her food, thinking there had to be more to the story for him to have written off the woman this way. "She's never asked about not having a mother?"

"She has friends with two mothers. Friends with two fathers. Friends with one of each. Friends with only one or the other." He gathered up the first sub bun with two hands to bite in.

"And she's okay with that?"

"I told her she used to have a mother but now it's just the two of us," he said, then chewed, swallowed, shrugged, and added, "I don't know. Maybe it's all crap. Maybe my mother's right, and she and my dad could do a better job with her. What the hell do I know about parenting, besides the fact that it's some scary shit. Honestly. Being solely responsible for seeing to it that little girl turns out to be a decent human being?"

"You may not always be solely responsible for her," she said, what remained of her appetite wasting away. "Light at the end of the tunnel and all."

He frowned at his sandwich, taking another bite and finishing with it before asking, "Have you dated since then?"

She'd heard his question, but it surprised her enough that she asked, "What?"

"Dated. Since your husband died."

"No, why?"

"Why not?"

Where did she even start? "Because I haven't met anyone I've been interested in."

"In two years?"

She pushed out of her seat to fetch the wine bottle she'd left on the counter. "Hope Springs is a small town. And two years isn't that long."

"It's not so small that people don't meet," he told her. "We met."

"I'm your daughter's teacher. We had a reason to meet," she said as she returned to the table and poured herself a refill. "And even before you came to class, I'd been in your shop often enough that we should have."

"I'm sorry I missed you," he said, holding her gaze as he brought his beer to his mouth.

She lifted her wine to hers, her pulse hammering for no reason that made sense. "I'm sorry, too."

Several seconds ticked by before he said, "You still haven't answered me about making chocolate tonight."

She'd actually forgotten he'd asked. "In preparation for the field trip?"

He shook his head. "Because I want you to know."

Wanted her to know what? The work he put in? The steps the artisan pieces required? "You're not making any sense."

"Will you come?" he asked, his eyes twinkling.

She swirled her wine in her glass and shrugged. "If that's what you want . . ."

"It is," he said, and chuckled, a deep, healthy sound that filled her kitchen until she wasn't sure if it was the man or the wine making her warm. "Though you don't need to make it sound like I'm sentencing you to hard labor."

"I just . . . I don't date parents of my students. I should probably put that out there." Even though she didn't want to. She really, *really* didn't want to.

"That's good. Because this isn't a date. Can you bring the wine?"

This time she was the one to laugh. He made it so easy to do so. "I thought you just said this wasn't a date."

"Wine doesn't mean dating. We're going to use it in the chocolate. And maybe drink the rest."

Monday, June 10, 2013

Brooklyn tugged the sheet and comforter to her chin and cuddled up to Artie's side, her head on his shoulder, her thigh draped over his. He wrapped his arm around her, pulled her close. He smelled like sweat and soap and clean sheets and sex.

"I don't want you to go." The words were an understatement. She could stay in bed with him forever, loving the warmth of his skin, his size, feeling

vulnerable and yet protected. He was so very strong, yet so very gentle when he touched her.

"I don't want to go." His voice was gravelly with lack of sleep and the wear of grunts and groans. "But we've been in bed most of the weekend, and last I knew, there was a bunch of little kids whose futures depend on you putting on clothes."

"I don't want to put on clothes."

He rolled on top of her. She grabbed the edges of the comforter and flipped it up over his head, cocooning them both. He wiggled, settling against her, leaning his weight on his forearms on either side of her head, kissing her forehead, then resting his on hers.

"If you never wore another stitch for the rest of my life, I'd be quite happy."

"You'd have to do all the grocery shopping, and pick up your own dry cleaning. Not to mention weed the flower beds and teach my class."

"How about I do this instead?" he asked, reaching down and slipping his fingers between her legs while covering her mouth with his.

Afterward, she fell asleep and dreamed of caterpillars and butterflies, then woke to her alarm, which Artie had obviously set. When she stretched to turn it off, she found a slip of paper on her bedside table. He'd drawn her a heart, adding eyes, a beak, deep brows with a tuft of feathers between, and tiny stick feet.

Smiling, she slipped the owl beneath the clock and sat up, smelling coffee. This husband of hers, seeing that she was on time to school and that she had coffee waiting when she woke. She lingered with her first cup, then rushed through her morning routine, wondering, with her second, why she was the one lucky enough to win his heart.

That night after dinner out with a friend, she picked up an Elizabeth Stuart novel from the counter near the kitchen door and opened a bottle of wine. While taking her first sip, the phone rang. Her mind was far away in ancient Britain, and she reached absently for the receiver.

"Hello?"

When the voice on the other end began to speak, then said the words she'd feared hearing for twelve years—fire, building collapse, every effort was made to save him, our deepest condolences—her knees gave out and she fell, the room spinning. The glass she'd been holding shattered on the floor as if blown from a window frame.

And the wine spread over the tiles like blood.

CHAPTER TWELVE

You brought the wine, yes?" Callum tossed the question over his shoulder as Brooklyn set her bag on the counter in Bliss's kitchen, the door whooshing closed behind her. He'd come in his truck; she'd come in her car. With all the groceries they'd brought, his bike would've been too unwieldy for the two of them to ride.

She pulled out a bottle and handed it to him while looking around the room he thought of as his second home. It was cold. It was sterile. It was his own operating theater. But that was what it was now. Give him five minutes and he'd have the Talking Heads blasting over the speakers. Give him an hour and the air would smell of fruit and alcohol and the best chocolate money could buy.

"It's so quiet in here," she said after several silent seconds had ticked by, both of them caught up in the possibilities.

"It's my favorite time to work. I love it when the place is empty. When I don't have to worry about making noise. If not for wanting to be home with Addy, I'd probably be up here every night till the wee hours," he said, digging through the sack of foodstuffs he'd brought with him.

It held peach and pear slices canned by Lena's mother last summer, and fresh apples and oranges. He'd picked up a new jar of Ceylon cinnamon when in Austin with Addy last week. That he pulled from the cabinet next to the fridge. Then he found a jar of honey from the Gardens on Three Wishes Road and a bottle of brandy. Some butter from the fridge and the chocolate from his bulk storage, and they'd be good to go.

"What are we making?" she asked, coming closer to examine the ingredients laid out on the counter.

He reached overhead for two trays of spiral cone molds. "It's called Punch Drunk."

Brooklyn picked up one of the molds and examined it. "I think you put one of those in the box I bought for Jean."

"Did she like it?"

Grinning, she set down the tray. "She asked if you could just make her a bowl of the filling."

He grinned, too. "I could, but since I'm about to reveal all my secrets, you'll be able to show her how to do it for herself."

"Then I'll pay very close attention," she said, but he was too distracted to respond.

"This wine," he said, frowning as he studied the unfamiliar—and obviously Italian—label. "This doesn't look like something you found locally."

"It's from Italy," she said, her gaze intense, and he wondered what it meant to her, this wine. "I've only got a few bottles left, and only a couple of wineries are still making it. It's definitely sweet so if you'd like something else, I can run home and see what I have."

"You sure you want me to use it?" he asked, though he was more than curious to see how it would taste; he usually worked with a Spanish red. But if it was important to her, if it held memories, if it made her think of Artie instead of him . . .

She went back to her bag, brought out a corkscrew and two glasses she held upside down by the stems. "You did say something about drinking the rest."

"Okay then." He smiled, held out his hand for the corkscrew. "Let's do this thing."

"Uh-uh," she said and waited for him to hand over the bottle. "My wine. I do the honors."

"Have I ever told you how much I like bossy women?" he asked, grabbing a cutting board and knife while she worked the corkscrew like a pro.

"Since you're brandishing a weapon over there, and mine's all twisted up in this cork, I'll give you that one." She poured the Sciacchetrà, but he swore her hands weren't as steady as before, and he didn't know if she was reacting to the innuendo in his question, or a memory connected to Italy and the wine. She sipped hers, handed him his, and said, "What's first?"

"The molds. We'll prep them with colored cocoa butter so they'll be ready when the chocolate is." He nodded toward the cabinet above the counter behind her. "Supplies are in there. I use the pearlized red for the airbrushing and spatter the one called Eggplant Garnet. Comes out looking pretty much like a bowl of sangria."

"You've got quite the artist's studio in here," she said as she opened the doors. "Paints. Brushes. Rollers." She glanced over her shoulder. "What else do you need?"

He showed her the scrapers and spatulas, along with the airbrushing system. Then, warming the solid cocoa butter, he took her through the process he used to decorate the molds.

She watched closely, asking only a couple of questions as he spattered them with the one color before airbrushing them with the second. No two candies from any batch would ever look exactly the same, and that was the point. Their uniqueness was what drew customers to the display case, the color, the shimmer, the gloss.

The design tools moved out of the way, and the molds placed on another counter, she asked, "Now what?"

"Now we temper the chocolate."

"And what does tempering do exactly?"

He took a second to decide the best way to explain. "Have you ever left a chocolate bar in a hot car and then tossed it in the fridge to save it? The consistency's not the same, right? It doesn't snap when you break it. It's not glossy anymore. It's streaky or blotchy or spotted. A little bit soft. That's all caused by the reactions of the crystals in the cocoa butter."

"And that sounds a lot like science," she said, her eyes behind her glasses sharp and bright.

"And here you thought I was just a pretty face," he said, reaching into the cabinet below the workstation for a five-kilo bag of 100 percent cacao mass discs.

"Those aren't the same as the chocolate melt discs you can buy in the grocery store, are they?"

He shook his head. "The stuff in the grocery store usually isn't even real chocolate. No cocoa butter. Partially hydrogenated oils. Trans fats. Run far, far away."

"And you only work with the real deal."

"Artisan-produced couverture."

"Couverture?"

"It's the Rolls-Royce of chocolates. Designated by the percentage of cocoa butter to cocoa solids. Rich flavor. Brittle texture. High sheen. Low melting point. Creamy." He stopped then because he was pretty sure he'd crossed from instructive into evangelical.

"Domori?" she asked, reading the name on the bag.

"The cacao plants are the Criollo variety." And now he sounded like a Wiki page. "They make the highest quality beans, pretty much a delicacy. Comes out of Venezuela. The chocolate itself is made in Italy.

This is the dude, Domori, I told you makes the unsweetened bar that's not the least bit bitter."

She opened the top of the bag and peered in. "Wow. I swear I almost smell coffee, too."

He thought back to the park when they'd talked about the soil where both coffee and cacao were grown. "You probably do."

"What does this bag set you back?"

He snorted. "Let's just say it's not cheap. But you've seen the price of the candy."

"Should we maybe work with one that's not so pricey?" she asked, her frown worried. "Since I don't know what I'm doing and don't want to waste something this valuable."

"Do you want to do it right?" When she nodded, he said, "Okay, then. We'll just use half a pound." He eyeballed the amount he wanted and poured it into his electric melting pot. "Besides, I don't have anything cheaper."

"You can't use a microwave?" she asked, looking at the chocolate as it began to warm.

"Yeah, but I'm old-school," he said, and handed her a digital thermometer. "We need to hit one hundred twenty-two degrees."

While she measured the temperature of the chocolate, he reached for his wine, working it around in his mouth and thinking how it would taste when reduced with the fruit. She was right. It was sweet, but not enough to throw off the rest of the flavors.

"Is that okay?" she asked. "The wine?"

He nodded as he swallowed. "Not what I expected, but I'm anxious to see how it turns out," he said, checking the chocolate's thermometer. "Okay. We're at temp. Now pour about two-thirds of what's in the bowl onto the marble counter. Spread it out. Then work it back into the center. It's how we equalize the temperature as it cools."

"I thought they made machines for this," she said, and when he arched a brow, she blew out a deep breath and added, "Right. Hands-on. Old-school."

That had him laughing again. She did that a lot, made him laugh. He hadn't realized how seldom he let himself relax enough to do so except when with Addy. "I actually do use the tempering machine most of the time. I just wanted to show you how to do it by hand."

"Sure thing, *boss*," she said, in such a near perfect imitation of Lena that he groaned as she lifted the pot from the warming element.

Then, focused on the pool of chocolate in front of her, she held the offset spatula and the scraper the way he'd demonstrated, and got to work, spreading out the warm liquid, bringing it from the edge back to the center with the scraper, repeating the process again and again until the chocolate reached the consistency that indicated the right temperature.

Since the first time he'd tempered chocolate, Callum had thought it an incredibly sensual act. It was a lot of work. It used a lot of muscles. The repetitive motion, the clicking sound of the scraper against the marble, the spatula against the scraper, the chocolate growing thicker as it cooled. But he wasn't sure he'd ever known the full measure of the sensuality until having Brooklyn in front of him, her hair pulled up in a net to match his, her long neck exposed, her triceps flexing with the motion of her arms, her back and shoulders flexing, too . . .

"Okay. That looks good," he said after clearing his throat and forcing his attention from her body to the reason they were here. He set the pot on a stool beneath the lip of the work surface, scraping the cooled chocolate into it to seed the rest into a tempered state, too. Then he poured the chocolate into the molds to coat them, draining the excess back into the bowl to use later, and leaving the shells to set.

"So that's the outside of the candies," Brooklyn said, waving a hand toward the molds. "I guess that means the filling is next."

"Yep. Now I get to try out your wine." He reached for the cutting board and knife, then the skillet, plugging in the countertop range he would use to reduce the fruit and the wine. Honey, cinnamon, and brandy would finish the sauce.

They made quick work of the ingredients, Brooklyn anticipating his next move and handing him one item, then the next. She asked smart questions, and he explained the entire process at length, probably giving her more information than she really wanted, but enjoying more than he thought he would talking to her about what he did. Since Duke and Lainie, he hadn't talked to anyone about what he did. Not in any depth.

Lena knew enough to advise customers, and his father had stopped by a time or two to watch him make a batch of one candy or another. He couldn't remember his mother doing more than walking through Bliss a day or two before it opened, commenting on the placement of this or that, asking why he hadn't chosen colors that were brighter, music that wasn't so loud, flavor combinations that might appeal to more people.

The memory had him laughing as he funneled the fruit mixture into the squeeze bottle for filling the shells, which had Brooklyn asking, "What's so funny?"

"This is the first time I've walked through making an entire batch of chocolates with anyone," he said, liking a whole lot, probably too much, that he'd done so with her. "Of course, it's also the first time I've asked anyone to come watch what I do."

"Then I'm honored," she said, her elbows on his worktable, her chin in her hands as she studied him. "Do you ever feel the urge to squeeze that into your mouth?"

He looked up from the tray of half-filled molds. "My mouth?"

"You know, like spraying canned whipped cream from a nozzle."

"Into my mouth."

"Don't tell me you've never done it."

"Never."

"Not once."

"Never," he repeated.

"You don't know what you're missing."

"Besides a sugar coma?"

"In this case," she said, reaching over to close her hand around the bottle above his and slipping her finger beneath the tip, then licking off the squirt of thick filling, "it would be more like a shot. If wine came in shots. Oh my God, that's so good. No wonder Jean wanted more."

Good. Nothing better than a satisfied customer. "Wait till you taste it with the chocolate."

"How long?"

"Till it sets?" he asked, and she nodded. "I'll top the molds with more chocolate, then let that harden. That'll give us enough time to get this mess cleaned up."

"Right. I forgot. I've been making candy with Mr. Clean."

"Funny," he said. He was in an unbelievably good mood.

Another thirty minutes and the chocolates were done. Callum set about storing the ingredients and wiping down the equipment. Brooklyn helped, scraping out the skillet and setting it in the sink with the spatulas and other utensils. When she turned suddenly, her hands full with the bowl holding the remaining fruit filling, her shoulder bounced off his chest.

He reached to steady her, his hands on her upper arms, squeezing before he let go to move the bowl out of the way. He set it on the counter behind him, his gaze still holding hers as they stood there, not speaking, barely breathing, the tension of the last couple of hours finally ready to break.

The bowl settled, the stainless steel ringing against the marble before coming to a stop. Brooklyn hadn't moved. She stood where she'd been, her hands empty, her gaze wide-eyed and searching, her pulse throbbing in the hollow of her throat, a tight drum skin, *boom, boom, boom.* Then she swallowed, and pulled in a shaky breath, and Callum was through waiting.

He threaded his fingers into her hair on either side of her head, exactly as he'd been wanting to do since walking into her classroom.

The strands slid through his fingers, corn silk, smelling like flowers and rain when he stirred them, and so he leaned down, nuzzling her beneath her ear, breathing her in, smelling green tea and lemongrass and ginger.

He'd think more about the combination later, and about what he thought was saffron, but for now he wanted only Brooklyn in his head: the texture of her soft skin, the flutter of her lashes against his cheek when she closed her eyes. The jittery rise and fall of her chest as if she'd been distracted from her need to draw breath by the way he was touching her.

He liked that. He wanted her to respond. He needed her to be as involved as he was, as compelled to explore this chemistry, if it *was* something that basic. A mix of flavors. A reaction of one ingredient to another. The science of attraction. Which wasn't simple at all.

This was complicated, this feathering of his fingers over her ear, her fingers curling into his biceps, pulling him to her as she lifted her chin. He gave himself enough space to look down at her as her eyelids shuttered down, as her lips parted, and then his mouth was on hers.

She tasted like chocolate, and like the grapes in the wine, like apples and peaches, like oranges. Like pears. It was his version of sangria, though it was different than he'd ever made before because of her wine. Her rare Italian and no doubt expensive wine. And he would forever think of her when he made the filling they'd created tonight.

Who the hell am I kidding? he mused, using his thumbs on her jaw to tilt her head. He'd be thinking of her every time he stepped into this kitchen. And he had no one to blame but himself. It was his choice to bring her here, to sacrifice solitude for her company.

Right now he didn't care. This kiss . . . he fell into it, losing himself, finding Brooklyn and something that could not have felt more right. That shouldn't have happened. Everything in his world was already right, wasn't it?

He took a hard step into her. She stepped back and he followed until she had no place else to go, the work counter behind her, his body in front, yet still he pushed, aligning their bodies, moving a thigh between hers, his hip bone pressed to her abdomen, his arm sliding around her shoulders to hold her.

She didn't try to get away, only to get closer, as if she, too, needed more of what they'd created. More of this heat nearly melting them. Sweat ran down his spine to the small of his back, and her hands were there, her fingers curling into the fabric, tugging it up so she could find skin, then touching him . . .

He wanted to laugh, but his tongue was tangled with hers, which was as hungry as the rest of her. She was moving against his thigh where he'd pinned himself between her legs, and he wasn't sure which of them was the first to realize where this was going and groan.

"Brooklyn—"

"Don't stop." Her hands had moved up his back to his shoulders, to his nape, to his hair, her fingers raking against his skull to the knot and tugging it loose. It fell around his face, around her face, a curtain hiding them from the hard truth of this very big mistake.

She was leaving.

He was staying.

He'd promised himself no more bad choices. He had Addy to think about. He had Bliss to think about. Thinking about Brooklyn would splinter his focus, but if he didn't think about her, he'd lose his mind. "We can't—"

"I know. I know," she said, cutting him off.

But he wasn't sure she did. Her mouth was still on his, kissing, nipping, and her hands had moved to his neck, and the buttons on his coat. He let her free one, then two, then three. At the fourth, he grabbed her wrists and stopped her.

"Brooklyn. We can't. Not here. Not tonight."

She dropped her forehead against his chest, gripped fistfuls of his coat while she stood there and breathed. She said nothing. And for the longest time he was afraid he'd hurt her feelings. But she had to know the time wasn't right for either of them, with all they had going on in their lives. None of that meant he didn't want her.

There wasn't a cell in his body that wasn't aching to strip her pants down to her ankles and off, hoist her legs around his waist and let her ride. Even painting the mental picture . . . he couldn't help it. He groaned. And Brooklyn spread out her fingers over his chest, as if feeling the sound echo.

"Do that again," she said, finally lifting her head.

Her eyes were damp, but not sad. "Maybe later."

"Will we? Later?"

How was he supposed to answer that? *Later* could mean anything. Tomorrow. Next week. Four months from now when he was still here and she was in Italy. "I don't know."

"It's been a long time for me."

"It's been a long time for me, too."

"I haven't . . . since Artie."

"I haven't since leaving the hospital with Addy in my arms."

He should've told her sooner, because those were the words that finally got her to let him go.

"You haven't slept with a woman in six years."

"Nope."

"No sex in six years."

"With another person?" He shook his head.

Her cheeks bloomed with color, but he didn't think her embarrassment had much to do with his admission.

"Six years is a long time," she said.

"So's two."

"Yeah, but I'm a—"

"A woman? And that makes a difference?"

"I don't know—"

"I think you do know," he said. There was no need to remind her that only moments ago she'd been the one begging.

"You're right. Celibacy's for the birds."

"Oh, I think the birds get theirs. Them and the bees."

"You're a funny man, Callum Drake. You're a nice man."

"You say that like it's a bad thing."

"It's a compliment," she said, circling to the other side of the center workstation. "My girlfriends tell tales of men who aren't."

"Kindness and respect, doing unto others"—he stopped, shook his head. "It's really not that hard."

"Funny, nice . . . all the things that make for a good father."

He reached up a hand, dragged it down his jaw. "Is bringing my daughter into the conversation your way of throwing a bucket of cold water?"

"Did it work?"

"To remind me she's at a sleepover and I'll be going home alone? I could've done without it, but yeah."

She pushed one of the filled trays toward him. "You *are* the one who put on the brakes."

"Maybe before I take them off, we could finish getting this cleaned up?"

"It's not the best offer I've had all day, but it's probably a good idea. I've heard the boss here doesn't like leaving the place in anything but tip-top shape."

"Sounds like a real jerk," he said.

"He's not. Trust me."

"You know him that well, do you?"

"Not yet. But I'm getting there."

"Too bad you're not sticking around," he said, because the two of them in this small room needed the reminder. "You could get to know him a lot better."

CHAPTER THIRTEEN

Sitting at her kitchen table with her Sunday morning latte, still wearing her yoga pants and the Austin Fire Department T-shirt she'd slept in, her feet in cozy socks, her legs crossed, Brooklyn thought of only one thing: that kiss.

Oh, that kiss. She brought her mug to her mouth, held it there, swearing she could still feel the press of Callum's lips beneath the steam from the espresso and very hot milk. The skin around her lips was slightly chapped from his beard, and she touched the most sensitive spot with the tip of one finger, closing her eyes and remembering the heat of his breath on her face.

What in the world had she been thinking, falling into him the way she had, his mouth, his hands, his body? Falling into the moment and wanting more of him? Falling into the fantasy of being able to have him when there were so many reasons she couldn't: her trip, his mother, Artie's ashes, his daughter, Bianca's need for a teacher, his focus on good choices.

The kiss was a bad one. A very bad one. Even so, she spent much of Sunday morning reliving Saturday night. Wanting to go back and finish what they'd started. Wanting to go back and not kiss him at all. Wanting more.

Kissing him had been . . . *amazing* wasn't a strong enough word. She was a teacher. She had an advanced degree in education, yet she couldn't come up with a description for what they'd done together, to each other, there in Bliss's kitchen. That was Sunday. All. Day. Long.

Monday's spelling lesson was a hit. Bees and beavers and bugs and bulls. Kelly Webber came up with *begonias*; she and her mother had looked at flowers over the weekend, now that the home improvement stores were stocking starter plants for spring. Luke Bean, grandson of Alva, offered *the Beatles*, explaining to the class how his grandfather played music on vinyl LPs.

Adrianne added *butterflies* and *berries*. While at Kelly's during the weekend, she, too, had gone plant shopping, where she'd seen the first, and then to the Gardens on Three Wishes Road with her father, where Callum, Brooklyn learned from his daughter, had bought the second.

The strawberries from Indiana Gatlin's greenhouse would be dipped in chocolate for a party at the home of local sculptor Orville Gatlin and his wife, Merrilee, who had judged the dessert competition at the Second Baptist Church carnival. Brooklyn knew about the soiree from gossip shared by Jean Dial. What she hadn't known until Jean had mentioned it was that Callum did that sort of catering.

Tuesday brought a quick call from Bianca. Artie's cousin had remembered another family heirloom Grandmother Zola had given him, an olive-wood mortar and pestle that Brooklyn recalled sitting on top of his bureau for years. She promised to find it and send it along with the vase.

Thursday saw two more fathers visit Brooklyn's class to read stories for her Dads Love Books, Too! reading program, and while the kids were as captivated by Dan Roth and Stephen Howard as they'd been by Callum Drake, Brooklyn was not. Both men were handsome, Stephen

Howard divorced from his son Stevie's mom and available. But she felt none of the attraction that had drawn her immediately to Callum.

She didn't necessarily believe in love at first sight, and she knew calling what she felt for Callum *love* was a stretch, but neither did she think such a thing was impossible. She and Artie had been inseparable from the day they'd met. And even if she and Callum weren't, she'd been thinking about him as much as, if not more than, she'd thought about Artie in those early days—a realization with which she was as confused as she was uncomfortable.

Was she falling for Callum? Was she falling in love with Callum? Was this a physical need her very hungry body had decided she couldn't live without? Or was this just her infatuation with—and her lust for—a very attractive man? After that kiss, his hands in her hair, her hands on the skin of his back, the taut muscles there, the sweat . . . his leg pressed between hers, the hardest part of him so evident against her belly.

She wanted to sleep with him. There. She admitted it. She wanted to get him out of his clothes and touch him in places she blushed to think about. She wanted to see his tattoos. All of them, not just the ones he'd shown her. To ask him about them: what they symbolized, where he'd had them done, why he'd chosen the colors. If he regretted any of them, or valued the quotes as much today as he did at the time he'd marked himself with them.

The last five days had passed like five months. It had been a long week of not seeing Callum. Not talking to Callum. Not hearing from Callum in person or by voice. The only contact he'd made with her had come on Wednesday through Adrianne, and the tiny Bliss box she'd carried so carefully in both hands to Brooklyn's desk that morning.

That time at least Brooklyn hadn't been blindsided, though she had still been surprised. After the butterflies settled, she could hardly wait for the end of the day to arrive so she could open it with no one around and see what he'd sent her, what he'd made for her, what about her he'd put into another one of his candies the way he had the coffee she loved.

The candy was shaped like a leaf, the veins a dark green while the rest of the surface was lighter, and shiny, as if catching the rays of the sun. It made her think of their day at the park, the sun and the breeze and the trees. That was what she'd expected to taste when the candy hit her tongue, a delectable representation of the day she'd spent with father and daughter, but the flavors that melted in her mouth with the chocolate surprised her.

The combination had tasted of citrus, lemon, maybe, and ginger, and what she thought was green tea. A spice she didn't know hung just beneath the rest; she'd have to ask him what it was, and what had inspired him. But when she reached for the lid to tuck the box into her drawer with the other he'd sent, her hair fell forward, and she knew exactly his inspiration.

She was slow to tuck her hair back behind her ear, first bringing a lock to her nose, smelling it, then lifting her shoulder and breathing in the scent of her morning's shower that lingered. Green tea and lemongrass and ginger. And the spice, the saffron, with which her soap was infused that remained on her skin.

He'd put what he'd smelled on her into the chocolate. He'd breathed her in and he'd remembered. He'd been close enough only one time to pick out the individual scents that made up the whole. Which meant he'd put their kiss into the candy. What the kiss had been for him.

Could she have done the same? Identified anything about him in that moment and latched on to it to remember? There'd been the chocolate, of course, but that was embarrassingly easy. The rest of him . . . she'd been so caught up in what he'd made her feel that she'd been barely aware of the rest of the sensory details. *His* sensory details.

Closing her eyes, she pictured his hair, the dark auburn that made her think of autumn leaves, of burnt sienna. How could she ever put that into a chocolate? She didn't think in the same way that Callum did. She thought like a . . . well, like the schoolteacher she was.

A schoolteacher who'd hung cutouts of leaves in October, who could name almost every Crayola crayon color in the ninety-six-count box. Who'd traveled to Ireland and read all of Nora Roberts's trilogies set there. Those were the bits and pieces of who she was. These were the words she would use to describe him, because she was practical, not creative. An educator, not an artist.

Finally, on Friday, once she was home and curled up in the corner of her sofa with a glass of wine and a book, she picked up the phone. She'd had meetings two nights this week, and spent the rest of her free hours packing.

She'd wanted to call sooner, to thank him for the gift, but the kiss made things so awkward. It shouldn't have; she was thirty-seven years old. He was thirty-four. She was a widow. He was a father. They were both adults, both professionals. Not high schoolers, experimenting, learning, curious.

Yet she was so out of practice, after Artie, because of Artie, that it felt exactly like that, leaving her to her silence. And to wonder why Callum hadn't called her . . .

"Bliss. What's your pleasure?" came Lena's voice on the line.

"Hi, Lena? This is Brooklyn Harvey. Is Callum available? Don't bother him if he's busy—"

"Yo. Boss. Phone," Lena said before Brooklyn could finish.

"Thank you—"

"Bliss," Callum said so quickly Brooklyn decided he was in the showroom instead of the kitchen.

"Hi. It's me. Brooklyn."

"Yeah. I know who me is. What's up?"

O . . . kay. "Thank you."

"For?"

"I think you know," she said, and waited one heartbeat, then another for him to respond.

He finally did. Saying nothing more than, "You're welcome," before adding, "My pleasure," then asking, "Was that all?"

What's your pleasure? It was how they answered the phone at Bliss. And that left her wondering if his response was rote, or if he'd truly found pleasure in making the candy for her, in their kiss . . .

"This is going to come out of the blue, but if the offer's still open, would you mind if I took a few things to your place tomorrow? I thought if I got them out of my way, for now at least, I'd have a better idea of what I have left to do." She couldn't imagine he was buying this. She sounded lame to herself.

"Sure. I can meet you out there. What time?"

"You don't have to. If you're working. Or busy with Addy. I could just stop by Bliss and get the key to the storage barn from you," she said, cringing when she realized how presumptuous she was being. What was wrong with her that she couldn't come right out and tell him she wanted to see him?

Hearing what she thought might be the door from the showroom into the hallway closing, and realizing he hadn't responded, she prompted, "Callum?"

"You called her Addy," he finally said, the echo of his voice confirming her hunch that he'd moved to a more private location.

"What?"

"My daughter."

"Isn't that her name?" she asked, confused.

"It's her nickname," he said, his tone softening. "No one uses it but me. You always call her Adrianne."

"Oh," she said, pressing her fingers to the flutter in her throat. "I guess it just slipped out."

"I like that it did."

Please don't read anything into it. "As much as you talk about her, it's no wonder I picked it up."

"Are you saying we've been hanging out too much?"

She was pretty sure they had, though his question had her smiling. "Hanging out. Is that what we've been doing?"

"Well, we're not dating, so *hanging out* seems to cover it."

Oh, boy. "I can't date my students' parents."

"I hope not. That would make for a hell of a schedule to keep track of."

She found herself wanting to laugh. "You know what I meant."

"Sure. Okay. But we can still be friends?"

"Of course we can still be friends." The thought of his disappearing from her life . . . she couldn't even imagine it.

And then he asked, "What about kissing?"

She closed her eyes, blew out a slow breath. "That's probably not a good idea."

"Doing it again? Or doing it the first time?"

"Both."

"You disappoint me, Brooklyn Harvey. I thought you were more adventurous than that."

If she were adventurous, wouldn't she have continued to travel on her own? Wouldn't she have done more the last two years than watch movies and read books? Wouldn't she have figured out how to have fun without Artie?

"Listen," Callum said before she could push away the thoughts and find a response she could live with. "I need to go check on Addy. She's been coughing and sneezing all afternoon."

"Really?" No wonder he'd sounded distracted earlier. "She seemed fine today at school. Does she have a fever?"

"I took her temperature when we got here, and she was fine. Had to get Lena to run to the pharmacy for a thermometer."

Brooklyn thought a moment, then asked, "Does she have allergies?"

"Nothing serious like peanuts or ragweed. Could be she just got into something in the storeroom, dust or whatever. I need to get my child laborers back in there to clean it up."

"It didn't look dirty the other night." The night she'd kissed him. The night she'd tried to get beneath his clothes and find him. Find why she wanted him. Why she needed him. Find herself.

If his mind had made the same leap, he thankfully kept it to himself. "I haven't had it scoured since the Valentine's Day shipping rush. Who knows what she picked up back there. Look, I'll talk to you later, okay? If Addy's all right, my mom's picking her up in the morning at nine, so I could meet you at nine thirty, unless that's too early for you."

"It's fine, but we can do this another time. And really," she said, realizing it would've been so much easier to be honest and admit she wanted to see him, "we don't have to do it at all."

"Tomorrow's fine. My work schedule's pretty light. Lena can handle things till I get in."

Then he hung up, leaving her to wonder if friends was what she wanted to be with this man, or if she wanted to break the rules that were nudging her shoulder, pushing her out of the bubble she'd been living in all these years.

Pushing her toward him.

∼

Addy
Friday Night

If I had a mommy, I would want her to be just like Ms. Harvey. I don't ever tell Daddy, but sometimes I pretend that's who Ms. Harvey is. Daddy says there are some little girls who don't have a daddy, and some little girls who don't have a mommy, and some little girls have both of them and LOTS of them.

And sometimes I think it would be nice to have a kitty, too. Because a kitty and a little girl and a daddy and Ms. Harvey for a mommy would be the best family EVER. I want a big gray and white kitty. And I want to name her Pikachu. I promised Daddy that if we got a kitty I would never EVER sneeze.

Achoo!

"I heard that."

I pull my covers down away from my itchy face and see Daddy looking at me from the door. I don't want to be sick. If I'm sick, I can't go to school and I HAVE to go to school. That's where Ms. Harvey is. "It was just a tickle in my nose. It's not there anymore."

"That's because it's all over your sheets now."

"Daddy! Tickles can't get on sheets."

He walks close to the bed and sits down. Then he puts his hand on my forehead to see if I feel like a fireplace.

"I'm not hot."

"You're warm."

"Warm isn't hot. Warm is like cool."

He shakes his head. "Warm is not like cool."

"Ms. Harvey says it is."

"Does she now?"

"Uh-huh. Warm hasn't made it all the way to hot yet. Like cool hasn't made it all the way to cold yet."

"I see," he says, and he rubs his beard like it tickles. "Is that how Ms. Harvey tells it?"

I can't remember Ms. Harvey's real words, but I nod anyway. "If you don't like it you can take it up with her."

That makes Daddy laugh.

He's so funny when he laughs. But then I want to laugh and it makes my throat hurt, and then my tummy hurts because my throat gets all tight but I am NOT SICK.

"Sit up a second. You need a spoon of the purple medicine," he says.

The purple medicine is yummy, but it's not candy so I pretend I don't like it too much. And it is hard to swallow. My throat wants to close up and feels all sticky.

Daddy puts the top back on the bottle. "You didn't eat much dinner. Sometimes when you don't have an appetite that means you're getting sick."

"I do too have an appetite."

"I didn't see it tonight."

"I kept it in my tummy because I ate too many of Grammy's sugar cookies when she came to see me at Bliss."

Then Daddy says some bad words I'm not allowed to EVER REPEAT. But I hear them in my head and I want to know what they mean and when I'll be old enough to say them.

"Listen, pumpkin. I know you love your Grammy, and Grammy loves you, but it's okay if you just eat one cookie and save the rest for after your dinner."

"If I eat my dinner I'll be too full to eat them."

"Yeah. That's the point."

"What is a point? Like a pencil?"

"Nothing, sweetheart. Never mind." Then he puts his hand on my forehead again. "Does your throat hurt when you swallow?"

"I don't have anything to swallow. If I had a piece of ooey gooey cake I could swallow it." I really, really want a piece of ooey gooey cake.

"You can swallow your spit."

"Daddy, you are just yucky."

"Here. Drink some water."

I do, and it hurts a little bit, but I don't want him to know because then he won't help me make an ooey gooey cake.

"That's what I thought," he says, when I open my eyes after the hurt stops.

"Are you going to make me stay home from school tomorrow?"

"I am. Because it's Saturday."

"Does that mean I don't get to see Ms. Harvey?"

"Saturday is the weekend, pumpkin. It's Ms. Harvey's day off."

"Is it my day off, too?"

"It is."

"And Grammy's? She's going to take me to look for an Easter dress."

Daddy shakes his head and tugs at my hair. "You're not going anywhere if you're still sneezing."

"I won't be. I promise. Can you come with us, too?"

"I would love to come, but I have to work. This week I don't get a day off till Sunday."

"How come you have to wait till Sunday?" I don't like it when Daddy works so much.

"Because people who don't have to work on Saturday like to come buy chocolates. I have to be there to sell them."

"But Lena sells them. You just make them."

"You make it sound so easy."

"It's just candy, Daddy. Candy IS easy. It's not hard like ooey gooey cake."

He moves my hair away from my face and touches the end of my nose. Then I scoot down so he can pull up my covers and tuck me in like a cozy bug in a rug before he reads me a Pete the Cat story. "If you're running a fever in the morning, you're staying home."

"That's okay, Daddy. I don't mind."

But I would mind if I had to miss school and not see Ms. Harvey.

CHAPTER FOURTEEN

Rather than sitting on Addy's bed and leaning against the brick wall at the head as he usually did for story time, Callum perched on the edge of the mattress, figuring as bad as she felt with her allergies, and with the medicine due to kick in, he wouldn't be here long. He was right. He didn't even make it through half the book before she fell asleep.

Leaving her with a brush of his lips to her brow, then lingering at her doorway with a prayer that he not screw up this parenting thing, that he help her become a well-rounded, decent, and productive member of the human community, he headed for the kitchen and the small offset pantry where he stored his chocolate-making supplies.

Since opening Bliss, he rarely made candy at home. He didn't keep any but the most basic of ingredients in the loft, and his best molds were at the shop. But there was just something about going back to his roots that settled him. And tonight he was feeling the need to be settled. Plus, he'd be seeing Brooklyn tomorrow. He'd been terse on the phone with her earlier, concerned about Addy, and he made his best apologies with chocolate.

Okay. Brooklyn didn't date men whose kids she taught. He got it, and he could respect it, though it made for a bit of a hurdle; by the time

Addy was no longer one of her students, Brooklyn would be on her way out of town. She might return, she might not, meaning he had to make sure she knew his interest went beyond last weekend's kiss. A kiss that had thrown him far enough off-kilter he'd been afraid to touch base all week: afraid he'd gone too far and she wouldn't want to see him again, afraid seeing her again would have them going even further when sex at this stage of the game wouldn't be smart. She wasn't ready, and, he feared, she was too hung up on the past.

No, the best thing to do would be get her to change her mind about leaving for good—though that wouldn't be fair to either of them. She had to do what she had to do; he knew without a doubt she'd regret staying, and he'd regret persuading her. Her loyalty to her husband and the man's family was admirable, and he couldn't compete. He didn't want to compete.

What he wanted was for her to choose him because he was the one she now wanted. At least he didn't have to worry about physical attraction, though he'd been pretty sure all along that wouldn't be an issue. The issue was a lot more complicated than that: his rival, though he hated thinking of a dead man that way, was a ghost, and Brooklyn still haunted.

The fruit bowl in his kitchen yielded but one lone banana. He and Addy had split the last orange this morning. He'd sent an apple for her lunch, and brought the remaining one to Bliss for her to have after school. Hmm. She must've left it there, too full after eating his mother's cookies. Whatever else he did this weekend, Sunday he had to buy groceries.

The freezer contained frozen raspberries, blueberries, and cherries, the refrigerator two plump lemons. He'd already given Brooklyn the lemongrass candy, and he'd be making truffles with crème de framboise, crème de myrtille, and crème de griotte next week, so . . . Bananas, er, *Banana* Foster it was.

Digging a skillet from the cabinet, he set it on the stove, then grabbed a cutting board and a knife. Leaving those on the counter, he reached above the fridge for a bottle of dark rum and one of banana liqueur. From the pantry, he snagged the Vietnamese cinnamon he kept on hand for French toast and a box of brown sugar. The few molds he had were on the same shelf as his retired tempering machine. Retired from Bliss anyway.

The only cocoa butter he had turned out to be a jeweled ivory. Close enough to the yellow he usually used. More interested in the flavor than the color or the shape, he went with one that was a sort of trapezoidal prism. The edges and angles were great for showing off the shimmer of the shell.

He'd watched Brooklyn down the Queen Cayenne and witnessed her appreciation for the chocolate as much as the pepper's bite. The Bananas Foster recipe yielded an equally taste-intensive experience: the caramelized brown sugar and banana, the tickle of the cinnamon, the headiness of the rum, and the extravagance of the butter and cream.

Unlike the last two candies he'd made her, this was one he kept in the shop during the summer. The ingredients brought to mind the tropics and clear skies and blue waters. He thought it appropriately symbolic of her trip to the Italian Riviera, and figured making it would show his support, when her going to Italy was the last thing he wanted.

Measuring out just enough chocolate for the half tray's worth of filling he'd get out of his single banana, he tossed the discs into his tabletop tempering machine, then checked the bottle of cocoa butter warming in a bowl of hot water. The outer ring had melted, so shaking the seed of the solid center brought the liquid to a tempered state.

On the phone this afternoon, she'd called his daughter Addy, he mused, swirling the barest glaze of cocoa butter into the molds with his fingertip. Addy, as if it were the most natural thing in the world. Obviously she'd heard him use the nickname, but she'd continued to call her Adrianne, putting up, he supposed, some sort of wall since Addy was in her class.

He wanted to change that, but didn't want to make things hard on Brooklyn. As far as he knew, her stance on dating was her own, not a school regulation; she obviously had her reasons. He was going to have to find a way to get her to ditch them without causing her any grief.

~

After yesterday's phone conversation with Callum, Brooklyn wasn't sure what mood she'd find him in when she arrived with her boxes. In order to get to Artie's books, she'd needed to move her keepers out of the way. Those would be staying with her, not traded in or donated, and she liked the idea of storing them at Callum's. She was trusting him with something important, something valuable, even though he wouldn't know.

She'd almost backed out. Almost called this morning to gauge his frame of mind; if she found him short-tempered again—Was that what he'd been yesterday? Had she caught him at a bad time? Had he not wanted to hear from her? Was he regretting the kiss and the candy? Or had he indeed simply been worried about Addy?—she would cancel. But she hadn't called. And she hadn't canceled. She'd come here as if yesterday hadn't happened at all because she wanted to see him.

It was as simple as that.

Instead of pulling to the front of his house in the circular drive, she'd stuck to the driveway's extension that led to the storage barn at the back of the lot. It sat next to a second barn that was used to keep lawn and pool equipment, and from the outside didn't look any different. But this one, Callum had told her, was insulated, temperature-controlled, hardwood-floored, and appeared to have been used in the past as an office or a study. Even as small as Hope Springs was, she wasn't sure if she'd ever known who lived here before.

She imagined it as a library, walls of shelves with the very books she'd brought over, and the hundreds more she had left to pack. The idea of having all of her books in one place, organized, any title she wanted at her fingertips . . . heaven. When she pulled to a stop, she glanced in the rearview mirror to see if the smile on her face looked as big as it felt.

The door to the storage barn opened, and Callum stepped out just as she shut off her car's engine. As always, he wore jeans and boots, and this time, instead of a ragged T-shirt, an oxford shirt left untucked, with his hair pulled back in a knot. Stuffing his keys into his pocket, he stepped out of the building and walked toward her, his expression worrisome.

Her smile faltering, she opened the door and climbed out. "Thanks for this," she said, and waved an arm. "How's Addy feeling?"

"She's fine." He wrapped his hand over the top of her door. "Sorry for being short yesterday. When you called. I was afraid I was going to end up at the clinic with her today."

"No need to apologize," she said, the pressure in her chest easing. "Is she with your mother?"

"She felt better today. A good night's sleep. A dose of meds. So yeah. Easter-dress shopping as planned." He ground out the words, nearly pulverizing them.

"You don't sound too happy about that." Talk about an understatement.

He lifted his gaze, staring into the distance. "It's nothing."

"Nothing except you wanted to be the one to buy her a dress."

Responding with a humored huff, he said, "And here I thought I had a handle on that being so transparent thing."

She liked that he was human, vulnerable. A dad with feelings. "The fact that you don't makes it a whole lot easier to read your mind."

He brought his gaze back to hers, beginning to grin. "You been doing a lot of that?"

She shrugged, reaching into the car to pop the trunk and unlock the back door. "I try. I don't always succeed. And you can buy her a dress, too, you know."

"I hadn't thought about that." He glanced into the backseat as she opened the door, then followed her around to the trunk and stared at the boxes there. "You know today's the last day of February, right? That tomorrow it'll be March?"

"I stayed late yesterday afternoon to hang shamrocks and leprechauns above the classroom cubbies. So, yes. I'm well aware of the date." But she knew what he was asking. Knew, too, that he probably saw through her ruse of needing to get boxes out of her way. She wasn't particularly thrilled at the deception, but was even less thrilled that she hadn't pulled it off.

He looked at her, back at the trunk, then at her again, and arched a brow. "Since you're leaving in a little over three months, and this is all you've brought over, I wasn't sure if you'd lost track of time."

Not likely. She was leaving on June 5, five days before the second anniversary of Artie's death. Two years. He'd told her no more than two years. He'd made her promise not to become Queen Victoria. "No. I know how much time I've got to get everything done. This will help. Thank you."

"You're welcome," he said, reaching for the first box, labeled "A." Not "A-C," or even "A-B." Just "A." "Let me guess. Margaret Atwood. Isaac Asimov. Jeffrey Archer. Aristotle."

"Try Jane Austen," she said with a laugh, adding, "And more Jane Austen. Louisa May Alcott. Lara Adrian. Cherry Adair. Michele Albert. Judith Arnold. Shana Abé."

"Got it," he said. "I guess you've got at least twenty-six of these then."

No. She had a whole lot more. She followed with a second, smaller box, also labeled "A." He took it from her before she could step into the building, realizing when she did that he'd already turned on the air conditioner.

"We haven't talked money—"

"No money," he said, straightening from where he'd stacked her box on top of his. "I'm not using the space, so it's no inconvenience."

Not the point. "You're paying for the electricity and you're not even living here yet. I'm going to reimburse you for that at least."

But he shook his head. "I'm not going to figure out the square footage and kilowatt-hours just so I can take your money."

"Then I'll pay you what a comparable storage unit would cost me."

"You say that like you could find another place with the same amenities. Trees, a swimming pool, a killer kitchen."

She waited for him to add *me*, but he didn't, which was probably for the best, so she said, "A killer kitchen would have food. And dishes for eating. Chairs for sitting. A corkscrew."

He chuckled and came toward the door where she stood. "I was thinking of doing some shopping for this house this weekend. Tomorrow, actually. Addy's going to a craft show or carnival thing in Gruene with my mother. Face painting, cotton candy, animal balloon races or some crap."

"You don't sound too excited about that."

"It's just the usual," he said, hopping back to the ground and offering her his hand. She took it and stepped down, then reluctantly pulled away. "All these plans get made while I'm working, then when I decide I want to do something, Addy's already excited about what my mother has going on."

"Have you asked your mother to check with you first?" Surely he had. It seemed so obvious.

"Only once every week at least. I don't get it. She gets in my face about my responsibility, then she schedules things for the two of them to do, knowing I won't want to disappoint Addy."

"Your daughter will forgive you, you know. Eventually."

"Yeah. Then there's the part where balloon animals sound like a whole lot more fun than furniture shopping, even to me."

"So go with them." Because that seemed obvious, too.

"I really need to get this done. I just don't want to do it alone."

"Misery loves company?"

He frowned as he asked her, "Do I make you miserable?"

"You? No. You dragging me to store after store after store . . ."

He laughed, then he groaned. "You mean we have to go to more than one?"

"Do you want to get it over with?" she asked him as she headed back to her car, ignoring his use of the word *we*. "Or do you want to do it right?"

"Depends if you're talking about shopping," he said, following her, reaching her, leaning close as she reached for a box in her trunk. Nearly brushing his mouth to her ear when he said, "Or sex."

That damn kiss. The way she'd climbed all over him. The way she'd let him see how hungry she was for what she knew without a doubt he could give her. Even thinking about it now . . . his arms, his legs, his chest pressed to hers, the hair on his very flat belly . . .

She cleared her throat, wishing for a big glass of water. Or a big glass of wine. "I'm beginning to wonder if shopping's really what you've got on your mind."

"Unfortunately, it is," he said, taking the box from her. "But sex is there, too. Trust me on that."

Now she was going to spend the day wondering about the things he was thinking. "If you say so."

"Curious?"

She stacked a third box in his arms, her hands trembling, heat pooling between her legs until her skin flushed. "Or about what it would be like to have sex with you?"

He laughed. "Brooklyn Harvey. I think you just surprised me."

And now she needed to change the subject. Talking about sex with Callum Drake was probably the worst idea in the world. "Well, it's not like I can surprise you with a chocolate that tastes like me kissing you . . ."

"I wondered if you'd figure it out," he said as he turned for the barn.

"Not at first," she said, following. "But then I caught the scent of my shampoo. Thank you. It was lovely. And such a great combination of flavors. Surprising, really."

"I'm glad you enjoyed it. I had another one to give you today," he said, from inside the building before returning to the door, "but I was in a rush this morning and forgot to bring it."

"You need to stop with the candy," she said, lifting the box she held for him to take inside with the rest. "Really. I sit at a desk too much to make your chocolates a regular thing."

"They've got about fifty calories each. I think you can afford it."

She laughed. "Well, sure. But there's afford, and then there's *afford*."

"Anytime you're in the mood for one, swing by the shop."

"I'll keep that in mind," she said, turning back for the car. "Right now I'm in the mood to get these boxes unloaded."

"And tomorrow?" he asked, hefting the largest box out of the trunk. "You think you'll be in the mood to go shopping?"

She did not need to be spending so much time with him. She did not need to be looking to him for her fun. "Sure. I'd love to."

"You want me to swing by and pick you up?"

"On your bike?"

"Absolutely."

Meaning every one of her neighbors would know who she was with, and she did not need that bit of gossip spreading, though after his help in her garage it was probably too late. "It's better if I come to you."

"You want to do breakfast first? Malina's? Or we can eat once we get to Austin."

Neither of his suggestions gave away what he was thinking, but she couldn't help feeling uncharitable when she said, "Let's do that."

"Right." This time his tone was caustic. "Less chance we'll run into anyone we know."

And now she'd hurt his feelings. That was the last thing she'd wanted to do. "Callum—"

"No. It's okay," he said, carting the final box to the barn. "Hope Springs is a small town and teaching puts you in the public eye. I get you not wanting the scrutiny."

"I wouldn't think it would be good for you, either." Though really. Did it matter what Shirley Drake and the residents of Hope Springs thought about her personal life?

"Are you kidding?" Callum asked, on his way back to her car, his dimples cutting deep as he grinned. "To be seen with the teacher everyone loves? My reputation could use a little of that juice."

"How long have you been here now?" she asked, swallowing the flutters tickling her throat. "I've never heard a bad word spoken about you. Curious words, yes. But nothing I can see doing your business any harm. In fact, I'll bet some customers want to see the big bad biker for themselves."

"And you wondered about the one-way glass," he said, slamming the lid of her trunk. "So, eight o'clock? Or maybe eight thirty would be better, since my mother's coming for Addy at eight."

"Eight thirty. I'll do a slow crawl past the alley and make sure the coast is clear. Ooh, we could have a signal. You could text and say that Elvis has left the building. Or Operation Buy-a-Bed is a go."

"All this mocking," he said, shaking his head. "Keep it up, and I might just think you want to be seen with me."

Strangely, no matter her protests, she wanted exactly that.

Brooklyn's Banana Bread Spice Cake

For the cake:
2 1/2 cups all-purpose flour
1 1/4 teaspoons baking powder
1 teaspoon salt
1 1/2 teaspoons cinnamon
3/4 teaspoon nutmeg
1 teaspoon cloves
1 2/3 cups sugar
2/3 cup shortening
2 large eggs
1 teaspoon pure vanilla extract
1 1/4 teaspoons baking soda
2/3 cup buttermilk
1 1/4 cups ripe, mashed bananas (about three medium)

Preheat oven to 350° (F). Grease and flour three 8-inch cake pans, or one 13 x 9-inch baking pan, and line with parchment paper, coating with nonstick spray.

Sift into a large bowl the flour, the baking powder, the salt, the cinnamon, the nutmeg, and the cloves.

In another large bowl, cream the sugar and the shortening. Add the eggs and mix well. Add the vanilla.

In a small bowl, dissolve the soda in the buttermilk. Stir the buttermilk/soda mixture into the sugar/shortening/eggs/vanilla mixture. Add the bananas and mix well.

Add the flour mixture a little at a time until well mixed and pour into pan(s). Bake 25–35 minutes or until inserted tester comes out clean.

For the frosting:
1 stick butter
1 packed cup light brown sugar
1/4 cup milk
1 3/4–2 cups powdered sugar
1/2 teaspoon vanilla

Melt the butter in a large saucepan over low heat. Add the brown sugar and cook until the sugar is dissolved, beating together the butter and the sugar well. Do not allow to boil. Remove from heat. Add the milk and the vanilla. Gradually add the powdered sugar until frosting is of a spreadable consistency. Beat until smooth and cool. Spread over cake.

CHAPTER FIFTEEN

Being seen with Callum would've been a whole lot more fun, Brooklyn decided, had they taken her car or his truck. Instead, they'd ridden his Harley from Hope Springs to Austin, then from store to store, her hair looking worse with each stop. Putting the helmet on, taking the helmet off, the wind blowing as they rode. Then there were her aching legs . . .

She'd worn jeans and ankle boots, so she was well-protected, but no matter how often she told herself to relax, tension was making itself known in her lower back. Her hips and knees were just as full of complaints. She had to face it. She was not cut out to be a biker chick, or biker mama, or whatever the term was.

But she wasn't going to have to worry about that, was she? Just like she wouldn't be the one using the furniture he bought, or the one living in the house where the furniture would be delivered. The one to sleep in his bed, make him pancakes, drink the perfectly brewed cup of Sumatran coffee he handed her each morning.

And why wasn't she going to be the one? Because she was scared to death that falling for Callum made her disloyal to Artie. That somehow it diminished what she'd felt for Artie. That she couldn't care for Callum when Artie still took up so much of her heart. Two-year deadline or not, and no matter the promise she'd made, she couldn't move on if it meant losing any of what Artie had been to her.

She was going to fail in his request of her; she just knew it. Culling their possessions . . . no, she didn't need to keep what clothes of his she hadn't cleared out of the guest room closet, and going through his tools hadn't been as hard as she'd thought it would be. It helped that they would end up belonging to others whom she knew would get good use from them.

But the pictures, the books . . . the owls. She could store the pictures in the cloud and look at them from time to time. She could think about Artie turning the books' pages as he read her his favorite parts. She could group the owls together on the bureau's top and remember where each had come from, but she could never live without them.

Those thoughts had weighed heavily all day, while she and Callum had shopped, and along with repeatedly having to untangle her hair and shake out her aches, had made her less than the ideal shopping partner. Plus she was starving; they'd been at it most of the day, and it was nearly six.

"Can we call it a day now and get the hell out of here?" Callum asked as if reading her mind.

They were in a store that specialized in bedrooms: bunk beds and futons and sofa beds and mattresses with adjustable air technology.

Judging by the tone of his question, he wasn't any happier to be here than she was. Not that she could blame him; after seven stores and too many attempts by salesmen to hard sell them, calling it a day sounded like a plan to her, too.

"Hey, this was your idea. Not mine."

He answered with a snort.

So far, he'd outfitted Addy's room, his man cave, and bought a kitchen nook table with a bench and four chairs. She liked the table a lot. And the chairs. All were made of a light, rustic pine, and the matching bench had a tufted red seat that made her think of a diner.

When they'd been shown the same bench with a seat of forest green, Callum had looked at her and shrugged. It wasn't her house. It wasn't her kitchen. But she loved red, so she'd made the suggestion. If he'd given any indication of leaning the other way, she wouldn't have.

And maybe she'd been wrong to suggest anything. He was the one who'd have to live with the choice. She didn't want him blaming her if he hated it. Green, being darker, would hide more sins—

"Just tell me which bed you like and I can knock out my bedroom. That'll just leave the living room. And the dining room, I guess. And whatever the hell I decide to do with the extra rooms. Guests, maybe, or an office, or a playroom for Addy. Hell. Staying in the loft is sounding better and better."

"It's a little bit late for that, isn't it?"

"As long as I don't tell Addy about the house—"

"Callum Drake. You are not going to deprive your daughter of that house and yard."

He muttered under his breath. "So which one do you like?"

"It doesn't matter what I like. I'm not going to be sleeping in your bed." The moment the words left her mouth she wanted to call them back. Not because they weren't the truth, but because the idea of any other woman sleeping with him, especially in a bed she'd helped him choose . . .

She couldn't bear it. She was going to Cinque Terre on a one-way ticket. Her familial ties to Hope Springs, to Texas, were gone. She could live in Italy as long as she wanted to. But now that she had all the time in the world, she didn't want to go. Not when Callum, and Addy, would be here.

She grabbed for the bed's footboard post and sank onto the padded bench butted up against it. Callum loomed over her, then moved to sit at her side, his legs spread, his forearms on his thighs. He toyed with the ring on his right hand, turning it around and around and around.

"Maybe this wasn't such a good idea," he said, at the same time she said, "I'm sorry."

"You don't have anything to apologize for. I've never shopped for furniture before. I have zero taste when it comes to anything but chocolate. That's the only reason I asked what you liked. I wasn't beating around the bush, trying to get you into my bed. If that was the case, I would've come out and said so. I'm not exactly the most subtle guy, in case you haven't noticed."

"I have." And then because she absolutely could not help herself, she asked, "Do you? Want me in your bed?"

He laughed. Not loudly. Not with anything resembling humor. Not at her. Not even at what she'd said, it seemed, as much as at what was going on in his mind. Things no more suited to this time and place than her question.

She wasn't stupid. The way he looked at her. The way he touched her. The way he'd kissed her. Yet not being stupid hadn't stopped her from asking something that was.

"Callum—"

"Yes, Brooklyn. I want you in my bed, but you know that. I want to undress you," he said, his voice barely above a whisper, the pitch low and hungry, making her ache. "I want to see you naked, and look into your eyes when I cover you and push into you."

It took so little of her imagination to feel him between her legs, parting her, entering her, and she shivered with the sensation as much as with the realization of how much he wanted her. That he would say so to her here, in this store, where he could be overheard, as if the possibility was nothing compared to his needing her to know how he felt.

He laughed again, a deep, painful sound, a wounded sound, as if he were suffering. "Thinking about having you in my bed takes up way too much of my time. But what's the point of starting something that's going to make your leaving even harder than it's already going to be?"

She closed her eyes because she was so afraid she was going to cry. How was she going to survive leaving him? How had her carefully made plans become so terribly unappealing? What in the world was wrong with her? "Sometimes I wonder . . ."

"What?"

"If I really want to go."

He hesitated for a very long moment, as if his waiting would get her to repeat the words with more conviction, then finally said, "A little late for that now, isn't it?"

"I do want to go," she said with a heavy sigh. "I know that. I haven't seen Artie's family in far too long."

"You're just not sure if you want to stay and teach."

"I thought I was sure," she admitted, raising her gaze to his.

He moved closer to her on the bench, their thighs pressed together, and his eyes were so close, and his mouth, and she couldn't help it. She lifted her hand and laid it against his face, cupping his cheek, then his jaw, stroking him with her thumb before letting him go.

Tucking her chin to her chest, she closed her eyes, still feeling the scruff of his beard on her palm. But before she could make a fist and hold it in, his hand was on hers, his fingers lacing with hers.

"From everything you've said, it sounds like this trip, for however long it lasts, is important to you—"

"It is important. I should never have let so much time lapse between visits."

"Then it's probably not the trip responsible for the second thoughts. More like it's selling the house, or giving up your job here."

"Well, I can't be in two places at once, so the job had to go. As far as the house"—she shrugged—"renting would've been too much of a hassle with me living abroad. Even with a management company handling things."

"Not the house, not the job, not the trip."

Was he baiting her? Trying to get her to admit she wanted to stay for him?

"You're giving up the life you've lived here for twelve years," he finally said. "Of course there are going to be nerves and doubts and all sorts of what-ifs floating around in your head."

She looked down at the scuffed and peeling hardwood beneath their feet, at the equally scuffed toes of his heavy black boots. "Did you have the same? When you decided to move to Hope Springs?"

"Ah, that was different," he said, sliding his hand from hers and lacing his own together, his elbows on his knees as he leaned forward.

"How so?"

"For one thing, I had a newborn I needed to get the hell out of a crapfest of a situation. Coming here was about saving our lives."

"Is that what you really think?"

"If we'd stayed in California? If I'd kept working for Duke? I don't even want to imagine—" He stopped and cleared his throat, his voice quavering, the last word more of a strangled whisper than spoken. "The thought of Addy growing up in that environment . . . I can't even imagine who she would be now. And she's only six years old."

He went silent after that, staring at the throw rug beneath the bench, or at his boots, or at hers. She kept quiet, too. They'd both said enough, and she had so much to think about and was ready to go home.

"I like that one," she finally said, pointing to the mahogany suite in the alcove across from where they were sitting. "But that's just me and my love for sleigh beds. You might like a different style."

"I'll definitely need something without a footboard. Even with a king-sized mattress I tend to wake up with my feet hanging off the end."

Callum had four inches on Artie at least. "See? This is why asking me for furniture advice is a bad idea."

"A bed? Maybe. The rest? You've been a great help."

A great help. Yes, that was exactly what she wanted to be.

~

Once at the loft, Callum slowed his bike and pulled to the back side of his building. Brooklyn had parked behind his covered spot this morning, and he eased around her car.

She held on to his waist until he'd braked and shut off the engine, then she climbed off and handed him the helmet she'd used. If she were staying in Hope Springs, he'd buy her one of her own.

"You coming up?" he asked as she shook out her hair and smoothed it, her fingers catching in a tangle.

She gestured toward her car. "I should probably get going."

"C'mon. Just for a second." He tucked the extra helmet beneath one arm, held his in the same hand as he bounced his keys in the other, finding the one for his door. "I've got something to give you."

Wariness crept into her eyes, but she nodded and said, "Okay." The word sounded out with the same sense of caution.

Meaning he couldn't do anything that would scare her off. For some reason, she seemed ready to bolt. He wanted to know why, because it had to be more than furniture-shopping frustration.

The freight elevator opened onto the hallway of the building's second floor, where his loft took up the east side of the space, and another tenant's the west. He turned in his direction, and she followed, though she did so a lot more slowly than he liked.

"Listen. I know it's been a sort of rough day, but I promise I'm not going to make it any worse," he said as he reached his door and waited for her to catch up. "So it would make me feel a whole lot less like a case of the mumps if you wouldn't hang back like I'm contagious."

That made her laugh, a cute snort of a sound, and when he opened the door she walked through, saying, "I'm afraid you are."

Which was probably the last thing he needed to hear from her.

He closed the door, locked it, bounced his keys in his palm, then tossed them to the table that sat against the wall beside the door. They hit the surface and slid, knocking one of Addy's *Frozen* figurines to the floor.

He snatched it up and crossed to his daughter's room, giving Brooklyn time to relax and leaving the toy in the basket of things Addy had to earn back. She knew the rules. Toys belonged in their place. She could play with them in the big room, but they went back to their basket at bedtime.

Harsh, maybe, but as busy as the two of them were, messes in the loft would get out of control before he knew it if he didn't stay on top of things. And with the new house being the size it was, he couldn't have anything out of control. He'd never catch up. He'd never rein it in.

"I can see why you needed to buy furniture," she said, looking from the futon he still used as a sofa, and ended up crashing on too often, to the bar stools he and Addy sat on to eat. "I'm guessing you don't throw a lot of dinner parties?"

"This was only supposed to be temporary."

"I think there's something to be said for the scaled-down life. It will certainly make for easy packing."

"Maybe I should ditch everything I bought today. Just keep what I have," he said, instead of thinking about her going through the things of her husband's she'd lived with all this time. "I don't want the house to be all fussy."

"You'll do no such thing," she said, sounding bossy and proprietary and him liking it way too much. "All you bought were the basics, and not even all of those, really. It's going to take a lot more than that to get close to fussy."

She turned then, and caught him staring at her, her smile fading to something hesitant again, something that said she wasn't sure she should be here. Something that made him want to get her to change her mind.

But he'd already had this talk with himself more than once. He wanted her here, but only if the want was a mutual thing. Right now, her vibes were all about finding the fastest way to the door. And that had him on the verge of giving up.

He headed for the kitchen where he'd left the candy he'd made her, and before offering it to her, he put the bar between them, pushing the bonbon across it. "I meant to give this to you yesterday, but getting Addy out the door turned into a mini-drama yesterday morning, then this morning you were waiting downstairs by the time I was dressed, and I forgot to grab it."

She took it from him with a heavy sigh, picking it up and looking at it up, down, and sideways.

He finally said, "You're welcome," because the silence was gnawing a hole in his gut.

"Sorry. It's beautiful. But you've got to stop doing this." For a moment she looked as if she was going to eat it, then she set it back down. "You make me feel . . . guilty."

"Guilty of what?" he asked as her gaze came up.

"Not reciprocating."

That wasn't what he'd expected, but he gave her extra points for honesty, and for not looking away. "You think gifts are about reciprocity?"

"No, but I still feel as if I should be doing something for you."

Did she really not get it? How much she'd already done? "Like helping me pick out furniture? Like keeping my daughter from breaking legs at a church carnival? Can you imagine if Alva Bean had fallen hard on the gymnasium floor?"

"So this is a thank-you?"

"It's a chocolate, Brooklyn. It's meant to be enjoyed, not analyzed."

"Analyzing your chocolates is one of my favorite things to do."

Too bad she wouldn't be here to analyze more. "Then tell me about this one."

She took so long deciding, he thought she was going to say no, but then she bit off a third or so, savored, and finally swallowed. "I taste banana. And some sort of liqueur. Or maybe rum. Cinnamon for sure. I think all it's missing is the ice cream."

"There's cream in there, too."

"If I light a fire will it burst into flame?"

"It's not that kind of Bananas Foster. At least not anymore. The flames got a little dicey while I was cooking the filling, but that's because my head wasn't in the game."

"Where was your head?" she asked, licking a speck of chocolate from the pad of her thumb.

"Nowhere important," he said, the words a lie, but a small white one that felt better than telling her he'd been thinking how to convince her that they'd be good together. "You going to eat the rest of that or just see if you can get it to melt in your hand?"

Smiling, she bit off half of what was left, closing her eyes, her mouth still as she let the flavors settle.

"Good?" he asked as he came around the bar to where she sat.

"Mmm. You want to taste?"

"Yeah. I do," he said, taking the chocolate from her hand. He bit into it, let the chocolate melt on his tongue, moving in and lowering his head and covering her mouth with his.

She smelled like the sun and the wind, and like her shampoo that he loved. She tasted like chocolate and like Brooklyn and like the rest of his life. He was insane for putting himself through this, and yet *this* was exactly what he wanted. This passion. This response. This woman.

He hooked one arm around her neck, the other around her waist, and pressed his hand into the small of her back, wedging his thigh between hers that parted for him so easily. He wasn't going to take her to bed. He wanted to take her to bed, but not tonight. Too much stood unsettled between them . . . his past, her past, the future.

There was something about her trip to Cinque Terre that she wasn't telling him, and he would bet the bank it involved her husband. Again with the rival. Again with the ghost. The thoughts came at him like cold water, buckets of the stuff, and Brooklyn felt it; she began pulling away from the kiss before he did, her hands sliding from his neck to his chest, her smile uncertain, her gaze strangely timid as she let it fall and stepped back.

Yeah. Neither one of them had been on the top of their game today, both thinking too much about things gone wrong instead of working at what they had that was so very right.

"Now that we've had dessert, you want to do something about dinner?"

"That would be nice, as long as we don't have to go out to get it."

He groaned. "Right. Can't be seen in the company of an ex-biker hoodlum thug."

"I doubt you were ever a hoodlum or a thug," she said with a smile. "But you are the father of one of my students, though as long as I've been here tonight, I'm pretty sure that ship has sailed."

He wasn't going to set her straight on what he'd been. This wasn't the time. But he planned to enjoy the hell out of the fact that she hadn't split at the idea of being seen. "I can order pizza or Chinese."

"Or we can cook."

"Cook."

"Unless the pantry is bare?"

"It's fresh out of fruit for sure."

She tucked back her hair as she considered him. "If Addy were here, what would you two do for dinner?"

"It's Sunday night, so probably pancakes and bacon."

"I like pancakes. And bacon."

He grinned at that. "Do you want them shaped like Olaf?"

"I don't think I've ever had a snowman pancake before. So yes. Thank you. I'll take a stack of Olaf."

CHAPTER SIXTEEN

Almost a week went by without Brooklyn seeing or talking to Callum, a week that left her too much time to think about the kiss in his loft, the kiss in his kitchen, and to decide that, though their two busy schedules were completely out of sync, they were getting too close. The fact that he was on her mind as often as he was, when they'd reached the early days of March, and she needed to be getting ready for her trip to Italy, was more than enough proof.

Yet here she sat, Friday night, trying to come up with a legitimate reason to call him, or make the drive to Bliss. If they were just friends, hanging out would be simple. She'd drop by to see him and Addy. The three of them would grab a bite to eat. But her desire wasn't simple. And she was in no position to be in a relationship, though she feared it was too late.

So she stayed where she was—curled in the corner of the couch, her book on the arm, her phone on the lamp table—staring into space. Or at least staring at the full-wall bookcase across the room, the dozens of owls populating the shelves, and the several hundred titles waiting for her to give them away, or pack them away, or throw them away because she would never in her life have time to read them all.

And what a waste that was: of money, that she could've spent so more wisely, much as Jean had bemoaned what her husband had spent on his hobbies. Of expectations, that the books she'd bought in increasing numbers over the past two years could give her what she'd had with Artie, when it had been Artie who'd saved her more than a decade ago from a life destined to be spent in the pages of academic texts.

When she heard the doorbell ring, she was so lost in thought, she jolted before getting up to answer the door, then frowned at the teenager standing on her porch wearing the black-and-orange logo shirt and hat of Fat Mike's Pies. "I didn't order a pizza."

The driver looked at the ticket. "Harvey, 262 Stardust Lane. Is that you?"

"Yes, but I——" And that's when she heard the approaching rumble of the big Harley. Heart fluttering, she took a rather unsteady breath and said, "Hang on. Let me get my purse."

"Oh, it's already paid for, but if it's not yours——"

"It's his," she said, gesturing into the distance and leaving the driver frowning as she fetched her wallet for a tip. She handed the boy a five and took the pizza, just as Callum rode into her driveway.

"Oh. *That* his," the boy said, then added, "Thanks," tucking the money into his pocket. Before he made it back to his car at the curb, Callum waved him over. He tugged off his helmet, digging for his billfold and tipping the kid a second time before climbing from his bike.

He shook out his hair as he secured his helmet to the bike, then reached up and wound the strands tight to the back of his head while walking to where she stood in the doorway drinking him in. Jeans and boots and black leather jacket, oxford shirt wrinkled, as always, beyond belief.

He was absolutely gorgeous. Breathtakingly so, with his eyes flashing, his dimples cutting into his cheeks like two smiles turned sideways, his mouth ready to laugh and holding back until he reached her, as if he needed to share what he was feeling before letting it go. She half expected him to lean down and give her a big kiss, and she wanted him to do just that, and so very badly she came close to lifting up on her toes to reach him.

Dear God, she mused, nearly crushing the pizza box in her fists, she was in so much trouble. So much trouble, and absolutely, positively in love.

The realization hit her as he reached her, and she had no time to process any of what she was feeling, only to enjoy it, to enjoy him, to step back and make room for him on the porch, his body so much larger than hers, looming over hers when the pizza box kept him from coming closer. Oh, but she wanted him closer.

"Good night for him," Brooklyn said, bumping the door open with her butt and backing into the house.

Following her in, he took the box, set it on the coffee table along with a small white sack she hadn't noticed, then opened his billfold a second time. "What did you give him? Let me pay you back."

"It was nothing," she said, adding, "It was five," when he shot her an *I'm going to win this battle* look. She took the money from his hand, then gestured for him to sit on the couch. "I'll get napkins and plates. I'm out of beer. You want wine?"

"That'd be great," he said, perching on the edge of the center cushion and flipping open the box. The smells of tomatoes and onions and peppers hit her nose, and her stomach growled before she made it to the kitchen.

"I heard that," Callum called, chuckling as he did.

She rolled her eyes, laughing, too, happy as she grabbed the wine, two glasses, and a corkscrew along with the napkins and plates and joined him, returning to her corner seat and curling her legs beneath her, every bit of her previous ennui gone—a mood swing she didn't even want to think about.

He handed her a plate with a monstrous slice, and she didn't argue. She was starving. "What are you doing here? Besides having dinner. And what's in the sack?"

"Thanks for not kicking me out," he said, shaking loose his own piece. "I'd have hated to eat all alone on your front porch. And the sack is dessert."

"Dessert?"

He nodded. "From Two Owls. I thought you might like a brownie."

"You brought me a brownie?" Had she told him how much she loved Kaylie Keller's creations, or had he watched her inhale the one she'd eaten the night of the church carnival?

"I brought you a half dozen."

Her grin grew huge, her cheeks aching with it, her heart aching a little bit, too, and in a very good way. "I think you just earned yourself the position of my best friend forever."

"I can deal with that," he said, his mouth full, the word a jumble of sounds as he chewed.

"Where's Addy?"

"I dropped her off at Kelly Webber's," he said, backhanding the grease from his mouth, then reaching for a napkin and his wine. "Lindsay called and invited Addy to eat with them right as we were leaving Bliss to go home."

"It's great that they're such good friends," she said, and bit into her pizza, thinking about the two girls, their heads close together during snack time. Then thinking about Callum with Lindsay Webber at the church carnival. "Addy's mentioned going over there a lot. Doing things with Kelly on the weekends . . ."

She let the sentence trail as what was probably the truth behind Lindsay's numerous invitations hit her, then said, "Oh," and reached for her wine.

Callum was closer and handed it to her, holding it for the few seconds it took him to say, "You know Lindsay's divorced."

"I just remembered."

"She likes my chocolates," he said, letting go of her glass.

"Yeah. I'll bet she does," she said, and drank.

He laughed at that. "You can't be jealous, considering you and I are just friends."

Friends. She didn't want to be friends. Or just friends. But telling him that now, when in three months she'd be leaving . . . *Great timing, Brooklyn, falling for one man when you're on your way to fulfill a promise for another.* "Actually, I think I am. A little bit anyway."

"Really," he said, adding an interested, "Huh," his brows in a deep vee as he sat back. "Not sure what I'm supposed to do with that."

"Do with it what you like," she said flippantly, when she didn't feel flippant at all, downing the rest of her wine and holding his gaze as she did.

"Oh, Brooklyn," he said, his eyes flashing again, his mouth grinning again, neither conveying the teasing from before, but saying things that were so much more potent when spoken without words. "Be sure that's what you want before you say it."

He was so still, sitting there on her couch, his chest rising and falling, his knees spread wide. One hand crushed his napkin in his fist. The other held his wineglass so tightly she feared it cracking and spilling the Sangiovese all over him. Yet nothing happened. The wine didn't spill. Callum didn't move.

Neither did he say anything more, or catch fire, which was what the heat in his gaze had her imagining. It was so very hot, that look, and she was already burning from the flush of the wine, and so she threw caution to the wind and tossed out more fuel. "I think the cat's already out of that bag."

In response, he groaned, a sound that rolled up from his gut as he pushed off the couch and crossed the room, finishing off his drink as he stood with one foot in the living room, one in the dining. She thought he might be trying to escape, and the very idea that she'd brought him to feeling the need . . .

She leaned forward and poured another glass of wine she didn't need in order to have something to do with her hands. He stared at the floor between his feet as she lifted it, shaking his head, his mouth working as if he didn't like the words he was going to say, or he needed more wine to say them.

"I think we both owe Lindsay Webber a very big thank-you right now," was what finally came out.

Of all the things she'd expected to hear, well, mentioning another woman when she'd pretty much just offered herself to him . . . "How so?"

"I told her I'd be back to get Addy at nine."

It was nearly eight now. "Oh."

"That cat's going to need more than an hour."

"Oh," she said again, barely able to get the simple sound up her throat. Sweat trickled between her breasts, bloomed in the small of her back.

"Yeah . . . probably best if you just forget I said that." He took a deep breath, blew it out in a whoosh, leaned his head against the doorjamb separating the two rooms. "After Sunday night at the loft, it's pretty clear neither one of us is in any position for things to get heated."

She gave him her go-to response, which was growing weaker with each use. "I don't date—"

"I got it," he said, scrubbing one hand over the stubble on his face. "We're not dating."

"Callum—"

"It's okay." He laughed. "Lainie once told me, after all the shit that went on with Cheryl, to keep it in my pants until I knew it was safe to let it out."

If she hadn't already been flustered, she was now, so she took the conversation in another direction. "Lainie. From the motorcycle club."

"Right. Duke and Lainie Randall. The couple I lived with after Addy was born."

"Was the club a social thing?" She thought about the fictional ones she'd seen on TV. "Or did it operate as a business?"

"Wolf Bane was registered as a business, though originally most of what the MC did was outside of the law. Duke played a big part in the club going legit, even if he was an outlaw at heart, and kept one foot in the off-the-books activities."

She glanced to the wolf's head tattoo on Callum's inner wrist, the parchment scroll with the Tennyson quote he'd had inked to cover up the goriest of the details. "How did you get hooked up with them anyway?"

"The truth?" He snorted. "Sex, drugs, and rock 'n roll. And before you ask, yeah. At eighteen? I really was that shallow. I shouldn't have been, considering where my parents came from."

She was more interested in where he'd come from, but rather than push, she asked, "Are they not from here?"

"I went to school in Dallas," he said, coming back to join her on the couch. "They moved to Hope Springs after I'd graduated. My dad was transferred to Dallas thirty years ago. He's an accountant. Telecommunications. Both he and my mom grew up in the Northeast. He went to MIT. She went to Boston College. I was born in Boston, but never went to school anywhere but Texas. And I only made it through high school. No higher education for me."

"That doesn't make you shallow," she said, thinking about her own parents and their focus on academia, how she'd toed that line so exactly she'd never thought of anything else. Not sex or drugs or rock 'n roll.

"Maybe not. It does make me lazy and unappreciative. I could've gone to school anywhere. I had the grades. Or I did until my senior year."

"What happened?"

"Girls and beer mostly. It was Texas, so the music was a lot of country. The drugs . . ." He stopped, scrubbed a hand over his jaw as if wiping the memory away. "Those came later. After I'd hooked up with the MC. I took off after graduation with some boys from school to work the oil fields in West Texas. Like I knew anything about oil. Or fields that weren't chalked off every ten yards. The money wasn't shabby, but the days were long, and all we did was work and drink and sleep. And not always in that order."

She smiled to herself, picturing Callum as a restless and reckless teen. "I guess that didn't go over so well with the boss."

"It didn't go over so well with my gut. Or my head," he said, with a self-deprecating laugh. "I started needing something stronger than the hair of the dog to kick the hangovers. Found it with some bikers in a Midland bar. You think the boss wasn't happy with the booze . . ."

"I can imagine," she said, staring into her glass, thinking about the young man Callum had been, his whole future ahead of him and nearly throwing it away.

"I'm not sure you can. Looking back, I have a hard time believing I got out of there in one piece. I was a rich kid from an upscale Dallas suburb. I knew about beer and watering down decanters in parents' liquor cabinets. I knew about pot. Boy, did I know about pot. I knew where to get my hands on coke and crystal, but I didn't. Not then anyway. Later . . ."

She didn't say anything. She didn't know what to say. She wasn't going to judge him now by what he'd done fifteen years ago. He wasn't that person. She knew that because twenty-two-year-old Brooklyn Harvey was certainly not who she was now at thirty-seven.

"I'm not proud of those years," he continued. "The things I did to get by. Some I knew were wrong. Some I didn't ask about. Others . . ." He shook his head. "Sometimes it really is better to go in blind. I did what I was told to do. I took the money they paid me. And it was good money."

"This was before you worked as a bartender?"

"And before I met Addy's mom. She came with more benefits than warming my bed. She was Duke's sister. She got me the job."

How was that even possible? He'd lived with and worked for his daughter's uncle? "I thought she told you in the hospital she wanted nothing to do with Addy."

"She did."

"What about Duke? Or their parents? They all just let you take Addy and go without promising to stay in touch?"

"Their parents had been dead a long time. And as far as Duke and Lainie . . ." He leaned forward and closed the top of the pizza box. "They knew I was getting out of club life, that I had a chance to make things better for me and Addy. And as much as they loved the idea of having a niece, they didn't want to mess things up for her, so they bowed out."

"Mess things up." She had so many questions: How? Why? "Because of their relationship with her mother?"

He shook his head. He was out of wine, and frowned down at his glass but left it empty. "They didn't have much of a relationship with her by then."

Everything he said made her even more curious. And more confused. "Cheryl and Duke must've been on speaking terms for him to have given you the job originally."

"A lot of shit went down between Cheryl getting pregnant and Addy being born. Honestly"—he sat forward, his elbows on his knees, and dragged both hands down his face—"I'm surprised that little pumpkin of mine was born with all her fingers and toes. I counted. It was the first thing I did." He stopped, pulled in a breath that had even Brooklyn shaking.

She pictured him, this tattooed man, this Irish rogue, this long-haired chocolatier, holding a tiny baby in his big-boned hands.

Callum cleared his throat. "I thought if she'd made it through with her fingers and toes maybe the rest of her would be okay. It sounds so stupid now. And I knew it was stupid then. But Cheryl was a drunk and an addict. Not so bad at first, so maybe that had something to do with Addy turning out okay. But later? She was running with some pretty bad dudes then. Got into some seriously bad shit."

Her mind went to the obvious. "But you know Addy's yours?"

"No question. The timing was right, and Cheryl said as much. But I paid for a paternity test to be sure."

"Do you think, if you'd found out she wasn't, you would've loved her anyway?"

"The minute I picked her up from the hospital bassinet, she was mine. Yeah, I wanted to know, to be sure, but she had this tiny pink screwed-up nose, and these big bowed lips, and blond fuzz that was longer at her crown and looked all punk. I might've regretted that she didn't have my blood, if the tests had showed that, but I'd been waiting to meet her for months, and I was a goner the minute I did. If anything, I wished then that she had a different mother. A mother who wanted her and gave a shit about her.

"It's hard to believe, you know. That something so precious and so innocent, something so pure could come from someone who was nothing but—" He stopped, the words seeming to choke him. "Addy's everything to me. I don't want to even think about losing her."

"Why would you?" she asked, her chest tight around the question. "You have custody."

He shrugged. "Cheryl could always change her mind."

"You had to have presented a strong case to win over the court."

"Yeah. And I'll be holding my breath until Addy turns eighteen that my *case* doesn't fall apart."

"Can it?"

"It's doubtful," he said, shaking his head. "But I never say never."

She let that settle. He didn't want to talk details, and really, that was fine. "Did you get a tattoo when she was born? Her name with the date or a baby rattle or something?"

He arched a brow. "A baby rattle? You think I'd wear a baby rattle?"

Ah, so he did have something sentimental. Too entirely cute. "Methinks the man doth protest too much."

"You're screwing up your *Hamlet*," he said, reminding her again of their shared love of literature.

"Show me. What is it?" And *where* is it, because if showing her required him taking off his clothes . . .

His hands moved to the buttons of his shirt, and he turned toward her as he freed them from his throat to his sternum. He stopped there, pulling the fabric to the side, and twisting on the cushion beside her to give her a better view.

The tattoo was of an illustration she knew well, a favorite childhood storybook character, a yellow bear holding the hand of a tiny pink pig. Over their heads floated a balloon bearing Addy's name and birth date, and another with a quote from the Milne book.

The sentiment brought a catch to Brooklyn's heart. Because it was inked right over Callum's.

"It's the truth, you know," he said, dropping his chin to glance down at his chest, his mouth pulled sideways in a goofy grin. "As soon as I saw her, there wasn't a doubt in my mind a grand adventure would happen." Then he looked up, the grin still goofy, his whole expression dopey, like a man so enthralled with the little girl who was his, it rendered him a fool.

She absolutely loved seeing this part of him, loved that he trusted her enough to be this vulnerable with her. Loved him. She loved him. "Has it been all you expected?"

"It's been one insane ride, that's for sure."

"But you wouldn't trade it for the world."

"You got that right," he said, smiling as he buttoned his shirt. "Not for a million bucks."

Two Owls' Crackle-Top Brownies

1/2 cup all-purpose flour
1/8 teaspoon salt
6 ounces unsalted butter, cut into pieces, room temperature
6 ounces bittersweet chocolate, cut into pieces
1 cup sugar
3 large eggs

Preheat oven to 300° (F). Grease an 8 x 8-inch baking dish and line with parchment paper, coating with nonstick spray.

Whisk together the flour and the salt. Set aside.

In a double boiler, or in a bowl set over a saucepan of barely simmering water, slowly melt the chocolate. Remove the chocolate from the heat, and stir in the room-temperature butter until it melts.

Using an electric mixer or a stand mixer with a whisk attachment, beat the eggs and the sugar until thick. Add the chocolate and butter mixture, then fold in the dry ingredients by hand.

Pour the batter into the prepared pan and bake 50–60 minutes, or until the top is crackled and a tester inserted into the center comes out with a bit of batter attached.

Transfer the pan to a rack and allow the brownies to cool completely before cutting.

CHAPTER SEVENTEEN

S ince eating pizza with Callum two weeks ago Friday night—their schedules refusing to mesh for more than a few phone calls in the meantime—Brooklyn had been thinking about his Winnie-the-Pooh tattoo. For years she'd kept a list of quotes she considered tat worthy, but she'd never thought seriously about sitting still for a needle long enough to have one done.

Until now.

Artie's ink had been image-heavy, but just as meaningful to him as were the quotes Callum had chosen for himself. She loved how both men owned parts of their lives so strongly they'd paid permanent homage: Artie to his career, the brotherhood of firefighters he called family, Callum first to his club, then later to himself, his daughter, the life he needed to live for her.

Thinking about that commitment was what had finally convinced her to take the plunge. She was changing so many things, why not a tattoo? As many sayings as she had in her collection, she could've covered her entire body with suitable adages. The problem was finding an inkman to trust, though it wasn't much of one: a phone call to Callum had solved it.

He'd even made the appointment for tonight, saying he wanted to talk to the artist first, then come along, rather than having her go in blind. Being seen with him in this case wouldn't be such a bad thing. In fact, she mused, tugging up on the jeans she hadn't worn in ages, being seen with him was exactly what she wanted. She was going to have as much fun as she could while in Callum's world tonight. And she wasn't going to think about her world at all.

∼

"Are you sure about this?" Callum asked, his hand on the door to the tattoo parlor on Austin's 6th Street, his gaze on Brooklyn's pale face. He hadn't seen her for two weeks, having been swamped with work and with arranging for everything Addy needed as part of the after-school program, though they'd talked twice to coordinate tonight's appointment. "It's a forever kind of thing, you know. You can't change your mind when you start itching and peeling."

"Thank you for the comforting thought, but yes," she said, adding, "I'm sure," as she scraped her hair away from her face and wound it into a bun she secured against the back of her head with a chopstick.

A fancy one, but it was still a chopstick. He was going to have to try that trick. See if it would hold any better than the bands he normally used. "Just checking. You know. Since that's what friends are for."

"A friend recommending a tattoo artist is one thing," she said, shrugging out of the hoodie she'd worn over a black, body-hugging halter top, the hem of which skimmed the dropped waist of her jeans, leaving a bare strip of pale skin he couldn't look away from. "A friend reminding me I'm due for a load of discomfort is something else."

"I'm a good guy to have for a friend." But damn if looking at her had him wanting to be something else entirely. Her body was killer. He'd known that from kissing her, but the outfit she was wearing . . . no, he hadn't known it. Even though he'd had her pressed up against him, he hadn't known it until now. "You're going to want to keep me around."

"So you keep saying."

"It's not just the itching and peeling. Don't forget the discomfort of the needle. And the jolt to your checkbook."

"Thanks, friend," she said, looking up at him as he reached for the door. "But I'm good on all counts."

There was something in her eyes, something fiery and challenging, that had him wanting to go all barbarian and throw her over his shoulder. Instead, he reined in the urge and said, "You'll like my guy. He's a good dude. He's done a lot of my cover-ups. Name's Geezer."

"Geezer?"

"Well, it's not his real name."

"I certainly hope not," she said, pulling open the door, since he hadn't managed to stop looking at her long enough to do it.

The windows on the front of the shop were tinted, giving the place a dark and brooding feel. The reception area was equally macabre, with its black walls and dim lighting and the decor's overwhelming use of skulls.

But the interior of Geezer's looked a whole lot like a barbershop or a dentist's office. Bright lights in an acoustical ceiling, a tiled floor that matched the speckled-black granite countertops. Three walls of cabinets and drawers. Three workstations with a sink at each. Three adjustable hydraulic chairs.

Two were occupied. The third was empty, the space Brooklyn's, and the artist standing at the counter behind—in black jeans, black boots, and a long-sleeved black T-shirt—was going through his supplies. He was tall and lean, his silver hair worn in a military buzz.

His mustache, on the other hand . . . Callum waited for him to turn. Yep. The longest Fu Manchu he'd ever seen, hanging to the man's chest. "Geezer."

"Cal. My man. Good to see you." They shook hands, slapped backs;

then Callum stepped aside to say, "Geezer, this is my friend Brooklyn. She's a needle virgin, so be kind."

"Brooklyn. Welcome to my little corner of hell," Geezer said, his laugh rather maniacal. "I mean, come on in, pick your poison."

"You're not helping things here, man," Callum said, but Brooklyn reached for his arm and squeezed.

"It's fine," she said, her gaze cocky as she looked from him to Geezer. "I know a bluff when I see one. I teach kindergarten, remember?"

"You. A kindergarten teacher." Geezer stepped back, looked her up and down. "I would've stayed in school for a teacher like you."

"Kindergarten, Geezer," Callum said. He knew the other man was teasing and trying to establish a connection with Brooklyn, but his own inner caveman was in rare form tonight, and he had this need to stake a claim.

"So what can I do for you, Brooklyn?"

She handed him a folded piece of notepaper. "Make sure you spell it right."

"Believe it or not, I've got a master's in art history. I do know how to spell."

Brooklyn watched Geezer open the paper, then glanced over. "Callum forgot to mention that part."

"I'm not sure Cal ever knew that part," Geezer said, moving closer to Brooklyn to talk over the details of the tat. "Show me where you're wanting it, and what you're thinking about lettering and decorative extras."

Callum gave them their space, dropping to sit on the bench that was part of Geezer's workstation. It didn't take them long to settle on the specifics; Brooklyn knew what she wanted, pointing out added design frills from his book, and others from his wall. There was no debate, no argument, no uncertainty. She was that way about everything. Or almost everything.

It was her trip to Italy, possibly staying in Italy, and dealing with the things that had belonged to her husband that were giving her grief.

She didn't talk about it, not in those terms. She didn't complain, but he knew she was having a hard time.

Not surprising, he mused, as Geezer got started. She was upending her life. Head over heels upside down. And though he understood why she was putting herself through the upheaval, he had a feeling she wasn't sure what she was doing was the right thing. Maybe it had been when she'd agreed or promised or whatever, but time had passed, things had changed.

He didn't have it in him to fix this for her, as much as he wanted to. She was going to have to deal with the ghost on her own. He looked over to where she sat hunched forward and facing him, her face pale. She winced once, as Geezer got started, then she opened her eyes and focused on his.

"You doing okay?" he asked, wishing he could make this easier for her, too, but it would be done with before the end of the evening, and there wasn't a doubt in his mind she'd be happy with Geezer's work.

She nodded and said, "Tell me about your first tattoo."

Now he was the one to wince. And not from the pain. "I don't even know if I remember my first."

Geezer looked up and scoffed. "Of course you do, dude. Everyone remembers their first."

"Fine," he said, sitting back and crossing his arms over his chest. "Then how 'bout I don't want anyone to know about my first."

"Yeah, I can see that," Geezer said, leaning close to Brooklyn's back. "If it was anything like mine, it was a piece of crap."

"Thankfully, no one can see it now."

"What was it?" Brooklyn asked.

And because he understood her need to be distracted, he gave in. "It was a terrible piece of barbed wire around my ankle. No depth. Cheesy design. Black ink. No better than a prison tat, really."

"Probably got it in prison," Geezer mumbled.

Callum rolled his eyes and made a cutting motion across his throat, which Brooklyn unfortunately looked up in time to see. "I didn't get it in prison, no. I got it not long after high school. But the ink was done by a guy whose clientele didn't care how much practice he'd had, most of them being on the inside. And it showed."

"I do great cover-ups," Geezer put in, leaning his head around Brooklyn's shoulder. "For a price."

"I know all about your prices. And it is covered up."

"But you have been in prison," Brooklyn said, bringing the conversation back to the spot where he'd dropped it.

Kinda late to try and hide it. "County a few times. A two-year stretch in the state pen when I was twenty, but that's all ancient history."

She didn't ask about his crime. She simply said, "What's on your ankle now?"

Of course she'd want to know. "Just some abstract art."

She nodded toward his leg. "Show me. I want to see."

"Yeah," Geezer added. "We want to see."

"You know, G, if you weren't so damn good, I'd be taking my future business elsewhere," Callum said, leaning down to hike up the leg of his jeans and unlace his boot. He pulled it off, rolled down his sock, and turned his leg, enabling Brooklyn to see the details of the wing that started near his arch in a sort of spiral, then uncoiled around his ankle and spread up his calf.

The artist who'd done the cover-up had taken liberties with the concept, and loose feathers drifted down to hide the old barbed wire. The wing itself appeared to have been inked with a fine calligraphy pen; the lines were that sharp, that defined. Shadowing was done with stylized dots, giving the tat the look of a sketch. Originally it had all been black-and-white, but over the years he'd had colors added so it now matched the phoenix on his chest.

"Mercury?" She lifted her gaze to meet his, hers appreciative, thoughtful. "Hermes?"

"Take your pick," he said, and shrugged. "I worked as a sort of messenger for a while. Got caught because I didn't have wings."

She let that settle, the buzz of Geezer's needle loud in the silence, until she asked, "Is that when you went to prison?"

He nodded. Seemed as good a time as any to confess his sins. "Possession of a controlled substance. But not enough to cost me a lot of time."

She took him in, her gaze seeing through his bullshit. "Two years sounds like a lot of time to me."

"It's better than twenty." And it so easily could've been worse. He'd just dropped off a package he'd been certain contained enough coke to send him away for life. "And I wasn't much more than a kid. A harsh way to learn the lessons that hadn't stuck when my parents had tried to hammer them home."

"Are they stuck now?" she asked, then sucked in a sharp breath.

Callum looked from Brooklyn to Geezer, but the older man was intent on his work. "Oh, yeah. I still make mistakes, but rarely of the stupid variety. Same with choices. I'm over the bad ones. Not saying I don't ever make a wrong one, but I look before I leap."

"That's good to know," she said as Geezer blotted his work and sat back.

Callum lifted his chin. "Can I see?"

"Not yet. A couple more tweaks," Geezer said, leaning forward one more time. Brooklyn closed her eyes and Callum waited the fifteen minutes or so until the other man gave a nod and turned her chair, offering her a hand mirror so she could check her reflection in the big mirror above the sink.

Callum had known that she'd chosen a quote, and knowing Brooklyn and her love of books, he'd figured it was something literary. But Geezer had turned it into a work of art: the script, the feather and floral embellishments, the swirls of font.

Know your own happiness.
Want for nothing but patience—
or give it a more fascinating name:
Call it hope.

"That's some damn fine work, G. Really, really nice," Callum said to the other man, then to Brooklyn, "I hate admitting that I don't know who that is, but it fits you."

"It's Jane Austen," she said, still looking in the mirror at the reflection. "From *Sense and Sensibility*. Mrs. Dashwood is talking to Edward Ferrars. He loves one woman, but is bound by honor to another, and he's in a *melancholy humour*, as Mrs. Dashwood puts it. She tells him 'that the pain of parting from friends will be felt by every body at times . . . '" She stopped, as if the same thoughts running through his head had made a synaptic leap into hers. "Anyway, I like the part about hope."

The pain of parting from friends. How about the pain of parting from someone whose friendship had become so much more? The idea of Brooklyn walking out of his life—

"Hope's a good thing to have," Geezer said, taking the mirror and bandaging up Brooklyn's shoulder while explaining how to care for the tat.

Callum supposed the other man was right, that hope was a good thing, and since it was all he was going to be left with . . . hope that Brooklyn wouldn't leave, or if she did that she wouldn't stay gone. That she would realize how good they were together and give life in Hope Springs a second chance. That this connection between them was strong enough to get him through the pain of parting . . .

"You ready?" she asked. She'd settled up with Geezer and was working her arms into her hoodie.

Callum helped her pull up the side that covered the bandaged area, then pushed open the door and followed her outside. "We probably should've brought the truck instead of the bike."

"Why? Because of me? I'm fine."

"You sure? You want to get a coffee or something before we head back?"

"Coffee, no. Taco?" She nodded. "Pain makes me hungry."

He laughed at that, glancing down one side of the street then the other. "Feel like walking? We can grab a bite on the corner there."

The bite they grabbed ended up being more than just a taco. They added beans and rice and enchiladas and guacamole to the mix and feasted on the best Tex-Mex he'd had in a while. Then again, he couldn't remember the last time he'd had any. Usually by the time he and Addy sat down to dinner, it was a rotisserie chicken and mashed potatoes made fresh in the grocery store's deli, if not something from someone else's kitchen.

He really did need to do a better job of cooking at home. He did manage to shun fast food; not hard to do in Hope Springs since he had to go out of his way to hit one of the joints. Most of the time it was Malina's Diner, or now that Two Owls Café stayed open till six, he was able to grab several servings of their casseroles to go, and have food for a couple of days. He did rely too much on Fat Mike's Pies, and there was a new burger joint downtown he wanted to try. He'd have to see if Brooklyn wanted to go.

Opening his mouth to bite into his taco, he met her smiling gaze. "What?" he asked, before his teeth cracked through the shell.

She shook her head. "Nothing. Just wondering where you'd gone."

"Thinking that I should probably hire a cook. Or look into one of those places that delivers precooked meals made out of fresh ingredients. I'm terrible when it comes to feeding Addy at the end of the day. We eat breakfast for dinner way too often," he said, thinking of the Olaf pancakes he'd made Brooklyn a couple of weeks ago.

"What about feeding yourself?"

"I eat, too."

"No, I mean, of course you want to think about what Addy's eating, but don't forget to think about yourself, too."

That had him smiling. "Are you worried about me, Ms. Harvey?"

"Not that you can't take care of yourself, but that you aren't. And that you won't."

Spoken just like a teacher. "You mean now? Or after you're gone? When I don't have you here to remind me?"

"You'll have your mother," she said, breaking into a laugh when he glared at her across the table.

"Thanks for that."

"She feeds you, doesn't she?"

He reached for his beer. "Spaghetti with guilt sauce. Pot roast with passive-aggressive gravy. Snark pie for dessert."

Brooklyn frowned as she reached for her beer. "Is your relationship with her really that bad?"

"If she weren't my mother, and if Addy weren't her granddaughter, let's just say we'd have no reason to cross paths. And I'm pretty sure my father would feel exactly the same. I'm wondering if Addy joining the after-school program is going to make a difference in their relationship. Not that I'd mind."

And wow, did that make him sound like a piece-of-crap son, but the truth was the truth. He and his mother did not see eye to eye about anything—they never would—and he hated seeing his father miserable.

"My mother died two years before my father," Brooklyn said out of the blue. "He never stopped mourning her. He never gave her up. He never let her go. He was still holding on when he passed," she added, her focus on her food, her frown telling.

"Is that why you're going to Cinque Terre?" he asked after a very long moment of turning over her words and thinking about the husband she'd lost. "Because you're like your father?"

"Artie told me not to."

"Not to go to Cinque Terre?"

"Not to be like my father. Not to mourn him. Not to stop living my life if he lost his. And I knew what he meant because it's exactly what I saw my father do."

"Do you think that's what you've done?"

"I don't know." Frustrated, she shoved her hands into her hair and pushed it away from her face. "Sometimes it feel like it. I'm still living in the house we bought together. And until I started going through all the rooms, I still had most of his things. I've accepted his death. I accepted it long ago. How could I not? I wake up every day without him. That's one thing my father was never able to do—come to terms with my mother being gone."

"Then what's wrong?" he asked, wondering if she wasn't ready to make the break after all.

"I feel like somewhere along the line I lost me," she said, scooping up a bite of guacamole with a chip. "Or maybe I never knew me. I left grad school and became Artie's wife and a teacher."

Hmm. "Did you teach because you wanted to? You said your parents were educators, right?"

"They were. But I love teaching. I might have chosen a different path if I hadn't grown up under their influence, but I don't regret a moment of my career."

That was good to hear. "Why did you choose to teach kindergarten?"

"Because of Addy," she said, sipping from her longneck. "Obviously not Addy specifically, but because of the questions kids that age ask, how excited they are to learn. How hungry they are to learn. I love being a part of that. Showing them what it's like to discover answers to their questions, and giving them the tools to do so."

"Makes sense you'd want to keep doing it. In Italy," he said, so damn glad this woman was teaching his daughter.

"You'd keep making chocolate if you moved."

"Yeah—"

"And I'm not sure I will teach. Bianca and I have talked about it, but I don't yet know if her program will be a fit."

Did that mean she might not stay? "Did you ever think about moving? After he died? From Hope Springs?"

"Not until last summer after talking to Bianca. I love it here. Artie and I had been married a year when we came here from Austin, but since he stayed in Austin so much of the time . . ." She scraped her rice toward her beans and concentrated on mixing the two. "Hope Springs has been my home more than it was ever his, but I still picture him mowing the lawn behind me while I'm pulling weeds from the flower bed. Or hear him singing in the shower when I first wake up. His voice was this big baritone. I loved lying in bed and listening to him."

Callum frowned down at his plate, breaking off a chip in his beans. "Sounds to me like you have a ghost."

"If I believed in ghosts, I'd say you're right."

"Then selling the house is probably the right thing. You say it's yours more than it ever was his, but if you can't be here without him being here, too . . ." He shrugged. "It's not my place to say, but that pretty much sounds like a given."

"Or further proof that I really am in a rut."

"Why do you say that?"

"Doing the same thing over and over again?"

"I think it's called a routine," he said, finishing off his food. "Work. School and church and family, or whatever a person does."

"Going to work. Going home. Reading books and watching movies?"

"Why not? If that's what makes you happy and gets you through."

"I want to travel again."

"Then travel," he said, wanting to punch himself, but adding, "Instead of staying in Vernazza to teach, fly to Madrid, or Vienna, or Prague. Soak in the culture, gorge on the food, drink wine until you can't stomach another drop, absorb the atmosphere, and then come home."

She'd been looking at him while he talked, and she continued to hold his gaze when he was done. Her eyes grew misty, and she blinked, then asked, "Is that what you want? For me to come home?"

He couldn't say it. Not tonight. Not when she was on the verge of tears. Not when she had her husband on her mind. "How about I take you home?"

The ride took forty-five minutes, and as he guided the Harley into her neighborhood, he wished again they'd taken his truck. No doubt every single one of her neighbors could hear his bike, and were he to glance at their houses, he imagined he'd see curtains fluttering, porch lights flickering on, doors being cracked open to satisfy the curiosity of those inside.

Brooklyn didn't seem bothered at all when he pulled into her driveway and cut the bike's engine. She handed him her helmet and allowed him to help her off with her hoodie; then she draped it over her arms and turned, waiting for him to go.

"I'll see you Monday then," he said.

"You will?" she asked, frowning.

"In your official capacity as Ms. Harvey."

"Oh, right. Your first parent-teacher conference." She grinned as she said it. "I kinda put Ms. Harvey away for the night."

"Are you going to need help putting her on come Monday? The shoulder and everything?"

"I think I'll be fine," she said, though she winced as she flexed the newly inked skin.

"If not, you've got my number," he said, and she nodded, smiling, then waved and turned away. He waited until she was inside before starting his bike. Then he headed for his parents', even though it was late and the Harley might wake them, because he wanted to see his girl.

CHAPTER EIGHTEEN

Coming to Brooklyn's classroom on official school business had Callum feeling uneasy. His last visit here, six weeks ago, had been all about fun. The idea of hearing about Addy's progress, what he'd been doing wrong, how he could do better . . . though for all he knew he'd hear about what he was doing right. For some reason he'd conditioned himself to expect the worst.

From day one he'd made sure Addy had a bedtime story every night. Even then he left books under her extra pillow when he tucked her in, and left her bedside lamp turned low. No harm he could see in her discovering the joy of reading herself to sleep. Whether or not she grew up to be a reader would be out of his hands, but he was planting the seed.

They had fun with numbers, too. Money and measuring ingredients and telling time. He had no idea how much of what they worked on stuck, but why not let her count out her own carrot sticks for lunch? Or the columns in the spreadsheet on his screen while he worked with her in his lap? She'd only be young enough to want to do so another year at most, probably less.

He did his best to answer all of her questions in ways she'd under-stand. It wasn't always easy, and a lot of the time he would've preferred to change the subject. Who wanted to explain to a six-year-old what rape was?

And, yeah. She'd wanted to know, having heard the word on her Grammy's twenty-four-hour news station, even after he'd asked his mother repeatedly if she could turn off the sound and turn on the closed-captioning when Addy was in the same room. She'd said she would. She never did. And it didn't matter now. Even if Addy couldn't hear the words, she could read them.

"Are you ready?" Brooklyn asked.

She was sitting at her desk, and he was sitting across from her, not in the Addy-sized chair he'd sat in for story hour, but in a chair designed to make him sit up and pay attention. It was hard plastic, unforgiving, bright red. He wondered if it was the chair Brooklyn used for time-outs.

"Callum?"

"That would be Mr. Drake," he said, dragging one leg over the other and squaring his ankle at his knee. "Since this is us being profes-sional and all."

But he didn't want to be professional. He wanted to remember kiss-ing her, to think about her fingers in the small of his back, her lower body pressed to his thigh. About her mouth on his, her tongue hungry and tasting of wine, her hair smelling like lemongrass and green tea.

She rolled her eyes, pressed her lips tight to keep them from break-ing into a grin, and frowned as she looked down at the papers in front of her. "Mr. Drake, then. I'd like to go over your daughter's progress. We've got six weeks left in the school year, and we'll be spending most of that time in review. These are the places I think Adrianne could use extra work . . ."

Adrianne. Not Addy. Because . . . professional. He listened to what Brooklyn was saying, but found himself paying more attention to the tone of her voice than the words, and watching the movement of her lips while she talked. He'd always liked her mouth. She rarely wore bright lipstick. The only time he'd seen it was the night of the church carnival, when he'd first realized she had no trouble standing up to his mother.

For that matter, she had no trouble standing up to him. She seemed to have the most trouble standing up to the ghost of her husband, but he'd told himself he wasn't going to dwell on that; why should he, when it was up to her to solve that particular problem? Even if the problem felt like it was his, too. And it was, wasn't it? He wasn't going to be able to get what he wanted—Brooklyn in his life—until she solved it.

And he did want her in his life. He was crazy about her. The way she questioned him about his history but was never judgmental, as if understanding he was who he was because of where he'd come from, what he'd been through, the wrong steps he'd taken trying to find something . . . He wasn't even sure he knew now what he'd been looking for. Unless it was belonging. And until he'd had Adrianne in his arms for the first time, he hadn't known what it meant to have such a visceral tie to another human being. Much like the connection he felt with Brooklyn. To Brooklyn.

"That wasn't so terrible, was it?"

Bad enough that he needed a drink. Though most of that was due to his train of thought more than anything she'd said about Addy. His gut knotted, he asked, "Have you been to the new pub on Fortune Avenue? Want to grab a burger? A beer maybe? I'm sure they've got wine if you'd prefer it. Or coffee.

"And, yeah. I'm asking you out," he said, uncrossing his legs and sitting forward on the seat, leaning both forearms on her desk. He picked up a paperclip and frowned. "I get that dating one of your students' parents puts you in a fishbowl, but I'm pretty sure between you coming to Bliss, and me coming to your house on the Harley, not to mention our hanging out at the church carnival, that any gossip that's going to start has."

"I know—"

"And I'm pretty sure if my past was going to cause me trouble, it would've done so by now. Not the part with Addy's mother, but the rest. Bliss has a good reputation. Business is booming. Hope Springs is small. People know I'm the ex-biker behind the one-way glass."

"I know—"

"And I get that you're going to Italy, that you may stay in Italy. That whatever this is we've got going on couldn't have come at a worse time—"

"Callum?"

"Yeah?"

Her smile was soft and understanding and tickled. "I haven't eaten anything but an apple since breakfast. I'm starving."

She was starving. That had to be good. "That's a yes?"

She nodded.

"Okay." He took a deep breath, feeling light-headed, his blood rushing through his body in unexpected relief. "So Back Alley Burgers is good for an early dinner? Or a late lunch? Not sure what to call a meal eaten at four p.m. Unless you've got more conferences lined up . . ."

"You're my last of the day," she said, straightening the papers on her desk. "And since I spent my lunch hour prepping for this afternoon, I don't care what we call it as long as there's food."

"Even if I call it a date?" he asked, trying to play it cool. He wasn't. Not a bit.

She nodded again, smiling.

"Okay then," he said, and laughed. The laugh felt good, as did her answer. "We've reached a turning point."

"I guess we have," she said, and laughed, too. "Though I'm not sure I know what it means."

Because Italy still beckoned. "It's okay. We'll figure it out."

"One day at a time?" she asked, her hand shaking as she tucked back her hair.

"Something like that," he said, and then to make it easier on her, asked, "Would you still say yes if Addy joined us, though that makes it less of a date and more just food with me and the girl?"

"Of course," she said, almost sounding relieved, though that was more than likely his imagination. "Why wouldn't I? She's here, right? Is she enjoying the after-school program?"

"She's loving it. I owe you a ton for mentioning it."

"And your mother? Is she glad to see her granddaughter engaged with the other children? And not watching movies at her desk in your storeroom?"

Yeah, he mused with a huff. *About that* . . . "My mother has barely spoken to me since I enrolled her."

Brooklyn gave him a disbelieving frown. "You're kidding."

"Nope. First I deprive her of seeing Addy as an infant," he said, gesturing with one hand. "And now I keep her from their afternoon outings. You know, the ones that allow her to show Hope Springs her commitment to seeing her prodigal son's offspring raised right."

"Callum! You don't mean that."

"Sometimes I think I do," he said, getting to his feet, wishing things with his mother had been different, but doubting they would have been, even if he'd gone east to school instead of west to the oil fields. "Anyhow, I need to grab Addy, and I've got my bike, which isn't exactly built for three, so . . . meet you there?"

"Meet you there," she said, drumming her pencil against her desk in a way that had him wondering if she was rethinking their outing. But she didn't call after him, and by the time he reached Addy, he finally remembered to breathe.

～

Dinner with Callum and Addy made Brooklyn feel part of a family, and that was unexpected. She hadn't felt that way the day they'd all gone to the park, but she hadn't known him as well then; they'd just met, they hadn't kissed. That day he'd been Adrianne's father. Today she knew about his struggles with his mother, the life he'd lived—and left behind—in California, and he knew about Artie, about Italy, about her.

But she also felt out of place because they weren't a family. Callum was not her husband. Addy was not her stepdaughter. And the girl was in a mood Brooklyn didn't know how to interpret. First she hadn't wanted to get off his bike, and he'd had to lift her and dodge her kicking feet. Then she hadn't wanted to walk inside, and he'd had to carry her. At the door, he'd told Brooklyn Addy just needed a nap, but the girl had curled her face into his shoulder like it was more.

Callum had ordered her a bowl of mac 'n cheese, a corn dog, and applesauce, reminding her they were her favorites when she said everything was *yucky*. Then he'd eaten his burger, ignored her playing with her food, and asked her about her day. She'd done nothing but shake her head and drink her milk. They'd argued about that, too. She'd wanted chocolate. He'd told her she couldn't have dessert if she had chocolate with her meal.

His exasperation had tugged hard at Brooklyn's empathy. He was trying to be reasonable when his daughter couldn't have cared less about reason. She hadn't wanted to talk to Brooklyn at all, giving terse responses and only at Callum's insistence. Brooklyn had finally stopped trying. Something had happened between Addy leaving class this afternoon and Callum picking her up. Since the only place the girl had been was in the school cafeteria . . .

She looked at Callum. "When you left my classroom earlier, did the teachers mention anyone visiting after school?"

"Visiting?" he asked, and when she gave a nod toward Addy, he said, "Oh," and set what was left of his burger on his plate, reaching for his napkin and wiping his mouth before turning his attention to his recalcitrant daughter. "You never finished telling me about the hopscotch game you and Kelly Webber were playing when I came to get you."

"It was stupid. School is stupid. Kelly is stupid."

"Adrianne Michelle." Callum's tone was firm, his voice pitched low. "You know better. We do not call people names."

"Kelly said I was stupid."

When Callum frowned up at Brooklyn, all she could do was shake her head and shrug; she was clueless. "Why would Kelly do that?" he asked, returning his gaze to Addy.

"Because I wouldn't share the cookies Grammy brought me, but Grammy told me they were *'specially* mine," she said, then curled up into her father's side, pressing her face into his shirt as if it were a giant tissue for her tears and runny nose.

Callum muttered several choice words Brooklyn hoped Addy couldn't hear, wrapping his arm around the little girl where she sat next to him on the booth's bench. When he finally looked up, it was as if to say, *See what I'm dealing with here?*

"I wish I had an answer." It was all she could think of.

"It's my problem. Not yours. But thanks. Nice to know I'm not alone in this corner," he said, glancing down then back up. "So to speak."

She wished she was sitting beside him, too. He looked as if he could use a hug of his own. "You are doing a good job. Your mother's right about that."

He huffed. "Probably not the best time to be mentioning her."

"I get that," she said, her hands in fists on the edge of the table in front of her. "But there's a lot going on here, and it's obvious as far as she's concerned that I'm in the way."

His eyes grew dark, his mouth grim. And when he said, "You are *not* in the way," his voice was on the verge of breaking.

She was stopped from responding by their server arriving and asking, "Can I interest either of you in dessert?"

"I'd like a slice of key lime pie," she said absently, having seen it on the menu when ordering her food.

"Coming right up. Sir?"

"How about a piece of the *tres leches* cake?"

"Good choice," the young man said, leaning over the table to gather their empty plates. "And for the little one?"

"Tell you what," Brooklyn said, when Callum shook his head as if nothing would set Addy to rights. "Why don't you bring an extra plate and we can split both desserts three ways?"

"Very good, folks." The young man smiled. "I'll be right back."

Brooklyn waited until he was out of earshot, then glanced at Addy where she was curled half-asleep against Callum. "Maybe something else would've been better? A brownie sundae or something?"

"At this point I don't think dessert is the issue as much as whatever happened today."

That much was obvious. "We can cancel the order and just go if you want. I'm sorry. I wasn't even thinking."

"No. We're good. Being quiet for a few is pretty much what the doctor ordered. Speaking of which . . ." He nodded toward her shoulder. "How's the tattoo healing?"

She teased him with a partial truth. "Have I been leaning against the textured walls at home and scratching it raw, you mean?"

"Tell me you haven't," he said, holding her gaze as he stroked Addy's hair.

"I haven't," she said, watching the little girl's chest rise and fall softly. "But I've wanted to. It's better, but the next one will be in a place I can reach without going through all sorts of contortions to keep it clean."

"You know, I did volunteer to help with that," he said, his arched brow speaking volumes about his idea of help.

"I know." This wasn't the time for the things she really wanted to say.

"So the next one, huh?"

"We'll see," she said with a shrug, reaching for the rest of her iced tea. "Maybe when I'm back from my trip."

The words tumbled out of their own accord, surprising her as much as they obviously did him. She lifted her gaze, catching his wide-eyed and sparkling. "So you are coming back." He said it as if her response to the five words would make or break him.

She gave him what she could. "Apparently my subconscious has decided so."

The server arrived then with the two desserts and the extra plate. Brooklyn sliced her pie into three pieces, then when Callum nodded for her to go ahead, did the same with the cake. She gave him the largest pieces of both.

Then he gave Addy a nudge. "Want some pie or cake, pumpkin?"

She sat up, frowned at her plate, then looked at Callum's. "I want a big piece like you."

"I'm not sure your tummy's got as much room in it as mine does," he said, handing her a fork.

"Does so. I didn't eat my corn dog, so there's lots of room."

"Did you eat any snacks after school?" he asked, cutting into his pie. "Any of the cookies Grammy brought you?"

She reached for her milk again, put the straw in her mouth, and shrugged.

"Why don't you eat what Ms. Harvey gave you? Then if you want more, I'll give you some of mine."

At that, Addy slammed her milk glass onto the table. "Grammy would give me a big piece. Grammy loves me."

"Whoa, Addy. I'm not sure what's going on, but you need to remember your manners. Of course Grammy loves you," Callum said, his jaw so tight Brooklyn swore she heard it pop. "And I love you, and Ms. Harvey loves you—"

"She's just my teacher. Not my mommy. Grammy said so."

Oh, boy. Seems they'd reached the root of something. "Your grandmother is right. I'm not your mother. But that doesn't mean I don't love you."

"But I want you to be my mommy," Addy wailed, pushing her plate across the table so hard Brooklyn had to slam her hand onto the pie to keep the whole thing from hitting the floor.

She looked at the little girl who'd collapsed sobbing into the seat, Brooklyn's own eyes welling as she raised her gaze from Addy to Callum. He had one hand shoved back through his hair, and was staring down as if seeing a monster. "I don't even know . . ."

It was all he got out before Addy scrambled out of the seat and ran. "Shit." He bit off the word and followed, Brooklyn waving him on and calling out, "I've got the bill," then finding a napkin to wipe the pie from her hand. Good grief, she mused, tossing the napkin to her plate and draining first her tea, then the rest of the water in her glass.

Most of the time she and Callum had spent together Addy had been elsewhere. Selfishly, Brooklyn hadn't minded; she saw Callum's daughter every day. She saw him much less often. So where Addy had gotten the idea of Brooklyn being more than she was . . .

Unless it was Shirley Drake telling the girl that Brooklyn was *only* her teacher—

"Is everything okay, ma'am?"

She looked up at their server. "Yes. Just a tired little girl. Can I have the check please?"

"Of course," he said, pulling the folder from his apron. "Did you need a to-go box for the cake or the pie?"

"No." She shook her head as she counted out enough cash to cover the bill and the tip. She didn't want to wait for him to run her card. "Thank you."

She scooted out of the booth and hurried to the parking lot. Callum was already straddling his bike, Addy on the pillion behind him, her helmet in place.

"I'm so sorry," he said, frowning down at his helmet instead of looking at her.

She didn't know who was more distraught: father or daughter. But she stepped close to Addy, took her in her arms, and gave her a great big hug. The girl hugged her back, and though Brooklyn didn't know how much Addy could hear through her helmet, she whispered, "I love you, Adrianne Drake. It doesn't matter if I'm only your teacher. I love you very much."

Then she stood and placed her hand on Callum's face, saying, "I'll see you later," before she leaned in to kiss him on the mouth. It was a quick kiss, and she didn't care if everyone in Hope Springs saw it.

Back Alley Burgers' Tres Leches Cake

For the cake:
1 cup all-purpose flour
1 1/2 teaspoons baking powder
1/4 teaspoon salt
1 cup granulated sugar
5 large eggs
1/3 cup whole milk
1 teaspoon pure vanilla extract
1 can sweetened condensed milk
1 can evaporated milk
1/4 cup heavy whipping cream

Preheat oven to 350° (F). Grease a 13 x 9-inch baking pan and line with parchment paper, coating with nonstick spray.

In a large bowl, combine the flour, the baking powder, and the salt.

Separate the egg yolks and the egg whites into two large bowls.

Beat the egg yolks with 3/4 cup of the sugar on high speed until the yolks are pale yellow. Stir in the milk and the vanilla. Pour the egg yolk mixture over the flour mixture and stir gently until combined.

Beat the egg whites on high speed until soft peaks form, then add 1/4 cup of the sugar and beat until the egg whites are stiff.

Fold the egg white mixture into the batter very gently until combined. Pour into the prepared pan and spread out evenly.

Bake for 35–45 minutes or until an inserted tester comes out clean. Turn the cake onto a rimmed baking sheet or a serving platter and cool.

In a small bowl or pitcher, combine the sweetened condensed milk, the evaporated milk, and the heavy cream. Using a fork, pierce the surface of the cooled cake in several places. Remove and discard 1 cup of the milk mixture, and drizzle the rest onto the cake, paying close attention to the edges. Allow the cake to sit for 30 minutes, absorbing the milk.

For the frosting:
3 tablespoons granulated sugar
1 pint heavy whipping cream
1–2 tablespoons rum (if desired)

Whip the pint of heavy cream with the 3 tablespoons of sugar and rum (if using) until thick. Spread over the surface of the cake.

CHAPTER NINETEEN

Sunday night two weeks later found Brooklyn in the kitchen at Bliss, prepping for a run-through of Callum's Monday-morning demonstration for her class. Since holding the attention of fifteen kindergarteners longer than half an hour was out of the question, he was going to have to shortcut the entire process. He'd asked her to come by and help. And since she'd had no chance to see him since the end of their first official date, both of their schedules keeping them busy and the timing at odds, she'd accepted. Plus, she'd missed him.

Their *date*. What a fiasco that had been. Poor Addy. What in the world had Shirley Drake been thinking, saying such a thing to her granddaughter? She knew Callum had talked to his mother; he'd told her so on one of the several times they'd talked, but he hadn't said anything about the outcome. And Addy hadn't mentioned the incident even once.

"I decided not to do the Root Beer Float candy," he said. "If that's all right with you."

"Okay," she said, having to jar herself back to the present. What was it they'd been talking about?

"I mean, if you're set on that one I'll do it," he said, both hands spread out on the island counter between them. "But it's more complicated than some of the other flavors in that the layers need time to cool and set. I thought something simpler would hold the kids' attention better. And the Root Beer Float isn't very colorful, though I could change that up."

He was so cute when he rambled. She reached up to tuck back her hair, thinking of kissing him in the parking lot of Back Alley Burgers. Wanting to kiss him again now. But not wanting to cause any additional trouble for him and his mother and his girl. And so she looked at the ingredients he'd set out, including the package of Oreos, and asked, "What were you thinking?"

"Cookies and Cream. A white chocolate filling. A dark chocolate shell. I mean, what kid doesn't like Oreos? Except those with allergies, I guess." He looked at the same ingredients and frowned. "Do you clear that kind of stuff for parties and field trips? What the kids can eat? Because I use a lot of peanuts here. I don't want to send anyone into anaphylactic shock."

"I do," she said, nodding as she pushed her glasses up her nose. "It's district policy. And all the children in my class are cleared to visit."

He grinned, a big show of dimples and teeth. "You get all protective and professional when you talk about your job, you know."

"You're just as professional," she told him. "And I think you may be equally protective."

"Protective of what?" he asked, frowning.

"This kitchen, for one thing," she said, as she looked around. "You're always looking for something you've missed. A cookie crumb or a chocolate shaving or a spot of cocoa butter."

"That's just common sense," he told her. "Clean now, I won't have to remember it later."

"I know that," she said, an eye-roll implied in her tone. "But you clean as you go. I would think doing that would interrupt your flow."

"I guess it comes from where I started." He shrugged, crossed his arms, leaned against the counter behind him. "I was in a kitchen a quarter this size if that, and it wasn't dedicated to making candy, so I had to be sure I wasn't getting coffee grounds in my ganache."

"Do you ever miss that?"

"Are you kidding?"

"Not the kitchen itself." Though she had no idea what this Duke's place had been like. "But I don't know. The discovery," she said, and waved one hand. "Figuring out what worked, what you liked. The success of something finally turning out, and not really being sure why. Assuming you had more than a failure or two."

"I had one or two . . . thousand."

"I don't believe you."

"It felt like that." He gave a self-deprecating laugh. "Stupid mistakes, and I'm not talking hot buttered rum popcorn, but things like thinking I could skimp on the quality of the chocolate. Learned that lesson in a hurry. So I do miss some of that, yeah. But I don't want to go back there again. Not to California. Not to the kitchen. Not to any of it."

"You don't miss your friends?"

"They weren't friends. Not really," he said, turning to plug in his tempering machine. "Well, Duke and Lainie, but they were the only ones who were."

She started to ask about Addy's mother, if he'd considered her a friend, or if their relationship had been more about what they'd shared in bed. Which had her wondering if they'd even bothered with a bed. Which had her asking, "Have you ever had sex on your motorcycle?"

He turned slowly, looking at her over his shoulder as if he couldn't believe what had come out of her mouth. "Did you really just ask me that?"

She shrugged and moved on, because really. What was wrong with her? "It had to be an interesting life, belonging to a club."

"Brooklyn—"

"I know. I'm sorry. I don't mean to pry. But I have been known to watch the occasional episode of *Sons of Anarchy* . . ."

That made him laugh. But all he said when he finally spoke was, "Yes."

"Oh," she said, her skin growing flushed. "Okay. So it is possible. But while parked, right? Not while riding?"

That had him laughing harder. "Parked, yes. The closest I've come to doing it on the road would be getting hard thanks to the woman behind me."

Her eyes went wide. "Oh. Is that . . . normal?"

His mouth pulled sideways as he fought a grin. He was enjoying this way too much. "Are you asking if I've been aroused when riding with you?"

Was that what she was asking? Did she really want to know? Her own body's reaction to riding with him . . . it was so personal, yet letting her imagination run wild, she could see herself touching him in ways that had nothing to do with her holding on.

"I'm sorry. That was totally inappropriate. I don't know why—"

"Yes," he said again, though this time he was answering his own question, not hers, because she hadn't asked, and she didn't want to know, and she wasn't sure if either statement was the truth or a lie.

She looked away, not sure how to respond. *Be careful what you ask for, Brooklyn. You might get what you want, and then what are you going to do with it?* "Can we go back and pretend I never asked such a stupid question?"

"We can. Or we can face the fact that it's a whole lot of fun for a guy to have a gorgeous woman pressed to his back and hanging on for dear life."

He thought she was gorgeous. The words had her skin warming and prickling from the heady rush of her blood. Then again, he could've meant any number of the women he'd ridden with; she was certain there had been more than a few. He'd left Texas at eighteen. He'd been

ALISON KENT

twenty-eight when his daughter had been born. Ten years. Single. Tattooed. Bearded. Long-haired. She wondered how many women there
had been.

She didn't ask, but what she finally said, as lame as it was, as benign,
was, "You're fun to hang on to."

The groan that rolled up his throat nearly undid her. And when he
came for her, she thought she just might die from the need in his eyes.
He didn't ask permission, or wait to see if she was ready. He slid one
hand into her hair at her nape, and cupped her neck with the other.

"You gonna hold on now?" His words were gruff, his mouth inches
from hers, his breath warm, his hands warm, too.

He smelled like sugar and chocolate and as many sweet things as
ones that were dark, and those were the ones she wanted. "Where?"

"Anywhere you want," he said, and she reached for his wrists, sliding her hands beneath the sleeves of his chef's coat to his elbows.

"Can you get rid of this? It's in my way. I can't get the grip I want."

He looked between them, down to where his chest was rising and
falling rapidly, and his voice was gruff when he said, "Buttons are right
there."

The sound was like fingertips running from the base of her spine to
her neck, and she shivered as she slipped her hands down his forearms
and pulled them free of his sleeves to reach for the front of his coat.

He kept his hands on her shoulders and watched her, not her hands
but her face; she could feel his gaze move from her lips to her eyes and
back again, and she smiled as the first button popped free.

She'd seen part of his chest when he'd shown her his tattoo of Piglet
and Pooh, but she'd been too caught up in the emotion of the moment
to appreciate the texture of his skin, the hair that dusted his pectorals,
this more ginger than that on his head, and covering more tattoos. She
was curious about the art—

"I'm beginning to think you're just here for my ink," he said after
clearing his throat.

"What ink?" she asked, all innocence and tease, tracing a nail along the edge of an abstract design in blue and green spreading right from his sternum to his shoulder. Buried in the colors were more words, but she would need better light to make them out, and she didn't want him to move.

A bird, maybe? A phoenix, or a raptor, in the same colors as Mercury's wing on his leg, its talons extended to strike. She outlined one, then another, and when she flicked over his nipple, he hissed.

His hand on her neck tightened. "Are you done with my buttons?"

His coat hung all the way open. She could see the spine of the dragon arching above his fly, and the bear and his piglet behind the fabric on the left. Discovering the rest of his ink could wait. She wrapped both of her arms around his neck and pulled his mouth down to hers, whispering, "I'm done with your buttons," before parting her lips against his.

His groan echoed off the small room's walls when he backed her up against the door, his leg sliding between hers and pushing them apart. She obliged him, and ground down when he shoved himself hard to her sex, moaning into his mouth, her hands traveling . . . up his neck, into his hair, down his shoulders, to his chest, around his ribs, under his waistband.

And then he was under hers with one hand, the other taking his weight as he leaned against the door. He fought with her pants' back zipper, getting it down far enough to give him access, and then his hand was in her panties, and his fingers sliding up and down, arousing her, playing her, bringing her up on her toes as she moved against him, inviting him in with the tiny sounds she made, with her tongue on his, with her hips writhing.

She kicked off her shoes and went to work on his belt. He finished her zipper and tugged down her pants. She ached, and she was so very wet, and this was such a terrible idea, but she wanted him too much to care about anything but right now. Well, almost anything.

"Do you have a condom?" she asked, tearing her mouth from his.

"Front pocket," he said, his forehead against hers, his breathing rough and ragged. She reached into the right, got an "Other front pocket," and reached into the left.

"Got it," she said, so glad he'd been thinking about this enough to be ready.

Then he was tugging down his pants, and she was tugging off hers, and he sheathed his erection while she kicked her panties away. He cupped her bottom and lifted her, and she wrapped her legs around his waist, and he pushed into her, stopped, pushed farther, pinned her to the door with his weight, and held her there, unmoving, panting, his mouth at her ear.

"I didn't want it this fast."

"I know." He was inside of her. He was filling her. He was stretching her and was glorious and thick and full, and she hurt with how long it had been and how much she loved him.

"I wanted a bed and I wanted you naked and I wanted hours."

"I know." She wanted to cry. She wanted to laugh. She wanted to climb on top of him and slide up and down and feel every inch of him, and never forget anything about now.

"I have to finish."

"I have to finish, too," she said, and he let loose a string of curses fit for a biker and slammed into her, stroking her, moving where she told him she needed him and rubbing her until she came.

She nearly screamed with it, the release, the pleasure, the absolute joy in giving to him and taking from him, and she shuddered, and he grunted, growling as he let go, surging into her, rough and demanding and bold.

He scraped his beard against her cheek, making desperate sounds and needy sounds, nearly purring, then shuddering to a sigh, flexing his hips one last time. "I want to stay here forever."

"I don't want to move."

"My thighs are about to give out."

"My back is killing me."

They were a mess of satisfaction and tangled clothing; her hands were inside his open jacket, one arm around his neck, the other beneath his arm that was still holding his weight. She began to let him go, and he eased from her body, a withdrawal that left her bereft as she straightened her legs to stand.

He turned away to take care of his clothing, while she grabbed her panties and pants from the floor. "I'm going to . . ." she said as she reached for the door's handle. "The restroom."

He nodded. "Yeah, me, too. But you go ahead."

She scurried out the door, the air cool on her bottom, the tiles cool on her feet, her face burning, and when she looked in the mirror, she saw why. Her cheek was red from the chafing of Callum's beard, her jaw nearly raw.

And then it hit her. Tomorrow she'd be back at Bliss with fifteen kindergarteners and three chaperones, looking through the window into the kitchen, where twelve hours earlier, she'd been pinned to the door, Callum's pants around his ankles, her pants in a puddle with her panties on the floor.

She giggled, though the sound was as much of a hysterical cry as anything. She was absolutely crazy, thinking she'd be able to make it through tomorrow's field trip without giving herself away.

Groaning, she hung her head, and was almost presentable when she heard Callum talking to himself in the restroom on the other side of hers. Somehow, his being just as rattled made her feel not quite so alone.

"Seems the Cheshire Cat was right. We're all mad here," she told her bright-eyed, sex-drunk reflection, fighting another burst of giggles as she did.

~

Since Bliss didn't open till ten, Brooklyn had arranged with Callum to come by first thing. That meant eight thirty, before she had too much time to work herself into a frenzy, or do something drastic like call off the whole thing. So as soon as she finished with roll call at eight, she and the parent chaperones lined up the children and saw to the loading of the bus.

The trip was short—thank goodness, because the closer they got to the confectionery the more rebellious her stomach grew. The driver let them out in front of the shop before pulling away from the curb to park in the alley behind it. Once everyone was in line and she'd done a quick head count, Brooklyn led the way to the door.

"Remember today's rules, class. No talking unless you raise your hand to ask or answer a question, and only when it's time. No touching anything without permission. Stay next to your trip buddy, and stand exactly where you're told. I want everyone to be able to see and hear Mr. Drake."

Seeing Callum, hearing Callum . . . her face began to heat, her stomach to tighten. She lifted a hand to her jaw, hoping her makeup had adequately covered the bruise she'd found this morning. *Deep breath, Brooklyn. Deep breath. No one but Callum knows.* But wasn't that the worst part? The fact that he did, and would no doubt be thinking about what they'd done?

Three hands went up, which was about three less than she'd expected. "Yes, Kelly."

"Do we get to eat any candy?"

"After the demonstration, you will get one piece each. Yes, Andrew?"

"What if we don't want any candy?"

Because, of course, he had to be contrary. "Then you don't have to have any. Yes, Adrianne?"

"Can I go play at my storeroom desk, since I know all about the candy already?"

"No, you'll stay with the rest of the class and pay attention just like everyone else. When we get back to school we'll talk about the demonstration, and if I ask you any questions, you'll want to be able to answer them. Yes, Adrianne."

"I can answer all your questions now," the girl said, her brow creased as she thought through her logic, "and you won't have to ask them when we get back to the school. That way I won't have to watch."

It took Brooklyn a moment to realize she was holding back on being stern with Addy because she was Callum's daughter, because the girl had cried about wanting Brooklyn to be her mother, because she loved Addy as if she were her own, and that just wouldn't do.

This was why she didn't date a student's parent. This was why even being Callum's friend was a very bad idea, much less being in love with the man. And this field trip? An even worse one, she mused, a shiver fluttering down her spine. What in the world had she been thinking? Up against the kitchen door?

Oh, who was she kidding? Her feelings for him had leapfrogged her rule as if it didn't exist. She thought she might be more excited than the children to get inside. And that just wouldn't do, either. Especially since she and Callum would both be under the scrutiny of the chaperones. And she couldn't imagine he'd forgotten a single moment of what they'd done last night.

"Class?" She held up her hand to get their attention. Once everyone was quiet and focused on her, she asked, "If any of you break field-trip rules while we're away from school, what will happen when we get back to class?"

Fourteen hands went up. Addy Drake's did not. "Bashir."

Bashir Zaman wore the most solemn expression she'd ever seen on the boy, his black hair catching the morning light, his brown eyes big and wide and dignified. "The time-out chair."

"Thank you, Bashir. Class? Did you hear that? Anyone who breaks the field-trip rules will have to take a turn in the time-out chair. Does everyone understand?" Fourteen heads nodded, leaving Brooklyn to ask, "Adrianne? Do you understand?"

"Yes, Ms. Harvey," the girl said, her eyes downcast, her bottom lip quivering, her tiny shoulders slumped.

255

Brooklyn took a deep breath. If she made it through this day . . . "Okay then. Let's go inside and see how Mr. Drake makes candy."

∽

Addy
Monday

Daddy says I should always pay attention, but that it's not nice to stare. Sometimes I don't know if I'm doing it right. Paying attention means I HAVE to stare. Like now, when I'm looking at Ms. Harvey when she's looking at Daddy. And looking at Daddy when he's looking at her.

They look at each other a LOT. Even more than they did the day we went to the park with our ice cream and books. Or when I was sad about what Grammy said and forgot to eat my cake and pie.

Sometimes Daddy forgets what he's saying about the candy, and then Ms. Harvey tries not to laugh, and Kelly Webber's mom looks like she's mad at the WHOLE WORLD.

I don't think Kelly Webber's mom likes Ms. Harvey anymore. She asks me TONS of questions when I go to their apartment. She wants to know if Ms. Harvey sleeps over at our loft, but I tell her we don't have enough beds.

Then she asks if we go to Ms. Harvey's house. That is just so SILLY! How can we go to Ms. Harvey's house? We don't know where she lives!

I tell her about the park and the ice cream and the kitty who lives at the bookstore—but I don't tell her that Ms. Harvey LOVES ME—and how much I really really REALLY want a kitty of my own. She says doing things with Ms. Harvey is TOTALLY INPROPRATE. I don't know what that means but it sounds like she doesn't think I need a cat.

Now Daddy is talking about the Oreos and Andrew raises his hand. Ms. Harvey tells him he can ask questions later, but I know all he wants to say is that he doesn't like Oreos. Kelly Webber told me her mom said

Andrew's mom is crunchy so he's not allowed to have cookies or candy or ice cream unless it's made out of bananas or coconut milk and that is just the YUCKIEST.

I like Daddy's Oreo candy, but he makes them ALL THE TIME and I know all about how he crunches the cookies into little pieces. Sometimes I get to crunch them, and I want to raise my hand and tell Ms. Harvey I know how.

But we can't ask questions on field trips until she says so. I hate rules. I hate time-out chairs. I don't like it when Kelly Webber's mom looks at Ms. Harvey. I think she wants to yell at her, because she has a mean face.

But Daddy's face is happy, and Ms. Harvey's face is happy, and that makes me happy, even if I have to listen to BORING stuff about making candy when I could be playing at my desk with my Olaf and Anna and Sven and Elsa and Kristoff toys and watching *Frozen* on my tablet.

Then I feel Ms. Harvey's hand on my shoulder, and I look up and her eyes tell me I'm not paying attention, but she smiles, too, and she looks happy, and I wish I could hold her hand, but I don't want to hear Kelly Webber's mom say TOTALLY INPROPRATE again because I really want a kitty.

I don't want Ms. Harvey to stop smiling so I put my eyes on Daddy and listen to all the words he says. He's smiling, too, so I smile. And it feels good to be happy with Daddy and Ms. Harvey. I think my kitty's name will be Candy.

CHAPTER TWENTY

Brooklyn had agreed to meet Callum at Bliss after the shop closed on Saturday three weeks later, and go with him to show Addy their house. He'd asked her a few days after she'd taken her class on their field trip. She'd been as surprised as she'd been honored; she'd thought for sure he'd want to share the moment with his daughter alone.

But, no. He wanted her there because she'd helped him pick out the furniture that had finally been delivered—a bit of a stretch, since all she'd done was tag along and make suggestions. He'd argued the point, and he'd cajoled, but he hadn't needed to do much of either. She'd known when he'd asked that she'd say yes.

Her attempt to beg off had allowed her to hide her excitement. She didn't want to appear too eager, since she was seeing him less often these days than she had the first month they'd met. During February, and even early March, they'd crossed paths a lot, and on a few occasions made actual plans.

Now, however, she was busy with her house, and he was busy with his. And what a metaphor for their lives that was: her selling and leaving, him buying and staying. Her looking for her life, his already found. It sure would've been nice if she'd met him when she had things figured out.

Then again, she had a feeling figuring things might take longer than a lifetime. All she had to do was look at Jean Dial to realize that. Jean, who had family to keep her from being lonely, and friends with whom to share gossip, and a male dinner companion to fulfill another sort of need.

Jean Dial, who at seventy-three years old had admitted to never moving beyond the loss of her love, but who had never stopped living. Brooklyn was going to miss Jean more than any of her friends. Except for Callum.

Angling her car into a parking slot in front of the empty storefront next to Bliss, she shifted into park, glancing up as Callum pushed open the front door and walked out behind a woman. They were deep in conversation, the woman gesturing expansively and Callum laughing.

If Brooklyn hadn't known who he was, she wouldn't have any trouble imagining the two as a couple, exiting a shop where they'd gone to pick up a gift, laughing over a story the store's chocolatier had told them, caught off guard by the prices his chocolates commanded and rushing to escape.

This woman, whoever she was to Callum, and other women, too, like Lindsay Webber, or the room mothers who'd so appreciated him at story hour, would be here to keep him company and . . . other things, when Brooklyn was not.

She was going away. For Artie. To see his family. To teach with Bianca. To scatter his ashes. To prove that she was over her mourning and moving on with her life.

What had happened to doing things for Brooklyn?

And why was it so hard to ask herself that? Why did doing so seem so selfish when it was anything but?

Once she returned from abroad, if she returned from abroad, in a year, or two, rather than finding a small terraced home overlooking the Mediterranean and staying on, she had no reason to come back to

Hope Springs at all. Her job was gone. Her house, with its sale pending, would be gone. Her friends were already out of touch.

Except she did have a reason. And she was looking at him now. Her Irish rogue. Her chocolatier. The man she loved. The man she knew loved her.

She swallowed hard, blinked back the threat of tears. How in the world was she going to be able to get on that plane next month? How was she going to be able to stay and work with Bianca when Callum would be on her mind?

Opening her car door caught Callum's attention. He raised a hand. He grinned. He waved her over.

"Brooklyn Harvey, this is Juliana Bower. Her daughter Grace is going to be Addy's sitter for the summer. Brooklyn is Addy's kindergarten teacher."

"It's nice to meet you, Ms. Harvey." Juliana held out her hand.

"Brooklyn, please," she said, and took it, so pleased that he'd found reliable help. And strangely relieved that the woman's connection to Callum wasn't anything more.

Just then, Addy came out of Bliss with a teenager wearing red athletic shorts, white socks and sneakers, and a gray T-shirt with the Hope Springs Bulldogs mascot and logo.

Addy ran for her father and he swung her up in his arms. "Ready to go, pumpkin?"

"Ms. Harvey! Daddy's got a big surprise for me!"

"I know," she said, grinning as she hiked her purse strap higher on her shoulder. "He told me."

"Do you know what it is? He won't tell me!" the girl said, gesturing dramatically with both hands.

"If he told you, it wouldn't be a big surprise, would it?"

Addy pouted. "I don't like surprises."

"Oh, I think you'll like this one," Brooklyn said, laughing along with Juliana while Callum rolled his eyes.

"Can Grace come, too?"

"That's not up to me, sweetie." Brooklyn looked from Addy to Callum to Grace, who shook her head.

"I can't," the teenager said. "I've got to go wash some cars."

"You don't have to wash cars, silly," Addy said, as if it were the most obvious thing in the world. "You can drive through the washoteria."

Grace laughed, her black ponytail bobbing. "We're doing it to raise money for a band trip next year."

"Can I come? On the trip? I like to take trips."

"Well, you have to play an instrument, and you have to attend Hope Springs High, and you have to be at least fifteen."

"I'm almost fifteen. I'm six already."

"C'mon on, Addy," Callum finally said. "You'll have plenty of time this summer to go places with Grace. But she needs to get to her car wash, and you have a big surprise waiting."

"Is it a kitty? Is it the kitty from the bookstore?"

Callum glanced at Brooklyn as if to remind her why he hadn't told his daughter about the new house before now. "No, pumpkin. The bookstore kitty lives at the bookstore."

"Kitties don't even like books!"

"The bookstore kitty does. He reads *The Cat in the Hat* every night when the store's closed," he told her, waving at Juliana and Grace as they headed the opposite way.

"Oh, Daddy. You're so silly sometimes. At night, there's no one there to turn the pages."

Addy's reaction to the house was classic six-year-old: excitement as she rushed through the rooms with no real grasp of what it meant to move. After all, she hadn't done so since she was an infant. "But what about Olaf? Can I bring him, or does he have to stay at the loft?"

Callum stood in the doorway of the library, his fists in his pockets as if trying to keep himself from grabbing her before all her running sent her crashing through a wall. "We'll be bringing everything, pumpkin. All your clothes and toys. All the food in the kitchen."

"And Olaf, too? And all my books? And your motorcycle? And a kitty?"

He leaned close to Brooklyn, who stood opposite him, and said, "Notice how she slipped that cat thing in there?"

"And your bike," she pointed out. "I told you you're going to be the most popular dad on campus."

"Campus. Ugh." He reached up and dragged both hands down his face as if he were the weariest man in the world. "That makes me think about her leaving elementary school, and things like braces and makeup and . . . bras."

He added the last with a shudder, this big bad biker so out of his element that Brooklyn couldn't help but laugh. Loudly. He was too adorable for words. "Just keep doing what you're doing and you'll be fine."

"Is that your opinion as a professional educator? Because I gotta say, that cackle of yours doesn't instill a lot of confidence."

"It's my opinion as someone who's seen the two of you together several times the last three months. Trust me. You're a good father. And that's speaking as both a friend and an educator. Because I've seen bad. And indifferent. And you may not like my laugh, but I know what I'm talking about."

"I know you do, and I love your laugh, and it's a bit of a relief to know I haven't effed things up completely."

She looked down at the bamboo hardwood they both stood on, her pink floral ballet flats so at odds with his tough black boots. "I don't have a single worry about Addy's future."

"The first time I buy her the wrong bra and you hear her screaming all the way across town, I'll remind you of that."

"They have bra-fit specialists, you know," she said, instead of reminding him she wouldn't be living across town anymore.

"Seriously? That's a job?"

Shaking her head, she pushed away from the door, catching a glimpse of Addy as the girl ran down the hall into her room. The library sat in the front of the house. A big bay window took up the front wall, and across from it, a pass-through fireplace opened to the den on the other side.

She hadn't seen this room since he'd outfitted it, and he'd done that without her input. At least verbal input. He'd shopped with her. He'd seen her classroom, her house. He knew what she liked. Knew her taste in things. Or so she surmised; how else could he have come up with . . . this?

It was her. The whole room. The lampshades. The throw rugs. The end tables and the coffee table and the chair-and-a-half with the ottoman in a rust and pine green and navy tartan, and the complementary one in a dark paisley floral. The copper spittoons on the fireplace, one holding cattails, one the fireplace tools. The scrollwork on the grate made her think of Jane Austen.

"Did you do this?" She stopped in the middle of the room, the carpet beneath her feet like marshmallows, and looked at him. "The decorating?"

"Yeah, well," he said, coming into the room, his hands still in his pockets, shuffling, "with some help from Lena, Dolly Pepper, your neighbor Jean, and about a hundred salesmen."

She held his gaze, her heart racing, his expression so hopeful that it stole her breath. Then he added, "I thought you might need a place to come back to. You know, when you got tired of Italy and needed somewhere to land."

Somewhere to land. Did he know what those words did to her? Hearing them come from him when he was where she wanted to be? When she wanted nothing more than to close her eyes, lay down her head, and rest?

Her eyes burning, she turned away, pressing her hand to her mouth. How was she going to leave him? How was she going to walk away?

He hadn't asked her to stay, but he wouldn't because his doing so would make things harder. He knew how important this journey was for her, how vital that she reach this destination she'd been preparing for for a year.

Except she didn't think it was. Not anymore. Not because any of what she wanted for Artie mattered less, but because it wasn't what *she* wanted for herself. Artie was gone. And she'd done the very thing she'd promised him she wouldn't: she'd stopped living her life when he'd lost his.

Taking a deep breath, she shook off the melancholy; this was not the time or the place. Callum and Addy had this gorgeous new home, and if she ever wanted a quiet place to sit and read—

"Wait a minute," she said, crossing to the closest of the wall-to-wall shelves and running her fingers along the books' spines, reading the titles, pulling one of the hardcovers from the shelf and opening it to look inside. "These are my books, aren't they? The ones I brought over to store?"

He nodded, then shrugged. "I figured since it's a library, and a library needs books, and I've been too busy with the furniture and Addy's things to pack mine . . . anyway, I heard it's not great to store them in cardboard. Silverfish. Roaches. Sorry," he said, as if he didn't want her to think about her books being eaten by bugs. "I thought they'd get some air in here, and it's not like they're in the way, and when you're ready for them, I'll pack them back up. I'm not holding them hostage for any nefarious ransom or anything creepy—"

"It's not that," she said, shaking her head. The day she'd brought over the boxes . . . she'd thought then that he'd never know how important to her the books were. She'd been wrong. Because he did. What he'd done in this room proved it, and for a very long moment she found it hard to breathe. "It's just . . ." She stopped, tried again, struggling for the words. "You saw the shelves they came off of. They were never this neat and organized."

"That control freak thing. Rears its ugly head even when I don't want it to."

"I love that you're using them. I do, really. They deserve a nice, OCD, bug-free home."

"Good," he said, clearing his throat. "I was worried you'd turn it into a big deal, thinking I was trying to keep them so you'd stick around or something."

"That might've been nice." She tried for a grin, not sure it came out the way she wanted. "Except for it being creepy."

"So," he said, facing her, his oxford shirt wrinkled, the lowest two buttons undone, the very edge of his dragon tattoo exposed in the open placket, "you don't want me to try to convince you to stick around?"

What was she supposed to say to that? "You know I can't."

He looked at her like he didn't know it at all. "I know you have a ticket to fly. That doesn't mean you can't stay here. It's just money. The airline isn't holding your firstborn hostage or anything."

She thought about his Pooh Bear and Piglet tattoo. The promise of a grand adventure his life with Adrianne Michelle Drake had lived up to. She wondered, and for not the first time, about his love of literature. How he had come to find solace and absolution and joy in the words of others.

Then she took him in, head to toe, wishing she could save this moment and take it with her, because she didn't want to ever forget. *You don't have to forget. There's this thing called a camera.* "Don't move," she told him, digging into her jeans pocket for her phone.

His mouth quirked. "You're going to take my picture."

"Why not?" She centered him on the screen, then took a step to the right, taking her time setting up the shot. She wanted it to be perfect, though seriously, with her subject matter, how could it be anything else?

"Weren't we just talking about creepy?" he asked, one brow going up, one dimple deepening. The light from the front window lit his hair until the hint of auburn was no longer a coal but a flame.

She took a shot and said, "This is not creepy. This is me commemorating the moment I realized you and I are kindred bibliophilic spirits."

"Thought you might've realized that when I showed you the Nietzsche and the Tennyson." He started to pull his fists from his pockets; she stopped him with a sharp shake of her head. "Or when you saw the Frank Herbert. Though, really, Pooh should've clinched it."

"I didn't know you as well then," she said, wanting to get closer, to photograph the words on his wrist, the ones on his neck. "I thought you might've just pulled quotes out of the air. Or off the Internet."

"Not to burst your bubble, but a couple of them, I did."

"What?" She looked away from his framed image to the man in front of her. "Say it isn't so."

He shrugged. "Can't keep it all in my brain. No matter how big my head is."

She centered him again and touched the button. She wanted to capture all of him: his boots, his jeans bunched around them and hanging low on his hips from the weight of his fists. The strip of his abdomen and the text from *Dune* that showed above his jeans' copper buttons.

She took another shot. She wanted every wrinkle of his shirt. She loved his wrinkles. This shirt was a faded-to-white pink; she liked that he'd owned it in its original color. The collar was twisted, the sleeves cuffed up his forearms; both allowed for more of his tattoos to show.

She lined him up once more. She wanted his dimples and his grin and the scruff on his face. His sharp cheekbones. His blade of a nose. His green eyes and long lashes and his brow that even when frowning wasn't heavy.

But mostly she wanted his hair, every ginger-brown strand. The ones wound into the knot he always wore, the ones sticking out, the ones hanging in twists that made her think of his daughter's corkscrew pigtails.

She didn't want to forget anything about him, or lose a single memory of their time together, or get to Italy and wonder if she'd made the right choice for fear of losing what she'd had with her first love.

"Got it," she said at last, because she couldn't stare at him forever. At least not the him across the room in the flesh. "And your head's not that big. So I forgive you for having to cheat."

"Like you had that Jane Austen bit memorized."

"Actually, I did," she said. The quote had stuck with her for a very long time. The idea of hope being equated with patience . . . funny that patience was a concrete emotion within her control while hope seemed so ethereal, yet they were so closely related as she looked ahead.

"How's it healing? The tat?" he asked, walking toward her.

"It's good," she said, tucking her phone into her pocket.

"Show me."

She brought her gaze up slowly, her pulse quickening, the look in his eyes bringing to mind the first time he'd kissed her, the second time he'd kissed her, the third time . . . and how none of them had been kisses between friends.

"Now?" she asked, because to show him she'd have to lift her shirt to reveal her back and her shoulder, and it seemed too much a tempting of fate with his daughter liable to run into the room.

"It's just your shoulder," he said, stopping in front of her, one brow going up, his tongue in his cheek as he tried not to grin.

"This isn't funny. Me baring skin in front of you is not a good idea. Addy could come in at the worst possible time."

"That being me looking at your tattoo? It's not like I haven't seen—"

"Don't," she said, shaking her head. "I can't. We can't. Not now."

"Hey, Brooklyn." He frowned as he said her name. "I'm teasing. If you don't want me to see—"

"Oh, Callum. It's not that," she said, but she didn't say more, because she wasn't sure she could explain what she was feeling without losing the very tenuous hold she had on her composure. "It's just . . ."

"What?" he asked, his concern making things so much worse. "Just tell me. What did I do? What's wrong?"

"That's just it," she said, burying her face in her hands. "Nothing is wrong. Absolutely everything is right. Except I'm not going to be here to enjoy this room, or you, or Addy . . ."

"Oh, baby," he said, stepping closer and wrapping her up in his arms. "This room isn't going anywhere. I'm not going anywhere. Addy on the other hand . . ."

She laughed, nuzzled into his chest, breathed him in, and let go of the doubts and worries that felt like walls closing in. She had patience. She would get through the next month. And she would cling with every ounce of strength she had to the hope that the rest of her life would fall into place.

Wednesday, February 14, 2001

Closing her eyes, Brooklyn leaned back on her pillows, needing the break from the books spread across her bed. As hard as it was to believe, she was tired of reading, the exhaustion the fault of the research required for her dissertation. Even the title was enough to put her to sleep: The Use of After-School Programs in Aiding the Development of At-Risk Youth.

A juicy medieval-set story. That's what she wanted. Knights and castles and bloody battles. A fair maiden. A noble steed. Sighing, she sank deeper and closer to sleep, her forearm thrown across her forehead to block the overhead light. Just five minutes. Make it ten. No more than fifteen. Her eyes ached. She was starving. She swore she smelled pizza.

Then came a knock on her bedroom door, a sharp rap of knuckles that only one person ever used. "You can come in if you have food."

Artie opened the door wide enough for the pizza box he led with, then peered around the corner. "Pepperoni, bacon, onions, olives, and fresh jalapeños."

"Real bacon. Not that ham that likes to pretend."

"Real bacon. Exactly the way you like it."

He knew her so well. She shoved the books to the foot of the bed, making room for him to join her. "Is it all for us, or did you have to share with my parents?"

"I offered but they both declined."

"You know," she said as she lifted a slice from the box he opened, winding strings of cheese around one finger, "I'm not sure I've ever seen my father eat a slice of pizza."

"He does seem to be more the broiled chicken and broccoli type."

She laughed at that. "He's the type who doesn't think about food as anything but nourishment."

"Yeah, well, I may be only half Italian, but it's the half that knows there's more to food than that," he said, finishing off his slice, then dusting crumbs from his hands over the box. "Hope that's okay with you."

"Why wouldn't it be?" She bit into her slice, wondering why he'd ask such a thing. Unless he was thinking about the future, the two of them being together, his eating them both out of house and home.

That made her laugh. She didn't know how to cook. How would she ever feed him? Because no matter what he said about being Italian and loving his food, one of them would need to be able to do more than pick up the phone and order takeout. Though she was getting way ahead of herself. And doing so today, of all days . . . She laughed again.

"What's so funny?"

"Do you know what today is?" she asked him, having caught sight of the date on the calendar above her desk.

"The happiest day of my life?"

He was always so dramatic. "The date, I mean. February fourteenth. It's Valentine's Day."

"Are you kidding me?" He frowned and glanced at his watch. "This has got to be the first V-Day in years I haven't taken a shift for someone."

"I can't believe you didn't know what today was."

"I do know. Like I said. The happiest day of my life." He reached into

his pocket, then pulled out a jewelry box before he scooted off the edge of the bed and dropped in front of her to one knee.

His face, freshly shaved, she noticed, grew somber, his eyes wide, nearly misty. He swallowed, as if fearful he would choke. "Today's the day I'm asking the woman I love more than life itself to marry me. The day I know she's going to say yes because she was made just for me."

"Oh, Artie." She pressed her hands to her cheeks, blinking back tears as he opened the box. The diamond solitaire was simple, no unnecessary extras, just the round-cut jewel on a white gold band. "It's beautiful."

"It's yours. I'm yours. If you'll have me." He took the ring out of the box, then reached for her finger. "There's going to be a lot of worse to go with the better, I fear, but that's part of being a firefighter, and I'll make it up to you the best that I can. I hope we'll both be as rich as thieves, and never know a day of anything but the best of health, but I'm not frightened by illness, or being poor, and Brooklyn Olivia Nilsson, will you be my wife?"

"Yes, yes, oh, yes!" And once he'd slid the ring onto her finger, she wrapped her arms around his neck, her legs around his waist, and kissed him until neither of them could breathe.

CHAPTER TWENTY-ONE

Two weeks later, Callum was mostly moved into the house and making all the living-in-a-new-place adjustments. The biggest one was doing a better job managing his time. Luckily, school was almost out, because getting Addy to class on time, then himself to Bliss, meant his alarm went off thirty minutes earlier than it had for the last nearly five years.

Thirty minutes didn't seem like a lot in concept, but when dealing with a sleep-loving six-year-old, it felt like hours. Still, the ride to town on his bike was his favorite part of the day, eclipsed only by the ride home. Three Wishes Road meandered through some gorgeous acreage, and something about it had him feeling all one with the earth, a thought he kept to himself because it was too ridiculous to put into words. Still . . .

How far he'd come since loading his bike into the back of his truck, securing Addy in the car seat that had been a gift from Duke, and getting the hell out of California. He'd been pins-and-needles panicked in those early days, thinking the mistakes he'd made would catch up with him, that he'd lose his girl, that no matter his choice to raise Addy on his own, that he'd fail. So many of his choices had sent him down a very bad road . . .

He wasn't quite as excited about the new place as he'd thought he might be. Proud of it? Sure. He'd worked damn hard to get here, and it was a hell of a house. Thrilled at how much Addy loved it? Without a doubt. Seeing his girl's excitement as she ran out the back door and through the huge yard to her swing set gut-punched him every time.

Being able to give her an acre of yard, instead of the limited time at the park they'd made do with, three thousand square feet instead of the loft where running was outlawed because their floor was a neighbor's ceiling . . . contentment wasn't even the half of it, but then he'd always had trouble defining the emotions that came with being a dad.

Pulling into his parents' driveway, he killed the bike, took off his helmet, and helped Addy out of hers. She ran for the back door and he followed, realizing the moment he walked into the kitchen that something was wrong. His father stood at the counter in front of an electric skillet flipping pancakes while bacon sputtered on the stove.

If his mother had been home, there would be no pancakes, no bacon, and whatever might've been cooking, grease wouldn't have been popping anywhere. "Where's Mom?"

His father turned to his left, then to his right, as if looking for Addy, who Callum knew had gone to check on the fish. Then he looked at the clock on the stove. "I'd say she's sitting at her sister's kitchen table with a big fat cup of coffee in hand, complaining about the waste of her life spent married to me."

Callum frowned and tried to find something to say. "Come again?"

"She's in Connecticut. She left me." The older man flipped the pancakes. "She's divorcing me."

Whoa, what? His heart thundering, Callum moved to his father's side and leaned against the counter. "I know I didn't just hear that."

"You did. You want pancakes? Bacon? Coffee?"

"Dad—"

"Callum, I'm fine," he said, sliding his spatula beneath one pancake, then another, and slipping them onto a plate. "Your mother and I haven't been much more than roommates for years. You know that." He turned to set the plate on the table. "Addy! Breakfast!"

Roommates. Callum sighed, thinking his father too blasé for a man whose wife had left him. "When did she leave? When did she tell you she was leaving?"

"Yesterday evening. She came home in a huff after stopping by Bliss. I guess you and Addy weren't there."

"We left early." They'd been doing that a lot since moving. Addy was having a ball at the new place. "What did she want? Did she say?"

"No clue. Could be she wanted to tell you in person. By the time she got home, she was going on about all the sacrifices she'd made so you could make your chocolate, her words, not mine, and you couldn't even bother telling her you'd bought a new house until after the fact, not to mention keeping her from her granddaughter until Addy was almost a year old."

What the—that was old news. Nearly five-year-old news. The Addy part anyway. "She's blaming this on me?"

His father pushed his glasses up the bridge of his nose and gave him a look. "Not you as much as Ms. Harvey."

Wait just the hell a minute. "How in the world did she make that stretch?"

"Something about gossip she heard that Brooklyn didn't want children," he said, slicing Addy's pancakes into bites. "And your mother never getting to hold a newborn grandbaby—"

Crap on a cracker. He had to be kidding. "Give me a freakin' break. She said that? Brooklyn and I aren't anywhere close to talking about children." Though the idea of having a baby with her . . . it was like a jarring blow to the head. A brother or sister for Addy? Brooklyn the mother of his child?

His father arched a brow as he poured Addy a puddle of syrup. "I never claimed her reasons made any kind of sense. Addy! Breakfast!"

"I'm here, PopPop," she said, hopping up into her seat. "Do you think fish like pancakes? And bacon?"

Callum's father chuckled. "Well, if they had teeth, they just might."

Addy picked up her fork. "If they don't have teeth, how do they eat their food?"

"Those little flakes you sprinkle into the water?" he asked, making the motion with his free hand. "They melt on their tongues. Like candy."

"Nu-uh," she said, shoving a big bite of pancake into her mouth. "Daddy, PopPop is silly just like you."

"Your daddy is even more silly than me," her grandfather said when Callum continued to stand there, rooted to the floor; why was he having so much trouble processing what didn't seem to bother his father at all? "He's got a job he needs to get to and he's just standing here like a bump on a log."

"There's a bump on the log in the 'quarim," Addy said, her mouth full. "I've seen the fishes go in and out of it."

Tuning out his daughter's fish chatter, Callum told his father, "You're coming to the house tonight for dinner. I'm not taking no for an answer."

"And I'll look forward to it," his father said. "But right now I've got to get back to the pancakes before I burn down the house like your mother was always afraid I would do."

Frustration gnawing at his gut, Callum pulled his father into a quick hug, dropped a kiss to the top of his daughter's head, and left the house, digging his phone from his pocket before he climbed on his bike, and pacing until Brooklyn answered. "What're you doing this evening?"

"Hello to you, too, Callum," she said, her voice husky with sleep. "Nothing, why?"

"You want to come over for burgers?" he asked, not stopping to analyze his need to have her there. He just did. Black-and-white. Simple. "I thought I'd cook out on the patio, let Addy run wild."

"Sure. What time?"

"I'm going to try to get out of Bliss early." His dad was dealing with enough, no matter what he said about Addy taking his mind off things. "My dad's coming out, too. My mom's . . . she went out of town last night."

"Oh, sure. Okay. What can I do to help?"

"Would you feel like grabbing stuff for burgers?" *Nice. Invite the woman over to eat food you don't even have.* "Like, you know, the burgers? Meat, buns, cheese—"

She laughed quietly. "I guess this means your kitchen's not stocked yet?"

"I've got eggs, bacon, cocoa butter, and chocolate."

"Hmm. A breakfast bonbon. That's probably one of those not-such-a-good-idea things."

This woman . . . man, he liked her. He liked her a lot. And that was only the beginning of the things he felt. "Six okay for you?"

"It's perfect. I'll see you then."

∾

Brooklyn bought everything she could imagine anyone wanting on a hamburger, including bacon and sliced jalapeños and blue cheese. She had no idea what Callum or his father or Addy might like, so thought back to some of the cookouts she'd been to with Artie, and the firefighters who'd never met a condiment or a topping they could get enough of.

Callum hadn't mentioned anything about sides, but she went all-out there, too, knowing the chips and potato salad and baked beans, if not eaten this evening, would be there for leftovers tomorrow. And because she knew how Addy felt about ice cream, she also splurged there: cones for scoops taken straight up, caramel, chocolate, and strawberry sauces for sundaes.

By the time she made it down Three Wishes Road, it was six fifteen, and pulling into the driveway, she found herself wondering if Callum had lighter fluid and charcoal, or even a grill. He'd lived for nearly five years in a loft, after all, with room for nothing but a balcony-sized hibachi for cooking outside.

She found him and his dad sitting at the picnic table in the side yard with Addy's swing set in view. She was draped across one of the seats, chattering to no one in particular as she pushed herself back and forth, dragging the toes of her shoes through the dirt beneath. She was the first to see Brooklyn arrive.

"Ms. Harvey! Ms. Harvey! We're over here!"

"So I see," Brooklyn said, shifting her grocery bags between her hands and nudging the car door shut with her hip. From the corner of her eye she saw Callum approach, and she offered him the bag with the perishables. "The ice cream needs to be put in the freezer asap."

"I can do that," said the older man with the same burnt sienna hair who'd walked up behind him. He offered her his hand, his eyes behind his wire frames as green as his son's. "It's good to see you again, Ms. Harvey."

"Mr. Drake. Hello. Please call me Brooklyn."

"As long as you'll call me Vaughn."

"Can I call you Vaughn, too, PopPop?" Addy asked, running up beside them.

"No you may not," Callum said, swinging her up onto his hip, and taking the second bag Brooklyn held. "You can call him PopPop. You can call Ms. Harvey Ms. Harvey. And you can call me Weird Beard McGee."

"Daddy!" She giggled out the word. "Don't be so silly!"

"What? You don't think my beard is weird?" he asked, glancing over her shoulder to where Brooklyn was shaking her head as Addy grabbed at his whiskers.

"That one's something, isn't she?" Vaughn asked from her other side, as Addy said something to her father.

Brooklyn started to respond as a teacher, telling Vaughn that kids Addy's age shared similar personality traits, but this was the girl's grandfather, and really, she didn't have to be such a stick-in-the-mud. Besides, she agreed completely. "She definitely is."

"I know Cal's hated leaving her with me and his mother as often as he's had to, but we've sure enjoyed the extra time with her. We didn't get to see her as a baby. Didn't even get to meet her until she was already a year old. But I know he couldn't help that, either."

Not knowing what else to say, Brooklyn smiled and offered, "I imagine Addy enjoys your company just as much. She's lucky to have family close. Callum, too."

"What about you?" he asked, as they walked toward the back door. "You have anyone nearby?"

She shook her head. "It's just me since my husband died. What's left of his family is all in Italy."

"That's right. Cal said you're heading across the pond once school's out. Bet you're looking forward to that."

"I am," she said, though it felt as much like a lie as it did the truth.

Two hours later, the three adults were sitting at the picnic table, their meal devoured, scraps of buns and chips and chunks of uneaten potatoes littering their paper plates. Both men nursed Shiner longnecks while Brooklyn poured herself a third glass of wine.

She didn't need it, especially since she was going to have to drive herself home, but she was so relaxed, so unbelievably at ease . . . the night was cool, and it was too early in the year to be battling mosquitoes. The patio lights threw a bright glow over enough of the yard for Addy to play.

Oh, but she could get used to this, Brooklyn mused, listening to Callum and his dad talk basketball and home improvements, watching Addy wear herself out running around with a ribbon on a stick, twirling it, whipping it, spinning with it over her head, jumping up off the ground—

And then the girl screamed.

"Oh, crap." Brooklyn spilled her wine as she shoved out of her seat. Callum scrambled up behind her, leaping over the table while his dad circled the end and followed. They all reached Addy where she sprawled on the grass as her shrieks died and her sobs set in.

"Where's it hurt, pumpkin?" Callum asked, checking her face, her bare arms, and her legs beneath her shorts. "What'd you do?"

"My foot, Daddy," she said, and he reached for one then the other as Brooklyn cradled her head.

"I don't see anything. Did you twist your ankle?" He looked at both sides of each, tugging down her socks and running his finger over the bones. "I'm going to take off your shoe—"

"No, Daddy, don't. It hurts in my shoe."

"Look at the bottom," Brooklyn said, stroking Addy's hair from her forehead. "She may have stepped on something."

Frowning, Callum checked the soles of both tennis shoes, biting off a sharp curse that was drowned out by Addy's cries. "There's a hole here on the side of her heel. Looks like a nail puncture—"

"Here it is," his father said, picking it out of the grass. "Sixteen-D framing nail. Bet this got dropped by the crew when they built the new storage shed. Could be more, so be careful. Addy may need a tetanus shot."

"I don't want a shot!" The girl screamed the words, then began crying again.

"I know you don't, pumpkin. I'll call Dr. Barrow and see if you need one," Callum said. Then to his father: "She had a booster before the school year started, so she should be covered, but I'll check."

"Ow, Daddy," Addy said, reaching up to swipe at her nose. "It hurts!"

"I'm sure it does," he said, unlacing her shoe, as his father dropped to his hands and knees to search the ground. "But I still need to get your shoe off to see how bad it is. Dr. Barrow will want to know. If you poked a hole in your foot, she may need to see you and clean it up."

"Okay," Addy said, quieting. "But can Ms. Harvey look? And can you find my ribbon stick?"

"I've got your ribbon stick right here," Vaughn said. "I'll brush off the dirt and it'll be good as new."

"And I'm happy to look at your foot," Brooklyn said, thinking Callum had an amazing handle on this parenting thing, negotiating without sugarcoating the truth of what might happen. "But I can't do it until you let your daddy take your shoe off."

Addy sniffled, her gaze moving from Brooklyn's to Callum's. "Be careful, Daddy. Don't break my foot more."

"It's not broken," her father told her, fighting a smile that tugged hard at Brooklyn's heart. "It's probably just scratched. Could be all it needs is an Olaf bandage."

"And no shot?"

"That's up to Dr. Barrow. But she has Olaf bandages, too."

"And she has Olaf stickers."

"Sounds to me like Olaf makes everything better," Brooklyn said.

"Olaf does!" Addy said, nodding furiously. "If you had an Olaf you would never have to be sad."

"Oh, sweetie," Brooklyn said, her throat tight and aching. "I'm not sad. I'm just worried about you."

"But all your books are here," Addy said insistently. "You have to be sad."

Brooklyn frowned, certain the girl must be thinking about having her own books close. "They're just here because I'm moving out of my house and don't have anywhere to put them."

Addy's eyes grew wide. "Are you moving here? With us?"

Well, crap. This was not how she'd wanted this revelation to happen. She smiled at Callum's daughter, using her thumb to stroke Addy's tears from her cheek. "No, I'm moving to Italy. It's very far away. Across the ocean."

"On the globe?" Addy asked, her lips quivering. "On the other side?" Brooklyn nodded.

"I don't want you to move," Addy said, breaking into another loud cry, which turned into more screams Brooklyn wasn't equipped to deal with.

She moved out of the way as Callum scooped up his daughter and headed for the house, lingering until she had a better handle on her emotions. No need to reveal to anyone else how completely her heart was torn between the old life she was shedding, and the new one she wasn't sure fit.

~

"Sorry about that," Callum said, having returned from seeing his father off and tucking his daughter in, to find Brooklyn in the library, the light on the table at her side burning low. "That's one sure way to sober up quick." He'd lost every bit of his buzz the moment he'd heard Addy's scream.

Thankfully, once he'd coaxed his daughter out of her shoe and sock, all he'd found was a bloody gouge on her heel and nothing requiring stitches or a trip to the ER. He'd left a message with Dr. Barrow about the need for a tetanus shot. She'd assured him when she'd called back that Addy was covered. And his father, after ruining the knees of his khaki Dockers, never found another nail.

The wound was easily cleaned with soap and water, smeared with an antibiotic ointment, and covered with a bandage. Two bandages, actually, which made his daughter too happy to argue about going to bed without a story. He would've taken the time to read her one if he'd thought she'd have stayed awake, but her eyes were fighting the weight of her lids when he'd pulled the sheet over her shoulders. Besides, it was long past eight.

In fact, he realized, glancing at the clock on the fireplace mantel, it was nearly eleven. Seemed time flew during the not-fun times as well. He rubbed his hands down his face and groaned. Brooklyn sat curled into the corner of the sofa, three books open on the arm at her side, spines up, pages down, as if she'd read to the middle of each and stopped.

"Why are you apologizing?" she asked as he plopped beside her onto the center cushion. "You're not the one who dropped the nail in the grass. Or told her that you're moving halfway around the world. Is she okay?"

"She's fine," he said, stretching out his arms across the back. A lock of Brooklyn's hair fell across his hand. He rubbed it between his forefinger and thumb. "She's exhausted. She was snoring when I turned out the light."

"I don't believe for a minute that she snores."

"She doesn't blow the house down," he said in response. "But she can be noisy. Like a puppy."

Her mouth trembled, and she looked on the verge of tears. "Poor thing."

"She'll be fine," he said, giving a quick tug to her hair. "Don't worry about her."

"Of course I'm going to worry about her." She moved the books from the couch arm to the end table, frowning as she did. "I love her."

"Yeah?" he asked, his heart swelling up a couple of sizes.

"You know I do."

He thought again of having more children, having them with this woman. Then he got rid of the thought because he'd been ruined enough for one night. "You would've been a great mom, you know."

It was the wrong thing to say. She closed up as if she were a book, as if she didn't want him to read any more of her than he already had, and leaned forward, pulling away from his hand. "Well, it didn't happen, so the point is moot."

"I didn't mean to bring up a sore spot—"

"It's not a sore spot. Artie and I chose not to have children for a reason. A reason that unfortunately turned out to be prescient. And honestly, not everyone who has kids should."

He frowned. "I hope that wasn't a dig at me."

"Of course not." She shook off whatever she was feeling, and said, "You're an amazing father. But I can't imagine, with all that you've told me . . . when you learned her mother was expecting, did you ever have doubts?"

His doubts . . . they wouldn't have fit into a freighter's worth of containers. He'd even been the one to suggest Cheryl—how had he put it?—get rid of the problem. Funny, her standing her ground on abortion being wrong, when she had no trouble with embezzlement, or extortion, or running drugs.

The thought of not having Addy . . . "Yeah, well, turned out what I thought might be a complication, wasn't."

"But it could've been."

"And I would've dealt with it."

"Faced your fear?" she asked. "Let it pass through you?"

She was talking about his tattoo, the litany against fear riding the dragon's back. He'd been coming off one of the worst times in his life when he'd inked those words. A time he wasn't proud of, didn't want to talk about, didn't want her to know about. The life he'd lived . . .

There'd been drugs; he wasn't going to deny it. But she was scratching just a little bit too close to the mark for comfort. They were talking about his daughter, and he didn't want to think of how wrong things could've gone if he hadn't gotten straight. Total obliteration.

The words he'd had inked still gave him chills. "The fear's been gone a long time, Brooklyn. Only I remain."

All she did was nod, and he found he was out of things to say as well. He took a deep breath. "I should probably check on the munchkin."

"Do you mind if I do it?" she asked.

"Be my guest," he said, telling himself the tugging sensation in his chest had nothing to do with his heart. "You know the room. It's the one with the snowflake lights on the ceiling. And all the Olafs."

"Be right back," she said, her smile pensive, reflective.

Thirty minutes later he startled awake, surprised he'd dosed off. Surprised he was still on the couch, and alone. His heart thumping a worried beat, he pushed up and headed for Addy's room, slowing as he reached the door and heard more than his daughter's soft snores.

Seemed Brooklyn snored, too. Just as softly, more like whiffles of breath than anything. Hands shoved in his pockets, he leaned a shoulder against the doorjamb and listened. Brooklyn lay facing Addy, curled on her side, Addy similarly posed, their foreheads touching.

The bedside lamp cast a soft glow over their hair; the color of the strands was nearly the same, as was the texture, he knew, from toying with Brooklyn's earlier, and from battling Addy's daily. He'd never thought seriously about having more kids. Addy was a handful, and there was something about the circumstances of her conception and birth that kept him from wanting to make the leap.

But the thought of having a child with Brooklyn . . . that wasn't why he wanted her, but he did want her. To be his. Forever. Because for the first time in his life, he was in love.

CHAPTER TWENTY-TWO

Tuesday, May 26, on what would've been her and Artie's fourteenth anniversary, Brooklyn made his lasagne to serve to Callum and Addy. She'd watched Artie put the dish together dozens of times, but she'd never fixed it herself. Thankfully, she'd picked up the ingredients after school yesterday, because the preparation kept her busy all afternoon.

She chopped an onion, a carrot, a celery stalk. She sliced garlic and parboiled tomatoes, peeling off their skins before turning them into sauce. She parboiled spinach, too. She browned ground chuck and boiled lasagne noodles and drained ricotta cheese. She measured oregano and olive oil and wine.

It would've been easier to use a jar of pasta sauce, and no-boil noodles, and prechopped onions, but Artie would have died—no, Artie wouldn't have been caught dead—no, Artie would've put in the effort, because every minute of the effort was worth it.

And not just for the flavor. He'd believed with all his heart that a labor of love brought bountiful rewards. Brooklyn didn't know about rewards, but she did know she had to keep busy, and she couldn't be alone. The lasagne accomplished the first, Callum and Addy the second.

At first she'd thought about a dinner party. Nothing too large. Jean, of course, and Alva Bean, because the two were seeing more and more of each other, which made Brooklyn ridiculously happy. Dolly and Mitch Pepper, because Dolly was becoming an unexpectedly good friend—and just as Brooklyn was getting ready to leave Hope Springs, which made her ridiculously sad.

Lindsay Webber, so Addy would have a playmate, and because including Kelly's mother, who Brooklyn knew didn't have many friends of her own, even if she did have her eye on Callum, was something Artie would have done to be kind. Vaughn Drake, so he wouldn't be alone with Shirley still out of town. Except the way Brooklyn's numbers were working out, Vaughn and Lindsay would be paired as dinner partners, assuming Brooklyn claimed Callum for herself, which wasn't even a question.

In the end she didn't want to deal with Lindsay, or assumed pairings, or anything more than getting through the day. But she couldn't do it by herself, a lesson she'd learned last year when she'd tried; with the date falling on Memorial Day, she'd found herself in Austin for the opening weekend of summer blockbusters, staying at the cineplex for hours.

She'd wound up inviting just Callum and Addy. And she'd been a basket case since they'd arrived. All she could think about was Artie preparing this very same meal for her, and how stupid she'd been to think serving it to Callum would make anything easier.

She should've suggested they go out, or cook hot dogs at his place. Being a Tuesday made it more difficult than if it had been the holiday again; he'd had to work, too, then pick up Addy from the school, then go home and change. She'd told him, when she'd invited him, just to bring extra clothes; he could shower then change in her bedroom, but he'd declined. She didn't know why. Unless it was the idea of undressing in her house . . .

"That was amazing," he said, bringing a stack of plates to the counter beside the sink where she was rinsing out the salad bowls they'd used.

She watched pieces of romaine and radicchio and Addy's uneaten cherry tomato halves slide into the disposal. "Thank you."

"And no doubt it was a lot of work. Which you didn't have to do."

She shrugged, fearing the response came off as indifference when she was doing her best to flirt. Or at least not to break into tears. "You fed me hamburgers on Saturday. I figured it was my turn to feed you."

"Crap. I never did pay you back for all that food," he said, reaching for his wallet. "I got so caught up with Addy and her foot—"

"Callum, don't," she said, lifting a hand toward him. "I don't want your money. I just . . . the house is feeling kinda empty. With all my packing. Tonight especially," she added without thinking, then wishing she hadn't.

"Yeah? What's going on tonight?" he asked, but she shook her head.

"How *is* Addy's foot?" It seemed a much safer conversation to have than the one she feared they were heading toward.

"Nothing that ten Olaf bandages didn't fix," he said with a snort, leaning back and curling his hands over the counter's edge at his hips. He cocked his head sideways to look at her. "Brooklyn, not that I mind keeping you company, but you want to tell me what's up? Because a twenty-piece box of Bliss candies says something's wrong."

He'd probably mind if he knew the truth. She stopped with the dishes, looked out the window over the sink, but it was dark outside, and all she could see was her own ghostlike reflection. That's what she felt like tonight. Transparent. Insubstantial. Lost and caught between worlds.

"Artie and I would've been married fourteen years today."

"Say again."

She turned to face him, reaching for a towel to dry her hands, twisting it in front of her as she said, "Today would've been Artie and my fourteenth wedding anniversary."

Callum's jaw tightened. "And you invited me and Addy to dinner, what? To celebrate?"

"No. No. It's not celebrating." It wasn't even commemorating. It was simply getting through. "It's just . . . a hard day for me. It's only the second time he hasn't been here." Her throat swelled. Tears filled her eyes. "I needed not to be alone. I needed to be with you."

It was a tough admission to make. Not because of how she felt about Callum, but because she didn't want him to think she was conflating that emotion with what Artie had meant to her. And there was no possible way to prove that she wasn't; her heart and her head were both so confused.

Callum hung his head, his gaze on the floor, frowning. "Brooklyn, do you understand what you mean to me? How much I care for you? It's driving me nuts that you're taking off for Italy in a matter of days—"

"I'm not leaving for a week. Almost two." And why was correcting the timing more important than what he'd just said?

"Tomorrow . . . six months from now . . . it doesn't matter when you go." He looked up, looked at her, the emotion in his eyes cutting into her like daggers, like needles, like the tiniest pinpoints of pain. "What matters is that you're going for him, instead of staying here for me."

"I don't have a choice." She sobbed out the words. "I promised him—"

"You can ship the Bible," he said, gesturing with one arm. "Ship the vase, whatever else you're taking—"

"But I can't ship him," she nearly whispered, the words breaking into pieces as she spoke.

"What?" The question was a gasp of disbelief, of needing to understand, of fearing the answer.

"His ashes," she said slowly. "He wanted them scattered on the second anniversary of his death. In his family's olive groves, or in the Gulf or the Guadalupe. The Mediterranean. The vineyards his grandfather owned."

"Why?" he asked as he reached up and rubbed at his forehead. "I don't mean why there, but why the two years? Why not before now?"

"Out of respect for the older members of the family. Some still follow antiquated mourning customs."

"And waiting to scatter his ashes is part of that?"

"I don't know. I didn't ask. I don't really care," she said, retrieving her wineglass from the table and emptying the bottle they'd opened with dinner into it. "And it doesn't matter. All I know is that it's what he wanted, so it's what I'm doing."

"And then?" he asked, watching as she swallowed half the contents. She swallowed the rest before asking, "Then what?"

His eyes grew dark, his frown deep, his emotions sharp and hurting. "Is that when you let him go?"

She thought everything inside of her might explode. Her chest, her head, the core of who she was. "Excuse me?"

"Are you going to let him go?" he asked, walking toward her, his steps heavy in his big leather boots. "Move on with your life? You've told me more than once that's what he wanted—"

The sound of glass shattering in the living room kept Callum from saying more, and kept Brooklyn from losing her mind over the echo of his words in her head. How dared he. *How dared he!* He had no idea what it was to love someone the way she'd loved Artie, then to lose that someone to a nightmare.

Except, she realized as she looked at the remnants of their meal on the table, that wasn't fair of her, was it? If Addy's mother did indeed come after her and decide to challenge his custody, he could lose his daughter to a horror of another sort. Spousal love and parental love were different emotions: Both were powerful; both consumed. Both created heartache in the event of loss.

But for him to be so demanding—

"Adrianne Michelle! What did I tell you about visiting Ms. Harvey's house? What are the rules?"

Uh-oh. Dread slipping down her spine, Brooklyn found herself holding her breath as she finally followed Callum to the living room, stopping in the doorway with a gasp. The slivers of colored glass on the floor could have come from only one thing: the mouth-blown and hand-painted glass ball owls that Artie had given her their first Christmas.

She'd never hung them on any of their trees for fear they'd fall and shatter. Instead she'd lined them up on the bottom shelf of the living room bookcase. The only time they were handled was when she dusted them maybe once a month. Or when Addy Drake decided they looked like toys. Which, Brooklyn mused, to a six-year-old they probably did.

Callum scooped his daughter off the floor and deposited her in the closest chair. "Sit here. I'm going to clean this up, and I don't want you getting cut on the glass. Do not even think about moving."

Addy was sniffling, wiping her nose on her sleeve, rubbing at her eyes. She was tired, and probably more upset over her father's anger than what she'd actually done—which proved yet again the incredible bond the two shared. The respect Addy had for her father meant his being anything but happy with her was more punishment than a time-out chair could ever be.

"No. No. It's okay," she said to Callum as he stopped beside her on his way to find a broom. The little girl crying her eyes out was so much more important than the broken glass; she didn't need the ornaments to remember her first Christmas with Artie. "It really is. They're just owls."

～

Malina's Diner, a Hope Springs institution the locals knew closed at ten after breakfast and opened for supper at four, had recently added a dining room that seated three times the number of customers as their counter, tables, and red Naugahyde booths. Since it was a *private* dining room, it was used for large groups needing a meeting space and good food.

Folks booked it for birthday parties and baby showers, for committee meetings, for wedding receptions—anything and everything under the sun. Today, four days after Tuesday's wreck of an anniversary dinner, it was the site of Brooklyn's going-away party, and not an inch of ceiling was visible for the dozens of helium-filled balloons bobbing against it, their ribbon tails dangling in a rainbow of Crayola crayon colors.

Brooklyn had been teaching at Hope Springs Elementary for over a decade. It was the only teaching job she'd had. She'd seen other teachers retire, like Jean Dial, who today wore earrings that looked like fresh-cut red roses—the color, the shape, *and* the size—and she'd seen new hires, both seasoned professionals and new college grads, join the faculty's ranks.

She wasn't the only one who'd been at the school for so long, meaning she had a lot of friends, some close, some less so, but all wanting to wish her a bon voyage as she started this new chapter of her life. The room was packed, the noise level deafening, the aroma of Max Malina's chicken parmesan cutlets and garlic bread strong enough to seep into the fabric of her dress.

It was hard to decide if she was happy or sad. Such a wealth of love and memories and friendship. Standing at the front of the room with a small group chatting about vacation plans, she let her mind drift and glanced from face to face: at those mingling, at those huddled over plates of cake at the tables, at those checking out the pile of gifts waiting for her to unwrap.

Gifts. What was she going to do with more *things* when she'd just unburdened herself of all that she owned? Well, most of what she owned. What was left was with Callum. Meaning whatever happened during her year away, at least she'd have seeing him again to look forward to.

Because no matter the ridiculous friction between them Tuesday night—and it was ridiculous, both of them on edge, both fearful, neither knowing what to do with this thing between them—nothing about her feelings for him had changed. All she could hope was that they had a chance to set things right before she left. The idea of leaving without doing so . . .

"Excuse me a minute," she said, taking her leave from the group, who had moved on to talking about summer camps for their kids, and making her way through the room to where Jean Dial sat with Dolly Pepper at the end of one long table. Jean huddled over a plate of Italian cream cake, while Dolly cradled a cup of coffee. Both were frowning, heads down.

Frowning or not, their familiar faces were just what she needed right now. "Is this a private party, or is there room for one more?"

Both women looked up. Both smiled. Jean was the one to push out the chair to her side, while Dolly said, "Of course."

Brooklyn hesitated. The tone of Dolly's voice didn't sound as welcoming as her invitation, and Jean was back to frowning again. "Are you sure?" she asked, tentative as she sat. "I didn't mean to interrupt, but you both looked like you might need a little cheering up."

"We're not the ones needing the cheering," Jean said, digging a fork into her cake. "That would be Vaughn Drake, though more than likely he's just fine. We're the ones *doing* the cheering."

"Vaughn Drake? Callum's father?" Brooklyn looked from Jean to Dolly, only to find the second woman with her face buried in her hands, mostly likely due to Jean's outspokenness, which had Brooklyn wondering why her neighbor was cheering. And what it had to do with Vaughn. "Jean?"

"Shirley Drake left her husband." Another bite of cake, Jean's earrings swinging against her neck as she chewed. "Packed up her clothes and flew to Connecticut to stay with her sister, who I gather from what Shirley has said over the years is just as miserable a woman as she is."

"To Connecticut." Why hadn't Callum said anything? "For a vacation?"

Dolly was shaking her head. "She told him she wants a divorce."

Now Brooklyn was really confused. "I don't understand. I saw them several times together. They seemed to have a good marriage." And in all his complaining about his mother, Callum had never hinted otherwise.

"I think Vaughn thought the same thing, though I understand he's not terribly broken up over it. So obviously I don't know what I'm talking about," Jean said, sliding her fork through her cake for a bite of nothing but icing.

Brooklyn looked from Jean to Dolly and back. "Why would she just leave like that? What about Callum and Addy?"

When the two older women exchanged a quick glance, then Dolly went back to staring into her coffee and Jean at her cake, a frisson of dread crept its way up Brooklyn's spine. "This has something to do with me, doesn't it?"

Dolly gave a dismissive wave of one hand. "Of course not, dear."

"If that woman has an issue with you," Jean said, gesturing with her fork, "it's all in her mind."

"Jean." Dolly nearly bit off the word.

"It's okay," Brooklyn said. "I'd rather hear the truth."

"The truth is that Vaughn Drake is a saint to have put up with that woman all these years," Jean said, never one to hold anything back. "Good riddance, I say. And I mean it."

"Oh, Jean, no." Dolly reached across the table and patted the back of Jean's hand. "Yes, Shirley can be trying, but you know Vaughn's got to be hurting. And think about Callum and his little girl."

But Jean wasn't having any of it. "I saw Vaughn in HEB just yesterday. He's not hurting at all. Or he's doing a damn good job of hiding it."

"Not to take away from what Mr. Drake is going through," Brooklyn said, "but would one of you tell me how this involves me?"

Jean reached behind her for her monster-sized purse and pulled out a flask, doctoring her coffee with a big splash of bourbon. "Oh, some BS about how her son deprived her of having a grandbaby, since she didn't meet Adrianne until the girl was already a year old. And now that you've caught his fancy, she might as well write off the idea of ever being a grandmother again, since you don't want children."

Brooklyn waited for the reverberation of the sledgehammer to stop. Her head ached. Her heart ached. Poor Callum. Poor Addy. Poor Vaughn. "I never told him I didn't want children. I told him Artie and I had decided not to have them. It's the same thing I've told others when it's come up in conversation. But I can't imagine him telling his mother any of that."

"Oh, I don't believe for a moment he did." Jean pushed her empty plate to the side and lifted her coffee cup with both hands, breathing in the aroma of the added bourbon. "She either heard it elsewhere or she made it up. She's obviously jealous of the time he's been spending with you. It's nothing more than her being her usual petty self."

"Jean!"

"Oh, Dolly. You know I'm right. Pearl's will be a much quieter place Friday mornings without Shirley moaning about every pothole put in the road just to ruin her brand-new tires." She turned to Brooklyn. "You want a piece of cake, hon? A cup of coffee?"

Brooklyn shook her head. "When did this happen? When did she leave?"

Jean glanced at Dolly, and Dolly was the one who spoke. "I believe last Saturday morning. Or last Friday night. I didn't hear about it until Sunday at church."

So Callum had known on Saturday when she'd gone to his house, and on Tuesday when he'd come to hers. He'd told her his mother was out of town, but said nothing about her leaving his father. And Vaughn . . . he'd sat there and eaten hamburgers and talked basketball and crawled around looking for 16d framing nails without so much as a hint of anything bothering him.

Elbows on the table, Brooklyn rubbed at the pressure in her temples. "I saw them last Saturday night. I had dinner with them."

"With Callum?" Dolly asked. "And Vaughn?"

"And Addy. He bought a house out on Three Wishes Road. They

moved earlier this month. He cooked burgers. Addy stepped on a nail . . ." She shook her head. This wasn't making sense. "I saw them on Tuesday, too. Callum and his daughter. They came over for dinner. I cooked lasagna."

"Artie's lasagna?" asked Jean. When Brooklyn nodded, Jean muttered some choice words under her breath. "I can't believe I forgot the date when I agreed to host that Bunco party with Pearl. I should've invited you to come."

"What date?" Dolly asked. "What am I missing?"

Shaking her head solemnly, Jean set down her coffee cup. "Tuesday was Brooklyn and Artie's anniversary."

"Oh, sweetheart." Dolly reached over and took hold of Brooklyn's hand with both of hers. "I'm so sorry. If I'd known, I would've been there with a gallon of ice cream and a pan of fresh brownies."

Tears welled in Brooklyn's eyes and her throat ached with emotion. She was so very lucky to have such very dear friends. "Thank you both. I'm fine, really. I'm not so sure Callum is." She shuddered. "I still can't believe I thought it a good idea to have him for dinner."

"And did you?" Jean asked, her lips pursed against a grin. "*Have* him for dinner?"

"Jean!" Dolly and Brooklyn gasped the other woman's name at the same time.

Jean waved off their shock. "Just trying to lighten the mood. And wondering if he's as good in bed as he looks like he'd be."

Brooklyn blushed, and Jean said, "Aha," and then Dolly shook her head, saying, "I don't want to know. I don't even want to know."

"Well, I *do* want to know why he didn't tell me about his mother leaving," Brooklyn said. "Though for all I know he planned to. Until he found out I needed his company to get through my anniversary with another man."

"He'll get over it," Jean said. "And knowing the kind of man he is, I have no doubt he'll take it as the very real compliment it was."

"And you're still leaving next week?" Dolly asked, before Brooklyn could respond to Jean.

She nodded. "I think so. I fly out Friday evening."

Dolly and Jean exchanged a glance, then Dolly was the one to say, "That doesn't sound like you're sure about this trip you're taking."

"It's complicated. I need to go. I *have* to go."

"But you don't want to leave Callum."

Hearing the words come out of Jean's mouth . . . Brooklyn shook her head slowly, her stupid eyes filling with tears again. She was so tired of the tears. So tired of being torn between duty and honor and love, and not even knowing which emotion belonged to the past, which to the present.

Or which to which man.

Max Malina's Mama Mia! Italian Cream Cake

For the cake:
1 1/2 cups sweetened shredded coconut, toasted
1 cup buttermilk, room temperature
2 teaspoons pure vanilla extract
2 1/2 cups cake flour
2 teaspoons baking powder
1/2 teaspoon salt
1/2 teaspoon baking soda
12 tablespoons unsalted butter, cut into pieces and softened
4 tablespoons vegetable shortening, cut into pieces
1 3/4 cups granulated sugar
5 large eggs, room temperature
2 cups pecans, toasted and chopped

Preheat oven to 350° (F). Grease two 9-inch round cake pans and line with parchment paper, coating with nonstick spray.

Process the coconut in a food processor until finely ground. Combine the coconut, the buttermilk, and the vanilla in a bowl and let sit until coconut is slightly softened.

In a large mixing bowl, combine the flour, the baking powder, the salt, and the baking soda. Using a stand mixer fitted with a paddle, or an electric mixer, beat the butter, the shortening, and the sugar on medium-high speed until pale and fluffy. Add the eggs, one at a time, and beat until combined. Reduce the mixer speed to low and add the flour mixture, alternating with additions of the reserved coconut-buttermilk mixture, scraping down the sides of the bowl as needed. Fold in 3/4 cup of pecans.

Pour equal amounts of the batter into the prepared pans and bake for 28–32 minutes, or until a tester inserted in the center of the cake comes out clean. Cool the cakes in the pans on wire racks for 10 minutes. Remove the cakes from the pans and cool completely.

For the frosting:
12 tablespoons unsalted butter, softened
2 1/4 cups powdered sugar
1/2 cup cream of coconut
1/2 teaspoon pure vanilla extract
16 ounces cream cheese, cut into pieces and softened
pinch of salt

Using an electric mixer or a stand mixer fitted with a paddle, mix the butter and the sugar on low speed until combined. Increase the speed to medium-high and beat until pale and fluffy. Add the cream of coconut, the vanilla, and the salt, and beat until smooth. Add the cream cheese, one piece at a time, and beat until incorporated. Frost the cake and press the remaining pecans onto the sides.

CHAPTER TWENTY-THREE

Sunday night following Tuesday's disastrous dinner at Brooklyn's, when Callum had cleaned up the owls Addy had broken, then cleaned up the rest of the dishes while Brooklyn had held his daughter on her lap and read her a book on her Kindle, Callum met his dad at the back door of his parents' home, climbing the three concrete steps into the kitchen with Addy asleep on his shoulder. He'd hated getting her out of bed, but it couldn't be helped. Well, it could have been, but only if he'd decided to do this before she'd gone to sleep.

"I really appreciate this," he said to his father as the older man closed the door. "And I'm sorry for calling so late. How're you doing?"

"It's no bother. You know I'm a night owl." He gestured for Callum to follow him, shutting off the kitchen lights and leading the way down the hall to the spare bedroom Addy used when she slept over. "Your mother would've loved to wake to find Adrianne here, but now I get to have all the fun. And I will. So don't worry about me."

"I'll be back first thing," Callum told him, worried anyway, even though his father looked less wan and less stressed and less . . . stooped and old than he had in months. "Hell, I may come back and crash on the couch so you don't have to deal with breakfast. Addy's still acting out about her Grammy being gone."

"Then she needs to see exactly how much fun breakfast can be when we don't have to worry about our silverware matching while we eat pancakes shaped like snowmen." His father gestured toward the bed, where he'd pulled down the covers before they'd arrived. The lamp on the bedside table burned on low.

After laying down his daughter, Callum waited for her to roll onto her side before pulling the bedspread around her shoulders. His father was taking his mother's absence a whole lot better than Callum would've imagined. He wasn't even sure *he* was taking it as well, but then, he was dealing with Addy's emotions and outbursts, which influenced his own feelings about what his mother had done—and not for the better.

"I would say you don't have to spoil her with snowman pancakes, but maybe it's what she needs. God knows I'm not exactly doing the best job of figuring that out these days." Then again, he wasn't doing such a good job with any of his relationships except maybe with Lena, and that was because she didn't let him get away with shit.

"How's Brooklyn?" his dad asked as if reading his mind. "The two of you doing okay? Getting any closer to making things official?"

"You know me," he said, wiggling his daughter's backpack off his shoulder and tossing it to the seat of the corner chair. "I've been kinda snake-bit these last few years when it comes to making choices."

His father huffed. "Easy to understand when you get told you're making bad ones often enough."

"Took me until ten thirty-three tonight to make the one that brought me here." And then he'd called his dad at 10:34.

From the doorway where he stood, his father chuckled. "Marking the date and time for posterity, huh?"

"Not on purpose," Callum said. "I can't let her go. Not without her knowing . . ."

He let the sentence trail, and smoothed Addy's hair over the pillow. He was still on shaky ground, and wouldn't have his footing right until he talked to Brooklyn in person. He glanced at the clock beside the bed, his stomach tumbling. Time was ticking.

After kissing his daughter's temple, he headed for the door. His father backed into the hallway, waving him toward his study. *Ticking, ticking, ticking.*

"Dad, I really should go. It's late."

"Humor me for five minutes." The older man walked into the room, lit a bright aquarium blue, and switched on a lamp. "I know what you feel for Brooklyn has come on suddenly, but that doesn't make it suspect. There is such a thing as love at first sight."

Callum hoped his father was right, because he didn't want to think he was making a mistake, falling so hard and so fast. Falling in love—because he was. Completely. In ways he'd never known love existed.

"Dad," he said, his throat tightening around the words. "I'm going to ask her to marry me."

"Well, that's the best news I've heard in a while," he said, the big wide grin splitting his face quickly turning into a frown. "Except didn't you tell me the night we cooked burgers that she's flying out of here later this week?"

"She is," Callum said, nodding, his hands at his hips, the thought a monstrous weight dragging him down. "She's scheduled to, anyway. I'm hoping she'll change her mind. Or at least do what she needs to do and come back sooner than she's planning to."

"What is it she's doing?"

He gave a sharp snort. "Believe it or not, scattering her husband's ashes."

"Ah," his father said thoughtfully. "So changing her mind has some complications."

Callum nodded. They were complications he wasn't sure he could overcome. One thing was certain: he wasn't going to get anything settled standing here. "Dad, I really need to go."

"All right, but I've got something I want to give you first," his father said, making his way to his desk. "I've been holding on to it for a long time."

"Well, it can't be a piece of advice, since you never held back any of those," Callum joked as he walked closer.

"Funny man you've turned out to be."

"I had a good teacher," Callum said, his chest tightening as the realization of how much he meant it struck unexpectedly hard.

Closing his desk drawer, his father walked to where Callum stood and handed him a hinged jewelry box. "This belonged to my mother. And to her mother. She wouldn't tell my grandfather which stone was her favorite, so he gave her one of each. Your mother wanted to resize it and replace some of the stones, but I told her we'd just save it for you, since it never was to her taste."

Swallowing hard, Callum opened the box and stared down at the ring of gold and precious gems, picturing it on Brooklyn's hand. He couldn't imagine anything more perfect, more suited to her understated style. But even more moving was the very idea of his father saving this for him.

The older man, never physically demonstrative, wasn't one for sentimental gestures, either, and the surprise of his doing so, of his doing this . . . Callum cleared his throat as he closed the box, then wrapped both arms around his dad, who returned the hug, patting him on the back, then covering his own mouth with his fist as he coughed his emotion away.

"I hope she likes it," he said, having removed his glasses to rub at his eyes. "I hope *you* like it."

"I can't imagine she won't, and I love it. Thank you," Callum said, shoving the box deep into his pocket. "Now I just hope I don't mess this up. I know I did with a lot of things, early on, after high school—"

"Nothing that you haven't fixed since."

"I wish you and Mom had been there for Addy's birth. Or maybe not for the birth so much"—what had happened in Cheryl's hospital room had not been pretty—"but when we got home. When she was a baby. Those early days were something else. I was a wreck. Completely clueless."

His father took his time with his glasses, worrying the earpieces into place. "Someday you think you'll want to talk about Addy's mother?"

"I don't know. It's probably better if I don't. She's never going to be a part of Addy's life. Or mine."

Nodding, his father asked, "Anyone else know who she is?"

He thought back to the last time he'd seen Duke and Lainie. "A couple of people. Her brother and his wife."

"But you're not in touch with them."

"Not for five years now, no."

"You going to tell Addy about her?"

"One day, maybe. Or not. She's the one mistake I'll be fine never thinking about again."

"Then we'll just let things stand."

"Thanks, Dad," he said, taking a deep breath and blowing it out, surprised at the relief that he pulled in when he next inhaled.

Then the older man cleared his throat. "Though you can make up for me missing those early years by being sure I'm invited to the wedding."

"If there is one," Callum said, torn between laughing and launching into a string of curses. If he'd read Brooklyn right. If he hadn't waited too long.

"I've got a good feeling there will be."

∾

It was nearly midnight when Brooklyn heard the knock on her door. She wasn't sleeping. She wasn't even ready for bed. Not that she had a bed anymore. Or would be sleeping in what used to be her house ever again. She couldn't imagine her visitor would be anyone but Jean come once more to convince her to use her spare bedroom instead of spending the next few nights in a hotel. Unless there had been an emergency . . .

Heart racing, she hurried to answer it, reminded of the notification two years ago that had changed her life. This wasn't that. This couldn't be that. The thought of having to face such another such event, her entire world turned upside down, everything she'd come to expect as normal gone. And yet when she opened the door and saw him standing there . . .

Her world flipped. Her new normal vanished. This moment. Right now. The wild wings of her heartbeat told her nothing would ever be the same. She just wasn't sure where she'd find herself after. "Callum. What are you doing here?" He waited for her to invite him in, though she could tell it was a struggle. "Is everything okay? Is Addy—"

"She's fine. I left her with my dad—"

"Why didn't you tell me about your mother leaving?" she asked as she stepped back to let him inside. "I had to hear it from Jean and Dolly yesterday."

"I was too pissed off." He stood in the center of her living room, his hands at his hips as he shook his head. "I didn't want to unload on you."

"You should have. Seriously."

"Can we talk about this later?"

His voice was gruff, his tone impatient, and it worried her. She hugged her arms over her chest. "Sure. Of course."

"I didn't know if you'd still be here." He glanced at the only things in the room: her carefully packed carry-on, and the futon she was leaving for the charity truck to pick up tomorrow along with the boxes in the garage. Jean would let them in.

"I was just about to leave, actually," she said, though she'd been tempted more than once to grab one of the blankets out of the box beside the futon and curl up beneath it for hours. She was so incredibly tired. "I wanted to do one more walk-through, even though I've done about ten already." She waved one arm in a gesture meant to encompass the entire house. "With all the trouble I had getting started, I ended up finishing the packing days earlier than I needed to. I haven't found anything I've missed the last nine times. I'm not sure why—"

They were the last words she got out before Callum stepped into her, wrapped his arms around her, brought his mouth down hard on hers. He'd kissed her before. They'd had sex before. But this wasn't either of those times. And this wasn't a good-bye. It was almost brutal with need, but tender in execution, not hurtful, a consuming mating of mouths and breath and the tactile pleasure of touch.

That part she realized when the room's still air hit her back as Callum's warm hands lifted the hem of her shirt. She raised her arms and he pulled it over her head, then she reached for the clasp of her bra, but he beat her there, undoing it and sliding the straps from her shoulders. He held her, his big hands kneading her, all while he stayed with the kiss, slanting with his mouth, sweeping with his tongue, stirring her as he brought her body to his.

She gave him the contact he wanted, but for the briefest moment only, breaking free to undo the buttons of his oxford, and realizing she hadn't heard the rumble of his bike before he arrived. "You came in your truck."

"Easier to haul all of Addy's things to my dad's."

"So he knows you're here?" she asked, pushing his shirt from his shoulders.

He nodded.

"And he knows what we're doing?"

He shrugged.

"Does it bother you?"

"For my dad to know how much I love you?"

She stopped with her hands on his shoulders and closed her eyes. The words tripped through her like tiny little feet, landing over and over and over, but it wasn't enough. "Say it again," she whispered, looking up.

He looked down: at her hair where it feathered over his hand, at her ear where he cupped it, at her jaw along which he dragged the tip of his finger. At her eyes where he lingered. "I love you, Brooklyn. Heart and soul and forever."

"Oh, Callum." She shuddered with everything she was feeling. Lust and desire and fear of the unknown and obligations and promises and vows. But more than anything, she nearly shook with the love she had for this man. "I love you, too."

She ran her palms from his shoulders down his biceps to his fore-arms. The room was too dark to make out all of his ink, but she could see enough to know she wanted time to learn all of it. For now . . . "The day you came to my class that first time, not to read, but later. When you came back. You were standing in the door with your arms lifted, and I could see just a hint of this." She ran her finger along the dragon's back. "I could make out the scales, but that was it. I didn't know if it was an iguana or a turtle or a fish."

"A fish."

"I saw that it was a dragon that day in my garage. But in my class-room, all I could see were the scales." She read aloud the words about facing down the mind-killer that was fear. "But I couldn't imagine you'd be afraid of a fish."

He snorted. "It's not a fish."

"I know that," she said, running a fingertip along the dragon's spiky spine, and realizing he wasn't going to admit to what it was he'd feared. "Why the dragon?"

"You don't want to know."

"You don't want me to know."

"That, too," he said and then his mouth was on hers again and any other questions on the tip of her tongue were swept away.

He was hungry, and he was greedy, and she was both of those things, and her only fear was that she would never know this again. He'd built her a library, a room of all the things she loved, the colors and the words, and offered it to her should she need the respite. But he hadn't asked her to stay.

He hadn't said he wished she would forgo the trip and rescind her resignation to the district, if such a thing was even possible. He hadn't told her he wanted her with him forever. Neither had she said that with him was where she wanted to be, and that was her fault; she should have told him sooner.

But she had tonight, and his declaration of love, and this moment. And she refused to waste it regretting that she'd been so slow in coming to know her own mind.

She knew it now, and she tugged at the strands of his hair hanging free, and begged him, "Take it down."

He grinned against her cheek and did as she asked, the wild mass falling like a cloak on either side of his face. She thought as she had so often of Heathcliff, at least the Heathcliff of her imagination, painted with this smile and these eyes and this hair.

"What else?"

"Take me to bed."

They were naked and wound up in each other on the futon in seconds. She'd never thought of herself as particularly small, or soft, but with Callum she did. His body was hard. Everywhere. His thighs where they pressed between hers. His backside beneath her questing hands. His chest pushing down and his stomach pushing down and his mouth as he sucked and licked and bit her and kissed her. Then there was that very hard part of him, sheathed and pushing deep inside of her. He possessed her so fully she wasn't sure she still belonged to herself. She feared he'd claimed her in such a way that who she'd been was lost forever.

Her thoughts. She didn't even know what they meant. She was floating and elsewhere and this time didn't truly exist. It couldn't exist because she didn't understand any of it. Not what was going through her mind. Not what was happening to her body. Was this because she'd been alone for so long? This strange sense of surrender? Of being taken over as she did?

Or was this Callum? Just Callum? Only Callum? Callum, who was moving above her, whose abs contracted as he withdrew, whose chest hair rubbed over her like the softest down, tickling. His hair was soft. There, and on his head where it was loose and falling over her face, a curtain closing them off from all but their breath and their sighs and the sounds they made.

It was a language she hadn't spoken in ages, and yet she knew the moans and the grunts and the desperation. His. Hers. Theirs, shared and more powerful because of the uncertainty that brought them closer instead of working itself between them like a wedge—one sharp and damaging when the last thing either one of them needed was to be hurt again.

"You good? You okay?" He asked the questions while stroking her, his hips rolling, his hand braced on the outer curve of her thigh.

"I'm good. I'm okay." Her words were as breathless as his, as raw and honest and purposeful as his. Significant in their simplicity. Eloquent in all the emotion they conveyed. The hunger they conveyed. The truth.

She opened wider to give him more room to settle against her, wanting him nearer and profoundly buried and full. Wanting him here forever because he made her feel so many things, and beautifully good, and filled, when for so long she'd been empty and hollow and left barren.

"I don't want to hurt you," he said, grunted really, the sound gruff and raw.

"You won't. You can't." She was beyond hurt, she'd ached too much already, and she'd lived with the worst hurt she could imagine for far too long. "You can't. It's not possible."

"I'm not sure I believe you."

"It doesn't matter," she said, shaking her head.

"That I believe you?" he asked as he slowed, as he pulled far enough away to look into her eyes. "Or that I'm hurting you?"

"Please don't stop."

"I'm not stopping. But we're going to finish this conversation."

"Later then. Not now. I can't . . . not now." Her body was burning with the way she wanted him. Her soles were pressed taut to his ankles. Her shoulders knew the weight of his, and she felt the same in the places between. Her knees. Her hip bones. Her ribs she feared would crack from the pounding beat of her heart.

As much as she wanted to wait for him, to draw out her climax, to stay here beneath him and feel each stroke as he slid into her, she let go, exploding around him. Nothing existed beyond the place where their bodies were joined, and the pleasure consumed her, from her scalp to the tips of her toes.

Callum came with her in strong, mindless thrusts, shuddering, eyes closed above her until he was done, then rolling from the futon and heading for the bathroom. She shook her head and laughed softly. There wasn't even a bar of soap or a towel left in the room.

She heard the toilet flush, and he returned moments later, his face damp as if he'd splashed it, his hands damp, too. He curled up next to her, pulling her close as he said, "Talk about roughing it."

"If I'd known you were coming by . . ."

"I didn't even know until ten thirty-three."

She smiled at that. "Down to the minute, huh?"

"Yeah. It seemed important."

Speaking of important . . . she had so much to say to him now that he was here, but she could only think of one thing. "I'm sorry about the other night. The dinner thing. Not telling you in advance about the date. I didn't think it was going to hit me so hard, but the closer it got—" She stopped because she didn't want to ruin tonight with the memories.

But Callum seemed to have gone elsewhere, and her intuition

proved true when he said, "I want to ask you something, but I need to tell you something first."

Her stomach flipped, then clenched tight. "That sounds ominous."

"I hope not," he said with a huff.

"Then tell me." *So you can ask me.* Because those were the words that had started her heart racing again, yet she didn't want to get her hopes up too high . . .

He rolled up to sit, reached for his boxers, and pulled them on, then handed her his shirt, and while she was slipping her arms into the sleeves, said, "I told you Cheryl said if I didn't take Addy, she was going to give her away."

"Is that not the truth?" she asked, pulling the sides of the shirt close, her heart pounding.

"It is, but it's not all of it." Lying back, he tucked his arm beneath his head as a pillow and stared at the ceiling while she stared at him. "Cheryl was really prone to changing her mind. About not keeping her promises. Her word was pretty much worthless."

"You didn't believe her."

"I believed her in that moment. She would've signed away her rights to Addy and left the line for the father on the birth certificate blank." He snorted, shook his head. "She only filled it in when I agreed to never come to her for help. Not babysitting. Not a kidney. Nothing."

"Wow. I'm surprised she carried her to term."

"She was a load of contradictions," he said, closing his eyes, rubbing them, then opening them again. "She could tell me to take the kid and get the hell out of her life, but she didn't have it in her to abort the pregnancy. Don't ask me why. Turns out I didn't really know her all that well."

"Just well enough to . . ."

He looked over and for a moment, held her gaze. "I'd feel bad about it except that's all she wanted from me. She got the rest of what she needed elsewhere."

"How so?" she asked, bracing herself.

"The club ran a secondhand store. Furniture, clothes, pots and pans. It was actually Lainie's deal. She had the biggest heart. But it was also a front for the main part of the club's business. There was a big warehouse behind the store where folks dropped off all the stuff they didn't want. Lainie oversaw everything. The legal part of it anyway. Duke used the warehouse to store the things that weren't. It was easy to lose things in all that space. Hard for anyone to prove it was anything but what it appeared to be."

"The things that weren't legal?"

"Drugs, guns. It's amazing how much money's to be made off what the law says is illegal. And off medicines that aren't."

"I don't get it."

"Duke sold the guns, the coke, the crystal, the H. And he ran an underground clinic out of the warehouse office. Painkillers were the big moneymaker, but he sold anything there was a demand for. Antibiotics. Cancer drugs. Shit for erectile dysfunction. Birth control. People who can't afford the meds, or the insurance, lots of time can't afford to travel to get what they need."

"Mexico?"

"Anywhere and everywhere. China. Turkey. There's always a supply when there's a demand. Most of the meds were manufactured overseas and not FDA approved. Duke made a mint. Cheryl made a mint, too. Duke just didn't know it."

Uh-oh. "That doesn't sound good."

He rolled to his side and propped up on one elbow. "She helped him keep his books. But she was skimming, selling on the side. And I had proof," he said, toying with the hem of his shirt where it covered her thigh. "I told her if she ever came after Addy for anything, I'd use it."

"Good for you."

"She didn't believe me. She wasn't the least bit afraid. I half expected her to laugh, or tear up the birth certificate."

"What did you do?" Brooklyn asked, dropping her gaze to his hand, his fingers, shivering each time he brushed against her skin.

"The day I left California with Addy, I gave Duke the proof I had, even knowing what he might need to do to protect his business."

She suddenly felt very, very cold. "Callum—"

But he cut her off. "I've never told this to another soul."

"Do you know what he did?" she asked, though she wasn't sure she wanted an answer.

"No clue."

Leaving him as haunted by his past as she'd been by hers. "So the motorcycle you keep hearing . . ."

"I'll live with the sound the rest of my life, because a part of me will always wonder. But even more so, I can't stop thinking that I'm going to mess something up and lose my girl," he said, his voice breaking, his eyes growing damp. "Or that what I did then is going to catch up with me and backfire."

"You didn't do anything wrong."

"Oh, I did a whole lot of things wrong," he said with a humorless laugh.

"I'm talking about telling Duke what Cheryl was doing."

"That makes me a rat, Brooklyn."

"It's not what you did. It's why you did it." She reached for his hand and squeezed his fingers with hers. "Addy had her whole future ahead. You did what you had to do."

He looked at her for a long moment, searching her gaze for more than the words she'd spoken, and then he said, "You had your whole future ahead of you, too. You have it now. Do you want to make things right for a man who'll never know, or do you want to make things right for yourself?"

She looked at him, felt his words like a vine at her ankles, twisting around and around and tightening, tugging, keeping her from running away. Keeping her here, facing her past, his past, both of their futures, but most important, facing him. It was the only place she wanted to be, and yet she could not go back on her word to Artie, even while loving Callum.

She leaned toward him, sliding the fingers of her free hand into his hair and holding him still while she kissed him. She needed him to know that her leaving was inevitable, and had nothing to do with him, but everything to do with who she wanted to be for herself.

If she couldn't be her best for herself, how could she ever be her best for him? How could she be the shoulder he needed, the touchstone he relied on, the sounding board? How could she be his friend, his lover? How could she be anything without knowing who she was alone?

But in this moment, alone was the last thing she wanted to be, and she pushed him onto his back, braced the heels of her hands on his shoulders, and climbed over him, straddling him, looking down at the tendons and veins in his neck pop as he struggled to hold himself in check.

He moved his hands to her waist, just above her hips, gripping her there tightly enough to leave marks. She loved the idea of wearing the tattoo of this night, of being able to see for days to come the imprints of his thumbs on her skin, his fingers, even if the indentations blued into bruises in the end.

Leaning to the side, she reached down to the floor for a second condom packet, opening it and rolling the sheath down his erection while he watched. It was a strangely intimate act, her fingers working along his length to cover him and protect them both, though the idea of having a child with him . . .

She loved the thought of their creating a life from such a beautiful act—or she would were they committed and not just beginning to explore their feelings. And things for both of them would have to be so different than they were now; his focus was on his business, she was leaving, and her life was upside down because of it.

But in another time, another place . . . if the two of them were together, a couple, sharing more than a bed, sharing their lives in a way she knew so well was possible, a way she didn't believe Callum had ever experienced . . . she wanted him to appreciate how amazing such a partnership was.

"I'm still here, you know," he said, and she lifted her gaze to his, then lifted one wrist to backhand her tears from her eyes.

"I know," she said, but her voice broke, and she hated the sound because it smacked of weakness, and she was anything but. Not with him. Not when she'd learned so much about herself because of him.

"Brooklyn, baby. Don't cry. Please don't cry."

"I'm not," she said, crying, lifting herself up onto her knees, positioning herself over him, then holding herself still. "I'm not."

Yet her tears fell as she moved up and down, with him, against him, their two bodies one as they were meant to be. And even though she was leaving, she knew she'd carry this night with her forever, and one day she would ink it onto her skin.

We loved with a love that was more than love.

Because like Poe and Annabel Lee, they had.

CHAPTER TWENTY-FOUR

Brooklyn paid her cabdriver and tugged up the handle on her rolling carry-on. She'd packed as little as possible. Clothes she could easily wash in a sink and hang to dry: over a shower rod, a window balcony, a chair. Khaki and olive hiking pants that zipped into shorts at the knees. Soft T-shirts that doubled as tops for her long cotton skirts. A single pair of yoga pants that would serve as pajamas when paired with one of the tees.

It was the same with her shoes. She'd packed two pairs of fold-up ballet flats, one black, one taupe, and was wearing lightweight, slip-on walking shoes. All of her clothes had pockets that zipped closed so she wouldn't need to carry a purse. Cash, credit card, passport, cell phone. They were all easily tucked away. Her sunglasses hung from her neck on a lanyard.

She would buy what she needed once she was settled in Vernazza, or in Corniglia, or Riomaggiore; she could easily walk between the five Cinque Terre villages, so she could live anywhere. She'd stay a day or two with Bianca, while the other woman showed her where she'd be needed, and then decide where to live.

The idea of renting rooms in one of the pastel-colored houses, the windows looking out over the sea, the breeze off the Mediterranean cooling her as she slept, the sun sparkling off the blue-green water and greeting her each morning as she indulged in a deep, dark espresso . . . she'd call it *bliss*, but that word would forever belong to Callum in her mind.

She'd traveled often enough with Artie that she was a pro. And though she hadn't traveled since, and this was the first time she was traveling alone, little about the process was unknown. None of which explained why she had yet to take her place in the security line. She wasn't in danger of missing her flight; she'd arrived plenty early to make sure that didn't happen.

The danger keeping her from committing to the next step of this journey was more personal. She feared she was making a mistake, running from her future instead of toward it. She'd planned this trip for so long. She'd been so very certain this was what she needed to do: for Artie, for his family, whom she loved as if they were her own. For herself.

But she wasn't doing it for Artie at all. Artie was gone. He'd told her not to stop living her life because he'd lost his. And yet here she was, doing what she thought would make him happy. What he would want. Yes, she was doing something meaningful, something that mattered. She was giving of herself in a way that would leave her fulfilled. But it wasn't what she wanted. Not any longer. And that was the bottom line.

The airport wasn't particularly busy, and she found a seat in one of the small eateries after ordering a coffee she didn't need. The caffeine would only make her more jittery, when she was already dealing with a terrible case of nerves. Not about the trip; flying had never bothered her, and she had an entire library of books downloaded to her fully charged Kindle Voyage. She could read for the whole of the trip, lose herself in another world instead of thinking about the one she was leaving: the one where Callum Bennett Drake lived.

The one where his daughter lived. The one where he made the most exquisite chocolates, and rode a bike too loud for words, and made love to her as if she were the only woman in the world whose bed he ever wanted to share. How in the world could she walk away, when he was now her life, just as Artie had been during their time together?

She dug out her phone, her heart racing, and took a deep breath as she scrolled through her contact list and dialed. She hated doing this, but she had no choice. Callum was her everything, and the idea of leaving him, when she didn't have to go to Italy to do what Artie had asked of her, was more than she could bear.

"Pronto?"

"Bianca? It's Brooklyn. Did I wake you?"

"No, no, I'm awake. Are you on your way?"

"I'm at the airport, yes," she said, closing her eyes as she blurted out, "But I may not be coming."

"Is it the plane? Will you be delayed?"

"It's not the plane, no." She took a deep breath and shuddered. "It's . . . a man."

The silence on the other end went on longer than the normal delay of a transatlantic call, and guilt assailed her. Why couldn't she have made this decision before now? "Bianca—"

"Brooklyn, I am so happy for you! I have waited what seems like an eternity for you to find again the absolute perfection you had with Arturo. He was taken from us too soon. You lost years you should have had to share with him. Do not think twice about coming here until you can bring this new man with you for me to meet."

"You're not angry?"

"How can I be angry about my dearest cousin falling in love?"

"I will come. And I will bring the Bible, of course," she said, feeling giddy. "And I will send the vase, and the mortar and pestle, and everything else I've found."

"And Arturo's ashes?"

"He told me to scatter them in a place he loved. He loved so many. I chose the vineyard and the olive groves, but there's a river near our home that he spent hours and hours rafting on."

"That sounds absolutely perfect. I can imagine him floating there forever, enjoying the sun and the wind, though I'm making all of this up, having never visited your Texas."

"You must come. Seriously. You must."

"I will come for your wedding. I promise."

"You will be my maid of honor?" she asked, getting so far ahead of herself and jumping without thinking, but knowing having Bianca at her side when she married Callum—because she would marry Callum, she knew this with more certainty than anything in her life—would make the day perfect.

"I absolutely will. But what is this most fortunate man's name?"

"His name is Callum," she said. "Callum Bennett Drake. And I love him."

~

"Lena. I need you to do something for me," Callum said, flooring the truck's accelerator as he entered the ramp onto I-35 North, leaving Hope Springs for Austin and the airport. Brooklyn was due to fly in a couple of hours. He might have already missed her. He might have waited too long.

"Sure thing, boss."

"I'm not going to make it back today, and I'm not sure about tomorrow." Fridays were usually slow, though Saturdays . . . shit. Lena would just have to cover it. "If I don't show up, I'll pay you overtime for tomorrow. And when you close, put up a sign that we won't be open Monday. I'll let you know about the rest of the week when I've got things figured out."

"Uh, boss? Is there something you need to tell me?"

"I might be going out of town." Town. Country. Did it make any difference? Hell, who was he kidding? It was doubtful he'd be going anywhere but home again, though just in case . . .

"And you'll be back when?"

"I don't know."

"Because it's not like we've got enough inventory to fill online orders but for a couple of days of you being gone."

"Yeah. I know." *This is some kind of way to run a business, hotshot. Leaving your employee and your customers in the lurch.* Like he had a choice. "I'll do my best to update you this afternoon. Push comes to shove, we add a delayed shipping note to the front of the website."

Lena was a long time in responding. "V-Day being over, I guess it won't kill us, but you take too long figuring things out, it will."

"Yes, ma'am," he said, which had Addy's head turning from where she sat in her seat beside him.

"Is that Grammy? Hi, Grammy! We're going to the airport!"

Lena cleared her throat. "Airport, huh?"

The women in his life . . . "Like I said. We might be going out of town."

"Addy, too?"

"Yeah. Maybe. I don't know." If he went, he'd obviously take her, too, which made his thinking he was going anywhere extra-dumb. He just had to get to Brooklyn. "Look," he said, grinding his jaw. "I'll call you tonight, okay?"

"Sure thing, boss," she said, and then she rang off.

He hit the end-call button, then muttered, "C'mon, c'mon," under his breath. He was going to miss her. He was going to be too late. He shouldn't have moved so far from freeway access. He should've taken the Harley instead of the truck. He shouldn't have thought he could live without her and let her go in the first place. After last Sunday night on her futon—

"Daddy?"

At the tremor in Addy's voice, he glanced over to see her hugging her plush snowman so tightly his bulbous white head looked ready to pop off. "Yes, pumpkin?" he asked, nearly choked with worry.

"Do you think Ms. Harvey would stay if I liked Elsa better than Olaf?"

"What?" he asked, frowning. "No, sweetheart. Of course not," he added, trying to figure out what she was thinking. Trying, too, to keep his heart in one piece. This girl . . . "Ms. Harvey loves Olaf, too."

"But she doesn't love us, does she?" she asked, tears in the corners of her eyes, the words tiny and sad. "Because she's going away. Like Grammy went away because she doesn't love PopPop anymore."

"Ms. Harvey can go away and still love us," he said, because he knew that Brooklyn did. He'd felt it in the way she'd moved beneath him, but he'd known it long before then. Which made his letting her go, not asking her what he'd intended to, a ridiculously huge mistake.

For some reason she wasn't letting herself be happy. He wanted to know what was keeping her in the dark. "Addy? Do you know why you love Olaf the best?"

His daughter nodded fiercely, her curls bouncing. "Because he's so silly and funny."

Callum sighed. She said it as if she hadn't had enough silly and funny in her life, when he'd done his best to give her everything. Sure, her first year had been spent in a borrowed playpen in Duke and Lainie's living room. Or in their kitchen watching him making a mess as he learned to temper chocolate.

But his friends, who were also his bosses and his landlords and his daughter's uncle and aunt, had treated Addy like their own, spoiling her with pink girly-girl clothes, and frilly socks, and shiny shoes, and too many toys for an infant her age, until it had been time for good-bye. She'd had a wealth of attention, and she'd had a family of misfits in California who'd loved her, and she'd been doted on by his parents in Hope Springs.

Brooklyn's parents had loved her, and Artie had loved her, yet something in her life had been lacking all this time. The thing about it was, he couldn't give Brooklyn what she was missing. She was going to have to find that for herself. But maybe if he was there beside her, he and Addy, hell, at this point he'd even put Olaf to work if he had to . . .

Checking the clock on the dash, he parked the truck, rushed around the hood to Addy's door and released her seat belt, swinging her and her snowman into his arms. And then he ran. He knew the time of Brooklyn's flight, knew the airline and gate. His chances of catching her before she made it through security were slim. He'd be too late. She'd be gone.

Bursting through the doors, he moved from one line to the next, searching for black-framed glasses and blond hair and the body he'd learned so well, and the face that gutted him every time she broke into a grin. But she was nowhere. He couldn't see her, and he swung around again as he dug in his pocket for his phone. If he could reach her while she was still at her gate—

"Daddy, look! It's Ms. Harvey!"

Callum pressed the hand holding his phone to Addy's back and spun in the direction she'd pointed. Brooklyn was sitting at a table in one of the terminal's small shops, her hands wrapped around a paper coffee cup, her gaze focused intently on whatever she wasn't drinking.

"Ms. Harvey! Ms. Harvey!"

At Addy's cry, Brooklyn looked up, searching the crowd but quickly narrowing in on the crazy man Callum knew he must look like as he hurried toward her, his biker boots feeling like lead weights on his feet, his daughter swaying in his arms like a flag of surrender.

"What are you doing here?" Brooklyn asked, frowning as she smiled. She got to her feet and took a diving Addy from his arms.

"We came to see you!" the girl said, her arms going so tightly around Brooklyn's neck, Callum had trouble pulling her away.

"C'mon, pumpkin. Let's sit down. You're a little bit heavy for Ms. Harvey to hold." Once they were seated, Brooklyn in her chair again, and Callum in the one facing her with Addy on his knee, he took a breath, blew it out, and said, "Hi."

"Hi, to you, too," she said, reaching a hand across the table to grip his and squeeze. "But now are you going to tell me what you're doing here?"

"Addy's right," he said. "We came to see you."

"Is something wrong? Why didn't you call?"

"I was going to," he said, showing her the phone he still held. "But then Addy saw you—" *Get to the point, hotshot. The woman's got a plane to catch.* "You don't have to make this trip, Brooklyn. Not if you don't want to. Not if you're not ready. If you're not sure. You can visit later. Take the Bible to Bianca then. Skype with the students." He was sounding desperate. "I know you have Artie's ashes to scatter, and if you're set on doing that in Italy, I get it. But go and do and come back. Or I'll go with you."

"And then what?" she asked after several seconds, her voice breaking as she held his gaze. "We come back . . . I come back . . . I sold my house, Callum. Everything I own is in boxes. I don't even have a bed anymore."

"I have a house. I have a brand-new king-sized sleigh bed. I also have a guest room. Or . . ." *Think, Callum. Think.* Desperate wasn't getting him anywhere. "I have twenty acres of trees and lawn I'm going to have to buy a tractor to mow. I can build a guest house if you'd feel more comfortable with your own space. I can renew the lease on the loft in the meantime."

And how much sense was any of this making? She didn't need him for a place to live, and a guest house would take months, and he was about five seconds from scooping up both her and Addy and taking them home—

"I don't want to be your guest," she finally said, tears spilling to roll down her cheeks.

"Oh, baby. Don't cry. That's not what I want you to be either. In fact"—he scooted to the edge of his chair, set Addy on her feet, and dug in his pocket—"this is what I want."

She looked down to where he held a candy box from Bliss. "You want me to eat chocolate?"

"Just open it," he said, grinning, and sliding off his chair to kneel on the floor in front of her as she lifted the lid.

"Oh, Callum," she said, pressing her fingers to her trembling lips. "It's beautiful."

"It was my grandmother's." He reached into the box and pulled out the ring. It was a narrow gold band, a braided design with five tiny stones set into the twist: a diamond, an emerald, a sapphire, a ruby, a topaz. "My grandfather had it made for her. She would never tell him which stone was her favorite, so he included one of each. And it would be the greatest pleasure I could imagine knowing if you would do me the honor of being my wife."

"Oh, Callum," she said again, but was stopped from saying anything more by the loudest little girl in the world.

"Yes! Ms. Harvey! We want you to be our wife!"

Callum hung his head, shaking it, and Brooklyn laughed. The other travelers around them and those seeing them off or welcoming them home laughed, too.

"Well?" he asked, hoping he was reading her right, and that the nerves eating him up would be worth this feeling that he was about to lose his lunch.

She held out her hand. Her left hand. He took it in his and slid the ring on her finger. The fit was perfect, and he looked up at her, his eyes glazed with tears he had to wipe away with his sleeve. Seconds later she was in his arms, kneeling with him, her face against his as she hugged him and kissed him and laughed and cried with him until they nearly fell to the floor, which made Addy, who'd jumped into the hug with Olaf, giggle like a loon.

"I need to tell you something," Brooklyn said, once she'd made it back into her chair, toying with the ring as she did, Addy moving to lean against her. "I called Bianca earlier," she said, raising her gaze to his and wrapping an arm around his daughter. "I told her I wasn't coming."

Nothing she could've said would've made him any happier. "You did?"

She nodded. "And I asked her to be my maid of honor."

He'd been wrong. *This* was happy, his face about to split from his grin. "Well, then. Since you're not leaving, which means I'm not leaving, I should probably call Lena and let her know."

"Wait a minute," she said, as he stood to look for his phone. "You told her you were leaving?"

He dug into his back pocket, came up with his and Addy's passports, which he'd grabbed from his fireproof safe on the way out the door. "I was going to be that man who followed his woman across the world if I had to. With the munchkin in tow."

She gave an incredulous laugh as she got to her feet, her eyes widening. "You brought passports?"

"No suitcases," he said, realizing the truth of the adage *desperate times, desperate measures*. "But yeah. We've got passports. We're good to go."

"I want to go, too," Addy said, jumping up and down and wedging herself between them. "I want to get books and ice cream again!"

Brooklyn laughed, so Callum laughed; then he opened his arms and she stepped into his embrace, kissing him soundly.

"Well?" he asked, moments later, holding up his credit card and the two passports. "We can still go if you want. Buy what we need when we get there."

"What about Bliss?"

"Lena can put up a sign."

"You would do that?"

"For you? Anything."

"It's up to you," she finally said.

He thought about it a moment, then dug into his pocket for a quarter. "Heads or tails?"

"Why not?" She clapped her hands together in front of her chest. "Either way, we've already won."

Damn but she had that right. "C'mere, Addy," he said, hunkering down on one knee. "Ms. Harvey and I have a game for you to play."

~

They didn't go anywhere but back to Hope Springs. Callum followed Brooklyn there from Austin. They left her car and Addy at his father's house, Callum having decided it better not to have to explain to his daughter what they were doing, then drove together in silence toward Gruene.

Brooklyn sat in the passenger seat of his truck, the box holding the urn with Artie's ashes on the seat between them. Symbolic, really, she mused, as she'd been so afraid of losing what she'd had with Artie that she'd let her love for him come between her and Callum.

Lifting the box to her lap, she scooted to sit in the center of the classic pickup, straddling the gearshift and setting the box on her other side. Callum didn't say anything, but she caught the edge of his smile when she turned to buckle her seat belt. And once she had, he wrapped his arm around her shoulder and held her close until he needed both hands on the wheel.

He maneuvered through the small town's narrow streets, turning at the intersection just past Gruene Hall and the Gristmill restaurant, then driving across the bridge over the Guadalupe River and parking on the other side. Shutting off the truck, he got out and Brooklyn slid across to exit through his door, then she leaned in to pull the box toward her.

Knowing she'd be scattering Artie's ashes, she'd never invested in an urn besides the red rectangle the mortuary had given her. She held it tight to her chest as she and Callum walked to the water's edge. Once there, she opened the box and removed the sealed bag inside, toeing off her shoes.

Callum took the box from her hands. "You want me to come with?"

She shook her head. This was her journey. The end of one. The beginning of another. She waded ankle deep near the bank, the water breaking over rocks and tree roots before rushing to the deeper center. She took a half dozen short steps, then turned. "He would've loved knowing you. Riding with you. Downing Shiner Bock and grilling burgers. Not sure he would've had the patience to make candy," she said, trying to laugh, and struggling. Her face was a wash of tears. "I miss him," she said, choking. "I miss him so much."

Callum came to her then, wading into the water in his boots and his jeans and wrapping his arms around her. He said nothing. He didn't have to. He was there, and he was giving her exactly what she needed. And then he made it better by dropping a kiss to the top of her head.

"I'll be right here," he said, letting her go and backing away, crossing his arms over the box that had held her husband's ashes, the water flowing between his legs. "Take care of Artie. Take as long as you need. I'll be right here when you're done."

She nodded, backing her way through the shallow water, and holding his gaze until she finally had the strength to turn. She breathed in, filling her lungs with the clean, crisp air, the scent of oncoming summer, the water that grew deeper with each step she took. She could do this. Tell Artie good-bye.

Once she was knee-deep, she broke the seal on the bag with shaking fingers. And then she said, "Do you remember that chocolate shop in town? The one named Bliss . . ."

THE NEXT HOPE SPRINGS NOVEL

Don't miss Alison Kent's next Hope Springs novel, featuring
Dakota and Thea

Fall 2015

ABOUT THE AUTHOR

Alison Kent is the author of more than fifty published works, including her debut novel, *Call Me*, which she sold live on CBS's *48 Hours*, in an episode called "Isn't It Romantic?" The first book in her Hope Springs series, *The Second Chance Café*, was a 2014 RITA finalist. Her novels *A Long, Hard Ride* and *Striptease* were both finalists for the *Romantic Times* Reviewers Choice Award, while *The Beach Alibi* was honored by the national Quill Awards and *No Limits* was selected by *Cosmopolitan* as a Red Hot Read. The author of *The Complete Idiot's Guide to Writing Erotic Romance*, Alison decided long ago that if there's a better career than writing, she doesn't want to know about it. She lives in her native Texas with her geologist husband and a passel of pets.